ALSO BY RUSSELL BANKS

FICTION

Foregone

A Permanent Member of the Family

Lost Memory of Skin

The Reserve

The Darling

The Angel on the Roof

Cloudsplitter

Rule of the Bone

The Sweet Hereafter

Affliction

Success Stories

Continental Drift

The Relation of My Imprisonment

Trailerpark

The Book of Jamaica

The New World

Hamilton Stark

Family Life

Searching for Survivors

NONFICTION

Voyager

The Invisible Stranger (with Arturo Patten)

Dreaming Up America

THE MAGIC KINGDOM

THE MAGIC KINGDOM

RUSSELL BANKS

ALFRED A. KNOPF, NEW YORK, 2022

THIS IS A BORZOI BOOK
PUBLISHED BY ALFRED A. KNOPF

Copyright © 2022 by Russell Banks

All rights reserved. Published in the United States by Alfred A. Knopf,
a division of Penguin Random House LLC, New York.

www.aaknopf.com

Knopf, Borzoi Books, and the colophon
are registered trademarks of Penguin Random House LLC.

Library of Congress Cataloging-in-Publication Data
Names: Banks, Russell, [date] author.
Title: The magic kingdom / Russell Banks.
Description: First Edition. | New York : Alfred A. Knopf, 2022. |
Identifiers: LCCN 2021054982 | ISBN 9780593535158 (hardcover) |
ISBN 9780593535165 (ebook)
Classification: LCC PS3552.A49 M34 2022 | DDC 813/.54—dc23
LC record available at https://lccn.loc.gov/2021054982

Jacket image from the author's collection
Jacket design by Chip Kidd

Manufactured in the United States of America
First Edition

815 5777

To Chase, the beloved,
And for my brother, Stephen Banks

THE MAGIC KINGDOM

FOREWORD

The late Harley Mann, a semiretired speculator in Florida real estate, told this story to a tape recorder over several months in 1971. As the reader may wonder from time to time who edited and shaped the content of Mann's now fifty-year-old tapes into a more or less coherent narrative, it may be stated that it is I, Russell Banks, the named author of this book, who have taken on that task.

The reader may also wonder why the publisher of the book chose not to bypass said author and simply transcribe Harley Mann's narrative straight from the tapes word by word, just as Mann himself spoke them in 1971. Anyone who has read verbatim transcriptions of recorded memos, conversations, meetings, and phone calls or transcripts of wiretaps by the FBI and other intelligence agencies of conversations between suspected criminals and terrorists will understand the need for a figure like the author to stand between whoever has been taped or wiretapped and the reader. Unedited transcriptions convey neither the voice nor, in many cases, the meaning of what was said or the intent of the speaker. Also, the reader should keep in mind that when the late Harley Mann recorded his story, he was in his early eighties, a somewhat eccentric, crotchety, impulsive, and garrulous old man fond of digressions and personal asides, who, like all of us when speaking at length without a written text, could be repetitive, self-correcting, inexact, profane, irrelevant, and sometimes inaudible.

For those reasons, and since I am the person who discovered the tapes twenty-two years ago in a storm-soaked cardboard box in the basement of the St. Cloud, Florida, public library, the publisher thought it useful to have me edit, cut, and when necessary overwrite, annotate, and summarize the content. There may have been a bit of legal anxiety as well, which is why I was advised by counsel to change the names of certain still-living individuals.

Harley Mann's story came to my attention in the following way. Back in October 1999, when Hurricane Irene passed over the Florida peninsula on its way to wreak havoc on upstate New York and New England, the lakes of south and central Florida overflowed, and much of the city of St. Cloud was flooded. A month after the storm, at the end of a solitary weekend fishing trip at East Lake Tohopekaliga, before returning to my home in Miami, I stopped in St. Cloud for a lunch at Crabby Bill's, a local lakeside restaurant I favor. An hour later, emerging from the cool air-conditioned gloom of the restaurant into the sweltering glare of the midday sun, I was unexpectedly struck by the look of a building at 10th Street and New York Avenue surrounded by a clustered mix of live oak trees and cabbage palms on the far side of the parking lot. There was nothing especially attractive or architecturally interesting about the building, but I was somehow drawn to it and wondered why I had not noticed it before.

It was the Veterans Memorial Library, a foursquare tan-brick building that looked like a 1950s bank from my Massachusetts hometown. In south Florida in the final decade of the twentieth century, it seemed an architectural outlier, oddly out of place and almost antique. It would have seemed more natural, more authentic, I thought, in a Disney World Potemkin village, embellished by transplanted elm or maple trees in a mythic New England suburban diorama, than here at the heart of the postmodern semitropical city of St. Cloud, Florida.

Curious and mildly intrigued and inexplicably agitated, and for vague and unnamed reasons wishing to examine the building more closely, I walked across the parking lot and entered the library.

The dimly lit lobby and main reading room were cooled by air-conditioning and appeared to be deserted, except for a slim young pony-tailed female librarian wearing a flowered skirt and pink blouse and luminous, bright-blue running shoes. A hand-lettered cardboard sign taped to the wall at the east end of the lobby said Free Books. A drawn arrow pointed down the wide stairway to the basement.

The basement was dark and damp, twenty degrees warmer than the lobby above, due to a bulkhead door open to the backyard. Mildew and black mold crawled up the poured concrete walls. A dozen or so sodden cardboard cartons and banker's boxes filled with old books and magazines and quarterly periodicals were stacked nearby. Beyond the bulkhead door was a dumpster on the gleaming green lawn. The rotting books and magazines and periodicals were evidently set to be tossed into the dumpster and trucked to a landfill.

Casting a glance over the contents of the boxes, I saw nothing of interest—until I noticed at the top of one pile a packet of what looked like old-fashioned quarter-inch reel-to-reel tapes. The box was soaked through, but the tapes themselves appeared to have been protectively wrapped in clear plastic and undamaged by water. Someone with a wide-tip marker had written "The Magic Kingdom" on the packaging.

Whoever had been lugging the boxes of books and magazines from the cellar to the dumpster seemed to have gone on a lunch break. In any case, no one was present in the basement to see me slip the package of tapes into the wide side-pocket of my fishing vest and walk up the stairs to the main reading room.

The librarian asked if I had found anything of interest down there among the rubble.

Bringing her attention to the packet of tapes might make her want them back, I thought, so I said, "No, everything's waterlogged." I then departed from the library and returned to my parked car and boat trailer and drove back to my home in Miami.

In a limited sense, then, the tapes were stolen from the St. Cloud public library. I had no way to listen to the old-fashioned reel-to-reel tapes, however, and for several years they sat stacked forgotten among unread books on a shelf in my office. I did nothing with them. I did not even unwrap them. Finally, while reorganizing my personal library, I decided to put the tapes in the trash. But something like an invisible hand on my sleeve kept me from throwing them out.

Reluctantly, since I would likely never use it for any other purpose, I went ahead and purchased via eBay a working vintage reel-to-reel tape recorder. When the machine was delivered to my condominium and I was able to listen for the first time to the recorded voice of Harley Mann, I learned that my machine was uncannily like the Grundig TK46 recorder described in Harley Mann's Reel #1. It was in fact the same make and model. Purely coincidental, of course, but only the first of many unsettling parallels and resemblances between my own story and Harley Mann's and no doubt one of the reasons why I have gone to the trouble of transcribing the tapes and bringing that transcription to the public.

Harley Mann himself is presumed to have died shortly after completing his account. A few months after I first listened to the tapes, on the last of my several return trips to St. Cloud seeking biographical details from the life of Harley Mann that, for reasons of modesty, discretion, or guilt, he may have omitted from his account, I made the surprising discovery of what appeared to be his grave site.

By then the young librarian in the blue running shoes had become my part-time unpaid research assistant. She was especially helpful in locating the records behind the purchase of seven thousand acres of land in nearby Narcoossee in the 1890s by the Shakers of Mount Lebanon, New York, and the eventual mid-twentieth-century purchase of that same land by representatives of the Walt Disney Company. She prefers not to be named in this account, however.

From her I learned of the existence of what we initially thought was the Shaker burial ground. The true location of Harley Mann's body is unknown, but his death has been memorialized by someone who must have loved and admired him and somehow knew his story. In a northerly corner of the land where the Shaker colony called New Bethany once stood, there are three small, barely visible bronze plaques, one of which bears his name and dates, "Harley

Mann, 1890–1972," and the word "Shaker." The second is inscribed with the name "Sadie Pratt" and the dates "1883–1910" and, below the dates, "Shaker." The third marks the grave of Eldress Mary Glynn, 1838–1911.

One must assume that Harley Mann's grave is empty. Possibly all three are empty. Nobody has been buried in that cemetery, if it is indeed a cemetery, since the last of the Florida Shakers returned to upstate New York over a century ago. They are the opposite of unmarked graves. The land is now owned by the Walt Disney Company, and the burial ground itself is protected by Florida state law from disruption or appropriation or resale.[*] It is overgrown and difficult of access, located in the Animal Kingdom on a low hammock at the edge of a marsh several hundred yards southwest of the Rainforest Cafe, where no one but Disney security guards patrols the area. The guards are mainly concerned with keeping interlopers from sneaking into the Magic Kingdom by way of the Animal Kingdom without paying.

There was no further information there or elsewhere concerning the lives of Harley Mann and Sadie Pratt and Eldress Mary Glynn. It was almost as if, except for the words on the purloined tapes and on the grave-site plaques, the three had never existed.

[*] Section 497.284, Florida Statutes

REEL #1

This is Harley Mann talking. I don't know why I said that. The words just fell out of my mouth. I guess I'm not accustomed to this mode of communication. I'm recording myself on a brand-spanking-new Grundig TK46 machine that I purchased yesterday after I drove up to Orlando from my home here in St. Cloud for the official opening of Walt Disney's gigantic amusement park, which is what inspired me to finally tell everything I can remember of certain events that I experienced and witnessed in my childhood and youth in this region south of Orlando and west of Lake Okeechobee, this sprawling district of lakes and swamps and creeks and sawgrass savanna and pine and live oak woods and palmetto that once upon a time was the headwaters of the Everglades.

That's my statement of intention. I'll probably tell about a lot of other things, too. In any case, instead of writing it down, I've decided to talk the whole damn thing into a tape recorder, because I'm a talker, not a writer. Everyone says that about me, sometimes with admiration, sometimes not so much, although they agree that my letters and postcards and personal notes and even my business correspondence are very expressive and descriptive. Just not as interesting as my talk. Which is probably because when I speak I almost never know what I'll say next, but when I write, since it almost always concerns business, I do.

There will be a batch of tapes when I'm done. Maybe whoever inherits my house and the rest of my personal property will someday transcribe them. I've got a last will and testament sworn and written, so I know who'll end up with my money. But I have no idea who will end up with the tapes. I hope that whoever does, he or she will make a faithful transcription and donate it to the St. Cloud Veterans Memorial Public Library or one of the local historical societies, so that after I have departed this world for the other, the true story of the Shaker settlement called New Bethany[*] and the people who lived there nearly a century ago will be known. It's a scandalous story almost completely forgotten now, and when remembered at all is lathered in lies and error.

Also, having recently turned eighty-one years of age, although still of more or less sound mind and body, my departure time is fast approaching. It's why yesterday, after attending the official opening ceremonies of Disney's amusement park, I got back into my Packard and drove down to the Montgomery Ward store in St. Cloud and marched in and purchased the recording machine and two dozen reels of blank tape. It's why this morning, after I made and ate breakfast, I set it up on my front porch, and as if talking to a trusted friend who knows nothing of these events and remarkable personalities, I have begun talking into it. It's early and the sun is still too low to bake away the morning dew, and nobody has walked by the house yet, but soon enough they will, and when they do they will likely think old Harley Mann is talking to himself in a steady stream and must have finally lost his marbles from all those years of living alone.

I suspect I'll be out here on the porch for many days before my story gets told, as it's a long and tangled tale, and the world today is so different from the world of my youth that I'll have to swerve away from its main thrust often and at length to describe it properly, so that whoever eventually listens to it or reads a transcription—assuming one gets made—will understand why certain people back then, myself especially, behaved as we did, both badly and, on a few occasions, well.

[*] See John 11:1–46

Human nature doesn't change, but contexts and circumstances do, so let me set the context and describe the circumstances. It's been close to seventy years since my family settled among the radical Ruskinites at their utopian colony called Waycross, and we found ourselves living in communitarian squalor alongside White swampers and Blacks in the marshes and piney forests of southeast Georgia. This was where my family began its long pilgrimage from light to darkness to light again, as it seemed to my childish eyes, and then in later years to still deeper darkness that I thought would never end. And then it did end, leaving me alone here in St. Cloud for most of a lifetime, ending up on the front porch of this old clapboard shotgun house talking to an electric-powered plastic box about a world that existed before the common use of electricity or the commercial use of plastic.

I could begin there, with our arrival at the Georgia commune in 1901. Or even earlier, with our family's life in the original Ruskinite colony of Graylag up north, outside Indianapolis, where I was born. But it's not my story that I need to tell, it's the New Bethany Shakers', so I'll begin instead in 1902, around the time when we first met the Shakers, when my twin brother, Pence, and I were twelve-year-old boys and we Manns were living like slaves on Rosewell Plantation, sixty miles south of Waycross, over by Valdosta. Maybe later on, if I see the need, I'll return to Waycross, and tell how my parents got all the way to the Okefenokee Swamp from their native Indianapolis and the Graylag colony and so on, how they went from being American followers of John Ruskin's anticapitalist teachings to founding communitarians to schismatic Ruskinites—an interesting account in its own right, but a whole other story for a whole other occasion. For now, I'll just talk about how we got over from Waycross to the Rosewell Plantation, which is where we eventually connected with the Shakers.

We were four children, me and my twin brother, Pence, and our brothers, Royal and Raymond, who were two years younger than me and Pence. They were also twins, a coincidence that in the eyes of the women in both the Graylag and Waycross colonies made Mother the object of an ambivalent mix of envy and pity. With two sets of twins, she could be said to have got her childbearing done in half the time of most women, but the work of raising a single baby from infancy to childhood had been doubled twice. This was before our sister, Rachel, was born. When we buried Father and set out from Waycross for Rosewell, we boys had only just learned that Mother was newly pregnant and that Rachel, the last of Mother's children, would be born fatherless at Rosewell.

It may go without saying that we and all our fellow communards were Northern White people. Nonetheless, we had associated plenty with Blacks before we got to Rosewell Plantation. Out of habit I call them Blacks. I suppose it would be preferable to call them African-Americans, along the line of Italo-Americans, but that's probably got too many syllables to catch on.

Mostly, the Blacks we knew at the Waycross colony were workers and drifters and peddlers and small farmers, some of them ex-slaves, whose paths often brought them into proximity with us White Northern communards. But until Father died and the rest of the family decamped for what Mother believed would be a refuge at Rosewell Plantation, we had never actually lived among Blacks, or for that matter among Southern Whites, either. We children simply thought of ourselves as Yankees and spoke our English with our parents' Indiana accents. I still do, I'm told. It's hard to erase an accent acquired in childhood, and from birth we had lived solely among White Northerners and even a few from Canada, England, and Scotland, people who were well educated and socialist to the bone and more or less high-minded, like the Shakers we later came to live with.

At Waycross we resided in one of the colony's small, windowless cabins, cold and drafty and dirt-floored, with little enough room for the six of us. Father was already sick. I did not know it at first and attributed his lethargy and seeming lack of interest in the governance and administration of the colony to his disappointment in the decrepit state of affairs there. The Ruskinite colony at Waycross had lost its way long before we Manns and over fifty other men, women, and children from the original Graylag colony came down by train from Indianapolis. We were a remnant of a remnant, a lost tribe wandering in the wilderness of the southeastern United States, guided by a misinformed belief that we had been led there by men who were wise and informed, men like Father, brought to a place sanctified by a people who adhered more closely to the revealed truths of communistic living than those lapsed Ruskinites we had left behind at Graylag.

My brother Pence and I were old enough and had overheard enough of the adults' discussions to understand roughly the cause and purpose of our departure from the only home we had known so far, the place where we had been born and had gone to school and learned to read and write and compute at a level higher than the children in the Indiana villages and farms that surrounded our commune at Graylag—higher, indeed, than most of the local children's parents. Until the financial and ideological quarrels that fatally divided the community into two warring parties, our life at Graylag had been a pleasing mixture of freedom and order, play and work, reflective solitude and organized group activity. Holding no worries over how to fund this communal life and no need to advance or defend any social theory, we children were given all the benefits of socialism with none of the deficits.

I was never again as happy with life as in those early years at Graylag. Until Father and Mother became ideological schismatics and split off from Graylag and set out for Waycross, my life was pastoral bliss. I was old enough to have acquired a bit of conscious personal history, eleven years of it, or at least the nine years or so from when I emerged from the cloud of infancy and began to form my first memories. Year in, year out, my life at Graylag had been a gradual, steady, happy opening-up to the world that surrounded me, a process encouraged and protected and led by Mother and Father and the other adult members of the community. And what a paradise it was!

I wonder now if the dream of utopia, whether secular or religious, is only the dream of an adult who has never ceased resenting and grieving over his imperfect childhood and as a result spends his life trying to start it over and make it perfect this time. But what of someone like me, who actually had a perfect childhood? Someone for whom the transgressions and imperfections of life arrived later, but not so much later that his memories of idyllic perfection got displaced. Someone who could look to the past for perfection rather than to the future.

When we settled into our Waycross shanty—for that is all it was, a shanty—Mother hung a blanket down the middle of the cabin, and she and Father slept on a narrow bed on one side of the blanket and we four boys shared a pair of folding cots on the other. She soon appeared to be pregnant, and one memorable morning she felt compelled to announce it to us boys, though not with much joy.

"You'll soon have another brother or a sister," she told us. "I'll be taking breakfast here," she added, and instructed us to join the others at the communal dining hall. Father had been ill for weeks and had not eaten with the other colonists for several days by then.

"How soon?" I asked.

"By end of winter. Now run down to the pump and wash." She laid out the day's chores for us and retreated behind the cloth wall where Father still lay abed. We could hear his rapid phlegmy breathing and restless turning in the bed, as if he could not make himself comfortable no matter how he lay. The younger twins, Raymond and Royal, were to spend the day scouring the abandoned, half-sunken railbed for bits and chunks of coal to burn in the tin stove that heated our cabin and boiled our water and cooked the little food Father could manage to keep down. Pence and I were charged with walking after breakfast back along the railbed to the main railhead in the crossroads village of Waycross to buy salt and sugar at the trading post, which Mother said Father needed to help him purge his sickness. We were pleased by the chance to get away from the sad decrepitude of the colony and briefly see how the rest of the world was getting by, but tried not to show it.

Mother no longer believed Father was suffering from malaria, she said. It was typhus.

"I didn't know he was sick from anything," I called to her. Pence said nothing. I was the talkative twin and usually spoke for the two of us. "I thought he was just . . ."

"What? Just what?" she asked sharply from behind the curtain.

"I dunno. Tired. From malaria. Sumpin'."

Mother came back to us, her hands on her hips. "Speak clearly, Harley. Say you 'do not know.' Say 'some-*thing*.' You're starting to sound like the swampers and the Negroes."

"I do-not-know," I said and pointed out that it happened to be a knowledgeable woman from a Black family named Calliphant, an old woman known as Partitia, who had made the tea from the sweet Annie plant that Mother had been using to treat Father's malaria. Partitia claimed it was a medicine she had learned from the Indians, and many of the settlers said that it had cured their malaria.

"Knowing that is how I know he does not have malaria," she said. "Because he's no better for it. I don't want to talk with you any further, Harley. You're too smart for your britches. Go, go," she said, and she shooed us boys from the cabin, waving her hands as if at mosquitoes. She was red-faced and looked like she would cry.

It turned out that she was right and Partitia was wrong. Father did not have malaria, and soon it became evident that the rash and red spots on his body were signs of typhus, what they used to call ague and the local people called swamp fever. More than we knew, the colonists at Waycross had been enduring an epidemic of typhus. It was one of the reasons their population had diminished to such a degree and why those who had not died of it or fled back north because of it were so enervated and lethargic, why so many of the children roamed free and half-clothed as if returning to savagery, why the fields were not planted and old crops lay rotting on the ground.

I tell this from memories of events and conversations that took place nearly seventy years ago, and an old man's memory of his childhood is generally not to be trusted, especially when he has told his story many times over the years and has had numerous opportunities to embellish and elaborate it and excise from it anything unpleasant or that reflects unfavorably on him, until his story ends up displacing his memory. But these happen to be stories I've never told before, in most cases not even to myself. As a result, my memories are relatively untainted by repetition and revision.

And I remember that particular day at Waycross clearly, because it began when Mother told us boys that she was pregnant with her fifth child, who would turn out five months later to be our sister, Rachel. And it was the morning we learned that Father was sick with typhus, not malaria, and realized that he was probably going to die of it. It was the morning when I first saw how terrified Mother was of losing Father and of having to take care of her four, soon to be five, children alone in the wilderness.

It was the same morning, as I learned later that day after Pence and I returned from Waycross village, that the man who managed Rosewell Plantation for Mr. Hamilton Couper had ridden sixty miles north to Waycross to recruit disillusioned and desperate members of the Ruskinite colony to go back with him to the plantation to live and work there as skilled laborers and household staff. And when Pence and I returned with the salt and sugar we'd been sent for, we found Father and Mother in deep discussion of Mr. Hamilton Couper's manager's offer.

Father lay in their rope bed, feverish and gaunt, his face and arms covered in a rash with raised red blotches blooming like phlox. He spoke haltingly, with great effort, but firmly nonetheless, as if his mind were focused on one thing and one thing only, which was to have Mother and his four sons and the expected fifth child transferred to Rosewell. He did not say it outright, but it was clear to me that Father would not be going with us.

Not ever. At that moment I believed that I could read the future. I was the eldest, born ten minutes before Pence, and I knew that my childhood was ending and Pence's would soon follow. Mother sat beside Father on a stool and with a spoon administered salt and sugar diluted in warm water. She spoke to him in a low voice, as if not wishing to intensify their disagreement, but not willing to let it go, either.

"I would feel better if we stayed put," she said, "until you are well again. And then we'll all go together."

"No. You and the boys go now. While you are still healthy. I will follow."

"There's no one here who'll care for you if we leave."

Father named five or six people who had come from Indiana and joined the Georgia colony with us.

"They can barely take care of themselves," she said.

"Go now. Or others will get there before you. They'll fill up the positions and take the housing."

Mother was known as an accomplished seamstress, one of the skills supposedly needed at Rosewell for making and repairing the field and mill workers' clothing. Father's experience as a smith was also much sought after. Pence and I were regarded as old enough for small household tasks and some of the field work, and soon our younger brothers would be available to work alongside us. We were told that the plantation was an enormous agricultural and industrial enterprise, practically a town on its own, with many hundreds of employees and their families residing there. I wanted to go there. How could it be worse than Waycross? But I wanted Father to go with us.

Father at that moment turned his body and practically flung his gaze at me. "Harley, you will be the man of the family," he declared, as if it were a discovery, a sudden revelation, not a charge or command.

Mother said, "No. He'll be a child for a long time yet."

Father then closed his eyes and seemed to be smiling at something only he knew and understood, something too profound and true to be shared with us, something unwanted by his family, but something he nonetheless desired both for himself and for us. And wanted especially for me, his oldest son. Then, during the night, while my brothers and I slept and Mother kept watch at his side, Father died.

And so dutifully, even though Father was no longer able to enforce it, we followed his final bidding, and within hours of the lightly attended service at the colony's nondenominational chapel, where three or four of my parents' compatriots spoke admiringly of Father's character and his blacksmithing skills, they buried his body in the colony's marshy, overgrown graveyard. We packed our personal belongings and left on foot for the railhead in the village of Waycross.

It was close to a half day's walk under a winter sun and a blank blue sky. Like refugees, we carried our clothing and blankets and a few cooking utensils and a day's worth of food in twine sacks and a canvas tote. Having sold Father's blacksmithing tools and the last of the family furniture and household goods to the remaining settlers for pennies on the dollar of their true value, Mother carried a small amount of cash that, after paying for our train fare from the Waycross station to Valdosta, she hoped would suffice until the first monthly payday at the plantation. She had been promised a dollar plus housing and food for a six-day week's work as a seamstress. In addition, Pence and I were to receive twenty-five cents per week for our sunrise-to-sunset labor in the fields or at one of the mills and factories and shops that clustered about the main plantation house, where the Couper family was said to reside in old-fashioned pre–Civil War splendor.

We had not seen Rosewell in person, but had heard about its scale of operation and high level of prosperity from our colonist neighbors, some of whom envied our move and promised soon to follow. The swampers residing in and around the village of Waycross and the Blacks living nearby, like the Calliphant family and their mother, the medicine woman named Partitia, spoke less admiringly of Rosewell. Which we Manns attributed to envy of the rich by the poor and ignorant and, in the case of the Blacks, to superstition.

I say "we Manns" when I mean Father and Mother and their fellow adult colonists at Waycross, because when you're a child you passively accept your parents' and their friends' view of reality, no matter how distorted by ideology or religion, and I was still a child, even though Father had made me the man of the family. But I remember Partitia Calliphant, when she was treating Father mistakenly for malaria with the sweet Annie plant, interrupting Father's praise of Rosewell and telling him, "That place a slavery plantation, Mr. Mann. Even White folks shouldn't go there for any business at all. Might never come back."

This exchange occurred some days before Mr. Couper's manager came to recruit the malcontents. It was back when Father had first spoken of going on his own to the plantation to see if his services as a smith could be hired out on a part-time basis. It was one of the few ways he was able to generate cash money in that communistic society, where all the necessities were supposedly provided by the community or purchased with Ruskinite scrip. Members with outside sources of cash were free to embellish their necessities with luxuries, but only as long as those outside sources did not require an exchange of labor. An inheritance or a packet of cash sent by a relative back in the capitalist world was permissible, but Father's hiring out his services to a local farmer who needed his horses shod was forbidden. According to the writings of John Ruskin, it made him a labor slave. My parents and their associates were close readers of Ruskin's *Unto This Last*.*

Mother explained to Partitia Calliphant that this is the twentieth century and slavery has been illegal since the Emancipation Proclamation.

Partitia said nothing in response. She was a very short, round woman with smooth dark-brown skin and heavy-lidded pale-blue eyes that she kept half-closed, as if holding back a secret. She was of indeterminate age, somewhere between fifty and sixty. She knew, of course, that slavery had been made illegal and that she had been a free woman for nearly forty years, even in the south Georgia wilderness. But my parents were educated White Northerners with an affection for abstract thought. There was much in the real world that escaped their notice, much that they no doubt would have noticed if, like me, they had lived their whole lives in the Deep South. They would have known, as Mother and her four sons would soon discover at Rosewell, that at the end of the nineteenth century and even well into the twentieth, in many parts of the South the Emancipation Proclamation and the Thirteenth Amendment to the Constitution had not been implemented.

I probably shouldn't say it here, but I have seen and heard things in my time, seen and heard them right here in my town of St. Cloud, Florida, that make me wonder sometimes if slavery has ended yet. Or if White people have managed merely to call it by another name. When defending their allegiance to their Ruskinite socialistic credo, my parents constantly railed against what they called "slave-wage capitalism." If they were alive today, what would they call Mr. Walt

* The founding texts for the Ruskinite utopians in the United States and England, John Ruskin's *Unto This Last*, four essays published in *Cornhill Magazine* in 1860 and as a book in 1862, and *Munera Pulveris*, published in 1872, were broadside attacks on the classical economics theories of Adam Smith and John Stuart Mill.

Disney's vast enterprise up there southwest of Orlando, where a Black man or woman seeking legitimate employment at the theme park need not bother showing his or her dark-complected face? Everything changes, yet everything remains the same, as the French say. Slavery is as slavery does, I say. The Whites get to exchange their labor for payment, even if only for a tiny fraction of its worth, and the Blacks are chained and put to work for nothing in the prisons and on roadside gangs that people speed past every day in their air-conditioned cars.

All right, maybe I exaggerate. An old man's privilege, I hope. A consequence, too, of that early exposure to my parents' need to see the world through the cracked lens of political ideology. It's like religion. The lens clarifies, but the cracks distort the image.

I don't normally look at the world through my long-deceased parents' eyes, however. I don't ask myself what would Mother or Father think of Walt Disney's amusement park, for instance. Or of today's plutocrats living off the labor of others just as readily and profitably as the plutocrats of my parents' time or John Ruskin's. I almost never ask myself what my communist parents would think of me, their eldest and sole surviving child, who by the time I turned forty had made a small fortune buying and selling real estate and then lost most of it in old age, thanks to my greed and pride and the superior intelligence and education of men hired by Mr. Disney to buy my property at a cut rate under false pretenses, property that I probably never should have owned in the first place. What would Father and Mother say if they knew my story? What would the Shakers' fount of wisdom and piety, Mother Ann Lee, say? Or the late Elder John Bennett and Eldress Mary Glynn, those clearheaded, high-minded, dedicated communistic Shakers? What would they say to me now? If they could speak each to each, what would they say about me?

Theirs are the antique inner voices I've been hearing since I began telling my story, the story of my childhood and youth among the Shakers at New Bethany in Narcoossee, Florida, including everything that led up to the dramatic events that unfolded there in 1910 and 1911, after I became a man, and the sorrowful consequences that followed from those events. When I speak into my tape recorder, the voices of those long-dead men and women fill my head. They've even begun to infiltrate and shape my own voice, the words and sentences I'm using to tell my story. It's as if I never learned to speak like the man I have in fact become, one of those White, lifelong, small-time Florida businessmen with no noticeable religious or political enthusiasms and no discernible class affiliation. I'm the kind of Republican or Democrat who registers as an Independent, the lapsed Protestant or Catholic who checks Christian, the Anglo-American who thinks of himself simply as American, the male human being who thinks of himself merely as human, the White man who believes he has no color.

That's the person I have been for most of my adult life and who I have over the years come to sound like. But when I flip the switch on my Grundig TK46 recorder and rewind and play back today's account, as I have just finished doing, I don't hear that person's neutral, all-purpose, modern American voice. Instead I hear a voice that's never been recorded before, not even by Thomas Edison, a voice spoken in another century, the nineteenth, and another country, the south-central Florida wilderness, a voice from long ago and far away. A voice I can barely recognize. My voice.

REEL #2

Since I closed my office downtown I've told folks that I'm retired from the real-estate business. But I still dabble a bit in buying and selling property whenever a choice lot comes my way and no one else seems eager to take a chance on it. I keep up with the market news and gossip and rumors passed around by onetime colleagues in the trade. Which is how I learned this morning that, seventy years after my fatherless family first arrived at its doorstep, Rosewell Plantation still exists.

The information came in the form of a colorful brochure forwarded to my post-office box from my now defunct office address, inviting me to refer interested clients to a new development of luxurious Southern "great houses" built around an eighteen-hole golf course designed by Arnold Palmer. The development, to be called Rosewell Plantation, is said to be located in south Georgia twelve miles from the charming city of Valdosta amid lakes and a thousand-acre pine-and-cypress forest on the grounds of a legendary antebellum plantation.

I read the brochure carefully and examined the four-color photographs of the neocolonial column-fronted brick mansions—they're called "great houses" and "homes," not "houses"—with their three-car garages and kidney-shaped swimming pools and manicured, mint green lawns. I noted the bicycle lanes and riding paths looping through open forests, the fairways and greens of Arnold Palmer's golf course, the photographs of happy-seeming, fit, elderly, White men and women, affluent and semiretired—in other words, people like me. Except that they pedal bicycles and ride thoroughbred horses and dine on moonlit patios at the clubhouse and whack golf balls over water hazards and sand traps. As I read the brochure, I remembered the arrival at Rosewell Plantation in October 1901 of my visibly pregnant mother and me and Pence and Raymond and Royal, thirsty and hungry and footsore, sombered by the loss of Father, but confident that in turning ourselves over to the plantation, we had improved our lot.

We trudged north from the Valdosta railroad stop on the old Ochlockonee River Road between two parallel hedgerows of white Cherokee roses, past fruit orchards and almond and pecan groves and flooded rice fields and glittering green fields of sugar cane, cotton, corn, and grain, and vineyards overloaded with dark red grapes ready to be harvested. Black workers, men, women, and children, with some White workers scattered among them, bent over the crops, all the while watched by Black men and one or two Whites on horseback, overseers who carried rifles and whips. We heard the buzz and hiss of a steam-powered sawmill somewhere in the distance, and the whistle and chug of a train arriving or just departing.

The dusty red-clay road ended at a piled-up heap of sweet-smelling honeysuckle and clusters of wildflowers and an open gate that led us onto a long, white crushed-stone driveway with a row of red cedars on both sides. The driveway circled before a wide shaded portico that fronted a true antebellum great house surrounded by a broad rolling lawn with flower beds shaped like scallops at the base of each of its high twelve-paned windows. The building was larger and whiter than anything we had ever seen before. We felt very small waiting there on the portico at the base of the towering columns.

It was exactly what we had hoped to see, a vast, well-organized, rich plantation, and it made us feel relieved, if not exactly happy.

It took our minds briefly away from our grief. So when Mother knocked at the tall oaken front door of the great house, we were not prepared for the greeting we received.

A small White boy opened the door. He was sour-faced and seemed not in the slightest inquisitive and only mildly surprised to see a pregnant White woman and two pairs of twin boys standing before him on the polished marble steps with all their worldly possessions at their feet. The boy was pale, as if he'd been permanently shielded from the sun, and red-lipped, with an inverted bowl of blond, nearly white hair. He wore green velveteen trousers and a flouncy, wide-collared white shirt like an adult dandy and made me think of that old song about the frog gone a-courting. He was barefoot, and his feet looked soft and trim, as if he rarely wore shoes and never left the mansion. He appeared to be about my age, ten or twelve, but his cold blue eyes and papery skin made him appear much older.

"I saw you coming up the lane," he said to Mother in a flattened voice. "We don't tolerate no beggars or peddlers. You got to move on."

Mother said, "Mr. Hamilton Couper's manager told my husband, Mr. Harrison Mann, the blacksmith up at Waycross colony, to come if we wanted work and housing. We've come from Waycross."

"Why ain't your husband doing the speaking, then?" the boy said, rather impudently, I thought, and I began to hate him a little.

"He passed," Mother said. "Three days ago."

"Just the same, ain't no work for no White woman and her children here."

Mother explained that Mr. Couper's manager had told her husband that Mother's skills as a seamstress were especially wanted at Rosewell and that her two older boys could work in the fields and the younger two in the house doing small chores.

In a lowered voice I said to Mother, "Don't explain to him. Ask to see Mr. Couper or the manager." I spoke as if I were now indeed the man of the family, anointed by Father from his deathbed, and was saying only what Father would have said.

Mother looked at me with slight irritation and tightened her lips.

"Go round to the kitchen and one of the people there will take you to the quartermaster's commissary," the boy said, and shut the tall door in our face.

A minute later a young Black woman suddenly appeared at our side and delivered us in silence to an unpainted wooden warehouse a half mile from the great house. She told the White man there that Master said to put us to work, nothing more, and she left us standing before him and returned to the kitchen.

I record and linger over these small scenes, trivial in themselves, because during the seven months that we lived and worked at Rosewell Plantation, that pale boy and the quartermaster were practically the only White people that we exchanged words with. There were a few White managers and overseers who gave orders, but they did not converse with us, except to make commands. Most of the managers and overseers were Blacks; and nearly all the workers, except for us Manns, were Blacks.

Even the White quartermaster, when we presented ourselves to him, did not speak to us directly. He sat behind a wide desk strewn with ledgers and loose papers on the further side of a ceiling-high wooden rack of small divided mailboxes. Evidently the commissary also served as the plantation post office, and the quartermaster doubled as postmaster, the man who controlled the bits of news from the outside world that came in and the little that went out.

He was small and bald and pale and his glasses reflected the fading late-afternoon sunlight like large coins. He opened a ledger and ran a crooked finger down several columns of figures, then hooked his spectacled head toward the elderly Black man behind him, who was stacking blankets on a shelf, and without saying the man's name or ours told him to put us in tent number 47. "Set them up and show them where to be at sunup," was all he said to the man. He said nothing to us, as if we were newly delivered livestock.

The old Black man was somewhere in his late sixties or early seventies and bent nearly in half with arthritis. He handed each of us a thin gray blanket and a metal cup and plate and spoon off the shelves and said to follow him. We did as told and asked no questions of him or of anyone else.

It was strange, and is stranger still to recall these many years later, that we so quickly and easily acquiesced to the authority of the place—not to any individual person's authority, the boy at the door, the woman who led us to the commissary, the quartermaster, or the old man who distributed our necessities, but to the authority of the plantation itself. It was as if the plantation and everyone on it were together a great machine, and my family and I had instantly become integral, inseparable parts of it. Simply by appearing at the door of the great house and asking for work and shelter, we had turned our lives over to the needs and rules, the protocols and priorities, of Rosewell Plantation. We had crossed a line that divided one world from another, as if exchanging planets, and now our sole concern was to learn the rules and principles that governed this new world.

The planet we had once called home was situated in another universe. It was as simple as that. The old rules and priorities and principles and the old physical laws no longer applied, even as a measurable point of comparison. To survive we had to learn as quickly as possible a new logic and coherence that were making themselves known to us at every turn, for the plantation was nothing if not self-defined and self-enclosed and rigorously logical and coherent. It was like a vast, self-sufficient factory with no other purpose than to exploit the thousands of acres of land surrounding it, the entire known world, in the manufacture and sale and distribution of a hundred different products—of cotton and sugar and lumber and turpentine and tar, of almonds and pecans and peaches, of rice and grapes, of rope and smoked meats and butter, of pumpkins and yams and peas.

We had expected to find other Ruskinite refugees from Waycross there, for we had known of at least a half dozen who had abandoned the settlement for Rosewell before us, several of them personal friends of Father and Mother. Eventually, we would learn that they either had fled the plantation for parts unknown or else had died at Rosewell. It was unclear which, for whenever Mother asked after the absent Ruskinites, their flight and their deaths were spoken of in the same way:

"They gone. Took sick and gone."

"Gone off."

"Not here no more."

There were among the workers a few White people, women mostly, and some children of various ages, but none seemed willing to acknowledge any racial kinship with us. Nor, for that matter, were we eager to acknowledge it with them, either. I remember feeling early on something like shame for my and my family's presence in the Rosewell work force, and that the origins of my shame, if that is what it was, somehow lay in the color of our skin. This was an entirely new experience for me. Up to that point, I had felt like a member of a tribe, one that I believed made me and my family culturally superior to most other tribes, regardless of race, and in fact having nothing to do with race.

I believe this is typical of groups bound together by a shared commitment to an egalitarian ideology. Or perhaps to any ideology or religion. My family and I had felt as superior to the White swampers in and around Waycross as to the poor Blacks and Indians living there. But it was based on our superior education and our freedom, as we saw it, from superstition and religion and our dedication to the ideals and principles embodied in the teachings of John Ruskin and certain other enlightened philosophers, poets, and scientists. Even toward the many other communistic groups and sects that thrived in that era, like the Fourierists and Shakers, we Manns, as Ruskinites, felt culturally, and therefore morally, superior.

But when your worth as a human being is reduced solely to the value of your body's capacity for labor, you tend to overvalue meaningless physical characteristics, like your body's skin complexion or hair texture or the shape of your nose and lips. And to find ourselves suddenly in a situation where the old familiar cultural distinctions no longer mattered, where everyone was essentially the same, except in terms of the degree of power wielded in the plantation hierarchy, was disorienting. It focused our attention on our racial difference from the other workers. That in turn generated a strange new sense, not of pride, but of shame, for we knew in our hearts that those differences were meaningless.

White-skinned or black-, we were not slaves, of course. Not chattel slaves, anyhow. We were more like indentured workers, albeit for an indefinite and lengthening period of time, thanks to the accounting system used against our poverty by Rosewell and many other plantations and mining and lumbering companies throughout the South in those years. But unlike the Blacks, it was not our skin color that had made us criminally poor in the eyes of the state. It was Father's and Mother's longtime foolish dedication to the Ruskinite dream of a "coming nation."

I don't speak for Mother and my brothers, only for myself. But it was clear to me that all of us quickly began to give off a tense, withdrawn affect and acquired a slumped, defeated posture, even Raymond and Royal, who were only nine then. Like the Black workers who surrounded us and the few White workers who toiled alongside us in the fields and forests and shops and warehouses and barns of Rosewell Plantation, we moved without alacrity or enthusiasm. To the degree that our identity as Ruskinite colonists was drained of meaning, our kinship with the scattering of Whites was somehow strengthened. But as there were no advantages or privileges granted for being a white-skinned person at Rosewell Plantation, unless one's name was Couper, we looked upon our color as a badge of shame, as if we had failed to live up to our racial prerogatives, privileges, and responsibilities. And worse, we could not know or say how or why that had happened.

Over time we learned indirectly, through rumor and gossip, that the White men and women living and working alongside us were almost all convicted criminals and their illegitimate offspring. They were petty thieves, pickpockets, and prostitutes, or they were White men and women arrested for cohabiting with a Black man or woman, or they were people who were what were called in those days sodomites. All of them were poor people unable to pay their fines or court costs. Their fines and costs had been paid to the county sheriffs and judges across the state of Georgia and even into Mississippi and Alabama by Mr. Couper himself. The convicted man's or woman's debt was to be paid by the convict at a dollar a day until such time as the balance was zero. Which could easily be postponed into the indefinite future, as Mother learned by the end of our first month, when the cost of the food and shelter and necessary goods that she had purchased on credit at the company store to feed, clothe, and house her children was deducted from our pay. There was always a negative balance. That negative balance was considered a loan from the plantation, and she was charged interest on the total. Month by month, her indebtedness increased. It never decreased by a jot.

We were housed in tent number 47, one of many dozens of what appeared to be US Army surplus tents left over from the recently completed war against the Spanish in Cuba. It was as if a battalion of American soldiers had pitched their camp in a cottonwood forest close by the plantation and dug their latrines and built their fire pits and then had suddenly decamped for some distant battlefield, leaving behind tents, cots, mosquito netting, latrines, wash stands, and outdoor kitchens for the use of the refugees whose homes and villages had been destroyed by the war. The tents provided adequate privacy and shelter against the rain and autumn winds, but not the chill of Georgia nights as winter came on. We did not freeze, but we were never warm, except when at work.

It was harvest time when we arrived, and a great force was needed in the fields, or we might have been given jobs more suited to our abilities, for unlike most of the other workers, we were literate, and Mother was an excellent seamstress. We were given three narrow canvas cots, one for Mother and the others for us four boys to share head to foot, two to a cot. The tent was the size of a small room pitched on bare ground and tall enough that Mother and Pence and I could almost stand in the center. There was an outdoor dispensary where our daily ration of potato gruel and pork bits and lard and coarse greens was ladled onto our tin plates, but no common dining hall, so we followed the example of the others and retired to dine in our tent.

The interior of our tent was always dark and mostly silent, for we worked sunup to sundown and owned no candles or lanterns, and after the first day of our arrival from Waycross, the five of us more or less fell silent. That's what people do when they are utterly defeated. They stop talking. To complain would be to express hope for an improvement in the situation. We had no such hope.

I speak of these things because I believe that the months of my and my family's virtual enslavement at Rosewell Plantation affected my personality and attitude and manner more than any other event or sequence of events in my long life and help to explain what I did later at New Bethany among the Shakers. It's partly due to my very impressionable age at the time. I was too young to summon an adult's ability to contrast his fate with what is deserved and just. At the same time I was too old to possess a child's innocence and thus wasn't shielded by a child's ability to accept as natural and normal any bizarre reality that comes to him. Despite the incompetent application of communistic principles and governance at Waycross and prior to that at Graylag, I had been happy in those places. Happiness had once been natural and normal.

I hold those seven months at Rosewell as responsible in some way for my lifelong garrulousness and secrecy, my consanguinity and pessimism, my easy sociability and solitude—my paradoxical, conflicted nature. But it's not just because of my particular age at Rosewell that I was so affected. It's also a consequence of what I witnessed there. And I tell it to my recorder today, not to explain the formation of my personality and attitude and manner, which are of no importance to anyone other than myself and, at my advanced age, not of much importance even to me. I'm telling it in order to keep from going soft in my affluent old age and forgetful of the true nature of the larger world. Especially now, when Rosewell Plantation has been turned into a theme park—I almost said "dream park"—for rich White retirees. For people like me.

It wasn't the work or the lack of adequate shelter or food. My family and I were accustomed to hard physical labor, and thanks to the squalor of Waycross, we had known rough living conditions. But we had never endured having our labor and living conditions enforced with such brute violence as they were at Rosewell. The overseers carried whips, which they did not hesitate to use both as goads and as punishment for any minor infraction or slipup. Workers, women as much as men, even children, were stripped and beaten bloody, often for no other reason than to serve as an example for the rest. It was the first time that my brothers and I feared corporal punishment. No adult at Waycross or Graylag had ever been known to beat his child. Ruskinites were more pacifistic even than Quakers.

The workers, while we labored in the fields or loaded and unloaded wagons or stacked bricks or boards, were encouraged to sing, as it seemed to help us work in unison at a steady pace, and we Whites sang weakly along with the Blacks, or else a blacksnake whip got cracked near our heads. I remember some of those songs to this day, nearly seventy years later. Here's a piece of one I especially liked. I'll say it to my tape recorder, but will not sing it, as it would make me too emotional if I tried to sing the words.

> Harper's Creek and roaring river,
> There, my love, we'll live forever,
> Then we'll go to the Indian nation.
> All I want in this creation
> Is a pretty little wife and a big plantation . . .

I'm hesitant to describe all that I saw there. It's hard to believe that human beings can be so cruel to one another, especially when everyone, victim as much as victimizer, shares the same plight. For we were all imprisoned at Rosewell Plantation, regardless of position, from the lowliest laborer to the chief overseer and even to the few officers at the top, like the quartermaster and the paymaster. The keys to everyone's shackles were held by Mr. Couper and his family members, who we rarely saw, except at a distance coming from and going to the great house in fancy carriages or riding beautifully groomed horses with long flowing manes and tails.

And the shackles were not merely figurative. Many of the younger, surlier men had short chains clamped to their ankles that forced them to shuffle when they walked. These were men who had committed serious crimes and had been serving life terms or very long sentences when Mr. Couper bought their labor from the prisons and who thus were more likely to try escaping from Rosewell than those whose sentences were relatively light and were thought, however falsely, soon to be completed and paid out.

Escape from Rosewell seemed impossible to most of the workers. We Manns never talked about it among ourselves or with the others. While my family and I were there, a few tried escaping, but they were quickly recaptured and in front of everyone were stretched naked over a barrel and beaten until they fainted. Survival with the least amount of physical pain was everyone's sole concern.

There was nowhere to escape to, anyhow. The plantation was many thousands of acres of field and pine and cedar forest and swampland, and all the towns and villages in the vicinity were economically dependent on its smooth-running existence, and the larger, independent cities like Savannah and Atlanta were hundreds of miles away and might as well have been on a different planet. An escapee could no more reach one of those cities than he could get to Philadelphia or Boston.

I learned a lot about human nature at Rosewell that I did not want to believe, a lot that contradicted much of what the Ruskinites and later the Shakers tried to make me believe. Had I never learned it, I might well have been a better son and brother, a better Shaker, than I have been over the nearly seventy years that followed my time there.

I learned that people who have had everything stolen from them will steal from anyone who has not. Under degrading conditions there is no such thing as solidarity. That is why, after our second day of work, when we trudged back from the cotton fields, we discovered that our tent had been emptied of all the belongings that we had carried with us from Waycross. Even our blankets were gone, and if we had not followed the overseer's instructions and carried our tin eating utensils with us to the field, those items, too, would have disappeared. Mother went to the commissary and asked the quartermaster to replace the stolen blankets, and the cost, another five days' work for each of us five Manns, was added to her account. He told her that from now on, if she and her children wanted to keep our blankets, we should carry them whenever we left the tent.

I learned that people who are worked almost literally to death have little desire for the company of others. Like wounded animals, they want nothing more than to be left alone, to huddle in a corner and try to recover enough energy to continue living another day. There was no society at Rosewell Plantation, anyhow, except in the fields or on our way to and from the fields or when we sometimes exchanged sober greetings at the start of the day as we clambered aboard the rickety wagons that carted us to our labors. No one revealed anything of his past or how he or she came to be imprisoned at Rosewell Plantation. People who can't imagine a future have a hard time remembering a past, or at least of telling about it, for the past can't have been worse than the present and thus it would be an unwelcome and painful thing to describe and bring fully to mind.

I learned that children as much as adults, women as much as men, Whites as much as Blacks, in degradation degrade whomever else they can. There is a downward exercise of violence and theft, of sexual dominance and use, of manipulation and control, deception, extortion, sadism. I have never forgotten or had reason to reject what I learned about human nature at Rosewell Plantation.

Mother saw what I was learning, for I had begun to exercise the power of the small advantages I had over my twin brother, Pence, and my two younger brothers, Raymond and Royal, and she tried to stop me. One evening the old arthritic Black man who worked for the quartermaster came to our tent. His name was Hamish, I can still recall it, and he spoke with a rattled voice very slowly, as if his throat were scarred from some old injury and it was painful to speak. He pulled back the flap and asked Mother which of her boys was best with numbers and writing. Mr. Browne, the quartermaster, in order to check against thievery, wanted a clerk of the works to inventory the goods warehoused there.

"No way to know what's been taken 'less'n he knows what's there," Hamish said. "Master Couper, he making Mr. Browne accountable for what's stole. Mr. Browne doing a count that's exact, so he don't get blamed for losing what wasn't there in the first place."

I assumed that Mr. Browne wanted a child for the job, so as not to take away one of the adults, all of whom were needed in the fields, and probably felt that a child would be less likely than an adult to deliberately undercount the stock and then pilfer goods to match the count. And because we Manns were White and recently arrived and, as indicated by our speech, were Northerners, we were assumed to be capable of reading and writing and doing sums.

I wanted very much to get free of field work and become the clerk of the works. I stepped in front of my brothers and Mother and declared that when it came to doing sums I was the best of them. Royal and Raymond, I said, were only nine years old and had but three years of schooling, whereas I had five. I then gratuitously added that Pence was thought to be a little slow. "If you know what I mean, Mr. Hamish," I added in a sly low aside, as if to keep Pence from hearing me.

Pence heard, of course, and punched me on the back.

And Mother heard, too. She said to Hamish, "Harley is wrong. None of the boys have had any schooling. None of them is capable of being a clerk of the works. Though I myself, because of my condition, would be mighty grateful not to have to work in the fields until after my baby is born. And I am very good with sums."

Hamish nodded, not quite in sympathy, but understanding her complaint and helpless to address it in any meaningful way, even if he wanted to. "Mr. Browne say he want a child for the position." Hamish had been given a task, and he had completed it and could return now to the quartermaster's shed and resume folding blankets. Keeping a count of the blankets and eating utensils and tents and cots and all the other supplies and food stores was Mr. Browne's responsibility, not his.

When he had gone, Mother said, "None of you is to take advantage of your brothers or me. Remember, boys, as long as we remain here we have no one but ourselves for comfort and support." She was ashamed of me for having put myself forward, when I was the strongest of the four and was therefore the best able to tolerate field work. Had I not promoted myself at the others' expense, she might have volunteered Raymond or Royal for the position of clerk of the works. Now none of us would have it. "It is better that all of us be deprived of a luxury than one of us obtain it illegitimately," she said.

This was a Ruskinism that I had heard many times before, a rule that I was on my way to thinking no longer applied. At least not here at Rosewell Plantation. And if the real world turned out to resemble

Rosewell more than my parents' utopian dream world, then the rule, like the Golden Rule, no longer applied anywhere.

Royal, who was the most sensitive of us boys, began to sob, and his braver twin, Raymond—with twins one of the pair is always the braver—demanded that Mother tell us when we could leave this place. "Why must we stay here? Why can't we go back to Waycross?"

She sighed and sat her heavy body down on her cot. "It was a mistake for us to come here. I know that now. I do. But we owe Mr. Couper for our food and other necessaries. We can't leave, not until we work off our debt," she said.

"I think Father would want us to return to Waycross regardless of our debt," I said, pretending once again to be the designated man of the family.

"We have no money to buy back our shares in Waycross. A condition of our departure from the colony was that our shares be deposited in the general fund. So they cannot be redeemed. I don't think Waycross will take us back, anyhow, unless we repurchase our shares, especially if we arrive bearing a debt to Mr. Couper. The Ruskinites are not a public charity. They don't take in homeless debtors. Especially a widow with four little boys in tow and another on the way. After the baby comes, I will find a way to get us free of this place," she promised.

"It can't be done," I declared. "As long as we eat Mr. Couper's food and burn his wood in our cook fire, we'll owe him more money than we earn."

"I will find a way," she repeated, and I decided not to question her any further.

We continued to wake in the dark every morning at four o'clock to the clang of the brass bell at the top of the main barn—rung with a rope pulled by the manager of the plantation work force, Mr. Guy Daniels. His name comes suddenly back to me, after having lain in my mind unbidden and forgotten for decades. At the commissary we were fed our morning ration of milk and gruel and thin coffee and given the slab of pork fat and cold oatmeal that would serve as our midday dinner. At four thirty, still before dark, another peal of Mr. Daniels's bell hurried us to the central lot where the wagons and mules awaited us and where the overseers assigned the day's work to everyone and issued our tools from the main toolhouse, the hoes and spades, rakes and crowbars, axes and machetes, mauls and splitting wedges that would fill our hands for the next fourteen to fifteen hours. Men whose job was to plow tossed their plows onto the wagons and climbed onto the backs of their mules and with harnesses and chains clinking rode slowly from the lot out to the fields ahead of the wagons that moments later carted the field hands and woodsmen and factory workers to their dozens of workplaces, the cotton and tobacco and vegetable fields, the orchards and vineyards, the pine woods and lumber mills and warehouses and shipping docks and the rail yards and stables and cow barns and hog pens and henhouses.

This was all done under the supervision of Mr. William Spain, the chief overseer. William Spain was the man who had gone down to Waycross that fateful day to recruit Father and Mother. His name, like Mr. Daniels's, has burst into my mind for the first time since the last time I spoke it, probably to Mother or Pence, those seventy years gone.

By five o'clock in the morning the sky was turning pale, and when everyone else had left the main lot for the workplace, Mr. Spain stepped up to his buggy drawn by his favorite horse, a high-strung Texas horse that only he could handle. I remember how Pence loved looking at that horse, admiring the animal's pure shapeliness, the beauty of its stride, the strength of its spirit. Mr. Spain rode out to show the overseers the plots of land that needed laying off for plowing or for planting and the plots that needed to be cut with the harrow and burnt over or turned under. His method was to drive over the land with his buggy marking the perimeters with the tracks of its wheels. He went from field to field and forest to stream and pond, and when everyone knew his or her job, he drove his beautiful horse back to his office at the great house and left the management of the day to Mr. Daniels and the overseers and their whips.

My family and I labored in the fields all day long six days a week. Nights we huddled in our tent, and both day and night we witnessed many atrocities, some worse than others. Most of the worst we did not see in person and only heard about, so I choose not to cite them, but here are a few that we saw. Or rather, here are the atrocities that *I* saw. Mother and my three brothers each surely had their own lists, but in all the years that followed our months at Rosewell Plantation none of us shared our lists, and now it's too late, for they all are gone. Except for me, and this is my list. Or as much of it as I am willing to share with strangers.

Late one night, Mother sent me to the sawmill in search of wood scraps for our fire, but she forgot that the mill ran all night as well as all day, and when I got there I realized that if I were caught scouring for scraps, I'd be beaten and sent off. The sawmill was a simple roof on poles to protect the machinery from rain. The men worked in dim lantern light while I watched from darkness just beyond. I was about to return to the tent empty-handed when I noticed a tall, thin Black man on the catwalk, shirtless and staggering from some kind of sickness, unsteady on his feet and dangerously close to the spinning blade of the saw. The man's job was to guide the cedar logs along the chute to the saw and meet a second man on the far side of the blade, and the two of them would carry the squared log back for a second run and a third and a fourth, until the log had become a half dozen or more one-inch-thick boards of sweet-smelling cedar ready to be shipped to Atlanta or Savannah or beyond.

The shirtless man suddenly vomited and then slipped on his vomit. He was sick, probably from homemade liquor. Extending his arm to break his fall, he got it caught by the steam-powered saw blade and severed cleanly off above the elbow. I saw the man's arm come off his body, and I heard him scream and then go silent and fall in a heap, while the shining, blood-spattered blade whirred on, and the wood-fired steam engine that drove the belts that turned the blade hissed, and the piston rose and fell like a giant steel heart. For several long minutes no one came to help the man, who was beyond help by then, until finally his partner at the receiving end of the chute noticed his absence and looked along the catwalk and saw his body lying in a spreading pool of blood. The man bled to death on the catwalk next to the still-spinning blade.

I did not move to help him or even to sound the alarm. I was rooted like a tree to my spot in the darkness, until at last someone shut down the steam engine, and the blade was silenced and stilled, and I crept away unseen, unheard. Because I did nothing to help the poor man, I never told my mother or my brothers what I had seen. Until now, I have never told anyone.

I remember a day when I and the rest of my family were picking cotton in a field a mile and a quarter south of the main plantation buildings. Wrapped by an oxbow of the slow-moving Satilla River, the flat ten-acre field was ablaze with white cotton. At dawn when we first arrived at the field, a mist hovered above the river, and the workers shivered from the cold, and the work kept us warm until the sun burned off the mist, and now the heat was wearing us down. Five crews of five workers, each crew with its own row, moved machine-like across the wide black floodplain. Quietly, obediently, we Manns worked alongside one another, filling our rough sacks, pricking our fingers bloody, sweating under the noonday sun.

I was singled out by the sometimes-kind overseer named Little John to go to the water stand and bring a ladle and a bucket of water to share out with the others. The water stand was a barrel with a spigot at the far end of the field in a riverbank grove of cottonwoods where the five crews would end the day, the field picked clean. The barrel sat atop the wagon that had brought the workers out at sunup and would take us and our day's picked cotton back to the weighing station at sundown, where it would be ginned and baled for shipment.

When I got to the wagon, two overseers were there before me, drinking water, laughing and pretending to argue as men sometimes do when they have something serious to argue about but aren't yet willing to push it very far. They were Black men, one very light, the other very dark, and not young, both in their forties, I recall. They saw me approach, and the darker one waved me over. "Let the White boy settle it," he said. He asked me for my name and then said, "Okay, Harley Mann, we got us a dispute going on. We both want that same little gal over there, and neither of us is willing to share her. That's the rule. You take on a gal, she's yours to keep. Not to share. Right?"

I saw a young Black woman a short ways beyond them tied by her hands to a cottonwood tree—a girl, actually, only a few years older than me. Her feet were bare and she wore a thin cotton dress that she appeared to have recently outgrown. Her black hair was tousled and shaken loose, and her bare arms and legs were covered with dust and dirt, as if she had been wrestled to the ground before being tied to the tree. She looked defiantly away from us three males, but was otherwise expressionless, dead-faced. It was not an uncommon look at Rosewell Plantation, especially among the females, where a powerful man, as in a prison, often made a concubine of one of the younger, prettier inmates and in exchange provided her, or sometimes him, with protection and small favors.

The two men agreed to abide by my decision as to which of them would claim the girl. I told the men that I couldn't choose between them. I said it was up to the girl to choose which of the two she preferred.

At that moment they seemed likely to fight each other for possession of the girl. Both had belt knives and might have stashed a gun nearby, as most of the overseers carried firearms, although at the moment neither appeared to be wearing a sidearm.

I did not want one of them to kill the other. I knew that Mr. Spain and Mr. Couper, the master of Rosewell Plantation, would need to know how it happened, and I would be drawn in as a witness. If I told the truth, I would make an enemy of the killer. If I lied, I would be tied forever to the man I lied for.

I repeated my suggestion that the girl choose between them.

Both men looked at me with disgust. "You sound like some kind of girl yourself, Harley Mann," the dark-skinned man said. "Maybe the one of us who don't get the gal gets you instead. As a consolation prize." He laughed and said to the other, "Bill, you want this White boy keep you warm at night?"

I pretended not to hear him and went about the business of filling a bucket with water from the barrel. My heart was pounding, and my legs were weak and trembling.

"I'm thinking on it," the one named Bill said, and he laughed, too. "He too skinny, though. I prefer something with a little meat 'fore I bone it," he said. "Come to think on it, that little gal over there a little too skinny, too. I'm gonna let you take her, Bridge," he said, and clapped the other man on his shoulder and walked in the direction of the field east of the oxbow, while I grabbed a ladle and the bucket of water and silently stole off toward my crew, abandoning the girl tied to the cottonwood tree and the man named Bridge, who now owned her, body and soul.

I never mentioned to anyone what I had seen and heard that day. Until now, that is. At Rosewell Plantation, I got secretive about many of my experiences and nearly all of my thoughts and feelings. I stopped sharing them even with my brother Pence, my beloved twin, closer to me since birth than any other human being, closer than our mother and father, more trusted, more relied upon for support and understanding and loyalty, more known by me than by anyone else. I was a few moments older than Pence, and like Raymond I was the braver twin, but Pence and I had always been more like two halves of a single unit than a pair of separate, autonomous individuals.

In the past, before we went to Rosewell, I might have told Pence what I witnessed at the sawmill that night, without telling Mother or the others, perhaps confiding to my brother that I felt ashamed for not having made a move to help the poor man who lay bleeding from his terrible wound on the catwalk not ten feet away, that I had waited in the shadows while the man bled to death, until finally another worker noticed his helper's absence and strolled down to the fallen man too late to help, and I ran away.

And I might have told Pence what happened that noonday at the water wagon, the quarrel between the overseers over which of them would take possession of the girl tied to the tree, and of the strange feelings aroused in me by the sight of her, and the oddly tempting sense of power I felt for a few seconds when the two overseers asked me to choose between them, and the even stranger feelings that arose when the two men entertained the idea of making me a concubine to one of them. But I never told Pence any of it. I kept it inside and choked on it.

And there was much more that I was silent about, so much more that I saw and heard at Rosewell Plantation, and felt, especially that—feelings that I dared not reveal to anyone, not even to my beloved Pence, and barely to myself. It was the beginning of my falling away from the family that later came to cause them and me so much grief and confusion.

I wonder if Mother and my brothers really did know what horrors surrounded us at Rosewell Plantation. Was I the only one who knew? In later years, when I reflected on our time there, I realized that Mother's first concern had been her pregnancy, and her four sons' physical and mental conditions were close behind in second place, so it made a certain sense for her to avert her gaze somewhat in order to concentrate better on making sure that we all got enough food and kept warm at night and avoided falling ill like so many of the workers, who were malnourished and down and dying of dysentery and malaria and typhus.

Mother on her own cultivated the quartermaster, Mr. Browne, who was also the postmaster, and eventually he brought her on as the clerk of the works he had been seeking, which took her away from the fields and the hard labor that replaced field work after harvest season passed, giving her access to increased portions of food, including extra rice and salt pork, and a charcoal stove and fuel and blankets. An honest woman, Mother listed everything she took back to our tent at the end of the day and as a result ran up our debt at the commissary, which, after the birth of her baby and the welfare of her four sons, became her third preoccupation—our growing debt to Mr. Couper. Her clerical honesty made her irreplaceable to Mr. Browne and at the same time made her and our family permanent prisoners of Mr. Couper.

My brothers, on the other hand, did seem genuinely unaware of the dark violence of the plantation, or rather, they merely accepted it as normal, as the way the world is, as the only way it can be. They were children and had no other world or had not known another world long enough to imagine an alternative. I felt a great difference in age opening between them and me, even between Pence and me, as if I had become a young man and they were still little boys. I did not want to hinder Mother in her pregnancy or her devoted attempt to provide for her children by telling her what I saw all around us, nor did I want her to know the strange ways it made me feel. Nor did

I want to disillusion my brothers of their belief that while life may be hard, exhausting work, our fellow human beings, all appearances to the contrary, were as good and loving inside as us Manns. They would be disabused of that dream soon enough. No reason for me to tell them there's no Santa Claus. They would learn it soon enough on their own. You learn what you can bear to know only when you can bear it, not before.

I should get on with describing my first sighting of the Shaker elder John Bennett. It happened at Rosewell Plantation the month after my sister, Rachel, was born and Mother was allowed to continue working as clerk of the works for Mr. Browne, the quartermaster. I did not know it at the time, but as clerk of the works Mother had access to the plantation post office and was able to write and surreptitiously slip into the outgoing mail several letters directed To Whom It May Concern at New Bethany, Narcoossee, Florida, whose fellow-communistic existence she as a Ruskinite had long been aware of.

It was a fresh spring day, and Pence and I were feeding the fires used to boil cauldrons of water to scald and skin the hogs before the crew butchered them and smoked and salted their parts. Thanks to the smoke from the fires, the usual swarming savagery of the clouds of mosquitoes was diminished, I recall, and Pence and I were almost glad to have been chosen to witness and participate in this brutal chore. The hogs in their pen knew what was in store for them, and they roared in fear and protest and clambered over one another's backs attempting to escape, until, one by one, a single hog was selected for execution and lassoed and led from the pen through a narrow chute, which must have looked like a gateway to freedom, because the hog instantly went quiet, and then was shot in the forehead. The chief butcher was a White man from the village of Valdosta, very skilled at executing the hogs with a single shot for each animal, followed by a slash of his long knife across the animal's throat.

It was hard, hot, dirty work to keep the water in the half dozen cauldrons at the right temperature—hot enough to loosen the skin and hair but not so hot as to cook the meat beneath when the dead hog was dipped by a pair of strong men with a winch attached to a tripod above the steaming cauldron. On a good day they could process as many as twenty hogs. We boys who fed the fires ran from cauldron to cauldron with our armloads of split firewood, dodging gouts of blood pumped by the animals' still-beating hearts out their slashed throats. The fires had to be kept going and low for hours, and when the first half of the first day had passed, we knew exactly how many pieces and how large a piece of wood to add without being hollered at by the men hooking the hogs by chains to the winches and hauling them upside down by their hind legs to the top of the tripods, as if to a crucifix, and dropping them down headfirst into the scald, while the butcher with his gleaming knives and saw went from cauldron to cauldron testing the looseness of the skin, until it was ready to be slipped off the carcass like a glove from a hand, and he could begin his grisly work.

I was on my knees feeding one of the fires, dodging the spillage of blood from the bucket overhead. I felt a light tap on my shoulder and turned and saw a pair of large soft-leather boots, and looked up to trousers of plain blue linen or hemp, and still further up to a long, loose jacket that came to the person's knees, cut in an antique way with no collar or cuffs and made of the same material and color as the trousers, and onward to the bright, broad, suntanned face of a bearded White man. A stranger. He wore a wide-brimmed straw hat. I remember that the large buttons on his jacket were made of wood. The man's hair and beard were long and thick and dark brown with a reddish tint in the sunlight and covered his face and throat like a soft shawl. He was very tall and thick-bodied, larger than any of the Black men scalding the hogs and the White butcher wielding his rifle and knives, possibly larger than any of the men that I had seen so far at Rosewell.

From little more than a rising glance from below, something about the man at that first sighting gave me the sudden belief that everything was about to change, and that my family and I would be saved by this stranger. The man made a gesture for me to stand. I obeyed and saw Mother with Rachel in her arms standing behind the man, and for the first time since Father died, Mother was smiling. Pence stood beside her, spattered with soot from the fires and blood from the hogs. He looked puzzled and wary, as if he thought a trick were about to be played on him.

I joined Mother and Rachel and Pence, and the stranger said to the butcher, who was the obvious boss of the operation, "These boys are now in my charge. Find thyself another pair to keep thy fires a-burning." His voice was dark and deep, and he spoke in an old-fashioned biblical manner that gave to his words an authority that embellished the authority he derived from his great size.

The butcher nodded and turned to one of the overseers standing idly nearby, and the overseer left at once to find replacements for me and Pence.

Mother said to me, "This is Elder John Bennett from the Shaker colony down in Florida. He has paid our debt to Mr. Couper. We are now free to go."

We were not quite free. It was as if we had been paroled and Elder John Bennett were our parole officer. We were only free to leave Rosewell Plantation and go with Elder John south to a place called New Bethany, named for the city of Lazarus, raised from the dead, only located now near Narcoossee at the headwaters of the Everglades.

By the time Mother and Elder John had gathered up Raymond and Royal, who were at work in the riverside cotton field, and we four boys had been bathed in the river, I learned that Mother and her five children had become Shakers. She had not signed the covenant contract yet. That would come later, when we were settled in at New Bethany. But Mother announced it in so many words while we carried our few remaining belongings to the wagon and driver that Elder John had hired to bring us to the railroad station at Valdosta.

Elder John had gone into the great house to finish signing the papers and promissory notes in the presence of Mr. Couper, while we waited at the wagon. Mother said with a broad smile, "We are to become Shakers now."

It was hard to tell if she was happy about the conversion or simply happy that Mr. Couper had been paid and we had been given permission to leave Rosewell. I concluded it was both. Pence probably thought the same. The younger twins, Raymond and Royal, likely believed that she was happy and smiling, her face like a small sun, because we were all becoming Shakers, which made our becoming Shakers, therefore, a very good thing. But only I questioned Mother.

"Which pleases you more," I asked her, "us becoming Shakers or us getting away from this place?"

She turned and stared at me, no longer smiling. "Why do you ask such a question?" The others all looked at me as if they, too, wondered why I would ask such a question. What could it matter, so long as our lives were about to change and our mother was pleased by the change?

I admit that back then, even as a twelve-year-old boy, I was a hair-splitting moralist, judgmental and proud. It goes with what I call my guilt complex. Anyone with a lifelong guilty conscience is likely to be a hair-splitting moralist, especially when it comes to other people's behavior. I have often wondered about the early source of my guilty conscience, which was already in full flower and had bloomed possibly even earlier at Waycross. Though it's hard for me to remember my inner life that far back, with a little effort I can recall what it felt like to be Harley Mann when he was a twelve-year-old boy. My parents had long eschewed organized religion, so it wasn't religion that made me accuse and convict myself of secret crimes and misdemeanors. It had to be my parents' perfectionist utopian dream, the dream they shared with the hundreds of like-minded dreamers who surrounded them near and far, the dream that made me feel like a failure and weak and morally inadequate. Sinful even. So it might as well have been religion, despite the fact that we had none. Until we became Shakers, that is.

Mother never answered my question as to which pleased her more, becoming Shakers or getting away from Rosewell Plantation. And I never answered hers as to why I would ask such a question in the first place. When we had seated ourselves in Elder John's wagon outside the great house and were prepared to depart from the plantation, the barefoot, pale-faced boy with white hair who had greeted us on our first arrival came out onto the portico with Elder John. The boy crossed his arms over his small chest and stared at us. Elder John walked to the wagon and climbed up to his seat next to the driver. The boy's gaze was as hard and cold as a diamond.

Elder John called to him, "T'was a pleasure doing business with thee, Mr. Couper."

This was Mr. Couper? I had thought him a boy, but he was not a boy at all! He was a tiny man. And not a young man. His hair was white because he was a man well beyond middle age. The master of the whole vast plantation more closely resembled an eleven-year-old boy than a grown man! Until this moment the imagined figure of Mr. Hamilton Couper had loomed large and dark over my mind and all my workdays and nights. It shocked me to see that a miniaturized man could wield so much power over the lives of hundreds of human beings and animals, thousands of acres of land, dozens of buildings and huge machines and industrial installations. Because we had not seen him in the fields or workhouses or the workers' quarters and did not know that we had already met him, I had imagined that Mr. Couper was a large man, as large as Elder John, and as old, except fierce and calculating, cruel and unforgiving. How else to explain his power over us? I now saw that Mr. Couper's power came only from money, his control of an unimaginable abundance of money and our lack of it and the terrible, almost unfathomable distance between the two.

On the ride from the plantation to the railroad depot in Valdosta, Elder John sat up front with the hired driver, and we Manns sat on the wagon bed behind and kept silent. We four boys and Mother, who nursed baby Rachel as we rode along, looked out at the passing barns and warehouses and plantation factories, the fields and woodlands where we had spent the last seven months toiling from sunup to sundown under the threat of the lash or worse, exhausted and ill fed and frightened of inexplicable explosions of violence in the company of several hundred other poor souls, almost all of them Black convicts enslaved just like us by debt, but most of them convicted beforehand and indebted to Mr. Couper because of their race. Which was not the case for us Manns. When I remember my family's departure from the plantation in the protective custody of Elder

John, I call that difference back, and the warmth of my memory is chilled with guilt for it.

So began our journey out of Georgia south into Florida. My first impression of our savior, Elder John Bennett, was that despite his somewhat ecclesiastical language, his "thee"s and "thou"s, he was not much of a religious man. His speech seemed more an affectation than natural or even habitual usage, as if he were an atheistic farmer or woodsman inappropriately cast as a Puritan preacher in an amateur play about the Salem witch trials. His language did not match his Kentucky accent with conviction or musicality, so that this big, confident, physically certain, and by all indications highly intelligent man came off as inarticulate and emotionally awkward, possibly a not very competent confidence man. He sometimes dropped the Quaker mode of speaking as if he'd forgotten his scripted lines and was plunging ahead in a different play, one about a trial in which he was cast as a Kentucky sharecropper wrongly accused of a minor crime. He seemed more natural and honest then, a man speaking in his neighbors' and family's tongue.

On the road to Valdosta, Elder John talked over his shoulder to Mother, but not to us children. He described the journey we were about to take as if he were a tour guide on the morning of departure. We would be traveling for two nights and most of three days, he told us, first by wagon and then on the Atlantic Coast Line Railroad, then by steamboat along narrow canals linking a chain of lakes in south-central Florida, and near the end by wagon again, to where the road finally ends at New Bethany. We would see clouds of marvelous birds, he told us, and alligators and deer and panthers and possibly a bear or two along the way. We would pass near Seminole Indian villages and old Spanish trading posts on the banks of the meandering St. Johns River, where schools of fish pack the waters and practically beg to be caught and brought to the skillet. We would cross vast wetlands and marshes and swamps between wide sawgrass plains where great herds of semiwild longhorn cattle graze. We might see lightning-struck fires in the distance, burning thousands of acres of pine forests. South of Jacksonville there would be no human settlements that could pass for more than a village or a ranch or a railhead with only a ramshackle post office and general store and a ware-house where oranges and limes and melons are packed for shipment north. Elder John said that down there the soil is deep and black and rich, and the climate is frost-free year-round, and the flowers and fruit trees and almond trees blossom twelve months a year and give of the Lord's bounty in endless profusion and abundance.

He did not mention blinding clouds of mosquitoes. He said noth-ing of the long, torrential rainy season. He did not say that every few years a frost kills all the crops overnight, and by morning every farmer and rancher from Tampa to Fort Myers has to borrow a year's income from the bank and start over. He did not tell us about the hurricanes. He neglected to describe the brutal intensity of the heat in summer and the suffocating humidity from May to September. And he said nothing about the ne'er-do-wells, the outlaws and prison escapees, the gunmen and cattle rustlers and poachers, the thieves and con men and hustlers, who for nearly a century had been drift-ing south from Georgia and Alabama and Mississippi and from states further north and west to ply their criminal trades with impu-nity and near-anonymity. He left out of his narrative the presence of thousands of fugitive White sharecroppers off the plantations of Georgia and the Carolinas who came to Florida after the Civil War with their large families and no resources or money and little more than an axe and shovel and shotgun to stake a claim on life and found themselves in short order worse off than they had been in their dirt-floor cabins back home, their children suffering from dis-ease and malnutrition, unschooled, isolated, inbred.

Though I barely observed it at the time, I remember that the way Elder John advertised our journey in advance out of Rosewell Plan-tation down to Narcoossee and the Shaker settlement called New Bethany and described what we saw as we traveled along, by direct-ing his commentary almost exclusively to Mother and more or less ignoring us children, he was behaving suspiciously. It was as if his interest in Mother were kindled by something more than a desire to convince her of the value of living in Florida as a Shaker. It may have been erotic.

"Elder John was unusually attentive to Mother" is probably how I should phrase it.

Of course, it was also the case that in order to recruit her five children to spend their lives working the Shakers' fields and farms, Elder John needed first to seduce Mother, for she was the only one who could sign us over to the Shakers. People who joined the Shakers were required to give over all their property and possessions, and if like Mother they owned no property or possessions, but had young children, the only thing they could give over was their children, who were then bound to work as directed by the elders and eldresses until they turned twenty-one, if male, or eighteen, if female.

Beyond that pecuniary motivation, however, there was about Elder John a powerful, unmistakably masculine aura, such that any undue attention he paid to a woman seemed suspicious—to me today, that is, not back then, when I was a boy. Children can intuit these things about adults' attraction to one another, however, even if they have no experience or vocabulary to help them name it. I obviously could not view Mother the way a full-grown man could view her, in particular a man whose body and physical grace and power were so explicitly male—an unmarried, sexually abstinent man—but I was nonetheless aware that, compared to most women her age, Mother was attractive to both the male eye and the male mind.

She was tall and slim and despite many years of hard physical labor in the outdoors under the Southern sun, and housekeeping since girlhood with none of the modern labor-saving appliances that we now take for granted, and despite having borne five children, Mother at thirty was still fresh-faced and pink-skinned and healthy looking. When angry or amused, her blue eyes sparkled with intelligence. Her teeth were intact and large, and her nose and chin were prominent, and the clean overall symmetry of her face put her features into handsome perspective and right proportion, one to the other. She was decorous and controlled in her movements and was a comfort to behold and was in no way flashy or glamorous. When she walked, she tilted slightly forward, as if thinking hard about her purpose and destination, curiously contributing to her general good looks. She did not laugh or even smile easily, which could be construed as evidence of an angry or even bitter temperament. And who could blame her if, after all that she had endured in recent years, she had come up angry and bitter? But despite all that she had suffered—the rigors of communal life and the unexpected downturn at Waycross and the sudden death of Father and the difficulty of raising five young children alone and the poverty and indebtedness that drove her to Rosewell Plantation and kept her there so long—despite everything, her anger and bitterness were more self-protective affect than temperament.

After she joined the Shakers and settled at New Bethany, after her life softened somewhat and became stable and secure, her mien and manner became greatly altered. She became less unpredictable and lost the earlier threat of unprovoked anger and edginess that had given to her personality an off-putting sharpness, a sharpness that had perhaps first attracted Elder John, the attraction that I found so suspicious on our journey out of Rosewell Plantation to Narcoossee and New Bethany.

Speaking at such length of that long-ago journey south has brought to my mind how quick and easy and comfortable a journey it would be if I drove the distance from Rosewell to New Bethany today in my Packard. I love driving that huge, powerful vehicle. I bought it new at Nixon Butt Motors on North Orange Avenue in Orlando back in 1953. Paid cash for it, as I do for everything, even real estate. I avoid the credit system of finance, except as a lender-out. A pepper-green Packard Patrician four-door sedan, my car sluices its smooth way along the highway like a moving room.

I wonder how much of Waycross and Rosewell Plantation I would recognize today. Everything changes, but on an underlying level everything remains the same. I remember the real-estate brochure advertising Rosewell Plantation Estates with the riding trails and golf course and fancy clubhouse and the columned great-house "homes," and I fancy driving up there in my Packard to see the place in person, if only to find out if it will joggle my memory of the original Rosewell Plantation, where my family and I were imprisoned so long ago.

Compared to the two nights and three days by wagon and rail and steamboat that it took to cover the distance from there to here back in '02 with Elder John, in my moving room I could travel from my old Shaker home in New Bethany outside the village of Narcoossee back to my even older home at Rosewell Plantation in less than six hours—a time-reversed journey between the two worlds. I could depart now from this house just a few miles down the road from the original Shaker lands near Narcoossee, drive west on Route 441 to St. Cloud where it curls north to Orlando. I'd pick up Route 17 in Orlando and, keeping west of the St. Johns River, follow it all the way up the state to Jacksonville, then cross into Georgia, where it hits Route 1 north and drive straight to Valdosta and Waycross. I can be there before dark.

But why would I want to revisit a place that I regard as the opening wound in a wounded life?

REEL #3

The longest segment of our journey south to New Bethany—and for me, a twelve-year-old boy, the least interesting part of it—was the ride on the Atlantic Coast Line train from Valdosta to St. Cloud, where we transferred to a flat-bottomed, steam-powered barge and crossed the chain of shallow lakes and deep sinkhole ponds linked by canals to the frontier village of Narcoossee and the final few watery miles to New Bethany. On the train we Manns were more or less confined to a pair of slatted wooden benches that Elder John treated as a schoolroom and an opportunity to educate Mother and us four boys on the principles and requirements of our future life as Shakers.

It was a somewhat legalistic series of short lectures that he gave, but he kept them brief and informal enough to hold the interest of me and my brothers, who had not been in a schoolroom or received any kind of formal instruction since leaving Graylag in Indiana over a year ago. We were glad for the chance to listen to an explication of just about anything that did not concern hard physical labor and was not enforced by the threat of a whipping. We were naturally curious and intelligent boys, and Elder John was a well-organized and knowledgeable and self-confident lecturer who used many homely expressions and turns of phrase. He was logical, too—if you took away his belief in the divinity of the religion's founder, Mother Ann Lee, which was the bedrock that supported the whole superstructure of Shaker doctrine and principle. Mother Ann Lee was the second appearance on earth of Jesus Christ, this time in female form, he explained, and after passing from this earth back in 1784, she reigned now in heaven alongside her male manifestation, Jesus, in a relationship that corresponded, in some way that I never really grasped, to Adam and Eve. According to Elder John, there were two creations. The first, through Adam and Eve, was the old creation, with marriage and generation its basic law, as in "go forth and multiply." The fundamental law of the second, inaugurated by Jesus Christ and embodied by Mother Ann Lee, was virgin purity and regeneration,* rebirth through grace.

Luckily, Elder John did not dwell very heavily on the theological and metaphysical aspects of the Shaker religion. Their formal name, he explained, was the United Society of Believers in Christ's Second Appearing. Other people, outsiders, people of "the World," had long ago named them Shakers, because of the Believers' early practice of shaking and trembling when at prayer, not unlike the first Quakers and what I have read of certain Sufi sects, a practice evidently long since abandoned by the time our family joined them. I was able to think of Mother Ann Lee more or less the way I'd been taught to think of John Ruskin, the supposed founder of my parents' Ruskinite society and the purported inventor of its guiding doctrines and principles.

To me, if a society's doctrines and principles are good for humanity, it doesn't matter whether the founder happens to be a female deity or a male English author, and I believe that overall the Shakers, like the Ruskinites, were good for humanity. And since I was at the time barely twelve years old, I was not put off by their insistence on sexual abstinence. I was relieved by it. Among other things, it meant

* Ephesians 2:5

that I did not have to be anxious about Elder John's attention to Mother, even though, perhaps for other reasons, I remained somewhat suspicious of it.

Though I myself eventually separated from the Shaker community—for reasons that I will provide when in my story I get to the occasion for it—and have long disavowed any allegiance to their doctrines and principles, if not their behavior and decorum, I am still able these many years later to recall in their totality Elder John's and the others' teachings. They were inculcated, restated, and reinforced daily in conversation at work in the fields and shops and barns and on the Sabbath by all the Shakers, especially by Elder John and Eldress Mary Glynn and the other brethren, male and female, who lived at New Bethany. It's why I can recite them today, as if they were embedded in my cellular structure.

Shortly after leaving Valdosta on the train, Elder John in a soft, earnest way began to describe the three elemental Shaker doctrines—purity and community and separation. By purity, he meant a complete avoidance of carnal indulgence. At that age I was not quite sure what carnal indulgence covered, but I knew that it had to do with taking pleasure from the human body, one's own and the bodies of others. I did not think it would be difficult or a detriment to uphold this doctrine of purity, despite the occasional irruption of impure thoughts and desires, as long as I kept those thoughts and desires to myself and avoided circumstances and situations that might arouse them, which the Shaker way of life seemed uniquely designed to do.

The second fundamental doctrine, community, argued that the good of the community overruled the good of the individual. To me this was little more than a radical extension of the old Ruskinite principle of taking from each according to his ability while giving to each according to his need, a creed that in a sense emphasized the needs and gifts of the individual rather than that of the community. The fuzziness of Ruskinite socialism was replaced by the clarity of Shaker communism, and to my mind this, too, was a good thing. When you are young, you have less tolerance of disorder and contradiction and conflict, of intellectual and moral fuzziness, than when you are old. It's why, when I was a boy, I was good at math and music and memorization and why I was pleased to embrace the Shakers' communistic doctrine and why today, now that I am old, I will admit to being a fuzzy-minded socialist, and a weakly committed one at that, a socialist who looks down the ballot, shrugs, and votes for the Democrat candidates despite their shortcomings.

The third fundamental doctrine that Elder John explained to us was separation. Shakers were obliged as a community to cut themselves off from the rest of society. They had to renounce all allegiances and prior loyalties to family and party and church and state. At that time I had no allegiance, or none that I was aware of, to party, church, and state, but I cleaved closely to my family—Mother, Pence, Royal, Raymond, and Rachel, and the memory of Father, who on his deathbed had designated me as the man of the family.

Elder John explained that because of the doctrine of purity, the males by and large lived and worked separately from the females, that brothers slept in separate rooms with nonrelated males, and sisters were likewise separated from sisters and, except for nursing infants, from mothers, too. The New Bethany family, he told us, would be our only family. Over the course of that journey south, while the others slumped in their seats and slept, and the train rattled along the narrow-gauge tracks into the humid Florida night, I gave that third doctrine some serious thought. Separation from my family and adherence to the larger New Bethany family might prove difficult, for up to now Mother and Father and my three brothers and new sister had been my primary and sole adherence, unchallenged by all other calls on my loyalty. I had never run with a gang of boys, perhaps because I was a twin with twin brothers only two years younger than me, and thus had a gang of homegrown male family members to run with. My schoolmasters had been Ruskinite colleagues and friends of my parents, approved and validated by Father and Mother, their teachings authorized and corroborated by what Father and Mother taught us at home, so my loyalty was not to a school or its masters, but to my parents. Mother and Father had long since forsworn any allegiance to all political parties and religions. The only nation they pledged allegiance to was the Ruskinite dream of a "coming nation." My parents were loyal to their family and to their much-desired utopian future, but to nothing in between.

On the other hand, separation from my family would release me from having to be the man of the family. The Shakers did not expect me to be a man and would not treat me as one. Elder John treated me consistently the same as Pence and Royal and Raymond—as a boy, one who needed steady, constant instruction and adult authority over all his actions and behavior. Elder John carefully described the world that we were now to live in, both the material and the spiritual world as well as the social world, and explained how we were expected to live there productively and with happiness and contentment. It was comforting to hear. It might be a relief, I thought, to be separated from my family. I began to look forward to it. I would become a boy again, a child.

By the time we reached Jacksonville, Elder John had moved on from the three fundamental doctrines to an explication of the Shakers' twelve basic principles. It's easy to inculcate an ideology in the minds of the young when its principles are framed numerically and follow an internal logic and like a catechism are regularly recited to an interlocutor. At the age of eighty-one, I can still recite all twelve principles with ease:

> honesty;
> continence;
> faith;
> hope;
> charity;
> innocence;
> meekness;
> humility;
> prudence;
> thankfulness;
> patience;
> simplicity.

"No one of them is more important than the others," Elder John insisted. Before explaining the meaning and implications of each principle and the behavior required by each, he drilled Mother and us boys, until by the time we reached Palatka, Florida, we had memorized all twelve. For me it was no more difficult than memorizing the Ten Commandments and the Eight Beatitudes. Sometimes an enumeration becomes an accounting, so that whenever I recite silently to myself or say aloud the doctrines and principles of the Shakers or refer even in passing to the Ten Commandments or Eight Beatitudes of Christianity, however much I try to honor them, I can't help taking the measure of my failure to live up to them.

In the early years, when I was still a child, the easiest of the twelve principles for me to observe were continence, or celibacy, and hope and simplicity. The hardest were faith and innocence and humility. By keeping to the easiest three I was able to give the appearance of keeping to the hardest, all the while struggling visibly with the middle six—honesty, charity, meekness, prudence, thankfulness, and patience—probably because honoring these six was evidenced more by one's observable behavior than were the others. By the same token, they were more easily enforced by the members of the Shaker family, all of whom, especially the elders, were charged with being responsible for the education and training of the newly gathered members of the New Bethany family.

Elder John all but declared that Mother's four male children were his to instruct and guide and protect until we reached our majority and could decide for ourselves whether we would remain members of the Shaker community. "Until that time," he said, "you must look mainly to me for understanding and instruction in the Shaker way."

He explained in detail certain aspects of the Shaker way, and certain things he left out, several of which I learned independently and my brothers later learned in turn from me—such as Mother's having agreed at Rosewell Plantation in her earlier secret exchange of letters with the New Bethany Shakers to sign the covenant with them, making her an official member of the United Society of Believers in Christ's Second Appearing. The covenant was a legal contract that would take effect as soon as she arrived in New Bethany and confessed her sins to Eldress Mary Glynn and turned over all her property to the Shakers and dissolved her familial affiliations with us five children so that we could be raised by the larger family. She would also be required to take a vow of celibacy.

I was sure that Mother had few if any sins to confess—possibly a small thorny bouquet of sins of pride and vanity and envy was all. And she had no property to sacrifice for the common good, no land or house or heirlooms, nothing but the shabby clothing on her back and the backs of her children and the few remaining household goods that had not been stolen by our fellow inmates at Rosewell Plantation. As for the dissolution of her familial affiliations with her children, I felt that, with Father no longer present to help her raise four boys and a daughter, it might actually unburden her, especially if she were allowed to continue to nurse her baby a few months longer before turning her over to the other Shaker women to raise. Elder John assured her that would be the case, no problem. So in general I was not unhappy with her having signed the covenant. The contractual condition that pleased me the most was her promise to remain celibate.

It was early the afternoon of the third day when, still a dozen miles southwest of the Shaker settlement at Narcoossee, the train pulled into the village of St. Cloud, which was as near to New Bethany as we could get by train. Not having eaten anything since the previous night, when Elder John had purchased a sack of biscuits and ham slices and six oranges for us to share, we were hungry and thirsty, causing my brothers and me to complain and whine a bit. Mother shushed us as if embarrassed by us, but as soon as we had all boarded the steam-powered flatboat, Elder John produced a second sack, this one filled with roasted chunks of catfish purchased from a Black man tending his charcoal fire at the dock. We settled in a circle on the top deck of the boat while it was being loaded with freshly planed cypress boards. When Elder John unwrapped the golden-brown filets and spread them out before us, we boys and even Mother reached down and grabbed what we could and commenced to fill our hungry mouths.

For a few seconds Elder John watched our ravenous behavior in silence. He shook his large bearded head and took from us all the uneaten pieces of fish and rewrapped them in the greasy sheet of brown paper and placed the packet back into the sack. "This is a good occasion for me to begin instruction as to the proper behavior at table," he said. He ordered me to go below to the main deck, where I would find a bucket at the stern. I was to fill the bucket with lake water and bring it up to them.

When I had done as instructed, Elder John told us to wash off our hands and faces with the water, which we did. Then he bade us all sit near him in a row, including Mother, who was cradling baby Rachel in her arms. The boat was now moving away from the dock and out onto the broad, shallow body of water called East Lake Tohopekaliga.

Elder John said, "There is a proper and fitting way to accomplish every human act. Listen closely, children and sister. Listen, and recite after me." And here he began to say a poem that he said was composed by someone named Elder Daniel Offord, who was a member of the Shaker colony up at Mount Lebanon, New York. It was a poem specifically and specially rhymed and metered for ease of memorization by children, although its rules apply as much to adults' behavior at table as to children's, he told us, and looked directly at Mother.

> First, in the morning when you rise
> Give thanks to God who well supplies
> Our many wants and gives us food,
> Wholesome, nutritious, sweet, and good.
> Then to some proper place repair
> And wash your hands and face with care,
> And ne'er the table once disgrace
> With dirty hands or dirty face.

While the long, flat side-wheeler churned its slow path across the glittering lake, Elder John said the lines several times over, until we were ready to recite them correctly in unison. Except for the half dozen stevedores below who were handling the cargo and the pilot and captain in the wheelhouse above, there was no one aboard to hear us learn and recite Elder John's long poem. And it was indeed very long, close to one hundred lines, and we learned it in chunks of eight and ten lines at a time.

> When to your meals you have the call,
> Promptly attend, both great and small.
> Then kneel and pray with closèd eyes
> That God will bless these rich supplies.
> When at the table you first sit down
> Sit straight and trim, nor laugh nor frown.
> Then let the elder first begin
> And all unite and follow him.

Elder John was very patient with us—one might say he was tirelessly persistent—especially with the younger boys, who were slower to memorize the poem than Pence and I, probably because some of the words were unfamiliar to them. We treated the task of memorization like a game and competed good-naturedly with one another, including Mother, laughing and then helping when one of us forgot a line or stumbled over a rhyme.

The lake was smooth, and the low mangroves and palmettos that marked the distant shore were sharply etched against the bright blue cloudless sky. Anhingas and stick-legged cranes and herons cruised across the low greenery, and seabirds, gulls and pelicans wandering inland off the Gulf of Mexico, followed the boat's wake in lazy, watchful arcs.

The rules laid down in Elder Daniel Offord's instructional poem were simple and narrow and easy enough to implement. I sensed that the principles on which the rules rested were general, however, and profound. And as Elder John planted the poem in my mind, I began to understand that if I obeyed these new rules before, during, and after every meal, I would be led to apply the principles that underlay the rules to each and every one of my daily and nightly activities and not just to my behavior at table.

> Of bread then take a decent piece
> Nor splash about the fat and grease,

But cut your meat both neat and square
And take of both an equal share.
And of the bones you take your due
For bones and meat together grew.
If from some incapacity
With fat your stomach can't agree,
Or if you cannot pick a bone,
You'll please to let them both alone.

After the misery and disappointment of the Waycross colony and the heavy, life-changing effects of the death of Father and the gloom and silence and violence of Rosewell Plantation, I felt uplifted by our arrival at the broad, grassy, lake-strewn plain of the northern edge of the Everglades. The sky was an enormous bowl, almost as if we were at sea. The distant horizon was a clean ruled line, a thin green firmament between the sky above and the water below. Great clouds of gorgeously feathered birds crossed over the boat like thoughts tumbling into my brain too fast and too abundant to contemplate or reflect upon. Largemouth bass and catfish, which Elder John called black trout, swam through the water before the boat in schools so large as to cause the surface of the lake to swell and surge against the bow and part and gather again at the stern as it passed. I sat there on the foredeck of the boat with my family and learned and recited Elder John's poem, and for the first time in more than a year I was truly happy, and not just relieved. I felt like an innocent child again.

After Father died and we departed from Waycross for Rosewell Plantation, it was as if we had been cast out of Paradise to suffer and perish for having committed an unnamed sin. And now, for reasons no less mysterious and contingent, we were being welcomed back into Paradise. I remember promising myself to find a way never to commit that unnamed sin again. On that day I began to believe that Elder John and the Shakers would teach me how to name the sin and would show me all the ways to avoid committing it again. Memorizing the poem on the proper behavior at table was just the first step in a process that I believed was sure to be lifelong.

As we sang the lines back to Elder John, I studied the faces of my three brothers and Mother, and I wondered if they were hav-ing the same exultant thoughts as I. There was Pence, his twinned face matching mine, but compacted and frowning as he repeated the lines after Elder John, and I decided no, Pence's mind is anxious and elsewhere and not at all exultant. This doesn't thrill him as it does me. There was Raymond, pronouncing the words cautiously and with little understanding, and I knew that my younger brother was not sharing my delight in the moment. And there was Raymond's twin brother, Royal, watching his brothers' lips for cues as to the next line, as cautious as Raymond and understanding even less. He, too, had no notion of my joy today. Baby sister Rachel, asleep in Mother's arms, was content, because Mother was at last content. Mother said the lines after Elder John, just like the others, but her mildly smiling face was merely that of a woman awash in relief, and relief was not what I felt that day. What I felt was a mixture of glee and joy, and I swung my arms in time to the meter and rhymes of the poem like a drum major leading a troop of marching majorettes, and Elder John beamed at me with solid approval.

> Potatoes, cabbage, turnip, and beet
> And every kind of thing you eat
> Must on your plate neatly be laid
> Before you eat with pliant blade.
> Nor ever—'tis an awkward matter—
> Eat or sip from out the platter.
> If bread and butter be your fare,
> Or biscuit, and you find right there
> Pieces enough, then take your slice
> And spread it over, thin and nice,
> On one side only. Then you may
> Eat in a decent, comely way.

The lake narrowed, and the boat drew closer to land. I saw my first Florida alligators slumbering half submerged in the water among the mangrove roots along the mudded bank. They were larger and more abundant by far than the Georgia alligators that I had seen from time to time back at Waycross and Rosewell Plantation—the Okefenokee gators that the Blacks and swampers and Seminoles killed for their hides and meat and peddled to us Ruskinites, who were not vegetarians, but in a vague and confused way were on principle averse to killing animals. Whenever the Ruskinite colonists could afford to purchase meat from a swamper or Black neighbor, they seemed to relish the venison and beef and pork and even the metallic-tasting gator meat. This mild hypocrisy was typical of the Ruskinites and stood in sharp contrast to the Shakers, who made no bones about being meat eaters and bred and fattened and slaughtered their livestock for no other purpose than to provide human beings with food and leather and many other life-supporting products, even including the manure they used to fertilize their fields and gardens.

In the kingdom of the Shakers, everything was part of God's plan for humankind. Every plant and animal, fish and fowl had been placed on earth solely to nourish and sustain God's human children in good health until the day when Mother Ann Lee's incarnation of the Second Appearance of Christ was at last realized on earth. The Shakers' duty and constant intentions were to live every moment as if that Second Appearance had been ushered into the world.

The Shakers hated hypocrisy as fervently as I did, or as fervently as every thoughtful child hates hypocrisy, though I did not at that time have the name for it. When I was still a child, it wasn't so much that I loved justice as that I loathed injustice. I didn't so much love truth as I feared being lied to. And I didn't so much aspire to equality as I desired to eliminate inequality. A child knows himself to be powerless and thus the most likely member of the community to end up deprived of justice and truth and equality. The clarity and specificity and universal application of the rules for living together that Elder John was putting forth to me and my family were therefore a comfort and reassurance that here among the Shakers justice and truth and equality would at last control not just my own actions and behavior, but the actions and behavior of every member of the community as well, especially the adults, for the guide to children on their behavior at table applied as much to adults, even to Elder John himself, as to me and my brothers and baby sister.

For butter you must never spread
On nut-cake, pie, or pumpkin bread,
Or bread with milk or bread with meat,
Butter with these things you may not eat.
These things are all the best of food
And need not butter to make them good.
When bread or pie you cut or break
Touch only what you mean to take,
And leave no prints of fingers seen
On whatever's left, e'en though they're clean.

Elder John played me and my brothers and Mother like a banjo, leading us through the verses faster and faster, over and over, until we knew the poem by heart and could practically dance to it. His large, bearded face beneath the wide brim of his palm-straw hat was flushed with pleasure and from the small exertion of recitation in the warm glare of the mid-afternoon sun off the quiet lake water. He wore a broad, approving smile throughout that showed his large, clean white teeth to advantage. He was evidently not a man who used tobacco or snuff, and probably abjured alcohol, too. A healthy specimen in early middle age, his shoulders, arms, hands, and back were muscled and hardened by many years of disciplined physical labor, labor of a dignified sort, farming and lumbering and animal husbandry and managing the earth and water and building and maintaining the machinery and engines that cut and planed and crated and carted the crops that were so abundantly nourished by the Florida sun and waters and the loamy fields that the Shakers had literally created out of the endless sprawl of swamps and marshes with their dams and dikes and ditches and canals. His body had been made healthy and strong and symmetrical by work, the wholesome product proving the wholesomeness of the process that had created it, just as a body bent and broken and sickened by work proves the unwholesomeness of the process that bent, broke, and sickened it.

My growing admiration of Elder John's evident physical strength and health led me to admire what had given him that strength and health, and for the first time in my life I saw work not as merely a necessary, undesirable means to a desired end, but as an end in itself. Work was no longer an unwelcome, unavoidable duty, a price to pay, an activity to be eased or shortened or evaded whenever possible. It was something one looked forward to, something one anticipated with joy. One started as early as allowed by the sun and continued for as long as permitted by the light of the moon or lantern or open fire, until out of pure necessity, not exhaustion, one rested for a night or for one Sabbath day a week, not simply to rest, but to better oneself for work. If Elder John said it was also to better oneself for God and Christ and Mother Ann Lee, it was only because one's work pleased God and Christ and Mother Ann Lee, and setting aside one day a week for thanksgiving and contemplation made one a better worker. It made one a strong and healthy man, too, I observed. A man like Elder John. Hands to work and hearts to God.

It was a cascade of observations, insights, connections, and decisions that descended on me that afternoon, while my family and I crossed the lake on our way to our new home. One usually doesn't feel changed as a person until long after the change has settled in, but I knew I had changed as it was happening. On that afternoon in April 1902, I became a wholly different person than I had been before. I was no longer the precocious but powerless man of the family, anointed by Father. I was simply and determinedly a boy, an unformed male human being, anointed as such by Elder John.

Be careful when you take a sip
Of liquid, don't extend your lip
So far that one may fairly think
That cup and all you mean to drink.
Then clean your knife—don't lick it, pray,
It is a nasty, shameful way—
And wipe it on a piece of bread
Which snugly by your plate is laid.
Thus your knife is clean when you pass
It into plum or apple sauce
Or butter, which you must cut nice,
Both square and true as polished dice.

The loaded side-wheeler plowed on to the northeast end of East Lake Tohopekaliga, where it entered the shallow canal dug by gangs of Irishmen shipped down from New York State a generation earlier. Those Irish laborers had dispersed across the South, probably the conscious intent of the hundreds of land agents and bankers and lawyers speculating on Florida's development as a solution to the social problem of having thousands of unemployed Irish laborers roaming the streets of the cities of the North. The plan was to send the immigrants and their shovels south to Florida, where they could drain the vast tracts of swampland and clear the thousands of square miles of sawgrass prairie that had just been placed by the federal and state governments onto the open market. A land grab, followed by a plan for parceling out the land and the construction of new means of transport—railroads, paved roads, canals, and ports of call—accompanied by bags of cash to loan at larcenous rates of interest to otherwise penniless Irish buyers dreaming the American dream.

I knew nothing of this history until much later, after I had come to understand how the Shakers ended up owning seven thousand acres of land between the lakes and marshes of central Florida. At the time of my arrival there in 1902 I could see no history—all was as if it had ever been thus. As if the Shakers had always maintained a colony outside Narcoossee. As if the Atlantic Coast Railway had always ended at St. Cloud, and the steam-powered side-wheeling barges had always hauled people and lumber and sugar cane and livestock across East Lake Tohopekaliga to the canal that threaded together the smaller lakes and ponds as far as Narcoossee and beyond, where the wagons, as always, waited to carry the people and cargo on to the sawmill and the sugar factory and butcher shop and smokehouse that somewhere in the distant past were built, owned, and operated by the Shakers. And it was as if, for as long as the New Bethany community of Shakers at Narcoossee existed, everyone who settled there was obligated to memorize Elder Daniel Offord's "Advice to Children on Behavior at Table," just as my family and I were learning it now.

Cut not a pickle with a blade
Whose side with grease is overlaid,
And always take your equal share
Of coarse as well as luscious fare.
Don't pick your teeth or ears or nose
Nor scratch your head nor tonk your toes
Nor belch nor sniff, nor jest nor pun
Nor have the least of play or fun.

At this, Elder John made a hearty laugh, and everyone joined in, even Mother. Elder John repeated the line more loudly, *"Nor have the least of play or fun,"* stressing the final word and clearly playing and having fun and inviting all of us to play and have fun with him. By now I could see that Elder John's attention was directed mainly at me and my brothers and only in passing at Mother. It helped that Elder John no longer spoke in the Quaker manner as he had before at Rosewell Plantation and early in our journey by rail to Jacksonville and points south. Gradually he had let his natural Kentucky farmer's way of speaking take over, which warmed him and made him seem less ministerial and more of a big friendly bear of a man, jocular and gregarious, yet gruff in an ironic, slightly self-mocking way.

So we were no longer merely grateful to him for having rescued us from the darkness and deprivation of Rosewell Plantation. We were happy to be in his company for its own sake. We four boys stole glances at one another and good-naturedly, teasingly elbowed and nudged one another whenever one of us stumbled over the words of the poem or forgot or mistakenly skipped a line as we recited the poem again and again, from the first line to the last, until we had it down so pat that Elder John could go silent and smile and lead us through its length just by wagging his forefinger like a conductor swinging his baton before an orchestra.

If you're obliged to cough or sneeze,
Your handkerchief you'll quickly seize,
And timely shun the foul disgrace

Of splattering either food or face.
Drink neither water, cider, nor beer
With greasy lip or mucous tear,
Nor fill your mouth with food and then
Drink, lest you blow it out again.

The day grew hotter, and we all moved out of the sun to stand in the bow beneath the overhanging roof of the pilot's perch in the wheelhouse. The canal ran like a vein from the east end of East Lake Tohopekaliga through wide marshes linking a pair of circular lakes, little more than deep, water-filled sinkholes clotted with pickerel-weed, cattails, and masses of floating-heart lilies churned by the slow-moving barge named *Coquina*. Along the muddy shore of the second lake huddled a rough-hewn frontier settlement with a wide pier half underwater.

As the side-wheeler neared the pier, I made out two female figures standing on the shore, apparently awaiting the arrival of the *Coquina* and its passengers. My first thought was that we must be arriving at New Bethany, the Shaker settlement, and I was disappointed and saddened by the sight of the place. I had pictured a thriving farmstead and manufactory. The Shakers were famous and envied, even among the Ruskinites, for their enormous, meticulously tended fields and meadows and gardens and large, shining barns and dormitories and communal halls and their factories and mills. They were praised everywhere for their skill and energy as architects and builders. I remembered illustrations in the old Ruskinite newspaper *The Coming Nation* of the Shaker communities in Canterbury, New Hampshire, and Mount Lebanon, New York, and Union Village, Ohio, pictures of great barns and three-story-tall, foursquare buildings modeled on New England colonial town halls and college dormitories, large, bright, wooden and sometimes cut-stone structures as balanced and symmetrical and simple and free of gratuitous ornamentation as ancient Greek temples.

But this was a shabby collection of rough wood buildings, a motley patchwork of small, unpainted, shotgun-style houses and a half dozen tin-roofed warehouses and storefronts on spindly mud-brick pilings, beneath which lay sleeping yellow hounds and uncaged, sick-looking chickens and an occasional wallowing hog. A sign nailed over the window of one building advertised a tavern's wares—spirits, beer, wine, fried fish. A second had a sign that said Kendall's General Store. Above the door of a third, a hand-lettered sign signaled the presence of the Narcoossee, Florida, United States Post Office.

I was relieved. This was not New Bethany.

Near the half-flooded pier was a head-high heap of pine slabs, scrap wood unsuitable for anything finer than firing the steam engines of the barges that passed up and down the watery roadway from the railroad siding in St. Cloud to the smaller villages and settlements further inland all the way to the vast waters of Lake Okeechobee. The *Coquina* was stopping to take on wood for the boiler, Elder John explained, and to load the pallets of cut sugar cane stacked on the dock for shipping over to New Bethany. "We Shakers operate the only sugar mill in the whole region outside of St. Cloud," he added.

The pilot and crew jumped from the deck to the dock and, tipping their caps to the two female figures standing there, disappeared into the tavern. At first glance the women were an oddly mismatched pair. One, in her sixties, was much older than the other and round and short, with high color in her wide face and broad cheeks, wearing a long, dark skirt fronted by a coarse cloth apron more suited to the needs of a male carpenter or blacksmith than to those of a female worker. Though heavy, she was not so much obese as muscular and healthy and strong, almost manly. She wore an old-fashioned bonnet over her short gray hair and a white lace shoulder coverlet that identified her as an old-school Shaker lady.

The other woman was very young, still in her teens, I guessed. Later I would learn that, indeed, on the afternoon when we first met she was nineteen years of age. It was so long ago, nearly seventy years, that my first impression of Sadie Pratt has been obscured and overlaid a thousand times by my later, more complex and powerful memories of her, to the point where it's as if I have always known her, the way one feels toward close family members, as if there never was a first meeting and she was always a part of my life, even before she arrived in my life and long after she parted from it.

I remember that she was taller than me, for I had not got my height yet. In three years I would be taller than her by several inches. Now, when Sadie appears in my dreams, as frequently happens, she is again taller than me, the way she was that day at the Narcoossee landing, as if in my dreams I am still twelve years old and she is nineteen and we are meeting for the first time.

She was strikingly slim and frail-seeming and stood with her thin arms wrapped around her body as if to warm herself, although it was a seasonably hot and humid afternoon. She wore a dark red, long-sleeved dress, I remember clearly, and a lady's green felt hat with a long black ribbon tied beneath her chin—genteel, Yankee, store-bought clothing. Her hair was long and shining black, gathered into a plaited coil that fell below her shoulders in an arrangement that was both discreet and adventuresome, almost accidentally reckless. Her face was very pale and had a luminous quality that did not so much reflect light as generate it from an invisible source within. Its glow had the effect of diminishing the significance of the face of any person who stood near her. Her mild smile was closed to interpretation, as if she were amused by something that she alone had noticed and had no intention of revealing.

With the *Coquina* tied tight to the pier and the crew gone into the tavern, Elder John stepped ashore and greeted the two ladies and helped them aboard. Speaking once again in his Quaker mode of speech, he introduced them to us Manns. "I'm pleased to present to thee Eldress Mary Glynn, who with me leads our New Bethany family. And a dear friend of our family, Miss Sadie Pratt, of Providence, Rhode Island." He explained that Eldress Mary was returning to New Bethany from her weekly call at the Sunshine Home, a tuberculosis sanitarium not far from Narcoossee, where she served as vice president and where Miss Pratt was in residence. "We are grateful to escort thee the rest of the way home," he said to Eldress Mary.

Eldress Mary smiled and said, "A happy coincidence is all it is. God's will, Elder John. You can't take credit for it, I'm afraid," she said, and gave a jolly laugh. I liked her immediately.

Elder John turned to the younger woman and embraced her in a fatherly way, which did not alter her stance or expression. He said, "We are happy to see that Sister Sadie is well enough to visit with us again."

Sadie Pratt merely smiled and stepped clear of him and said nothing. It was strange to hear him refer to himself as "we" and "us" instead of "I" and "me," as if, having arrived in close proximity to the Shaker settlement, his individual identity had been absorbed by that of the collective.

Having introduced them to us, he then introduced us to the two women. "Sister Constance Mann," he called Mother. "A widow," he added. "And her children, Brother Harley, Brother Pence, Brother Royal, Brother Raymond, and little Sister Rachel." He added that we had just been memorizing Elder Daniel Offord's poem on the proper behavior at table. "They learned it right quick, too. I bet they could say the end of it for thee. Come, boys, come, Sister Constance, let's show Eldress Mary and Sister Sadie how smartly thou can say the end of Elder Daniel's poem." He wagged his index finger to set the meter, and we began, shyly, weakly at first, and then with growing force.

> Then straightly from the table walk,
> Nor stop to handle things, nor talk.
> If we mean never to offend,
> To every gift we must attend.
> Respecting meetings, work, or food,
> And doing all the things we should.
> Then joy and comfort we shall find,
> Love, quietness, and peace of mind.
> Pure heavenly union will increase,
> And every evil work will cease.

Throughout the recitation, try as I might, I could not keep myself from gazing at the cool, luminous face and graceful, slim figure of Sadie Pratt. It was as if I had never looked closely at another human being's face or body before, male or female, young or old, White or Black. Or as if, until that moment, my youthful vision had been smudged, the way in recent years it has gone all cloudy, making it difficult for me to read even the headlines of my daily newspaper or drive my Packard or recognize passersby on the sidewalk from my chair on the porch without tilting my eyeglasses up or down, altering and adjusting the angle of refraction.

That afternoon on the *Coquina* at Narcoossee, clouded scales seemed to fall from my eyes, at least when my gaze was trained on Sadie Pratt, as when Ananias in Damascus on the street which is called Straight went to Saul who had been struck blind and laid hands on him and Saul received sight forthwith.[*]

I still know my Bible, certain parts of it better than others, despite having been a nonbeliever since the end of my days as a Shaker and before that only a fake believer and a hypocrite. It's strange that one can shrug off the cloak of any and all Christian sects, yet still end up many decades later with one's words and thoughts and observations of the world and one's fellow human beings all encased by the Christian Holy Bible. Without the Bible, both testaments, I wouldn't know how to tell my story—to myself as much as to anyone else. Without the Bible, the King James Version, my story would be little more than a diagram or an algebraic equation. I'd be like old Zacharias, struck dumb by the angel Gabriel for his unbelief, unable to testify that he had seen an angel.[†] I always liked that story. Perhaps because I myself had seen an angel and have been struck dumb for most of my life.

A half hour or so after our meeting with Eldress Mary and Sadie Pratt at the water's edge at Narcoossee, the four stevedores and the pilot and captain returned from the tavern and loaded fresh firewood onto the *Coquina* and fired up the boiler again. Soon the sidewheels began to turn, and the barge pushed out onto the lake and made its slow way toward the canal that linked East Lake Toho, as the natives call East Lake Tohopekaliga, to Live Oak Lake, where

[*] Acts 9:10–18

[†] Luke 1:5–2:20

somewhere off in the marshes and mangroves the Shaker colony of New Bethany was located.

I moved in small steps away from the Shakers and my family and Sadie Pratt, until in a short time I found myself up in the wheelhouse alone with the pilot and captain. From this elevated vantage point I could stare down at Sadie and not be seen myself, and when I felt my throat begin to tighten and my legs go weak and wobbly, I turned away from her and peered out across the bow at the gleaming surface of the lake and the mangroves and cattails and reeds crowding the shore, extending my gaze to the pine forest in the distance and the veldtlike grassy plain beyond, all the way to the western horizon and the towering banks of storm clouds that rose off the Gulf of Mexico and slid toward landfall in the east.

The pilot and the boat captain both smelled of tobacco and old dried sweat and whiskey. They were observant and intelligent men and had noticed me staring cow-eyed down at the slim young black-haired woman in the red dress. The pilot, who was the older of the two, a sinewy, sharp-eyed man, dark complected, but not a Black, said to me, "So you all goin' to be Shakers, eh? Hmmm. Young buck like you, kind of a shame, I'd say."

The other fellow, the captain, chuckled and chewed on his cigar with increased vigor and smiled.

I said, "No, sir. It's my mother who has become a Shaker. And there's no shame in it," I added.

"She a widder?" the captain asked.

"Yes."

"Shakers'll take good care of her, then. They looks after widders and orphans real good," the captain said. He spoke kindly, as if it mattered to him.

The pilot nodded in agreement. "Not much in it for a young buck like you, I'd think. What with all them rules and regulations they keep. No alcohol. No tobacco. And separating the males and females the way they do. I heard they even keep the boars separated from the sows."

"They'll work you hard enough night and day, you won't have any strength left for sportin' after the gals anyhow," the captain said and nodded his head in the general direction of Sadie Pratt on the deck below. "That there's a pretty one, ain't she?"

I followed his line of sight and once again took in the face and figure of Sadie and felt my breath catch and my pulse race.

"She comes over to New Bethany quite regular," the captain went on. "Usually with the old woman, the eldress. Stays a few days with the Shakers and heads back down to the sanitarium over by Narcoossee by herself, where I understand she's a patient. Don't believe she's one of them, though. A Shaker. Probably just religious. Comes up for their Sunday service."

"Consumption?" the pilot asked.

"S'pose so."

"Can't be too bad. They let her out and about."

"They's all kinds and degrees."

"Of consumption? Yes. Pretty gal, though. Wouldn't you say, son?"

"No! I mean, yes, I guess so," I said, and decided to try shifting the conversation. I asked the pilot how long it had taken him to learn the channels and shallows all the way from St. Cloud to New Bethany.

"A lifetime," the pilot explained. "You never stop learning the water and where it meets the land. The channels and shallows and even the shorelines, they keep changing from week to week, month to month, season to season. And then the hurricanes scramble everything all over again. And sometimes fire and drought make you switch your notions of where you can take a boat and where you can't. These waterways," he said, "they're like a nest of snakes."

I asked him if he had learned the waterways and how to navigate them on his own. Or did someone teach him?

My question was sincere, not merely strategic. I was at that age when a boy grows curious about how much of adult life a person can learn on his own. It seemed to me unlikely, maybe impossible, that a person could figure out on his own where the water was too shallow for a boat or barge or where the canals passed through the thick clots of mangroves between the lakes. There were no markers or buoys to guide you, and if, as the pilot said, everything out here kept changing its position like a nest of snakes, twisting and turning and moving in tangled, ever-changing coils, then no chart or map could be considered reliable. I wondered aloud how the Shakers had found their way here, so far from their origins in upstate New York and New England and their bases out west in Ohio and Kentucky. Why did the Shakers settle in such a watery wilderness? Did they choose it deliberately, in order to isolate themselves from the many temptations of the fallen world, or was it a mistake?

"You'll have to get the Shakers to answer you that," the pilot said. "Elder John, the big feller, he knows most of it. And the old lady, the eldress, she's been here from the beginning, from back in the early nineties. But as to your other question, about learning my craft, my daddy, he was a Seminole, full-blooded. He took me out here to hunt and fish since I was a baby. He teached me more than I'd ever need to know for navigating a big old flatboat like this. I could put this gal in Okeechobee without once grounding her, assuming the captain wanted her there."

"Sure you could," the captain said, and laughed. "Sure you could."

"I damn well could! I could get you down to Fort Myers or over to the Gulf, if you asked me. Or up the St. Johns to Jacksonville. Or down the Miami River to Biscayne Bay." He explained that Florida is like the human body, and all the veins and arteries are connected, from the fingers and toes down at the Keys and the Glades to the top of the head up at Ocala all the way back to the heart, which is Lake Okeechobee. He asked me if I'd seen the big lake yet.

"No, sir."

Okeechobee was like an ocean, he said. So wide and long you can't see the opposite shore, even from a high wheelhouse like this. Interrupting himself, he told the captain to just keep her ten degrees to port and head straight in past the mangroves, hugging what passed for a shoreline. The *Coquina* slowly chugged around a long bend in the canal that opened into a new lake, and almost at once it entered a small bay, where there was a sturdy, wide pier and behind the pier a large foursquare barnlike warehouse open at both ends. The land all around, a dozen acres or more, was cleared and dry, cut on the diagonal by narrow drainage ditches that ran to the bay. A pale crushed-shell wagon lane led from the further end of the bayside warehouse in a long arc up the low grassy slope and disappeared behind a grove of almond trees. Beyond the trees I could make out the distant stilled blades of a tall windmill and a set of sharply angled, cypress-shingled roofs with brick chimneys poking through at the ends. Here it was at last, New Bethany!

The captain yanked a dangling chain next to the wheel, and the steam whistle shrieked. Without saying goodbye, I scurried from the wheelhouse and made my way down the ladder to the deck below, where the stevedores tied the *Coquina* to the pier posts. Carefully avoiding even a sideways glance at Sadie Pratt, I joined my family and the Shakers by the rail.

"Welcome to New Bethany," Elder John said. "Thy long journey out of darkness into light has ended," he declared. He stepped from the barge to the pier and turned and spread his arms wide, as if offering a benediction. Instead, he offered his large hand to his recruits, and one by one we left the *Coquina* and joined him and Eldress Mary and Sadie Pratt ashore—Mother and baby Rachel, my three brothers, and finally myself.

In the course of our journey out of Rosewell Plantation, we had become Shakers, and we had arrived at our new home at New Bethany, and I had met the woman who would become the love of my life for the rest of my life and the cause of untold catastrophic loss and pain to me and to her and to everyone else I loved.

REEL #4

And so began our new life as Shaker novitiates, eased by the deliberate—one might say "calculated"—kindness and good humor of our leaders, Elder John Bennett and Eldress Mary Glynn. They were our parent figures, our governors. They and the thirteen other brother and sister Shakers residing at that time at New Bethany clearly had long experience at making newcomers to the community feel welcomed and secure, especially newcomers like us Manns, thrashed as we were by circumstance and human cruelty, malnourished, impoverished, indebted, and at the time of our arrival utterly incapable of caring for ourselves on our own.

The Ruskinite communes of Graylag and Waycross, where we began our pilgrimage, had been ruled by consensus. They were fragile, dreamy, socialist democracies with no overall governing authority, except for the revered texts of John Ruskin and other like-minded philosophizing theoreticians. Rosewell Plantation, by comparison, was a despotism whose authoritarian power over its subjects was enforced by violence and deprivation and debt. New Bethany, in contrast to both, was a mostly benign oligarchy, one modeled on the structure of the two-parent human family—except that one could choose to be a member of the family or not.

That is, if you were an adult you could choose. But if you were female and under the age of twenty-one or a male under eighteen, and your parent became a Shaker and gave you over to the community for maintenance, education, and care, you could no more resign from the Shaker family than you can resign from your biological family. You might be found unworthy of life as a Shaker, of course, and be expelled. But you could not, one hot day while haying in the field, lay your rake on the ground and walk back down that crushed-shell lane to the pier and step aboard the waiting barge and sail back the way you came. Until you reached your majority, you were essentially the property of the Shakers, signed over to them by your parent the same as any bit of land or other holdings or assets that your parent might have previously owned.

But we did not care a stick about that, Pence and I. Neither did Royal and Raymond. And Mother, who had no assets other than her children, didn't seem to care, either. Not then, or ever.

Due to the prohibitions against sex and, therefore, procreation and the inevitable aging of their membership, the Shakers in the early years, long before our time, were always in need of fresh converts to work the land, so they could both feed themselves and market their produce and seeds and herbs and various handmade domestic and farm implements. Back then, when they still had plenty of cash money and vast tracts of good farmland in half a dozen Northern states, the Shakers numbered in the thousands and were still expanding. Their recruits were mainly orphans and children born out of wedlock, infants and youngsters literally left at the Shaker doorstep, and spiritually needy men and women plucked from the waxing and waning waves of religious enthusiasm that every few years swept over the nation, lost souls figuratively dropped off by their religion. The Shakers provided a stable, supportive family, a practical education, and a sustaining religion—physical security and mentoring and spiritual uplift.

Later in the century, as state and local governments began to take over the care of orphans and abandoned children and those waves of religious enthusiasm receded, the Shakers looked for apostates and schismatics, dropouts from the more secular and political communitarian groups, like the Koreshans and Oneidans and New Harmonists, and our Ruskinites. By coming to our rescue, Elder John and Eldress Mary hoped to recruit us Manns.

We may have needed rescuing, but we didn't need to be converted. We had not been abandoned or cast away by our parents. Quite the opposite. And we needed no substitute religion, for up to now we had been irreligious. At least we five children were irreligious. In the beginning, anyhow. But Mother? Even now, I cannot say.

In the spring of 1902, when we first resided at New Bethany, my brothers and I and our baby sister, Rachel, were the only children in the community. There were fifteen adults, including Mother and Elder John and Eldress Mary. Eight were males and seven were females. They were of various ages, from Brother Hiram, a shell-shocked veteran of the Spanish War in his early twenties, to Brother Theodore, who was seventy-four and had been a Shaker since his infancy in the early 1830s, when he was given over to the North Family in Mount Lebanon by a teenaged mother he never met. He claimed to know her name and age, however, gleaned from the scrupulously kept Shaker account books. When transmission of property and child custody were involved, the Shakers knew to make and archive carefully signed, witnessed, and notarized contracts.

Just as we had done on our arrival at Rosewell Plantation, we fell immediately into the routine and mentality at New Bethany, although it was a dramatically different and, of course, a much kinder sort of routine and mentality than Rosewell's. It was no less rigid and controlling, however. Looking back, I'm still amazed by the coercive power of those who, usually by mere happenstance, come to surround one. Humans are neither strictly pack animals like wolves nor herd animals like sheep, but when they gather together in tightly bound groups, they behave like both. They instinctively organize themselves so that one or two are positioned at the top, as in a pack, while the rest, with diminishing degrees of authority and independence, get stacked below. At the same time they make the more generalized aims and needs of the herd their own.

Inherently unstable, it's nonetheless how human societies organize themselves—simultaneous adherence to authority and to the group. And from the day we first arrived at New Bethany, that was me and my three brothers and eventually my sister, too. That was Mother. We followed our leaders and sought acceptance by the rest. It's probably why most of my life since leaving New Bethany I have been in reaction a solitary man. An isolato. A monad.

Not in those early years, though, when I was following Elder John around the colony from morning to night, from the dining hall to the shops and barns and fields, like a puppy trailing after the lead dog. I studied his posture and his gestures, his facial expressions and tones of voice. I tried walking with his long-legged loping stride, despite being then barely half his height, and cocked my palm-straw hat at the same slight angle as his, and when a week after our arrival I received my uniform of pale-blue muslin shirt and trousers and dark-blue neckerchief, tailor-made by the sisters of the colony, I buttoned and tied and half-untied them just as he did his. I learned and mimicked his way of speaking, his slow, careful articulation and his easy, quick shifts of diction and expression from high Quaker to Kentucky hill-country farmer. I imitated every aspect of his person that was visible to me, making myself into a miniaturized version of the man who, with his female counterpart, Eldress Mary, was in charge of the colony.

As if flattered by my eagerness to ape him, and no doubt mildly amused by it, for he was not without a sense of humor, he corrected me when my version of him was slightly off, bringing us into closer alignment, despite the possibly ridiculous differences in scale. I knew, of course, that he was gently mocking me when he adjusted the tilt of my hat or loosened my neckerchief, but did not feel rebuked. I felt instead acknowledged, seen, and, in a fundamental sense, taught. Elder John was teaching me in a kindly way to be more like him on the inside by shaping the ways in which I presented myself on the outside.

At the same time, but differently, I sought to gain the approval of my Shaker brothers and sisters, young and old. I learned their daily rituals immediately and followed them religiously, because they were in fact religious. There was no divide between the secular and the godly, the material world and the spiritual. The two were seen as one harmonic, overlapping whole. The integrated structure of the day and the seven-day week and four-season year, even here in south Florida, where the changes between seasons, though distinguishable, were slight, was meant to guide us to an understanding of the structure of the universe, just as the structure of the atom is seen to correspond to the structure of the solar system, the solar system to the galaxy, the galaxy to all creation. I was determined to become a true Shaker and thought that the best way to accomplish it was by imitating those who had already become true Shakers, my older brothers and sisters at New Bethany. The Brethren. I decided to follow their example, to make their rituals and routines my own and to excel at keeping them.

Perhaps I was merely an overly competitive lad, a typical firstborn male in a fatherless family. I have no memory of being motivated by a transcendent religious awakening, so I definitely wasn't trying to please God or Jesus Christ or Mother Ann Lee. And it wasn't because my own real mother asked me to follow the rules and rituals of New Bethany. There was no need for that. Though she was the one who upon our arrival had made her confession of sins to Eldress Mary and obtained full conversion, I fell into line even quicker than she when it came to living the life of a Shaker. Children were thought incapable of making a confession and gaining full membership and were granted a certain degree of latitude in following the religious line, but it was a latitude I refused to accept. I was driven solely by the felt, but unnamed, unacknowledged pressure of the behavior of the Shaker community, the adult men and women who surrounded me, to behave as they did. I wanted to do as the others were doing, only do it better. There was almost no variety among them in how they lived their daily lives, for everyone's days and nights were as rigidly scheduled and timed and strictly choreographed as a marching band's. As a result, it was easy for me to integrate myself into the community, to identify the pattern and cut the fabric of my life to fit. My brother Pence followed behind in a slapdash, distracted way with none of my focus and desire, and the younger twins, Raymond and Royal, did as they were told, but had no commitment to the routines and rituals and, like normal boys, when they could evade them, they did.

Throughout that first spring and summer, while I modeled my exterior manner and mode of being, my personality, after Elder John's and strove at the same time to make myself into the ideal Shaker boy, I was aware that deep within me my love for Sadie Pratt was blossoming. I gave myself over to it, but spoke of it to no one. The form it took in those early days was an obsessive interest in her intermittent presence at the colony, tracking her comings and goings between New Bethany and Sunshine Home, the tuberculosis sanitarium outside Narcoossee where she was a patient. I was like a hotel desk clerk, checking her in every week or two and checking her back out after her brief visits, usually no more than three or four days at a time, and knew at all times where she was located while at the colony. She knew little or nothing then of my obsession, but I'm sure Elder John noticed that whenever she arrived on the *Coquina* I managed somehow to be there at the dock to greet her, and when she departed I was ready at the main house where she stayed to carry her satchel down to the lake and wave her off as the barge pulled away.

Mornings for us four boys—after ablutions and prayers and break-fast in the common dining room and the daily homily, delivered either by Elder John or by Eldress Mary—were organized around classroom instruction in the main building. While the other residents were assigned their tasks for the day and went to work with the peculiar Shaker form of eager sobriety, my brothers and I were led by Sister Hazel, a pink-faced, rheumy-eyed lady in her fifties, to the small classroom on the second floor of the main house. Reading and writing and arithmetic exercises, along with instruction in animal and plant husbandry, woodcraft, weaving and sewing, and farm maintenance made up the curriculum, with hour-long courses designed not so much to educate us in a general way as to prepare us to take our place as dedicated, intelligent, productive keepers of the Shaker land and industries.

Sister Hazel instructed us solely in literacy and mathematics—reading and writing and arithmetic. The subjects of our other courses of instruction varied, depending on the instructors' special skills. For instance, Brother Hiram was a beekeeper, which seemed an unlikely specialization, since he suffered from constant tremors and overall physical and mental agitation, and beekeeping required great calm and control. Before his first presentation on beekeeping, we were informed in a sympathetic way by Sister Hazel that during the Spanish War Brother Hiram had been the cavalry officer in Cuba in charge of a herd of over one hundred horses and mules that were slaughtered in a Spanish artillery attack, and the suffering and deaths of so many beloved animals had left him unable to work close to large animals or he would break down and weep uncontrollably, as if he were witnessing the carnage all over again. We were told to listen patiently to him, for he stuttered and stammered, and when he lectured he faced the wall away from us and formed each sentence in his head before he uttered it.

Elder John early on had excused Brother Hiram from work in the fields and barns with the New Bethany livestock, the horses, mules, and cattle. He could not tend or work the large animals—not even the sheep, goats, and hogs—without wanting to embrace and protect the creatures from an imagined artillery attack. So Elder John put him in charge of building up an apiary, an industry that had previously been ignored at New Bethany, and the poor, tormented brother swiftly developed a profound understanding of the bees' nature and needs and capabilities. When he instructed us in our classroom on how to build and tend the hives and explained the social habits and requirements of his charges and the economics of honey, it was clear that he loved his buzzing, industrious bees as much as he had loved his bomb-slaughtered horses.

He explained how to build a movable-comb hive and diagrammed on the blackboard the precise necessary dimensions for the comb box and the quarter-inch bee space, aspects of apiary science that Sister Hazel later applied to our arithmetic and geometry lessons. He described the structure of a bee colony, how a queen sat at the center, the colony's sole breeder, surrounded by her thousands of female worker bees and male drones, which Sister Hazel referenced later in her descriptions of economic realities in what the Shakers called the World—that is, the society governed and inhabited by non-Shakers. She called the beehives "honey factories," and though she compared the worker bees and drones to the laborers and factory managers and the queen to the capitalist factory owners, to my mind there was a sharper similarity to Rosewell Plantation and to the other utopian communities that I was familiar with, and even to New Bethany itself, than to the world of industrialized capitalism.

I soon gathered that in her role as coleader of New Bethany—one might call her our hive's queen—Eldress Mary directed the colony's financial affairs and domestic housekeeping and in general was in charge of the tasks relegated to the women, which included food preparation, laundry, the making of cloth and clothing, the harvesting and packaging and labeling of Shaker seeds and herbs, and the like. She also received the female applicants' confession of sin. None of this work was viewed as demeaning or of lesser importance than the work done by the men.

Elder John in a sense was a coqueen, for he was in no way a king. He received the male applicants' confession of sin, superintended the farm- and fieldwork and the various building projects and maintenance and the care and feeding of the animals and poultry. He oversaw all work at the sugar mill and lumber mill and the orchards and vineyards and the fields and gardens from first planting to harvest. Though Eldress Mary did the pricing and kept the books, Elder John was in charge of the distribution and sale in Narcoossee and Kissimmee and St. Cloud of the abundant overflow of the gardens and orchards and the packaged seeds and herbs and the various tools and household objects manufactured by the Shakers. Mostly, these were tasks and jobs performed by the male members of the community— except when, twice a year, and with some crops three times a year, harvest time rolled around and everyone in the colony joined in the work. But in general, the division of labor was based mostly on the colonists' physique and natural inclination and experience. The men were physically more suited to farm labor than the women, and the skills they had acquired before they became Shakers usually dictated the kind of work they were asked to perform at New Bethany.

Mother, for instance, was immediately put to work as a seamstress, cutting and sewing clothing for the rest of the group. She was still nursing Rachel then and could keep the baby close by in a small wheeled cradle, a Shaker invention, while she worked. We boys saw little of our mother and sister now, for we were housed with the male Shakers and sat with them at table, and when we were not at school, we were being trained by one of the adult Shakers in a skill for which we were assumed to have some sort of inclination or visible talent.

Raymond was a sharp geometrician and dextrous and from a very early age liked to cut fabric and sew alongside Mother, but Eldress Mary did not think it right to gain instruction by working alongside his own mother, so he was apprenticed instead to Brother Ezekiel, the cobbler, and taught to cut and sew boots and shoes and belts and harnesses. Brother Ezekiel was a taciturn man in his mid-thirties who had worked from boyhood in a collar factory up in Troy, New York, until he lost three fingers off his left hand to a molding machine and was fired from the factory and turned to begging on the streets of Troy. Homeless and despondent, still a young man, he joined the North Family at Mount Lebanon and despite the loss of his fingers took up working with leather and in 1891 migrated to Florida with Eldress Mary and the North Family delegation that founded the New Bethany family.

Royal, who wrote a lovely cursive and was thought to be artistically inclined, was apprenticed to Sister Beth in the sign shop, which doubled as a print shop for the seed and herb packets sold by mail order and out of general stores in nearby villages like Narcoossee and St. Cloud. Sister Beth was a somber Black woman originally from the long-disbanded Philadelphia colony of mostly Black Shakers. She was in her late sixties then and somewhat brittle-boned and arthritic and was glad to have a strong ten-year-old boy to lift and lug the heavy trays of type and work the hand wheel of the flatbed press and operate the manual guillotine paper cutter. When he was not assisting Sister Beth with printing, Royal learned sign painting from her by repainting all the old, flaking signs in the place, most of which were designed to control the movements of visitors from the World who came out sometimes in crowds on Sundays for the Shaker services and the songs and marchlike dances, which were a particular draw. With all the guidepost signs, even though they were small and discreet, you might have thought that New Bethany was a kind of early theme park.

My brother Pence and I were not identical twins, and we differed greatly. He was a natural horseman, I was not. He rode bareback fearlessly and seemed to have an uncanny, almost mystical connection to horses and mules, so Elder John made him a herdsman, which in those days in south Florida was a kind of cowboy. He assigned Pence his own horse to work and care for, a four-year-old Appaloosa mare named Bosh, and attached Pence to Brothers Amos and George, who herded the near-wild cattle on the vast sawgrass plains that surrounded New Bethany's seven thousand watery acres. The open state, and federal grasslands, seemingly endless and unfenced, were shared more or less amicably by cattle ranchers and herdsmen across the region from Fort Myers in the south to Tampa in the north. New Bethany's cattle were branded with the letters NB inside a circle and were raised for beef, some of which fed the Shakers, but most of which was either butchered and salted at New Bethany and sold locally or carried in barrels to sell in Fort Myers or Tampa, with the remaining more or less feral cattle fattened in the grasslands and rounded up twice a year and driven in large merged herds to dockside warehouses on the Gulf and sold at auction for shipment to Key West, Havana, and New York.

Pence's ease with horses went back to his earliest childhood years, before the family decamped from Graylag for Waycross, when he and I were barely three years old. According to family lore, his equestrian gift first appeared in late September 1893, at the Indiana commune. Mother and Father and their fellow Ruskinites at Graylag were holding a community picnic on the banks of the White River to celebrate the news that New Zealand had just become the first country in the world to grant women the right to vote. The Ruskinites, male as much as female, were dedicated to women's suffrage, and this was for them an occasion that called for celebration.

Our parents and their cohort were letting the older children ride the huge, docile workhorses for pleasure, an unusual reprieve for the dozen or so children and for the bridled horses, a pair of Belgians and a pair of Clydesdales. Pence and I were little more than toddlers, and when Father lifted me up and placed me onto the back of the gray Clydesdale gelding named Dan, I resisted and began to cry. He shrugged and put me back on the ground. Pence, though, was delighted to be hoisted onto the horse's bare back, and once up there took the reins in hand and clucked, and old Dan strolled away from the people and made his way down along the riverside trail. Father and Mother watched proudly as their little boy rode the horse with natural ease, straight-backed, rocking back and forth in time to Dan's easy gait. Pence was too short to grasp onto the horse with his legs, so he sat with them splayed across the animal's wide back, as if he were on the flat ground playing a game of jacks instead of perched six feet above the ground atop a fifteen-hundred-pound beast.

All of a sudden, a black squirrel darted across the trail in front of Dan, and the horse spooked and broke into a gallop. Off he went at full speed, and in seconds he and Pence had disappeared into the cottonwood grove at the distant bend where the White River joined the Wabash. The picnicking adults all panicked and ran after Dan and Pence, calling in vain for them to come back. I still remember Mother racing after Father and weeping aloud, crying, "Oh, no! Oh, no!" sure that her child had been thrown from the horse and badly injured or worse. Then, just as the crowd reached the cottonwoods, here came Dan, walking now and fully controlled by the tiny boy, who later said that he had ended the horse's flight by pulling the reins with both hands sharply to one side, turning the animal's head and calmly asking him to stop.

"Weren't you afraid of being thrown?" Father asked.

I remember being told that Pence had answered, "No, Dan's a good horse, and he didn't want to hurt me. He probably forgot I was on his back because I'm so little. I just needed to remind him I was there by pulling on the reins."

When it came time for my own apprenticeship to be decided, we were in Sister Hazel's classroom, and Elder John had already given out my brothers' assignments. I asked him forthrightly if I could be allowed to work with Brother Hiram and learn beekeeping.

"I had thought to put you to work with Sister Rosalie," he said, "tending the geese and poultry and learning the egg business. Sister Hazel tells me that when it comes to numbers and finance, Harley, you shine. Sister Rosalie is not much at that, and the egg business will soon be booming. The migrants from the World who keep arriving in Narcoossee and Kissimmee and St. Cloud and settling on their little five-acre plots all around the towns, they're not farmers and are used to store-bought goods. Tell me why you want to learn beekeeping, Harley."

I said truthfully that I thought bees were the most mysterious creatures in the universe, certainly the most mysterious at New Bethany, and hidden in the habits and behavior of bees was a key that could unlock the still-deeper mysteries of mankind. That's the turn of mind I had when I was a boy, the kind that likes to link everything up. If I had been raised differently, I might have become a theologian or a philosopher, instead of a speculator in land.

I told Elder John that I hoped to emulate Brother Hiram's love of his fellow creatures, which was true. I did not tell him that I wanted to work someplace near the main house, where Sadie Pratt stayed when she came from the sanitarium to visit New Bethany. Brother Hiram's bee yard was located on a low, protected slope adjacent to the extensive flower gardens and a short, pollinating bee flight to the citrus orchards that lay between the main buildings of New Bethany and Live Oak Lake. There was a good sightline from the apiary up to the foursquare three-story house and down to where the barge from Narcoossee and St. Cloud tied up to drop off and pick up passengers and produce. From the bee yard I would be able to see Sadie coming and going. She often walked in the flower gardens alone after breakfast and cut and arranged flowers for the dining-hall tables and for Sunday services, and sometimes in late afternoon she sat in the shade of the wide porch of the main house and read from a book and now and then looked up as if searching for a lost memory and gazed over the orchards and flower gardens and the cleared and drained marsh-meadow past the apiary to the lake and the wide blue sky beyond. As much as possible I wanted to be able to look at her without being seen by her. Working in the bee yard alongside Brother Hiram was the best way to accomplish that. And I knew that if Brother Hiram happened to notice my constant interest in the lady, unlike the captain and pilot on the *Coquina*, he would not tease me for it. Nor would he report it to Elder John.

Elder John said to me, "All right, then. See if you can penetrate the mystery of the bees, Harley. Go and work with Brother Hiram in the bee yard and learn from him all that he has learned from them."

And so I turned myself over to Brother Hiram and the bee yard. My three brothers and I, ages ten and twelve, were now required to work five and six hours a day six days a week without pay. At that time there weren't any child labor laws. Looking back, I have sometimes asked myself if it was exploitative and unnatural and cruel to work children that way. Exploitative, yes. The profit to New Bethany from our unpaid collective labor was much greater than the cost of our maintenance and education. That was easy to compute. In fact, I made it a classroom project, but did not show the numbers to Sister Hazel. But it was not unnatural or cruel. In those days it was assumed that children should work without pay for as many hours a day as they were available and able, especially in farm communities and among the poor, and we were both. Besides, after five hours of confinement in Sister Hazel's schoolroom, we boys were eager to get outside and be physically active. And for all four of us, the work we were assigned was interesting and instructive and rarely as onerous or dangerous as work in a factory or mill would have been had we been living in the World. The men and women to whom we were apprenticed, the brothers and sisters we labored under, with a few notable exceptions, were kind and patient, and they taught us skills and Shaker attitudes regarding work that would prove useful to us for the rest of our lives.

Over the summer my obsession with Sadie Pratt deepened and began to distract me from my schoolwork and the bee yard. Brother Hiram seemed not to notice or care that I was often not paying attention to his instructions and guidance, but whenever I forgot what he had told me or ignored him, he merely repeated himself again and again in his sputtering way, almost as if he welcomed the chance to practice speaking aloud and was doing it for his own benefit. But in the schoolroom, when Sister Hazel saw me staring dreamily out the window and not looking down at my Shaker workbook or up at the columns of numbers on the blackboard, she often brought me sharply back to earth with a loud crack of the ruler against her desk, and sometimes, if I was not ready to recite the times tables when called on or the dates of the English monarchs, she made me go to a corner and turn my back to the others and practice my memorizations in silence. Since we four brothers were the only students in the New Bethany school and were close in age and reading level, each of us progressed at his own natural rate rather than by grade or level, following the Lancasterian System, in which the older students teach the younger. In the beginning I was first in all areas, the assistant teacher, as it were; but gradually, due to my distracted state of mind, I let Pence and Royal and Raymond catch up and even begin to pass me.

Much of our instruction in Sister Hazel's classroom was given over to memorizing the history and principles of the Shakers, along with their rules and regulations, as laid out in a forty-page pamphlet published in the 1830s. I still possess my schoolboy's tattered copy of the booklet, and just this morning dug it out of the boxed papers and records I've saved from my years at New Bethany. It's called *A Brief Exposition of the Established Principles and Regulations of the United Society of Believers Called Shakers.* There are no illustrations. Except for the purpose of illustrating religious visions, the Shakers eschewed visual representations. Apparently composed by a committee of elders from the Mount Lebanon and Watervliet families, the pamphlet had the stated purpose of making the Shakers' religious and social beliefs and practices known to the World. It was more a defense of Shakerism than a scriptural text, more legalistic and expository than hortatory. Along with the Bible, in particular the Old Testament, it was our classroom primer.

My obsession with Sadie Pratt grew as rapidly as I myself grew in size and physical strength, for I was entering adolescence ahead of schedule and at reckless speed. Pence now seemed physically a full year younger than me, instead of mere minutes. Without drawing undue attention to the nature or source of my inquiry, I tried to learn whatever I could about Sadie's health, her background and family history, and the nature of her relationship with the New Bethany family.

Surprisingly, the best person to ask, perhaps because of his child-like innocence and trust, turned out to be my beekeeping master, Brother Hiram. I would not have dared raise such questions with Elder John, who would have seen through me in a minute. In his Quaker mode he would have chastised me for pursuing private information that was none of my business. Or else in his Kentucky-farmer mode he would have mocked me for being a boy with an unnatural interest in a grown woman. Also, I had observed that Elder John, along with Eldress Mary, seemed to have an especially close and protective friendship with Sadie. When Sadie visited New Bethany, she stayed in a room reserved for guests in the main house, where Elder John and Eldress Mary kept their offices on the ground floor and their separate sleeping quarters upstairs at opposite ends of the building. I noticed at meals that Sadie was always seated front and center at Eldress Mary's table with the females, directly opposite Elder John's table on the males' side. The tables were arranged so that whenever the two looked up from their plates, they could not see each other plainly, and I took some small comfort from that.

One fine afternoon when Brother Hiram was showing me how to smoke the bees into calm submission so we could remove the trays of honey without disturbing the hives' inhabitants, I asked him how Sadie Pratt could be both a patient at the Sunshine Home tuberculosis sanitarium in Narcoossee and a frequent visitor here at New Bethany. It was a cool, windless day. We were burning dried coconut shells and shavings in smoldering fires set at the base of the hives, making pale clouds of sweet-smelling smoke rise through the hives and gather overhead in a gauzy canopy between our heads and the bright blue sky beyond.

He stammered a bit as if he didn't know the answer to my question, then burst out with a response that sounded like he had said it many times, or else, in anticipation of my question, had rehearsed it. "Oh, Brother Harley, her sickness, it comes and it goes. When it comes and she's weakly, she hunkers down there at the sanitarium with the other tuberculars," he said. "Eldress Mary, she's one of the people in charge of Sunshine Home. She studied accounting in the World when she was young in Albany. I think she volunteers to manage their finances, like she does ours, and goes off there every ten days or so, and if Sister Sadie ain't weakly and coughing, she brings her back here for a little holiday. Sometimes Sister Sadie comes over on her own, and mostly she just takes her rest and joins us for the services and the company. But she ain't a Shaker. Not yet anyways," he added.

In those late days a constant preoccupation of the Shakers from Maine to Kentucky to Florida was replacing family members who had grown too old to work or were dying or for religious or other personal reasons had decided to return to the World. Since the Shakers were forbidden to replicate themselves in the usual way of humans and other creatures, they had to rely on a steady influx of new Believers to have enough workers to manage their land and other property and to feed, shelter, and clothe themselves. And the younger and the sounder of mind and body, the better. Sadie Pratt was not of sound body, evidently, but she was young and appeared to be of sound mind.

I wanted to ask Brother Hiram many questions concerning Sadie, but did not want him to think my interest was more than idle curiosity. I mentioned that when we first met her in Narcoossee on our way here from Georgia, Elder John said that she was from Providence, Rhode Island. I allowed as how Sunshine Home in Narcoossee, Florida, seemed a long ways to go for a tuberculosis cure.

Brother Hiram agreed. "Guess she got family up there that don't want her and her troubles close by or something. Families can do that," he said. "They gets scared." His own family in Maryland was like that when he came back from Cuba, he added. The war had got into his head and he couldn't shake it loose, so he talked about it all the time and had terrible nightmares and even thought of shooting himself to get rid of the memories. His mother and father wanted to put him in a hospital for lunatics in Virginia, so he ran away. He was trying to get back to Cuba, but didn't know why, he said, and only got as far as the Fort Myers dockyard, where he ran into Elder John, who was setting up a way to ship New Bethany pineapples to Cuba. Elder John convinced him to come for a mental rest cure at New Bethany, and he never left. He took up caring for the bees, and the nightmares went away, so he made his confession and became a Shaker. "Maybe something like what happened with me and my family in Maryland happened with Sister Sadie and her family up in Rhode Island," he said.

"Maybe," I said. But I didn't think so. There was a certain small shame associated with tuberculosis back then, especially among the upper classes. I pictured Sadie deciding on her own, perhaps against her family's wishes, to take her illness off to the south Florida wilderness, where she could deal with it privately and not embarrass or discomfit the Pratts, whom I imagined as mercantile aristocrats descended from the Puritans. I visualized Sadie disguised behind a veil and under a large hat, riding alone one gray, rainy morning in a horse-drawn cab to the train station in Providence and departing for Florida, bringing with her little more than a trunk of her clothing and some personal possessions and a letter from her doctor introducing her to the head of Sunshine Home. A brave young woman, I thought, noble and proud, determined to spare her family the inconvenience and social ignominy of having to care for an invalided daughter. She would have her own trust fund, no doubt, to pay for her upkeep and medical care at Sunshine Home. And the New Bethany brothers and sisters and Elder John and Eldress Mary would seem an attractive, compassionate substitute for the family she had left behind. I imagined her writing long, falsely cheerful, reassuring letters back to her parents and siblings in Providence, describing the colorful beauty and abundance of south Florida, the warm, balmy climate in winter, the kindness and skill of the staff at Sunshine Home, and the saintly hospitality of the Shakers. I imagined her as sad and lonely, unable to return to her Northern family and home until her illness was cured. And if it could not be cured, she would never return to family and home. She would make the Shakers her family and New Bethany her home. And I, young Master Harley Mann, I would be there to assist her and become her constant companion.

REEL #5

This morning, before starting to make this new reel, I sat at my kitchen table and listened to yesterday's taping. I seem to have veered away from my original intention, which was to tell what happened some sixty and more years ago to Sadie Pratt and Elder John and Eldress Mary. And to the New Bethany Shakers. And to my family. And to me. It's a story that was a very big deal at the time, a national scandal, reported in many newspapers, even *The New York Times*, a story that in the intervening years has been almost completely forgotten. This is not to apologize, but the truth is, I had not anticipated taking so much pleasure from recounting my memories of the events and circumstances that generated the scandal, nor had I meant to describe them at such length. These memories warm and enlarge my cold heart and mind. So this is not strictly or maybe even partially a story with a mission, as I originally intended. Nor is it driven by a desire to set straight the record concerning an old, forgotten scandal. It began that way, perhaps, but I see that it is becoming something else.

For most of my life I have refused to recall and rethink the events of my childhood and youth. I've not told about them to anyone or shared and compared reminiscences with the people who were there with me, not even my brothers and sister and my mother. It's too late for that, anyhow. They're all gone—my beloved Sadie Pratt, who went first, and Eldress Mary and Elder John, and then my family, one by one. And I've certainly said nothing of it in public. It's been my own private store of memories and opinions and shame all mixed together in a disordered mélange that I have until now refused to order and examine. But having started, I seem unable to stop myself.

I've spoken several times of my obsession with Sadie Pratt. A person might ask how a boy of twelve or thereabouts could develop so quickly and sustain for so long a fixation on a grown woman as I had for Sadie. But in a sexless environment where celibacy was not merely enforced but celebrated, it was easy to call my fixation something else. Admiration, curiosity, aesthetic appreciation, even competitiveness—I do remember worrying at the time about my early attraction to Sadie and my constant preoccupation with her and, in order to comfort myself, attributing it to all these.

For instance, admiration. I admired Sadie's self-containment, her ability to be both present and absent at the same time, her easy acceptance of the attentions paid to her by the Shakers, especially by Elder John and Eldress Mary, and her refusal to court them. She had a sort of regal entitlement that I had not seen before in a woman. I had seen it in plenty of men; even my father had that quality. In a negative way, so did Mr. Hamilton Couper, the diminutive white-haired owner of Rosewood Plantation. It was a common characteristic of strong, self-confident, privileged men. But until I met Sadie Pratt and watched her interact with the inhabitants of New Bethany, I had not witnessed the female version, and it entranced me. For the first time I realized that women were as complex and formidable as men, if not more so.

And she aroused in me a new curiosity as to the cosmopolitan world that I imagined she had left behind in Providence, Rhode Island, a country boy's fantasy of the New England urban ruling class—men and women with university educations and trust funds passed down for generations, parlors with oriental carpets on parquet floors, antique mahogany furniture and vases from China, crystal glassware, memories of European travel, summer holidays in Newport and Saratoga Springs. I wanted to ask her about those cultural and economic accoutrements. Did they provide her with delight? Or did they burden her with guilt? Or both? And did she miss those comforts and embellishments here in the rustic, watery wilderness of south Florida and long to return to them as soon as her health permitted?

Also, I romanticized her illness. She was a beautiful young woman with unnaturally large dark eyes and pale skin, slim and delicate-boned, enervated and careful in all her movements. Despite her evident fragility and weakness, she walked slowly and gracefully, with perfect posture. Unable to contend with the physical demands of our commonplace working world, she needed the assistance of our dumb, indelicate strength in order to get through a simple waking day, which made us feel strong and necessary. When I looked up from the bee yard and saw her sitting in the shade outside the main house reading from her book, I imagined that it was a book of poems by a great English poet of the previous century, Browning or Keats, a book too subtle and refined for my crude, unformed mind to comprehend.

And I confess, there was also an element of sheer competitiveness that fed my fixation, evidenced by my constant awareness of the attention paid to Sadie by Elder John and the attention repaid by her to him. For instance, the morning in the classroom when I learned from our teacher, Sister Hazel, that Elder John had for a long time been writing occasional letters on Shaker farming methods for publication in the *St. Cloud Tribune*. The letters were intended to ingratiate the New Bethany Shakers with our neighbors and at the same time introduce them to the Shakers' scientific methods of agriculture. Sister Hazel told us that Miss Sadie Pratt admired his letters and was compiling them into a small book that would be printed in Sister Beth's printshop and sold by mail order and in the nearby towns. My brother Royal was setting the type for the book, she added, which made Royal grin with pride.

Sister Hazel handed out printed tear sheets for several of the letters, one on clearing the marshy land surrounding New Bethany of trees and brush and draining the land with ditches from the Indian hammocks to the lakes and preparing the muck for planting, and another on raising Hart's Choice and Lady Finger dwarf bananas for the market. We were instructed to write a paper emulating the style and form of Elder John's letters about an aspect of New Bethany with which we ourselves had become familiar. Pence chose to write about branding the feral cattle on the grassy plains, and Raymond said he wanted to describe every step of the process of making a pair of boots, from tanning the raw hide to fitting the inner sole, and Royal said he would write about setting the type for Elder John's book of letters to the editor of the *St. Cloud Tribune*. Naturally, I chose beekeeping.

Before composing my paper, I carefully studied Elder John's two letters and after ascertaining the writer's intentions noted the deliberate impersonality of tone and the precision of his descriptions and certain implied assumptions concerning his readers, i.e., that they were, like him, experienced mechanics and farmers and longtime residents of this region and were used to reading manuals and handbooks for instruction and inspiration. His language was plain and unadorned. His letters were brief, barely a page or two, and to the point. His tone was self-confident, but not self-admiring. Objective, but not cold or detached.

The following day when we read our letters aloud to Sister Hazel, mine was declared the best. She complimented my letter for the same characteristics that I had thought praiseworthy in Elder John's. After correcting a few misspellings and untangling a pair of grammatically snarled sentences, she asked me to write out a clean copy so she could show it to Elder John. This was exactly what I hoped she would do. And then Elder John did what I hoped he would do, he praised my letter and at the evening meal invited me to sit for a moment next to him at his table and informed me that he would be sending my letter, entitled "On Beekeeping at New Bethany," to the editor of the *St. Cloud Tribune* for possible publication.

A few moments ago, I shut off the recorder and went back into the house and rummaged through a file of papers I've kept from the early days at New Bethany—"1902–1911," the folder is labeled. I haven't looked into that file in nearly sixty years. There wasn't much, a small packet of letters and a copy of my initial deposition to the Osceola County prosecutor in August and the summons to the grand jury, none of which am I inclined to reread now. I will, of course, reread them when I get to that part of my story.

But as I suspected, out of vanity I had saved my only published letter to the editor of the *St. Cloud Tribune.* The clipping is dated July 23, 1902. It's a tattered, yellowed page torn from the newspaper, and no doubt, when I have gone to my reward, it will be destroyed or tossed into the trash with the rest of my papers. As a verbalized addendum or footnote, then, I record it now.

ON BEEKEEPING AT NEW BETHANY
By Harley Mann

In recent years the Shakers at New Bethany have been experimenting with raising bees for the purpose of harvesting honey, God's perfect sweetener, and using beeswax in the manufacture of candles, lotions, sealants and varnishes. The traditional methods of hiving bees in this region in logs and in roughly carpentered boxes have proven inefficient and troublesome, as well as subjecting the harvester to a barrage of painful and dangerous stings. It is therefore an under-developed industry here and elsewhere in the United States. Yet in south Florida, more than anywhere in the country, there is an abundance of flowering trees and plants available year-round for the lively industrious insects to feed upon and convert into their ambrosial product.

At New Bethany the beekeepers have utilized methods in the manufacture of their hives that were invented fifty years ago by the eminent apiarist, Mr. L. L. Langstroth of Philadelphia. They were described in detail and illustrated in his book, *A Practical Treatise on the Hive and the Honey-Bee.* As a result of following his instructions, while employing just one beekeeper and his young apprentice, the Shakers have established twenty-two working hives, and in the recent spring season alone have harvested four hundred forty-five pounds of honey and extracted seventy-seven pounds of wax. This quantity greatly exceeds the harvest in the same period of any known apiary in the state.

The key to Langstroth's method is removable combs, so that the bees are not disturbed when the apiarist opens the hive to remove the fruits of the bees' assiduous labor. When the combs have been designed and constructed according to Langstroth's exact specifications, they can be easily slid from the hive without cutting the combs or injuring or enraging the bees.

The second most important consideration is ventilation of the hive, so that it is protected against extremes of heat and cold and sudden changes of temperature, which admittedly are uncommon in southwest Florida. The injurious effects of dampness, however, are common to our region. For the bees to thrive and perform their labors, the interior of the hive must be kept dry, as well as free of a pent and suffocating heat. Thus proper ventilation is essential.

A third concern for the apiarist is protecting the hive against the influx of the bee-moth and its larval worms, which can ravage a hive. After building into the hive removable combs and sufficient air space and providing easy entry and egress for the bees, installing a bottom board that can be slid out and in quickly and smoothly will greatly diminish the likelihood of an invasion by this pest. The bottom board should be constructed so as to slant toward the entrance to facilitate the removal of the dead bees and other useless substances as well as any invading bee moths and their larvae.

Except where the theories of L. L. Langstroth have been applied, beekeeping on a commercial scale in this country has long languished. In our most blessed and bountiful region of flowers and citrus that bloom and blossom throughout all four seasons, we should by rights be leaders in this nascent industry, shipping high grade Florida honey and beeswax to every corner of the country, and even to Cuba and beyond. The Shakers residing at New Bethany near Narcoossee invite any of their neighbors in the area who wish to know more about beekeeping to come out to their apiary and examine the hives built there by Brother Hiram Wales and the writer of this missive according to specifications invented and perfected by Mr. L. L. Langstroth. His book can be obtained by mail order from J. B. Lippincott & Co., 227 South 6th Street, Philadelphia, Pennsylvania.

Rereading that little essay, composed when I was but a nervy, precocious twelve-year-old—my first and only published piece of writing—I'm awash with memories and long- forgotten, mostly pleasurable sensations. I'm almost as proud of it today as I was when it appeared in the pages of the *St. Cloud Tribune* nearly seventy years ago. I'm impressed by the range of my vocabulary at such a young age and my mastery of formal English grammar. But at the time my pleasure was tainted, because when writing it I was motivated by an egotistical desire to compete with Elder John for Sadie Pratt's attention and admiration. Consequently, when I actually succeeded in every imagined way, I was embarrassed by my success and a little ashamed of it.

I remember the afternoon when Sadie walked down to the apiary from the main house, holding the issue of the *Tribune* with my essay. She greeted me warmly, which had never happened before. Until that moment, she had dealt with me as if I were a stranger, a nameless person in a crowd, the way she had when we were introduced by Elder John in Narcoossee on our first arrival at New Bethany from Rosewell Plantation.

"Brother Harley, I read your article on beekeeping," she said. Her voice was soft and low, but firm, as if she were used to being attended to and were speaking to an adult, not a child. "It's very good."

I thanked her and stopped work. She stood ten or twelve feet off, for Brother Hiram and I were in the midst of transferring a queen bee and her thousands of drones and workers to a new hive, and the bees were swarming. We wore our hiving clothes—gloves and white canvas jackets and face veils beneath our broad-brimmed palm-frond hats.

She did not seem to be alarmed by the buzzing cloud of bees hovering around me and Brother Hiram. She held out the newspaper and asked, "Did you write this entirely on your own? Did Elder John aid you in any way?"

I excused myself to Brother Hiram and stepped away from the hive and approached her and doffed my hat. I thought to remove my veil as well, but somehow felt the need to keep myself partially hidden, so I kept it on and spoke through the mesh. I told her that I had first read two of Elder John's letters to the editor and had tried only to emulate his format and style.

"Well, you did an excellent job of it. When I read it, I thought that he had written it himself, but under a pseudonym. He assured me that Harley Mann was a real person and pointed you out to me."

I thanked her again. I felt my cheeks flush and my ears burn, as if I'd been caught in a lie.

"I would like to include your article in a little collection of Elder John's newspaper articles about New Bethany that I'm editing, but I'm told by the printer, Sister Beth, that the type for it has already been set. Perhaps in time there will be a second volume. If so, would you mind if I included your piece on beekeeping?"

I said I'd be honored, and she asked me if I planned to write more articles about New Bethany for the newspaper, but I said no, beekeeping was the only enterprise here that I knew well enough to write about. Which wasn't altogether true, since by then I had learned from Brother Hiram quite a lot about horticulture, due to the bees' dependence on the nearby availability of citrus trees and flowering plants. Brother Hiram's daily lectures on beekeeping included many aspects told from the bees' point of view, as was his wont, and tree blossoms and flowers were a big part of their world. It was one of his maxims that you can't properly care for creatures until you see the world as they do, an attitude that probably lay behind his well-known sympathy for the horses and other beasts that he had tended during the Spanish War in Cuba.

She said that I should continue to write nonetheless. She said that I clearly had a gift for it, and turned to leave.

"Miss Pratt," I said, stopping her. "If you ever wish to know more about the bees, come down when we are not hiving them like today, and I would be pleased to show you all about them. Bees are very interesting creatures," I said. "They build and maintain an entire society. A hive is like a whole city in miniature."

She smiled. "I would like that," she said. "Now that we are friends." Then she walked in her slow, graceful manner back up the low slope to the main house, and I stood watching her the entire way, until Brother Hiram called me back to work.

That summer, no, that very afternoon, I mark as the high point of my time at New Bethany. I have held on to those few moments in the bee yard and played them back in my mind over and over again. More than a decade later, when I moved across the lake to live alone in St. Cloud and began speculating in real estate, buying and selling plots of undeveloped land and foreclosed houses, even then I could still recall every second of my first true encounter with Sadie.

To illustrate, when I first settled over here in St. Cloud, I became obsessed with maps and plats, surveys and deeds. It was in the beginning a practical matter, a business tool. In the 1890s and early 1900s, vast tracts of federal land from Lake Okeechobee to the Gulf, especially in and around St. Cloud, had fallen into the hands of developers like the Seminole Land & Investment Company. By order of the United States General Land Office, banks were required to provide equity-free, low-interest loans, enabling homeless war veterans to buy a five-acre plot and build a house on it. Not surprisingly, many of the veterans proved unable to make timely payments on their loans, and some of the subdivided plots turned out to be marshy or underwater, and by the time I arrived, the banks and developers were calling in those loans and reselling the properties to the next generation of borrowers.

That's where I entered the game. As a young man and something of an outsider, I was at a disadvantage in and around St. Cloud and Kissimmee and Narcoossee, and to make up for it I acquired as much knowledge as I could of the location and history of every piece of private land in Osceola County and every structure, domestic, retail, wholesale, industrial, and otherwise. It quickly made me a shrewd buyer and seller of real estate, especially including the tracts originally purchased by the Shakers, for which, as a buyer, I had more than a merely pecuniary interest.

My obsession with maps and plats and deeds and liens linked to New Bethany became a pursuit for its own sake, my own private indulgence in nostalgia, and not just a realtor's due diligence. I collected old surveys of New Bethany made in the early 1890s before the Shakers came down from Mount Lebanon and Watervliet, and copies of the deeds and bills of sale as over time the Shakers acquired their seven thousand acres piece by piece. I tracked the liens that the lenders placed on the properties and the loans the Shakers paid off and those they didn't. Finally, I bought two eight-by-four-foot sheets of half-inch-thick plywood and fifty pounds of plaster of paris and a set of watercolor paints. I made with these materials an eight-by-eight-foot table and built, at a scale of one foot to a mile, a sixty-four-square-mile plaster-of-paris topographical relief map of New Bethany and the surrounding properties.

It was more than a map. It was a miniaturized twin of the land and buildings where we Manns had lived together as Shakers for nearly ten years. With my paints I colored the fields and forests, the gardens and citrus groves, the flowering meadows and marshes, even the lilies that covered the small ponds, as if it were early summer in 1902 and the first crops were coming in. I bought and renovated tiny toy buildings and hand-carved people and animals and manufactured myself those I could not find in the German's toy store in St. Cloud.

It is a view of New Bethany from an altitude of about five hundred feet. You can see the tree-topped hammocks and the cleared and drained meadows, the sandy lanes and winding, narrow canals, the ponds and lakes, and most of the larger man-made structures, the barns, sheds, and warehouses, the Shaker meeting hall and dormitories and the main house, where Elder John and Eldress Mary lived and worked. From that altitude, you can see hay wagons, the sugar mill and the steam-powered sawmill and the herds of cattle and milch cows and even the sheep and hog pens and the animals themselves. There is the henhouse, but not the hens, of course, as it's too great an altitude. You can make out the mules and a pair of oxen yoked to a wagon, six horses in a corral, and a drover astride an Appaloosa, either bearded Brother Amos or Brother George, the hostlers, or Pence, beardless. You can't tell which is which, because you cannot see the drover's face beneath his wide-brimmed hat. The vineyards, yes, but not the grapes hanging heavily down. The lattice-works shielding the pineapple plants from the burning sun, but not the sweet, delicious fruits beneath. The orange, lemon, and grape-fruit groves, but not the citrus globes themselves, even though the boughs are bent down by the weight of the early-summer crop, ready to be picked and shipped north from the railhead at St. Cloud. You can see the hives in Brother Hiram's and my bee yard. You can see Brother Hiram. And a few feet away, there am I, standing beside one of the hives. And facing me, there is Sadie Pratt.

For decades my miniaturized New Bethany was exhibited in the center of my realty office, an object of constant, amused interest to clients and colleagues and over the years the subject of several news-paper articles. Naturally, when the Disney Company agents, their lawyers and bankers, came knocking in 1959 and 1960, they showed a particular interest in my plaster-of-paris model of the original Shaker colony. I didn't know the prospective buyers were Disney people, however. I didn't know they were surrogates and frontmen. None of us who sold our land to them knew.

Later, when I shuttered my office in downtown St. Cloud and started calling myself retired, I carried my plaster-of-paris New Bethany over here to my little house and cleared out the dining room, where I have never dined anyway, and set it up. I had to split the eight-by-eight-foot table in half to move it, and there was some unavoidable breakage, almost as if it had endured an earthquake—very rare here in south-central Florida, where the ground is more subject to sinkholes and cave-ins than slippage and fractures. Half the small lakes and ponds are water-filled sinkholes. A few are very deep and lead to unexplored, serpentine underground waterways that erupt in springs miles from the sinkholes. Every year cattle and horses and motor vehicles, even buildings, are swallowed whole by the sudden opening of a sinkhole, never to be seen again, like the end of that opera by Mozart, *Don Giovanni.*

After I reassembled the platform and placed it on wooden sawhorses in the center of the dining room, I repaired the breaks and cracks caused by the move and carefully updated and upgraded the quality of paint and many of the tiny animals and people and various vehicles and the structures built by the Shakers. By then, the early 1960s, the quality of paints and materials were much improved over what had been available to me back in the early 1920s.

I'm unsure what to call it. A model New Bethany, like a model railroad? A miniaturized New Bethany, as if it were some kind of toy? It's more than a model, more than a toy, and more than a map by far. It's a solid, three-dimensional presentation of a specific moment plucked from the stream of time and memory and fixed like a butterfly pinned in a glass-fronted case. I stand and stare at it for hours, unconcerned with time past and time to come, filled with swirled feelings that I'm unable to name.

I think that most people have a clear, detailed memory of a place where a life-changing event occurred that was not understood when it happened, a place where turbulent emotions and confusion reigned, where everything except the place itself was in flux. One fixates on such a place, as if it were the key to unlocking the mystery of what happened there and before and thereafter, so that everything physical about the place—the rise and fall of the temperature over the course of a day, the opening-out of light at dawn and the closing-in of darkness at dusk, the surge and retreat of the land beneath one's feet and before one's eyes as one walks across the land, the trees against the sky silhouetted along the hammock ridge, the midday heat of the Florida sun, the sound of the late-afternoon breeze through the dry leaves, the smell of the freshly plowed field and the oxen and the mules and their creaking harnesses and the moist manure they leave behind, the birdsong and the grasshoppers and the crickets, the dew-wet grass in morning's first light and the smell of the day's food being prepared in the kitchen as in the toolshed one readies oneself for work, the sound of the grinding wheel against the blade of the scythe, the bleat of the new lambs and goats from the barn and the chuff of the steam-powered sawmill starting up and the splash of the bass spooked in the marsh by the alligator in close pursuit, a flock of egrets rising off the lake like a curtain opening to let the play begin—everything of that remembered moment in that remembered place has resonance, meaning, significance. Everything is cloaked in emotion and mystery.

Over the course of that first spring and summer and into the following year, my brothers and I settled happily into our life at New Bethany as novitiate Shakers, while Mother eased with seeming tranquility into hers. She was now known as Sister Constance, a true Shaker lady. As long as her youngest child, Rachel, remained an infant, Mother was allowed to keep her by her side when at work in the tailor shop and at mealtimes. As long as she was still nursing her, she slept her baby in a cradle next to her bed in the women's sleeping quarters. That would not last, of course. By the start of her second year, Rachel would be gradually taken from Mother to be raised by the New Bethany family, just as we boys were now being raised.

I think Mother's adherence to the beliefs and liturgical practices of the United Society of Believers helped to soften the double blow of Father's death and the hardship and terror afterwards at Rosewell Plantation. She believed, as the Shakers taught, that Father was now in Heaven with Jesus and Mother Ann Lee, waiting for Mother to join them. She had held on to the Ruskinite ethical system and contrarian politics, which weren't much different than the Shakers', but had discarded John Ruskin's secular, materialistic metaphysic and replaced it with a belief in angels and life after death and the imminence of the Second Appearing of Christ in ascendence with Mother Ann Lee, the female founder of the Society of Believers. My brothers and I were not expected to accept or deny these beliefs, merely to obey our elders and follow the Shaker way of life in all our actions and not expose ourselves to the ways of the World. We were not thought capable of responsible religious commitment. While we learned self-discipline and acquired basic literacy and served an apprenticeship in a trade, we were more or less allowed to think our own thoughts.

The Shakers' interpretation of the Bible and the afterlife and their belief in the coequal rule of the eighteenth-century Englishwoman Mother Ann Lee, residing now in Heaven with Jesus, and the songs and choreographed marches and solemnly chanted prayers that characterized their Sabbath and daily services, this all might have seemed unconventional or even a little bizarre to non-Shakers. But in the South back then, where Christians, Black and White alike, practiced many enthusiastic and variant forms of faith, the Shakers hardly stood out. Nor was their communistic society subject to disapproval or suspicion by the locals, who admired the Shakers' agricultural skill and animal husbandry and mechanical inventiveness, their work ethic and industry, and their commercial acumen and honesty and straightforwardness. The Shakers' insistence on keeping celibate was sometimes a subject for country humor and low mockery, but at the same time it safely removed any possible sexual threat or hint of scandal, which distinguished them from the other religious communitarians, like the Koreshans and the New Harmonists and the Mormons, whose sexual practices, real and rumored, alarmed most Christian citizens and sometimes provoked them to acts of violence.

Much of the social rigidity and religious intensity of the Society of Believers was an aspect of their distant past, their early days in America. Over time they had become more flexible and adaptable to the habits and needs of the World. Even so, Elder John and Eldress Mary governed their particular community—or family, as it was called—with military precision and discipline. Perhaps this was due to New Bethany having been so recently established as a satellite family, and also to its distant location, fifteen hundred miles south of the Mount Lebanon family in New York State, which functioned as a kind of headquarters or capital. New Bethany was the Shakers' frontier outpost. The temptation to go native, as it were, and join the World was likely to be greater here than at any of the other Shaker communities, which were mostly bunched together in the northeastern states and thus were more easily overseen by the leaders in Mount Lebanon.

The activities of the fifteen members of the New Bethany family were all the more closely guided and guarded, therefore, by Elder John and Eldress Mary. There was very little social life as such, and for most of us almost no contact with people from the World. Our activities for every hour of every day and night were predetermined and precisely calibrated and served to us in individualized portions. Except when in the schoolroom or when called on for labor that needed more than one laborer, we were alone with our mentors.

Day after day, I worked mornings in Sister Hazel's classroom and afternoons alongside Brother Hiram. Raymond in the leather shop worked only with Brother Ezekiel. Royal in the print shop saw no one but Sister Beth. We envied Pence—or at least I did, for we had little chance to speak of it among ourselves. He got to ride out every day at noon on his horse, Bosh, to join Brother Amos and Brother George on the plain, to share a midday meal with them and meet the cowboys from the adjoining properties and spend the afternoons moving cattle from one grassland to another, separating New Bethany cattle from the unfenced, merged herds of our neighbors' cattle, branding the calves, treating the sick or lame cows, and penning them in preparation for the fall roundup and drive to Fort Myers. He was learning to crack the ten-foot-long plaited-leather whip like a vaquero and to ride like a Comanche. And he was meeting and talking and working with men and boys who were not from New Bethany, who were from the real World. Not the world invented by the Shakers.

My constant awareness of the intermittent presence and absence of Sadie Pratt—as if my job, instead of beekeeping, were keeping track of her whereabouts—did not diminish over the summer months into the fall. I saw little of my brothers outside Sister Hazel's classroom and almost nothing of Mother and Rachel, except at morning and evening mealtimes, when we smiled across the room at one another. Looking back, this strange solitude in the midst of a deliberately isolated, self-governing community may be what initiated my early fixation on Sadie Pratt. For the first time in my life I was lonely. And Sadie was like a bridge to the World. She was an inconstant but returning reminder that it existed somewhere out there beyond the lakes and canals, beyond the marshes and the long, low ridges called hammocks and the sawgrass plains and the pine and cypress forests and swamps that surrounded New Bethany.

Because Pence and I were the firstborn, I was named after Father's father, Harley Mann, and Pence was named after Mother's father, and I sometimes thought that as a result, I took after Father in certain deep-defining ways and Pence's character was more like Mother's. Perhaps Elder John sensed that difference in us, too. He may have been thinking it when he assigned me to the bee yard and gave Pence the relative freedom of riding the range with Brother Amos and Brother George. The two drovers were native Floridians, one an ex-alcoholic cowboy, the other a disenchanted onetime follower of Cyrus Teed, the charlatan who led the Koreshans at their utopian settlement down near Fort Myers. Both drovers were relatively recent arrivals at New Bethany, unmarried men in their forties who had applied for full membership in the Society of Believers, possibly out of desperation, only to obtain food, shelter, and work, but had not yet made their confession. Due to having too much to confess, no doubt.

But Elder John must have noticed that Pence had something of Mother's dreamy trust in other people's force of personality. It's what caused her, a new bride back in Indianapolis, to go along with Father when he decided to throw in with the Ruskinites at Graylag and sold his blacksmith shop and the small farm she had inherited from her parents, and why she had followed him down to Waycross, and why, even after his death, she obeyed him and took us to Rosewell. Father had force of personality aplenty, and though he did not have perfect judgment, he was keenly intellectual. He was a true Ruskinite. Mother, by contrast, was withheld and did not take hard positions. She was an easy convert. Probably Elder John thought Pence would be a quick believer, too, and was therefore less likely than me to be corrupted by the proximity of the open range, where New Bethany and the World overlapped. So Pence got to ride the range with the rough-hewn Brother Amos and Brother George and mingle with cowpunchers and cattle owners and visit the port of Fort Myers and talk with people of the World, while I stayed back at New Bethany and tended the bees with Brother Hiram and had moody, solitary thoughts of Sadie Pratt.

More than a year passed that way, and I turned thirteen and began to get my height and musculature, and my voice dropped a register, and a shadow of a mustache appeared on my upper lip, and I started having sinful dreams that were hard to erase in daylight. Pence rode off on the cattle drive to Fort Myers late that fall alongside Brothers Amos and George. With Elder John in charge, they sold and shipped almost the entire herd to provide beef for the US Army troops based in Guantanamo Bay in Cuba. It was a great commercial success for New Bethany.

When he returned four weeks later, Pence seemed different—more grown up, definitely, but distant from me and Royal and Raymond, more attached to the cow herders than to his family members. He asked Elder John and Eldress Mary and Sister Hazel if he could be excused from any further schooling, so he could work full-time with the cattle. He was learning more useful things there, he said, than in the schoolroom. Sister Hazel acknowledged that he was not much of a scholar, anyway, and had already acquired enough reading, writing, and mathematical skills to get through life as a cattleman, so they let him go off with the adult workers full-time. After that we saw him only at mealtimes, but he did not sit at our table anymore, so we hardly saw him at all.

Then one cool bright morning in April of that year, Eldress Mary came to me at breakfast and said, "Don't go to the schoolroom today, Brother Harley. Or to the bee yard. I have a different task for you. I've already spoken to Sister Hazel and Brother Hiram, so you needn't worry."

I was not worried. Any break in my routine would have pleased me. But when she revealed the nature of the different task, I could barely conceal my pleasure. She wanted me to help her transport a trunk filled with newly woven, sewn, and hemmed cotton sheets and pillowcases to the Sunshine Home tuberculosis sanitarium in Narcoossee.

The trunk was very large and too heavy to lift or carry alone. Eldress Mary instructed me to bring around the two-wheeled cart with side rails that was kept in the main barn for moving stacks of hundred-pound bags of grain and corn. I asked Sister Rosalie to come over from the henhouse and help me load the trunk onto the cart, and I stepped between the drop heel shafts like a rickshaw driver. With Eldress Mary coming along behind me, I drew the cart down to the dock and hauled it aboard the *Coquina,* waiting to carry us to Narcoossee alongside a load of cypress boards harvested off Shaker lands and milled for Narcoossee and St. Cloud builders.

It was glorious out there on the deck of the slow-moving side-wheel barge as it crossed the first lake and then entered the narrow connecting canal between the next and on to the lake beyond, one after the other, like large stone beads on a slender string. Along the banks of the canals the palmettos and red mangroves grew so close to the gunwales of the passing barge that I could reach out and touch them, and did, even though it drew a scowl from Eldress Mary, not because it was dangerous, but because I was too clearly enjoying myself. She said nothing about it, though. Just turned her back to me as if offended and watched the opposite bank of the canal and the far shore of the glittering lake beyond.

Great clouds of birds, anhingas and egrets and herons, crossed overhead, darkening the morning sun for ten and fifteen minutes at a time, and when all the birds had passed beyond the barge and merged and rolled in a surging wave toward the tree-topped hammock in the distance, it was like a sudden second sunrise, a new break of day. Below, slumbering alligators lay on the muddy banks, half in and half out of the mangrove-darkened water, deadly eating machines, impassive, unsentimental links to the planet's primordial past, reminders of the cosmic wisdom of nature and the comically stupid nature of newly arrived mankind. When we are long gone, alligators will still be here, I mused.

I had not realized how eager I was to get away from New Bethany, even if only for a single day, or anticipated how happy it would make me. I was especially happy to be on my way to where Sadie Pratt resided, the sanitarium where, when she was not at New Bethany visiting her Shaker friends, she ate and slept and took her walks and read her books of poetry and accepted the medicines and exercises prescribed by the doctors and nurses working to cure her of her terrible illness. After today, at those times when I could not see her at New Bethany, I would be able to visualize her at Sunshine Home.

I intended to study and commit to memory as much as I could of the grounds and rooms and atmosphere of Sunshine Home, and if the opportunity presented itself, I planned to speak with Sadie. As we made our watery way to Narcoossee, I played in my mind both roles, hers and mine, in small colloquies between us, friendly two-party conversations by means of which I would gain Sadie's affection and respect, possibly even her admiration. I would make myself known to her, and in exchange she would make herself known to me. It would not matter that I was a thirteen-year-old boy and she a grown woman. In fact, it was our very age difference that made us accessible to one another. Or so I then believed. If Sadie Pratt had been a thirteen-year-old girl or I a grown man of nineteen or twenty, if we both had been the same age, we would not have been able to create the kind of friendship I was imagining for us that fine spring day on the *Coquina* to Narcoossee.

I spotted the pilot and captain who had brought us out to New Bethany the previous year, Salty Haversack and Captain Shea, and I climbed up the short ladder to the wheelhouse to say hello and to see the world from their elevated perspective. Even this early in the day, they smelled of whiskey and tobacco, as if it were in their clothing.

The pilot recognized me and said to Captain Shea, "Ain't this the boy we brung out with his family a while back?"

The captain looked me over. "You've done a good bit of growing in a single year," he said. "Shakers must be feeding you good out there."

The pilot said, "I heard they save the best crops for their own table and sell just the leavings. That true?" he asked me.

I peered out at the flat western horizon in the distance, where clouds were rising off the Gulf like a snow-covered mountain range. "Looks like it's fixing to rain," I said, ignoring his question.

The pilot said, "Them clouds'll empty out long before they get this far inland."

Captain Shea asked me what was I carrying in the trunk I'd brought aboard, and I said it was bed linens that the Shaker ladies had made for the patients at the Sunshine Home sanitarium outside Narcoossee.

"That's right nice of the ladies," the captain said.

"Bet they got a pretty penny for 'em, though," Haversack said. "The Shakers drive a hard bargain. They ain't much inclined to charity."

"From each according to his ability, to each according to his need," I said.

Then the pilot asked if the Shakers ever thought of using elephants out there at New Bethany to dredge and cut canals and haul lumber and so on.

I allowed as to how they may have considered it. "But they probably decided against using elephants because of the cost of feeding them," I said in a joking way.

He agreed, not hearing my tease. "Right. Elephants are big eaters," he said. He'd heard that they come from India and are happier than horses or oxen in hot weather and are intelligent and easy to tame for work. They can be dangerous, however. He'd recently read an article in the *St. Cloud Tribune* about a female elephant named Topsy that was owned by P. T. Barnum. She went mad and killed three people up in New Jersey and was convicted of murder by a jury and sentenced to death. "But they couldn't figure out how to properly execute old Topsy," he said. "Couldn't hang her, she was too big for that. So Thomas Edison, the famous inventor, he volunteered to execute her with electricity. He's got a winter place over in Fort Myers where he does a lot of his experiments, you know," the pilot said. "Thomas Edison was supposedly in the business of selling to the state prison systems up in New Jersey and New York these electrified chairs he'd invented for executions. He must've figured shocking Topsy to death would be good publicity for his electrified chairs."

I remember all this now because it was the first time since Father died at Waycross that I had heard anything like news from the World. Father, like all the Ruskinites, used to read newspapers whenever they were available and share them around the commune and discuss the issues and events of the day, talking and arguing political positions and candidates. It didn't matter that they were marooned in the south Georgia wilderness on the edges of the Okefenokee Swamp. But after Mother took us over to Rosewell Plantation we never saw a newspaper anymore or spoke with anyone who had recently read one. And the few workers who escaped the plantation did not return willingly or with news of the world beyond. They never got that far, and most of them couldn't read anyhow. At New Bethany, thanks to *The Established Principles and Regulations of the United Society of Believers*, it was hard to hear news of greater use or interest than clippings of Elder John's letters to the editor of the *St. Cloud Tribune,* which brought news about the Shakers, not the World. We had become conditioned to living as if everything that happened out there in the World had no value or relevance for us.

Now suddenly here I was, having a conversation that I could not have had at New Bethany, and it concerned the execution by means of Edison's electric current of an elephant convicted by a jury of murder, which I found to be of great interest. How strange and wonderful it was! It made my mind race. "So did Mr. Edison succeed in executing Topsy the elephant?" I asked. "Did his electrified-chair invention work?"

"Sure did. P. T. Barnum even sold tickets, and a huge crowd come out to see it."

I said to Haversack and Captain Shea, "If there was a fight between a big bull alligator and an elephant, who do you think would win?"

Haversack said, "Me, I'd put money on the gator."

The captain laughed and said, "Elephant's too smart to mess with a gator. You got to pick your battles, boy. I expect an elephant knows that."

"But if the elephant couldn't avoid a fight—like, say he and the gator got trapped in a gigantic sinkhole or something—couldn't the elephant stomp the gator to death?"

The captain said, "They might get along, though. Seeing as how they're both dealing with the same dire situation."

Haversack said he could visualize it happening. He'd seen sinkholes suddenly swallow a whole herd of grazing cows. "You let a five-ton elephant tramp around one of these sawgrass fields that're all cut up with springs and wet ditches, he might find himself suddenly trapped down in a hole with a fifteen-foot gator, and Mr. Gator, he wouldn't bother trying to get out. He'd just be eyeballing five tons of elephant meat."

The captain liked this turn. "That's too much meat even for a gator. Maybe Mr. Gator would say, 'Mr. Elephant, let's forget I'm a gator. You kneel down and let me climb up onto your back so I can get free of this here sinkhole, and I'll wrap my tail around a tree up there and pull you out by your trunk with my powerful mouth. I promise not to bite.'"

Haversack said a gator could do that. They can make their mouth gentle when they want to. He once watched a gator steal a half dozen duck eggs from a nest and not break a single egg and carry them off to his wallow hole one egg at a time to eat at his leisure.

The captain said, "When Mr. Gator gets free of the sinkhole, though, he turns around and grabs the elephant's trunk in his mouth like he's going to pull him out, and he chomps it off for lunch. He says to Mr. Elephant, 'Sorry, but us gators don't keep our promises. And up here I'm still a gator.'"

All three of us laughed. "That's a gator for you," the pilot said.

I caught sight then of Eldress Mary standing next to the cart on the deck below, signaling for me to come down from the wheelhouse. We were approaching the Narcoossee landing. I said goodbye to my friends in the wheelhouse and descended to the deck and waited for the barge to come up against the pier.

"What were you talking about with those fellows?" Eldress Mary asked me. "I saw you laughing together."

"They were just telling me a funny local story. It was about a gator and an elephant. Kind of a folk tale, I guess."

"Well, you'll have to tell me sometime," she said, as I rolled the cart off the *Coquina* on a pair of planks and onto the pier.

"Yes, I will," I said. But I never did tell her. I knew she didn't really want to hear it. In fact, until now I've never told it to anyone.

REEL #6

This is a new tape. The previous one ran out just as I was getting into the story about my first visit with Sadie at Sunshine Home. There's still plenty of daylight left, so I'll pick up where I stopped.

I remember that to get to the Sunshine Home sanitarium from Narcoossee we walked for about two hours along a raised crushed-shell lane across a marsh many miles wide, like an inland sea. The lane ran flat, passed an islet with a shack on it, then ran flat as a catwalk another mile or so and rose abruptly from the marsh to a high, unusually wide and long hammock that, as one approached it, resembled an island covered with ancient hardwood trees, some of them hundred-footers. Across the region, most of the tall live oak and gumbo-limbo and sweet gum trees on the hammocks had been cut and milled back in the 1890s to build housing in St. Cloud for the home-buying veterans, so it was rare to see old growth like that, even back then.

As we neared the island I could make out the tin roofs of a large white clapboard building and several smaller outbuildings among the trees and splashes here and there of bright-green lawn and multi-colored flower beds. The high, tree-topped hammock rising out of the low, pan-flat marsh was like an illustration of a tropical island seen from the sea out of a children's book, *Treasure Island* or *The Swiss Family Robinson*, and my heart began to race with excitement. The two of us—me in my woven-palm-frond hat and loose Shaker shirt and floppy trousers, pulling the two-wheeled cart with the trunk of gifts atop it, and coming along ahead of the cart, stout Eldress Mary with her embroidered Shaker-lady shawl and her tight white cap and walking stick—we must have looked to anyone watching from the island like a pair of old-time medieval pilgrims.

It was mighty hot out there on the treeless lane, and despite the quick climb that turned the cart heavy, it was a relief to enter the shade of the forested hammock. At the top the trees opened to a broad lawn surrounding a large, three-story main building with an open porch on the second floor that crossed the front. Several small cottages with verandas were nestled at the far edge of the lawn in among the trees and flower gardens, and I noticed nearby four or five white canvas tents, each the size of a single room. The end flaps were opened to the breeze, and I guessed the tents were for the use of patients who were well enough to take their cure outdoors. A half dozen people of various ages strolled the grounds alone or in pairs, mostly women dressed as if for afternoon tea.

The light, cooling breeze carried the burble of mourning doves toward us as we approached the main entrance. It was very peaceful and almost luxurious, a strangely placed estate, like a plantation house with no evidence of the plantation's source of wealth. If it had been by the sea, it would have made an excellent resort.

We were met at the door by Sadie herself, as if she were the lady of the house and not a patient. She and Eldress Mary embraced like cousins, and Sadie gestured for Eldress Mary to come in, which she did, and only then did Sadie notice me on the doorstep holding the shafts of my two-wheeled cart. She wore a long dark-blue skirt and a white blouse with the sleeves rolled up to her elbows. The top two buttons of her blouse were undone, exposing her slender neck and throat and collar bones. Her long hair was tied back behind her ears as if she had been doing some household chore. She was very beautiful.

"Brother Harley," she said, and smiled. "How lovely to see you here! Welcome to my Sunshine Home." Her tone was elusive, her meaning obscure to me. Was she merely being polite? Or was it indeed lovely to see me? Or just a surprise to see me? And was this really her home? Was she referring to it in an apologetic way, or was she being critical of it? Was she paying a compliment to the place or slyly criticizing it? I was bewildered. But with her elusiveness and obscurity and ambiguity, she had gained my complete attention.

She saw the trunk and said to Eldress Mary, "My goodness, what have you brought this time?" and smiled in a way that mixed curiosity with gratitude.

Eldress Mary explained that the trunk was filled with fresh new bed linens, a gift manufactured by the sisters at New Bethany. "It's quite heavy. Brother Harley will need someone to help him take it inside."

The two left me standing there and went in search of someone to help me unload and carry the trunk, and a moment later came a large, unsmiling, broad-shouldered White woman in a white-and-blue-striped nurse's uniform. She grabbed the front end of the trunk and I the other, and the two of us lugged it inside. She said not a word. I followed, she led, until we set the trunk down in a high-ceilinged, windowless room where linens and other household supplies were stored. She brusquely thanked me and commenced to unpack the linens and stack them on the shelves, leaving me standing by at the door, lost somewhere in the middle of the building. I had no idea where Eldress Mary and Sadie had gone. They must have assumed that I would return to my cart and wait outside for further instructions. I was not here as a guest, I was merely a laborer who had no meaningful business with Sunshine Home.

I carried the empty trunk back to the cart and stood beside it for a few moments, then wandered off and inspected the grounds. The trees had been cut and pruned and the lawns and plantings and crushed-limestone pathways were laid out in a way calculated to make the area seem larger than it actually was. The pale-gray paths looped in and out of the trees and alongside nicely tended azalea bushes, flowering dogwood, and sumac. Surrounded by neat plantings of petunias and asters and hyacinths and some flowers I did not recognize were three cabins, each as small as a child's playhouse. I paused before the first cabin but did not dare to approach it, and continued on my way. At the edge of the broad lawn were the open white tents I'd noticed on my arrival, and as I passed them I peered inside, hoping to see Sadie and Eldress Mary. In the first few I saw only empty cots and chests for clothing and other personal items. In each of the other tents a person lay in shadows on the cot, asleep or at deep rest.

Along the paths several of the patients nodded hello to me as I passed, and I nodded back and kept moving. The rest ignored me, as if I were a groundskeeper, so I ignored them, as if they were invisible. They were not, they were extremely visible, for these were Sadie's constant companions, except when she left Sunshine Home to visit New Bethany. She dined with them, and they conversed together in the evenings on the wide porch, and she walked these paths in their company. They were like well-dressed men and women in a painting, out for a leisurely noontime stroll in the park, and I imagined Sadie into that painting, wearing a long light-blue silk dress with matching gloves and a white lace shawl covering her shoulders and a fashionable wide-brimmed hat and small parasol to protect her fair skin from the sun. I remembered seeing rotogravure pictures of people like that, cosmopolitan Europeans, men and women of leisure.

Then suddenly, without forethought, I decided to return to the main building and find Sadie and Eldress Mary. It was Sadie I wanted to find, not Eldress Mary, but I expected them to be together. There was a back entrance, and I entered that way and found myself in a long, wide hall that bisected the building, with a stairway and landing at the far end leading to the floors above, where I assumed the more seriously ill, bedridden patients were housed. I doubted that Sadie had a room up there. She must stay in one of the little cottages set in among the trees, or in one of the empty tents.

As I passed along the wide first-floor hallway, I glanced into the adjacent rooms. First was a large kitchen, where a pair of Black women were hard at work, preparing the patients' midday meal, I supposed. Across from the kitchen was an empty dining room with six or eight square tables set with tablecloths and silver and glassware. Then a lounge or living room with chairs and sofas and reading tables and two very thin middle-aged White women, one with a heavy lap robe, the other wearing a wool sweater, as if even in this balmy climate they needed protection against the cold, and a gaunt, pale-skinned man who coughed constantly. The three were seated far from one another, each reading what looked like a very old periodical. And finally, a business office, where I saw Eldress Mary, pencil in hand, seated at a desk, bent over a ledger with her back to the open door. But no Sadie.

Eldress Mary spoke sharply to someone out of my line of sight. "I said to bring me the accounts for '02. The entire year. This just covers the most recent quarter of the current year." I knew she could not be speaking to Sadie that way.

I moved beyond the door of the office without Eldress Mary seeing me and approached the stairway. I heard a door close above and the click of footsteps as someone walked away. When I reached the top of the stairs I glimpsed Sadie's dark-blue skirt and white blouse as she entered a room at the far end of the long hallway. It was silent up there, except for the sounds of coughing and the struggle to clear throats and chests. There were doors on both sides of the hallway, most of them half-opened, and as I passed I saw in each room, lying in bed or slumped solemnly in a chair beside an open window, men and women of various ages, one sick person after another. These were the true consumptives, as we called them then, those who were wasting away and knew they would not recover.

I stood at the open door of the room that Sadie had entered seconds before. She sat in a straight-backed chair beside the narrow iron-railed bed, wiping the face of a woman near her own age with a small cloth. The young woman's body was covered loosely with a sheet. Except for her face and head, she was very small, the size of a ten-year-old girl, and thin, skeletal, emaciated-looking, and she appeared to have been weeping. Her straight blond hair was sparse, and the bones of her face pushed against her pale-blue skin. Sadie was tenderly wiping away the woman's tears and speaking softly to her, so softly that I could not make out her words, but I knew they were words of comfort.

I was silent and still for several minutes, struck by the sight, and I felt Sadie's compassion and sadness warm and fill my own heart, which until now had been cold and empty of feeling for these people. It was very strange, a direct transference of feeling from one person to another, something that I had never experienced before. What Sadie felt for that poor dying young woman in the bed, I felt, first for Sadie herself and then for the woman in her tender care. I was not shamed by her example or corrected or instructed by it; I was briefly transformed by it.

Until now the sick and dying residents of Sunshine Home had existed for me as little more than complements to Sadie's presence, her social context, so that I had perceived them only as enhancements of my perception of Sadie. That was their sole meaning and value for me. Now, standing silently at the door, I was beginning to see them the way she saw them, as suffering human beings, each a unique individual who was facing an imminent, painful death. Alone, all alone, but for Sadie's quiet, comforting witness to their dying.

I thought of my father's dying and how I had not truly imagined it, and I was ashamed. He had his family surrounding him his last day and night, but my brothers and I had not comforted him or felt compassion for his suffering and the terrible solitude of dying. We felt only our own loss. We were boys then, children. At this moment, watching Sadie and feeling myself fill with sympathy and sadness for her and for a dying stranger, though I was still a boy, perhaps I was emerging from my childhood, like a butterfly molting inside its chrysalis, preparing itself for flight.

Sadie must have sensed my presence at the door. She looked straight at me, and without smiling or frowning, she simply, slowly, shook her head no. I stepped away from the door and returned to the top of the stairs, where I waited. After a few moments she came out of the room and approached me. She made a slightly worried smile and said, "Harley, you probably shouldn't be up here."

This was the first time she had addressed me solely by my given name, and it felt both unfamiliar and strangely intimate. I had grown so used to being addressed as Brother Harley by everyone that I'd almost forgotten my former name. It was as if there were two of me, one named Harley, the other the Shaker novitiate named Brother Harley. Even my own mother and my real brothers called me Brother Harley now.

"I'm sorry. I got a little lost," I said. "I was looking for Eldress Mary and thought she might be up here."

"I'll take you to her. She'll be in the business office downstairs. You must have passed her without knowing."

"Tell me, Sadie," I said, trying out her given name for the first time. "The people in these rooms, the patients, are they under your care?"

"No, there's a doctor, Dr. Cardiff. He comes out from St. Cloud daily, or nearly every day. And two nurses who reside here full-time six days a week. But it's a small medical staff for this many residents, so I try to fill in when I can. Especially in looking after those who are . . . dire," she said. "They're so sad and frightened, Harley."

"That's very kind of you."

"No. You would do the same, I'm sure."

"Yes," I declared. "I would. Now that I've seen the ones who are, as you said, dire. I am sorry that I wandered up here," I said again. "But I'm also glad. It's given me an understanding that I needed and didn't have before."

"Good, then," she said and reached out and placed her hand on my shoulder. Then she removed her hand and descended the stairs and I followed, my shoulder burning where she had touched it.

When we entered the office, Eldress Mary was still at the desk with several open ledger books in front of her. She turned in her chair and saw me standing behind Sadie just inside the door. "Brother Harley, you should wait for me out front by the cart. I'll be along shortly."

I took my marching orders and went out of the office. As I left I heard her ask Sadie if I had been accompanying her on her rounds upstairs. I wanted to stop and listen for Sadie's response, but thought better of it and walked quickly back to my cart, where I resumed watching the residents stroll the grounds of Sunshine Home and pretended to myself that I was in Paris, France, waiting to meet Miss Sadie Pratt for our appointed afternoon walk in the park. The infusion of compassion for the patients that I had received from Sadie earlier had now dissipated, and I was a child again, a callow youth inside a chrysalis of self-interest.

It was not long before Sadie and Eldress Mary came out of the main building and joined me at the cart. Eldress Mary was in the midst of speaking to Sadie with some seriousness. I quickly surmised that the subject was the finances of Sunshine Home. Sadie looked worried by her words, but I could not quite catch their meaning. Eldress Mary said, "It's a very simple but painful reality. No institution without an endowment or a wealthy benefactor or state support can survive an imbalance like this for long. Briefly, yes, maybe a month or two. But then one has to borrow in order to bridge the gap. Which adds to overhead. And one can't keep cutting costs, or one will no longer be doing the very work the institution was created for."

Sadie said, "I'm sure you'll find a way, Eldress. Dr. Cardiff will find a way. The board will come up with a solution."

"You're sweetly optimistic, my dear. But without a product to sell and a market to buy, no public institution can long survive. Not even us Shakers," she said, and laughed. "Where would New Bethany be if there were no market here and up north and in Cuba for our crops and citrus and our beef cattle and even our little seed packets?" She glanced over at me and added, "And Brother Harley's wonderful honey and beeswax."

"Yes, we must be grateful for Brother Harley's wonderful honey and beeswax," Sadie said.

Eldress Mary promised to bring a large supply of honey when she next came to Sunshine Home, and the two women embraced and said goodbye. Sadie and I exchanged a little private parting wave, and she went inside.

Eldress Mary and I made our way down from the hammock and back across the wide, oceanic marsh on the straight, sun-baked lane to Narcoossee. She walked ahead, as before, and I followed along with my cart and its much lightened load—pilgrims returning from the shrine.

At one point I stopped and looked back at the distant, tree-covered hammock, which I now viewed as the magical island of Sunshine Home, the place where Sadie Pratt was tending to the sick and dying patients. It was the island where she was a patient herself, though the development of the illness in her case had been mysteriously halted. But perhaps it was not so mysterious. Maybe, when she arrived from Rhode Island, her illness was still in its early stages, and the warmth of the south Florida climate and the fresh breezes off the Gulf that blew onto her inland island and the ministrations of the medical staff at Sunshine Home were enough to slow and even stop its fatal progression. It's also true that the Shakers regularly prayed for her recovery, and I could not say that did not help.

Though it's one of the human species' most ancient diseases, there was not much known about tuberculosis in the early 1900s, and no vaccines or antibiotics. Physicians grouped many different respiratory illnesses together under the name of consumption and treated them all as if they were indeed the dreaded, almost always fatal tuberculosis. But perhaps the illness that had brought Sadie to Sunshine Home for a cure was not tuberculosis, but was instead one of the pulmonary diseases that could be cured, and eventually she would recover her health completely, and she would be well enough to leave this semitropical island home and return to her old life in the cold, damp climate of Rhode Island. I did not want that to happen, however. I did not want her to leave Sunshine Home. It meant that I would never be able to see her again. Which meant that I did not want Sadie to be cured of her illness.

And yet I surely did not want her to sicken and die. I stood there on the lane looking back toward Sunshine Home and shuddered at the thought of Sadie suffering and wasting away in one of those upstairs rooms like the bedridden woman she had comforted earlier.

Eldress Mary had stopped and was watching me. As if she could read my conflicted thoughts, she said, "I think, Brother Harley, that you have been paying undue attention to Sister Sadie Pratt. She is very kind and sympathetic, but you must not take advantage of that."

"It's just that I like her very much. And she is very intelligent and well educated," I added, as if that justified my "undue attention."

"You might consider making your confession to Elder John," she said. "Even though you are not old enough to become a Shaker, you're not as young as your years, I'm afraid."

I nodded in apparent agreement, but I had no intention of confessing to Elder John what I had not yet confessed to myself. Eldress Mary said that we should hurry along if we were to meet the afternoon barge at Narcoossee in time to be back at New Bethany for the evening prayers and meal. Also, a special service was planned for tonight, she said, and we would not want to miss it. An important visitor was to speak to us.

She resumed walking, and I followed, and after a few moments I asked her who was the important visitor.

"A delegation come down from the Mount Lebanon family," she said. "They're expected to arrive today. We may meet them on the afternoon barge from St. Cloud when we reach Narcoossee." She said no more about them, and I didn't ask further. I assumed it was an inspection tour from Shaker headquarters and could tell from her clipped words and tone that Eldress Mary was anxious about their visit.

An hour after we reached Narcoossee, the side-wheeler *Coquina* steamed in from St. Cloud, and there on the foredeck stood four elderly strangers, the Shaker delegation from Mount Lebanon, two women and two men, dressed as if for a formal portrait. Piled at their feet was their luggage, four large satchels and several smaller cloth bags. The women wore long black dresses, embroidered shawls, and white Shaker-lady caps. The two men, both with long white patriarchal beards, had on black suits and dark-brown, wide-brimmed felt hats. The taller of the two leaned on a cane. All four were pale-skinned travelers from the sun-deprived North, and they looked uncomfortably warm in their heavy clothing.

The crew tied the *Coquina* to the bollards, and Eldress Mary stepped aboard and greeted the women warmly with embraces, like old friends. To the men she offered a detectable curtsy. I came along behind with my cart, and she introduced me as Brother Harley, and said the full names of the others. They were Eldresses Elizabeth Sears and Annie Mason, and Elders Thomas Halsey and Morris

Hicks. I guessed all four to be in their mid-seventies or maybe even older, but due to my youth, I wasn't very good at guessing the age of anyone over fifty. To me, everyone over fifty looked to be in their mid-seventies.

They acknowledged my presence with polite smiles, but did not offer their hands. Eldress Elizabeth was very small, shorter and slighter than our Eldress Mary, with a tightly closed, gray face, even when smiling. The other woman, Eldress Annie, was stout and with her twinkling eyes had more light in her face than Eldress Elizabeth. Elder Thomas, the one with the cane, was tall and lean and angular. Elder Morris had the squinty look of a lifelong bookkeeper. The two men showed little interest in me, or for that matter in Eldress Mary, either.

As if puzzled as to where they had landed, the delegation kept looking around at the ramshackle storage buildings and shops and houses of Narcoossee and the half dozen local small farmers and shopkeepers who had emerged from the buildings and were coming down to the pier to retrieve the boxes and barrels of manufactured and canned goods they'd ordered from St. Cloud. The Shaker delegation seemed particularly interested in the four men, two White and two Black, shirtless and sweating, who were lugging bound stacks of fresh-cut sugar cane and burlap bags of corn from a dockside tin-roofed warehouse onto the barge.

Eldress Mary noticed the visitors' interest and explained that the cane and corn were being shipped to New Bethany to be pressed into sugar syrup and ground into grain there. She took the occasion to boast a bit and added that New Bethany owned and operated the only steam-powered sugar mill and gristmill in the region. "The mills were designed by Elder John Bennett," she said. "And their construction was overseen by him personally. The steam is made by burning the crushed sugar-cane stalks after they dry."

Elder Morris said he assumed there was a charge for this service, and Eldress Mary hemmed and hawed a few seconds before admitting that, yes, a modest fee was attached. "But it costs the growers far less to have their milling done at New Bethany," she added. "They won't have to ship their cane and corn through middlemen in

St. Cloud all the way to Tampa or Fort Myers for milling, where they would be charged a second time."

"So you are undercutting the millers in the World," Elder Morris stated.

"Yes," Eldress Mary said.

On our upriver trip to New Bethany, I took shelter in the wheelhouse again with my friends, as I now thought of them, the captain, Bernard Shea, and the pilot, Salty Haversack. I didn't ask him why he was called Salty. I sensed that beneath his crusty overconfidence he was shy and insecure, and I didn't want to pry into his personal life. Years later, after he was killed in the boiler explosion of an excursion boat that he was piloting on Lake Okeechobee, I learned from his obituary that his real name was Haversack Dunchanchellin, and when he was a boy, he and his father, who was a full-blooded Seminole Indian, had worked for the Confederate Army in the salt distilleries on St. Johns Bay. His name must have come from that. I regret my reticence. I would have liked to ask him about the Confederates he worked for and many other things that he'd experienced back when he was piloting on the lakes and canals that meandered between St. Cloud and New Bethany.

Later that evening at New Bethany, after our communal meal was finished, we were dismissed from the dining hall and told to reconvene in the meetinghouse, where the Society's prayer services and general meetings were normally held. We were not a large group that evening, as it was not the Sabbath and there were none of the frequent weekend visitors from Narcoossee, Kissimmee or St. Cloud—only the fifteen resident Shakers and Mother's five children, plus the newly arrived delegation. We lined up as usual, men and boys on one side, women on the other, and walked—at the natural, nonmilitaristic pace we had been taught—from the dining room out the paired doorways to the wide porch and across the lane to the meetinghouse.

It was not yet dark, but someone had already lit the candles in the tin sconces. The light from the fluttering yellow flames softened the whitewashed walls, and the smell of the palm-oiled pine-board floor sweetened the air. The women, including Mother and little Rachel, held by the hand, tottering at Mother's side, entered their door and took their chairs down from the pegs along the right-hand wall and set them in a line on that side of the large room, while we males entered our door and took our chairs down and placed them on the opposite side. The meetinghouse was my favorite New Bethany building, not because of what took place there, but because of the way its interior struck the eye. I loved the way the room came to life when lit, whether by candlelight at night or the sun by day. I loved its perfectly squared symmetry and open, unhindered space and the warm relations between its length, width, and height, and the small things about it that pleased me, like the way the twin doors at the front mirrored the pair of high windows at the rear.

When all were seated, Elder John walked to the speaker's space in the middle of the room, and Eldress Mary followed and stood next to him. The four emissaries from Mount Lebanon had posted themselves like sentries just inside the two entrances to the room. Elder John introduced each of them by name and said that they wished to speak to the entire New Bethany family directly. As a family, he said, not individually. He told us they were trustees from the North Lebanon family, which, from our classroom lessons, we knew placed them at a rank higher in the Shaker hierarchy than Elder John's and Eldress Mary's. A trustee to an elder was like a cardinal to a bishop, Sister Hazel had once explained.

The four visitors came forward now, and Elder John sat down between me and Brother Hiram. Pence was sitting restlessly on my other side. Elder John, who was looking a little uncharacteristically downcast, gave him a hard look, and Pence stopped fidgeting and sat up straight, but I knew he was only pretending to pay strict attention to the visitors. Pence was better at that than I. Pretending good behavior came hard to me.

Eldress Mary sat across the room from me, and I noticed that she kept her head low and looked steadily at her ample lap, as if embarrassed or ashamed. All afternoon, since their arrival from Narcoossee, the visiting trustees had been huddled with our two leaders in the business office in the main house. I had expected the visitors to be taken on a tour of New Bethany's clean and orderly outbuildings and barns and shops and the mills and the many kinds of flourishing gardens and orchards that surrounded the place, but that had not happened. While I was finishing out my long day trip to Sunshine Home by working with Brother Hiram at the bee yard, I looked up every now and then at the house, hoping to catch a glimpse of them, but they never appeared. I wanted them to come down and be impressed by our apiary. They had a formidable presence that made one want to please them, even when they were silent and otherwise occupied.

It was Elder Thomas, the tall one with the cane, who took the floor first to speak for the trustees. He had a low, authoritative voice and spoke slowly and distinctly, as if he was used to sermonizing. He had a pleasingly flattened New England accent. I like the way New England women speak, but don't normally care for the men's version, too nasal and tinny. Elder Thomas's voice, though, was deep and came from his chest, not his face.

He thanked the elder and eldress and the brothers and sisters of New Bethany for welcoming him and the other trustees, and he apologized for not having come down to visit us in recent years to see in person the wonderful work we were doing here for the United Society of Believers. It was a great distance and an arduous journey, and he and the other trustees at Mount Lebanon were no longer young. He said that, personally and on behalf of the entire community of Shakers, he wished also to thank us for the many boxes of oranges and other excellent fruits and strawberries that we regularly shipped to Mount Lebanon. They were much appreciated by all the brothers and sisters, he said, especially during the winter months, when fresh fruit was not available to them. Everything done here at New Bethany, he reminded us, was done for the entire community of Shakers, for all the families of Believers, from Ohio and Kentucky to New Hampshire and Maine. As we at New Bethany prospered and grew, so did every other family prosper and grow. We were indeed a single branch of a great and bountifully blessed tree, the tree of faith.

From here he began speaking with metaphors and symbols that gradually revealed an underlying dissatisfaction with the very work he had just characterized as wonderful. He told us that the produce from our citrus orchards and banana groves and expansive gardens, our livestock and poultry and sheep and swine, even the honey given up to us by the praiseworthy industry of our bees, these were the seeds and acorns that drop from the tree of faith in autumn so that, with the coming of the spring rains, new saplings will emerge from the ground. The remuneration we received in exchange for the pine-apples and beef cattle in Cuba and for the citrus and other crops that we carried to the wholesalers in St. Cloud, Fort Myers, Tampa, and elsewhere and as payment for the valuable services that we pro-vided to our neighbors in the World, this was the life-giving sap that flowed upward from the trunk of the tree of faith, reaching all the branches, even to the tiniest and frailest twig.

He said there were four winds that from time to time blew through the branches of the tree and threatened to break them off and pos-sibly topple the tree. They were the winds of disputation, deception, dissension, and disunity, he told us. The first wind, disputation, is a common errant breeze that blows through the community almost daily, and it refreshes and cools us. But if disputation among fam-ily members is not ameliorated by palliation and compromise, it can lead to deception, which is a much more destructive force and signals the presence of a gathering storm, which if it comes our way becomes the storm of dissension. Dissension breaks the smaller limbs and cracks and weakens the greater branches of the tree. It often evolves into a hurricane, as those who live in this part of the world know all too well from experience. The hurricane is disunity. To save the very tree itself from its fury, the branches that have been cracked and weakened by dissension must sometimes need to be cut off from the trunk altogether.

Elder Thomas continued for some time in this manner, often quot-ing from the Bible and lapsing into the old-fashioned mannerisms affected occasionally by Elder John. I don't recall the exact verses cited, but the emphasis on common ownership of property and self-denial was evident. Speaking of the need to model ourselves on what he called "the primitive church," he said: "The multitude of them that believe who were of one heart and one soul, neither said any of them that any of the things which he possessed was his own, for they had all things in common. Neither was there any among them that lacked, for as many of them as were possessors of lands or houses sold them and brought the prices of the things that were sold."[*] Another verse he repeated several times was: "Whosoever he be of you that forsaketh not all that he hath, he cannot be my disciple."[†] And in order to clarify further, although clarification did not really seem his intent, he said, "He that loveth father or mother more than me is not worthy of me, and he that loveth son or daughter more than me is not worthy of me."[‡]

This led up to a closing peroration in which he enumerated the seven guiding principles of the United Society of Believers, starting with the need to live a life of abstinence from all sensual and carnal gratifications and ending with the principle of truth, which he said was opposed to falsehood, lying, deceit, and hypocrisy. These seven principles—abstinence; love of one another; pacifism; justice and honesty in all our dealings with mankind; dedication of our persons, service, and property to social and sacred uses; doing good to all mankind; and dedication to the truth—these seven principles, he told us, are the roots of our institution, planted by its founders, exhibited in all our public writings, justified by scripture and fair reason, and practically commended to the world as a system of morality and religion, adapted to the best interest and happiness of mankind, both here and hereafter, Amen.

At that, Elder Thomas limped to the wall and took down a chair and set it at the end of the line of men and my brothers and me and sat down with what appeared to be relief to be off his feet and silent again. He folded his large, arthritic hands over the top of his cane. I assumed the meeting was now over.

But Elder Thomas had been immediately replaced at the center of the room by the diminutive and dour Eldress Elizabeth. Almost before he was seated, she was talking. She spoke without emotion, like a typewriter, all her words uttered rapid-fire at the same impersonal, midscale pitch. She said that she and the other trustees had

[*] Acts 4:32, 34

[†] Luke 14:33

[‡] Matthew 10:37

spent the afternoon hours in conference with Elder John and Eldress Mary, examining the ledgers and financial statements that were kept at New Bethany, along with certain legal documents, such as the deeds to four five-acre tracts of land in St. Cloud purchased for three hundred dollars each from the Seminole Land & Investment Company and usurious liens against those tracts held by the same company, in the possession and name of Elder John Bennett. They have compared said account books and contracts and deeds to the quarterly financial reports made by Elder John and Eldress Mary to the Mount Lebanon trustees, she said, and they have discovered numerous troubling discrepancies between them.

She paused for breath, then continued in the same way, as if reading from a legal document. She said that to his credit Elder John, without being prompted, voluntarily provided the deeds and liens in question, suggesting that he was unaware of the forbidden nature of his speculative investments and the prohibition against the practice of usury, and that, in using funds taken from the remunerative income of New Bethany as down payment for the loans in order to purchase those five-acre tracts, he was more naive than deceitful. The trustees believed that he was not trying to benefit himself monetarily, but that he was, as he claimed, trying to increase the value of New Bethany's equity in landholdings.

She said that this does not mean that Elder John, in concert with Eldress Mary, having withheld the fact of these transactions from the quarterly financial reports made to the trustees of Mount Lebanon, did not violate the trust placed in him by the United Society of Believers and the trustees of Mount Lebanon, who have acted since its founding twelve years ago as guarantors of the New Bethany settlement. Nor does it mean that he did not violate the Believers' firm injunction, in imitation of the primitive church and in obedience to the Word of God, against participating in the practice of usury, whether as a lender or a borrower. As stated in the Book of Deuteronomy, chapter 23, verse 19: "Thou shalt not lend upon usury to thy brother; usury of money, usury of victuals, usury of any thing that is lent upon usury." And just as it is forbidden to lend upon usury, so it is forbidden to borrow, the reason given clearly in Proverbs, chapter 22, verse 7: "The rich ruleth over the poor, and the borrower is servant to the lender."

Except for the dual prohibition against lending and borrowing at interest, much of what she said went over my head. Given how rapidly and legalistically Eldress Elizabeth had spoken, most of it, if not all, was probably lost on the rest of our community as well, including Mother. None of our people, except for Elder John and Eldress Mary, had experience with business matters.

Though their honesty was not questioned, it sounded like Elder John and Eldress Mary had neglected to include all of their financial transactions on behalf of New Bethany in their regular reports to the Mount Lebanon leadership. Which was understandable, given the great distance between south Florida and upstate New York and the complexity of New Bethany's accounting methods and the vagueness and variety of autonomy given to the many branches of Elder Thomas's tree of faith. Though Elder John had apparently confessed to speculating in real estate in St. Cloud, it was not for personal gain, which at the time I believed, and so apparently did the trustees. But neither he nor Eldress Mary had reported that particular use of a small portion of New Bethany's income from the sale of its cattle and pineapples and other produce. And there was the religious issue of his having engaged in a usurious relationship with the Seminole Land & Investment Company.

Eldress Elizabeth continued: "Therefore, we the trustees of the Mount Lebanon community have asked Elder John to step down temporarily from his leadership of New Bethany for an extended period of self-reflection. We recognize his much-needed abilities as an engineer and architect and his management skills in supervising the complex operations of a farm this size with its many workers and variety of crops. Also, as a native of Kentucky and his now twelve years' residence in Florida, his experience and knowledge of this particular environment is irreplaceable. He will continue, therefore, in his role as a practical day-to-day manager of the New Bethany property, in collegial consultation with his brothers and sisters. His role as elder, however, will be taken up by Elder Thomas Halsey, who has agreed to resign his trusteeship at Mount Lebanon. When we depart for home, he will remain here with you as your elder."

Then she turned to the sentencing of Eldress Mary. It was to be a suspended sentence, as it were. In not reporting to Mount Lebanon the relatively small amount of one hundred twenty dollars taken from the New Bethany account and paid to the Seminole Land & Investment Company as a down payment for the four five-acre tracts, the eldress had simply made a bookkeeping error. She had explained to the trustees that she had not counted that money as an expense per se, since the grace period for full payment of the remaining one thousand eighty dollars, plus 10 percent compounded annual interest, was five years from the date of the sales contract made in the name of Elder John Bennett. At that time, five years hence, the tracts could be sold by him, presumably at a profit, with the money deposited to the credit of New Bethany, or the tracts could simply be added to the seven thousand acres of land already owned by New Bethany. This explanation was acceptable to the trustees, she said. Eldress Mary's oversight would be corrected with the next quarterly report.

It was necessary, however, for the trustees to issue a warning to her, and to the community at large, that the Society of Believers is not a competitive, profit-making business, and thus they do not seek to undercut the costs of those who live in the World merely in order to save them the costs of doing business with the World. It is fine if the products of our labor, if offered for sale at the same price as our neighbors' products, exceed in quality those products. If they prove to be more desirable for purchase in the open marketplace, it only confirms the value of our having dedicated our hearts to God and our hands to work. By and large, New Bethany has observed this obligation, Eldress Elizabeth said.

However, by the same token and for the same reason, the New Bethany community of Shakers must not provide services at a cut rate to their neighbors, like grinding their corn and milling their sugar cane. That makes New Bethany a profit-making enterprise competitive with the businesses of the World. Their business is not our business, she said. Our business is with the Lord. The trustees believe that Eldress Mary now fully understands these mild prohibitions, and they are confident that, in concert with Elder Thomas and with the continuation of farm management under Brother John, New Bethany will thrive in this climate and will begin soon to attract many new members from the North who wish to live in Shaker communion on lands with abundant sunshine and water and fertile, rock-free soil and frost-free winters.

For the first time since I saw her in Narcoossee on the foredeck of the *Coquina*, Eldress Elizabeth smiled. But it was a thin, forced smile, almost a grimace, and I wondered if she might envy old Elder Thomas a little for his newly acquired semiretirement in Florida and was already planning a return trip, ostensibly in order to extend her investigation, but in reality to spend as much of her winters as possible in a climate that was kind to elderly, arthritic Shakers.

REEL #7

Well, that did not happen. Eldress Elizabeth succumbed to pneumonia the following autumn at Mount Lebanon without having returned to New Bethany and lies buried up there in that cold, stony ground. I don't know the fates of the other trustees, Elder Morris Hicks and Eldress Annie Mason, but they, too, never came back to New Bethany. Evidently, the delegation's report to the leaders of the Society in upstate New York and elsewhere was sufficient not to warrant any further onsite investigation. Or perhaps, despite the attraction of wintertime warmth and sunshine, without the excuse of needing to inspect the ledgers, the journey was too arduous for the elderly Shakers.

Elder Thomas Halsey lived on with us for another two years, until March 1905, when he died one night in his sleep and went peacefully to Heaven, where I assume he still resides alongside Jesus and Mother Ann Lee. His earthly body was shipped back to Mount Lebanon, however. Among us, in his last years, he enjoyed spending his days in a straight-backed rocking chair on the front porch of the main house. He was a benign and usefully ineffectual coleader of our community. Usefully ineffectual, because he allowed our true leaders to do their work without interference. He was like an old retired monk living on at the monastery he had once led. We, his brother and sister residents of the monastery, honored and deferred to him, but because his opinions were mostly abstract and general, we ignored him. He preferred the company of little Rachel and my younger brothers, Raymond and Royal, and the new children as they arrived, to that of the adults and me and Pence. He enjoyed inculcating the younger children with Shaker beliefs and principles and enumerating the many Shaker restrictions on their behavior, which they listened to and obeyed as if they were receiving the wisdom of a sage. His manner was kindly and simple and scaled to each child's level of understanding, even Rachel's, who, as a three-year-old, was proving to be a preternaturally intelligent and verbal child. She had been taken from Mother's care when she turned two and placed in the hands of the other women in the community, who were raising her jointly with such true loving-kindness that she did not seem to miss Mother's maternal love. Nor did Mother, after raising four sons for so many years, seem to miss dispensing it. Raymond and Royal were becoming teenagers by then, but they were not as quick, restless, and skeptical as Pence and I, so they fell easily under the old man's gentle spell.

For the most part, Eldress Mary and Brother John, as he was now known, continued to run New Bethany much as they had before. I don't think either of them consulted much with Elder Thomas. Eldress Mary continued to run domestic operations and oversee the community's finances. Brother John still laid out each day's work and organized the crews and designed the various new structures and pens that had to be built to accommodate our growing herds and flocks, for he was still as much chief engineer and architect and general superintendent as he had been in the past. If he bore any resentment for having been demoted or felt any humiliation by it, he never revealed either. He seemed to view it as temporary and necessary, as if accepting it were merely part of his job as our leader.

In those years, as Eldress Elizabeth had foreseen, our reputation for efficiency and productivity and the fruitful nature of our land and the pleasures and healthfulness of our climate spread among the Shakers and the World, and we began to receive new members migrating down from the North, some of them lifelong aging Shakers needing to warm their cold bones, in addition to dropouts from the several other communitarian and utopian societies that had settled in Florida and Georgia and had proven unable to thrive economically or ideologically, like the spiritualist colony of Cassadaga over in Volusia County and Cyrus Teed's Koreshans down in Fort Myers, who believed that the Earth was hollow and we lived inside the globe and not on its surface. Even two Ruskinite families from our old home, Waycross, came down to join us and apply for membership in the Society of Believers, thanks to letters from Mother extolling the virtues and overall good health of our life here. The shift from a failed, secular, communistic society to a thriving, religious one did not seem to bother them any more than it had bothered Mother, who by that time had become round and soft and content with her life. In some ways, she had become a stranger to me, which is probably typical for a boy of fifteen and his mother anyhow, but I was glad that she was happy.

There were now seven other children of various ages in Sister Hazel's schoolroom, making me, the eldest of the students, an assistant teacher, specializing in mathematics, although I continued my afternoon work in the bee yard with Brother Hiram. On a given day in those years, there were as many as fifteen new adult residents at New Bethany who were seeking membership in the Society of Believers. But if truth be told, the majority of these supplicants were seeking reliable shelter and regular meals rather than everlasting life. If the price was abstinence from sex and all other stimulants, communal living and participation in Shaker rituals and customs, along with hard manual labor in the fields and with the livestock and in our various shops and manufactories, they were willing to pay it.

But it made Brother John's managerial skills all the more crucial to the smooth running of the operation. He now had enough workers to begin growing bananas in quantity and to expand production of pineapples for export, especially as the Cuban market opened up, which meant that more acreage had to be drained and converted from marshland to dry, arable farmland. Brother John had redesigned the ox-drawn Fresno canal digger and reduced its size and weight to make it an effective digger of drainage ditches manned by one worker and drawn by a single horse, greatly reducing the old labor-intensive pick-and-shovel method of making farmland out of swamp. Beyond this and superintending each day's work in the existing fields and gardens, barns and shops, to accommodate our growing population, he had to design and oversee the construction of two new dwellings and expand the dining and food-preparation areas and the laundry and bathing and toilet facilities.

With the death of Elder Thomas Halsey, Brother John's status as elder, by order of the trustees in Mount Lebanon, was restored to him. Other than his name, however, nothing much changed, except that he could now consult with Eldress Mary as an equal and coleader and was again allowed to hear the confession of sins by those male residents who were applying for membership in the Society of Believers and to offer religious counsel to the resident brothers and sisters.

It was overall a prosperous time for New Bethany. Eldress Mary, in compliance with the wishes of the trustees, had made her financial reports more thorough and detailed. She had discontinued undercutting the prices charged by the mills in St. Cloud and Tampa and was now offering the service of our mills to grind the Narcoossee farmers' cane and grain at the going rate and making the mills available only when they were not needed to grind our own cane and grain. It added little to the Society's income, but was seen as a virtuous solution to a complex theological problem, and for the Shakers, despite their reputation for frugality and hard bargaining, virtue was its own reward.

Over at the Sunshine Home sanitarium, however, things were not going so smoothly. I was no longer invited to accompany Eldress Mary on her regular visits there, which saddened but did not surprise me. My interest in Sadie Pratt had been obvious, and though I myself saw nothing wrong or unnatural in it, I knew that in Eldress Mary's eyes it was inappropriate. She never said anything about it to me directly. Simply, when she needed help carrying gifts from New Bethany to Sunshine Home, which more and more often were of basic food supplies and flour and butter and vegetables, she asked one of my younger brothers, Raymond or Royal, to pull the cart.

Sadie continued to visit New Bethany every few weeks for two or three days at a time and as before stayed in a room set aside for guests up at the main house. Our relations were friendly and warm and courteous, and she often came down of her own volition in late afternoons to visit the bee yard and chat with me about the bees, but also about other things that were of more interest to me, and I think were of more interest to her as well. Talking about the bees and bee culture was mainly a way for the two of us to introduce a different kind of talk about things like the Shaker songs, which she greatly admired and enjoyed singing herself, for she had a lovely soprano voice and had perfect pitch, and the dances, which she also admired, but did not participate in, due to her health. I, too, liked the songs and dances and had committed many of both to memory and sang and danced and marched enthusiastically along with the more devout brothers and sisters, for whom the singing and dancing and marching was a unifying, religious experience. But for me and Sadie, I think it was more of a purely musical experience.

It was Royal who let me know how bad things were over at Sunshine Home. He was then thirteen, almost fourteen. One summer evening after he had been on a morning visit to the sanitarium with Eldress Mary, we were walking from the meetinghouse to our respective rooms in the men's dormitory. The sun had not quite set over the fields in the west, and the buildings cast long shadows over us as we walked side by side. Bats darted close overhead in erratic loops and swallowed up the swarms of mosquitoes.

I asked him if all was well at Sunshine Home.

He said, "Why do you ask?"

I said, "I noticed your cart has lately been loaded with basic food-stuff, instead of the crafted items that Eldress Mary used to carry over there."

He was silent for a moment, then said, "I'm not supposed to say anything. Eldress Mary told me not to gossip about Sunshine Home or anything else. She dislikes gossip of any kind, you know."

I explained that I wasn't asking for gossip or rumor or hearsay. I only wondered if there was a shortage of food over there, and if so, then perhaps we at New Bethany should be addressing their needs more generously than we have been.

"Oh, yes, Harley, you're right to think of that. You should maybe bring it up with Elder John and Eldress Mary," he said. Though I was only two years their elder, Royal and Raymond and sometimes even Pence tended to treat me as an adult, probably as a result of Father's having tried on his deathbed to make me the man of the family. That charge had permanently changed both my behavior toward my brothers and theirs toward me.

"Lately many of the patients have departed or died," Royal continued. "And there are fewer patients to care for. So the doctor doesn't come out from St. Cloud as much nowadays. And those few who are left are either getting worse and dying or going elsewhere for help. And today I heard Eldress Mary and the one remaining nurse complain that the state had cut off its support. The nurse said they might have to shut down Sunshine Home altogether. Wouldn't that be sad, Harley?"

"What about Sadie Pratt? What will she do if they close the sanitarium? Where will she go?"

"Sister Sadie? I don't know. It's not really my business. But you should ask her when she comes over here next time. Or ask Eldress Mary. They talk together a lot, you know."

I said I would do that, and we walked on in silence, though the voice in my head, my own voice, was calling out in alarm to Sadie, imploring her not to leave Sunshine Home. Please, Sadie, don't go off to some distant sanitarium or return to your home in Providence, Rhode Island. Don't make it so that I cannot see you again!

The following Saturday morning she came over from Narcoossee aboard the *Coquina*, and that afternoon she walked from the main house down to the bee yard. She greeted me with her usual warm smile and extended her hand for me to hold in Shaker fellowship. I pulled off my netted hood and gloves and for few seconds held her hand in mine. It was long and thin and cool to the touch, her skin smooth as glass. As if rescuing a captured bird, she gently removed her hand from my much larger, work-roughened paw and settled herself on the grassy slope a short ways off from the hives, and I came and sat next to her.

Brother Hiram called over, "Hello, Sister Sadie. Ain't this a lovely day?"

She agreed, it was, and asked him to explain what he and Brother Harley were up to. "It looks complicated," she said. "As if you're destroying the hives."

We were rotating the combs that day and preparing to move a quarter of the queens to new settlements. "Destroying their settlements in order to save them," I said. "It's called splitting the colony. You take out some of the brood combs, which are full of eggs covered and nurtured by the nurse bees, and you move them to a new hive where there's plenty of honey and pollen but no queen bee, leaving the old queen and the rest of the combs behind. The nurse bees then use the eggs to build new queen cells, and soon there'll be a whole new colony with its queen and workers for gathering pollen and making honey and drones for breeding with the queen and making more bees."

Brother Hiram said, "There's lots more to it, though. Bees are complicated. And no two are alike, even in a hive with thousands and thousands of bees. Ain't that true, Brother Harley?"

"I'll be right with you in a few moments, Brother Hiram," I said. "I just want to ask Sister Sadie something."

"Take your time, brother. The good Lord willing, we got time. Oh, yes, we got time to spare," he said, and gave one of his short, nervous, snortlike laughs.

"What do you want to ask me, Harley?" she said. "You look unhappy. Are you unhappy? I hope not."

"No, no, not at all. Just . . . I'm just worried."

"About?" She gave a light, almost mocking laugh, as if I had nothing to worry about, which, compared to her, I suppose I didn't.

"About Sunshine Home," I said. "I understand that it may have to close. Is that true?"

"Yes, I'm afraid so."

"What will you do, if Sunshine Home shuts its doors?" I tried to sound merely curious, not plaintive.

"I'm not sure, Harley. I'm not well enough to return home. In fact, in the last few months I've felt a weakening in my lungs. If I may be frank with you."

"Oh, yes, please, be frank with me," I said and looked at her more closely. Her usually lustrous, near-black eyes had darkened and dimmed since the last time I saw her. Her skin was paler than usual.

"This climate overall has been kind to me, and the care I've received at Sunshine Home has been a great help. And of course the comfort and prayers I've been given here at New Bethany have contributed to my rising health. Though I'm nowhere near cured, Harley, I'm much improved over how I was when I first arrived. It's just that lately I've gone through a slight decline. No doubt due to the stress of my . . . my situation. Well, you don't want to hear all that," she said.

"Of course I do. Please, tell me. I want to hear everything, Sadie."

She sighed and looked away, as if to hide tears from me. "I don't know what I should do, Harley. I can't stay on at Sunshine Home. In a few weeks it will be closed. I'm not well enough to go back to Rhode Island, and I don't know of any other sanitarium nearby. Sunshine Home has been where I have slept most nights and taken my meals. It's where I've received medical care and where I have cared for others. But in an odd way, in the three years that I've been here in Florida, it's New Bethany that has become my true home. And the Shakers, you included, Harley, have been my family. I don't want to leave home and family again, Harley. It was hard enough the first time."

"You must try to figure out a way to stay close by."

"Elder John has suggested I move over here to New Bethany. He said he would put up a tent on the grounds for me to sleep in, the same type of tent as I have had at Sunshine Home. The air here is as light and fresh as there, and Eldress Mary, whom I love, is here."

"That sounds like a perfect solution."

It was not perfect, she said. Because she was not a Shaker. And much as she loved and admired their gentle ways and enjoyed being with them, especially Eldress Mary and Elder John, she did not want to join the Society of Believers and become a Shaker herself. "I'm not ready to commit myself to their form of life, Harley. I still hope that if I recover from this illness, I'll be able someday to marry and have children. A family of my own. I can't do that if I'm a Shaker, can I?"

"No. But if Elder John and Eldress Mary have invited you to stay . . ."

"I'd be accepting their hospitality under false pretenses," she said, cutting me off. "I can't do that, either." She was vehement about it. Elder John and Eldress Mary assumed that she was ready to make her confession and become one of the Believers, she said, or they would not have invited her to live at New Bethany, especially since she was still too ill to contribute anything to the community in the way of work. Some of the others living at New Bethany in those days were not likely to become Shakers, either, but they were at least, unlike her, able-bodied workers.

I did not know her exact age and wondered if she was even old enough to become a member of the Society of Believers. Maybe she was not yet eighteen. I was old enough by then to think that I was close to Sadie's age, whatever it was. Closer by far than when we first met. "If you don't mind, may I ask how old you are? A female can't become a Shaker until she's eighteen, you know."

"I'm twenty-two, Harley. More than old enough."

"Oh. Twenty-two. Have you told them that you don't want to become a Shaker? That would cancel out any false pretenses, wouldn't it?"

"I haven't dared. I don't want to disappoint them that way. Not after accepting their hospitality and care for so long, not after allowing them to make me a sort of honorary Shaker, not after spending so many days and nights at New Bethany without making any kind of contribution to the life here. After all that, they have every reason to expect that I will become a Shaker. I never should have done it. Never. I feel I have misled and deceived them."

"They may be disappointed if you tell them the truth, yes. But surely they won't withdraw their offer to let you live here."

"That would be charity, Harley! I can't accept their charity. Not after all they've already done for me." She laughed at that idea. She had no money of her own, she said. Eldress Mary and the board members who governed Sunshine Home had allowed her to live there and be treated as a patient without charge in exchange for performing useful, nonstrenuous tasks, like reading to the very sickest patients and writing letters for them and consoling them when they were dying. It was a fair exchange, not charity. She had nothing equivalent to offer New Bethany.

"Couldn't your Rhode Island family help pay New Bethany for your room and board?"

She laughed at that idea, too. "My family! Oh, Harley, if only I had a family who could help me, how relieved and happy I would be, in spite of this terrible disease!" She said that her father, who was alcoholic, had abandoned her mother and brother and three younger sisters and had later turned up dead in a ditch. She had dropped out of school at fourteen to work in a paper mill in Warwick, Rhode Island, to help support her mother and siblings, and then she got sick with tuberculosis. She came to Sunshine Home when the doctor in Warwick who had been treating her offered to pay for her first year there.

"I'll tell you more someday," she said. "But suffice it to say that as soon as I left Warwick, the good doctor forgot his promise. Now, you better get back to helping Brother Hiram," she said, and got up from the grass and brushed herself off and shook her long hair loose. I stood next to her and saw that I was now several inches taller than she, which pleased me. She took both my hands in hers and thanked me for listening to her troubles. "But you needn't worry, Harley. God will find a solution. He always does," she said, and turned and walked back up the slope to the house.

Apparently, He did find a solution, because the very next morning Elder John came to the schoolroom, where I was instructing the younger children in the Pythagorean theorem by having them draw and measure the sides of right triangles and parallelograms. "Brother Harley," he said from the classroom door. "Sorry to interrupt, but when you've finished today's lesson, please meet me in the side yard. I have a pleasant and practical way for you to utilize your knowledge of geometry," he drawled in his Kentucky accent.

Within minutes we were standing side by side in the high, dry section of the yard, where he told me he planned to install a tent for Sister Sadie Pratt.

"So she will be living here at New Bethany, then," I said.

"Yes. The sanitarium is forced to shut down, and the poor girl has nowhere else to go."

"Will she become a Shaker?"

"That's between her and God, Brother Harley. Between Sister Sadie and God. We don't do any coercing. We're merely giving her a healthy place to live, and in exchange she is giving us the pleasure of her company and the good counsel of her intelligence. Of which I know that you, in particular, have from time to time been the beneficiary, eh, brother?"

I wasn't sure of the tone or intent of his remark, so didn't respond to it. Instead I asked him what he had in mind for me concerning the tent.

"I want you to design it for us," he said. It would be eight feet square, he explained, eight feet high at the center line, pitched to six feet high at the two opposite sides, and flat at both ends. I was to design a sturdy mortise-and-tenon wood frame for the tent, which he and Brother Edwin Moore, the head carpenter, would cut in the carpentry shop, and a pattern for the canvas panels that Mother and the other sisters in the sewing shop would cut and hem and stitch together. The tent should fit snugly over the frame, he added. He and Brother Edwin would start today building an eight-foot-square platform to be set on flat stones for the base. "The tent itself needs to be strong enough to withstand wind and rain," he said. "But it wants to be light and airy feeling, too. We need to be able to roll up the sides and tie them there, and the back and front have to be split and also able to be tied back, so that breezes can pass through side to side and front to back or any combination of the four. We also want to be able to disassemble the structure and take it down quickly in case of a hurricane. Do you think you can manage it, brother?" he asked and clapped a heavy hand on my shoulder.

I said I would have him his designs by the end of the day and went straight to work. Two days later the frame was up, and the white canvas tent was sewn and stretched tightly over the frame. Elder John and I carried a narrow cot and bedding and a small chest and a reading chair and side table from the house into the tent, and Sadie took up residence there. It was situated at the side of the house with a view of the bee yard below and the lake beyond, high enough for a steady off-lake breeze to reach it, keeping the tent freshly aired and free of morning dew and evening mosquitoes and other insects. It was an ideal spot for Sadie, her own private sanitarium.

I now saw her not just on weekends every few weeks, but practically every day, at mealtimes and when I was at work with Brother Hiram and at evening and Sabbath services in the meetinghouse. I tried not to make my attentions noticeable, because I knew that I was being watched somewhat warily by Eldress Mary and Elder John. Sadie did not actively seek me out and solicit my attentions more than usual, or more or less than she sought the company of any other resident at New Bethany, as she was a naturally gregarious and kind person, and almost everyone there easily warmed to her.

The person she appeared to spend most of her socializing time with was Elder John, or so it seemed to me, and whenever I saw them talking or walking together, the sight agitated me enough to draw me forward toward them, and I would try to join them in conversation, as if I were competing with Elder John for her affection and regard. Which I suppose I was, despite our difference in age, his and mine, and his stature as co-leader of the community compared to mine as a lowly novitiate—a secretly skeptical, potentially subversive novitiate at that.

Not that I actively tried to subvert Mother's deepening religious commitment or undercut my younger brothers' and sister Rachel's growing adhesion to the Shaker faith. Nor did I point out to Pence that, despite his delight in his hard work as a herdsman out on the range and the pleasure I took from beekeeping and teaching in the school, we and our brothers and Mother were all laboring long hours six days a week without pay and being remunerated only by room and board. I made no invidious, admittedly unfair comparisons between New Bethany and Rosewell Plantation, though I frequently made them to myself. And I told no one of my growing religious skepticism, not Pence, who I suspected was as secretly skeptical as I, and not even Sadie, although I did now and then in our private conversations hint at it.

But it was absurd for me to feel in any way competitive with Elder John for Sadie's attention and regard. I was in most respects still a boy. He was a formidable presence, a large, physically imposing man in his mid-thirties, intelligent and forceful, learned in the ways of Shakerism, a skilled self-taught architect and engineer, a man raised on a Kentucky farm with wide knowledge of the South's climatic and environmental peculiarities and potentialities, as well as a clever, amused, and surprisingly tolerant observer of his fellow human beings and their failings and weaknesses.

I sometimes wondered how deeply his religious beliefs and adherence to the Shaker way of life really ran. If he had chosen a secular life instead of this monastic one, he could easily have been very successful in the World. He would have been a pillar of whatever community he chose to inhabit. He had a patriarchal manner and a natural masculine ease with governing others, and I could well imagine him surrounded by a doting wife and a large brood of loving, obedient children, running a business with many devoted employees.

Despite his commitment to abstinence and pacifism and self-restraint, Elder John clearly liked the company of non-Shaker men, even rough-cut, irreligious men who drank and swore and used tobacco and made no secret of their coarse lustfulness. By the same token, he liked the company of women, too, Shaker and non-Shaker alike, and enjoyed evoking their admiration and interest by treating them as fully human and not how they were used to being treated by men, which was as examples of a slightly inferior *Homo sapiens* subspecies. And he liked children, though it was hard to tell if it was because he enjoyed their company or because he could instruct and easily organize them. Whichever, he did not ignore the children the way most adults do, especially men. He gave them a direct gaze and called them by their preferred names and remembered all their previous conversations with him. Children repaid him with loyalty and obedience and an almost desperate desire for his approval. I myself, when first arriving at New Bethany, had fallen under his spell. Now, of course, as an adolescent, I had begun to look for his faults and inadequacies.

The first chance I had to speak privately with Sadie, she had been living in her tent for about a week. She had greater freedom of unobserved, unscheduled movement than I, so we were able to meet only when she initiated it, which more or less limited our meetings to the bee yard, and Brother Hiram was always present there, so a private conversation between us was exceedingly difficult to arrange. But one Sunday, our day of rest, instead of engaging in Bible study after the midday meal like the rest of the community, I took myself on a solitary walk. I retrieved a few barbed hooks from my kit and cut twenty feet of drop-fishing line and dug a tin of earthworms from the manure pile behind the barn and grabbed a bamboo pole from a batch stacked outside the carpentry shop and walked across the sawgrass fields where the milch cows grazed, down to the canal that connected Alligator Lake to Live Oak Lake.

Mostly, we fished the lakes once or twice a week in groups of four with seine nets strung between two rowboats, harvesting barrels of lake bass and other meaty fish like channel cats and flatheads to be consumed by the community as a whole. But I liked on occasion to fish alone with a pole from the banks of the canals. An afternoon's catch, even of a thirty-pound catfish, could not feed all our diners, so solitary pole fishing was discouraged. Just about any form of self-satisfying, individualistic activity was frowned upon at New Bethany, although much positive emphasis was placed on meditation and reflection and study. Fishing alone from the bank of the canal with a bamboo pole fell somewhere between what was discouraged and what was encouraged. I did it rarely, and so far no one had overtly disparaged it. My catch, when it was a good one, was usually made into a chowder shared out among all the Believers.

Down along the canal, well out of sight of the New Bethany buildings and windmills, I took up a position where the water ran deep. I cut a willow wand with forked ends, propped my pole against it, and set the pole to bottom-fishing on its own and soon fell into a meditation on Sadie Pratt. I often found myself, when not otherwise distracted, conjuring her image in order to commune with her and have imaginary conversations with her, conversations that could never take place in real life, in which I was able to speak fluently and amusingly of things I barely understood, like the new rebellion in Cuba and the terrible earthquake in San Francisco and President Theodore Roosevelt's plan for a canal in Panama to link the Atlantic and Pacific Oceans, and in those conversations Sadie finds me intelligent and even charming and in appreciation places her hand on mine and smiles warmly into my face and even lays her head on my shoulder and tells me to go on, keep speaking to me, Harley.

Then, suddenly, there she was in real life! She, too, had wandered off on her own and had ended up walking on the canal towpath and had come up behind me without my hearing her. She said, "Harley, I thought that was you. Have you had any luck?"

"Not until you arrived," I said.

She laughed. "You're becoming a smooth talker, Harley. Be careful."

All at once I was self-conscious, and that was the end of my smooth talking. I turned to asking questions of her, which set her to talking and freed me from my usual tongue-tied state in her presence. I asked if she was comfortable and happy with her tent and managed to add that I was the one who had designed it. I told her I had modeled it on the tents at Sunshine Home specifically for her. I did not mention that Elder John and Brother Edwin had built it, although she surely knew as much.

She said the design was brilliant, even better than the tents at Sunshine Home.

I asked her how was her health. The last time we spoke at length she had told me that she was weaker than before and had blamed it on the stressfulness of having to leave Sunshine Home. Now that she was settled at New Bethany, the stress must have abated. I hoped that meant her health was once again improving. She did look stronger, and she had walked all the way over from her tent, close to a mile through tough sawgrass pastureland and down the steep slope to the towpath.

"No, I'm about the same. Or possibly a little weaker," she said. "The disease is progressive, Harley. Until it's not. And then . . . ," she trailed off. "Well, fresh air and quiet and rest, that's about all one can do to slow and, if one is lucky, to stop its progress."

I asked how she had managed to make Elder John's and Eldress Mary's offer of hospitality acceptable, when not so long ago she had been adamantly opposed to it.

"Was I? Really? You mean, to come and live here at New Bethany? Why would I refuse their generous offer to live with them at New Bethany as a permanent guest? As permanent as my illness will permit, I mean. In my situation, one does not make long-range plans," she said, and made an ironic tsking noise with her tongue.

"Have you changed your mind, then, about becoming a Shaker? About wanting to marry someday and have a family?"

"Oh, my, Harley, why would I want to marry and have children? I can't inflict my fate on someone else, especially on an innocent child, when there's a very good chance, even a likelihood, that I won't live long enough to meet my wifely and maternal obligations. That would be selfish and wrong and cruel."

"Yes, I suppose that's true," I said. But I didn't understand how it could be true today, when a week or so ago its opposite was true.

"They're really two separate questions, anyhow," she said. "Whether I will join the Believers and become a Shaker, and whether I wish to marry someday and have a family. As long as I suffer from consumption, I know the answer to the second question," she said. "But as for the first . . . well, it's complicated. I suspect it's complicated for you, too. And possibly for the same reasons. Am I right, Harley?"

I nodded yes, but did not elaborate. Instead, I pointed out that I still had a little over five years before I could choose one way or the other. Until I reached my majority, it didn't matter if I wished to join the Believers and become a Shaker or choose a secular life instead. For me, until I turned twenty-one, the question was moot. I asked her if it was complicated, as she said, because of the Shakers' religious belief or because of the strict requirements of their life.

I did not say it, but at fifteen I had no argument with the need to adhere to a life of moderation in all things and abstinence and avoidance of sensual stimulation and pleasure, or with communitarianism. At that young and impulsive age, the Shaker way of life was useful to me and useful to others as well. It provided a disordered and undisciplined teenaged boy with order and discipline. In a sense, it was all I had ever known, anyhow, from Greylag to Waycross to Rosewell Plantation to New Bethany. Until I arrived at New Bethany, I had been but a child, compelled to follow in my parents' tracks. The path of my life had therefore been circumstantial and unavoidable, rather than, as it had recently become, ideological and elective. Though not yet fully an adult, I was nonetheless old enough now to choose my way of life, and I had no hesitation in choosing to follow the Shaker path. No, for me, at fifteen, the complicated question was the religious one.

"I, too, believe the Shaker way is the best way to live," Sadie said. "Especially given the conditions imposed on me by my illness. It protects me."

"Protects you? How?"

"By leading me not into temptation," she said. Then she pointed behind me and said, "Oh, look, Harley! You've caught a fish!"

I turned and, indeed, the line was being tugged and released and yanked again, and my bamboo pole was about to be pulled from its forked stand. I grabbed the pole with both hands and gently worried the fish, probably a large, slow catfish, not a black bass, leading it back and forth and side to side to tire it. The opaque, slow-moving water was the color of gray opal, and I could not see the fish and hoped that it had not swallowed the hook and I would not have to tear its innards in order to land it. Better to take a rock and kill the fish with a single sharp blow to the head as soon as I had it ashore than to eviscerate and torture the creature in the water, flooding its flesh and membranes and nerves with blood and pain.

REEL #8

For the first time since I began telling this tale, I've been kept away from my tape recorder for longer than a night's sleep, plus the little time it takes to prepare and eat a couple of simple solitary meals a day. The time-out was necessitated by the sudden appearance three days ago of a small sinkhole in the driveway leading to the garage where I keep my Packard. I had to arrange for the delivery of nine yards of crushed stone to fill it, and yesterday I had the pile flattened with a roller, so I could free my car from the garage and park it safely out front. I'll get the driveway repaved one of these days.

Probably none of that's worth mentioning, as sinkholes are fairly common hereabouts. People call them "sinks," and it would seem of no particular relevance to the story I'm trying to tell, except that the sink in my driveway reminded me that back in the day they were an unwelcome fact of life at New Bethany. Then I remembered one in particular.

Starting in the early 1890s, in order to link up the half dozen lakes on their property and facilitate the transport of produce from the fields to Narcoossee and Kissimmee and St. Cloud and beyond, the early Shaker settlers, under the direction of Elder John, added miles of deep new subsidiary canals to the existing network, which had been steam-shoveled and blasted out of the limestone a decade before by Hamilton Disston's Atlantic and Gulf Coast Canal and Okeechobee Land Company. Elder John designed and built his version of an ox-drawn digging machine called the Fresno scraper, a more efficient and kindly way to slice up the land with canals. Once the canals were dug and the lakes connected to Disston's canals, the Shakers cut thousands of ditches by pick and shovel and plow and Elder John's miniatured version of the Fresno scraper to drain the water off the marshes and wetlands into the canals and lakes, creating those much-admired, bountiful, dark-dirt Shaker fields and meadows.

They produced thousands of acres of newly arable land that way, just as they had in upstate New York and elsewhere. But their extensive excavations and extractions here in south Florida, combined with Disston's original canals, had the unintended effect of diverting surface and subterranean rivers and streams of southerly runoff from Lake Okeechobee and the upland swamps and springs and lakes further north all the way to the Okefenokee—waters that we now know are the headwaters of the Everglades. The diversions created a venous below-ground network of unmapped caves and tunnels with porous limestone roofs that occasionally collapsed from the weight of rain-saturated topsoil. A herd of cattle could suddenly get swallowed by the earth, or a shed or barn or outhouse would begin to lean dangerously and one morning would have fallen into a pit that did not exist the night before.

The collapsing pavement in my driveway made me remember the winter I turned seventeen, when a sink opened on a flat grassy stretch between the apiary and the Live Oak Lake landing. There was no structure or grazing livestock on that small plain, and sinks were fairly common at New Bethany, with one appearing somewhere on the Shaker land every few months. So this would not have been an event worth telling about if something unusual and consequential had not occurred there, something concerning me and Sadie Pratt.

The area had been ditched, drained, and cleared the previous winter for the eventual planting of a grapefruit orchard, the location chosen, among other considerations, for its proximity to the apiary. Brother Hiram was hoping to establish a line of honey flavored solely by grapefruit blossoms. Sadie, on her regular mid-afternoon walk-about, had left her tent and passed by the apiary, where she briefly stopped. As Brother Hiram was working nearby, we exchanged a few friendly, slightly formal words, all very decorous and prim, with me addressed as Brother Harley and she as Sister Sadie. After a few moments, she moved on.

By then it had become necessary for us when we were near one another to rely on strict formality and scripted words, not just to discourage suspicion and rumor among the residents of New Bethany, but also to protect ourselves from stumbling into a reckless intimacy. I speak more of myself, perhaps, than of Sadie, for I could not know at the time what she was afraid of stumbling into. Only later did she reveal to me her true feelings and fears back then.

But I was now at an age when a rising male lustfulness is impossible to ignore and difficult to repress. My night dreams often left me shattered with guilt and remorse when I woke; and my willed reflections on what were proper thoughts and what improper, what was permissible and what forbidden, and all my attempts to govern my wild impulses with honest self-analysis and vigilant self-restraint were under constant assault by my wicked desires. My mind was like an oak tree being repeatedly struck and split by lightning, and my body seemed to have a mind of its own, similarly struck.

I watched Sadie as she strolled in her elegant, slow, straight-backed way from the bee yard down the gentle slope beyond, her slender arms bent at the elbow, her high, slim waist turning in a languorous quarter-circle as she moved, narrow hips swirling slightly in time to her careful steps across the rough ground, all her movements so familiar and entrancing to me, who had been observing her from near and afar for over five years now. She wore a dark-purple, almost black dress that day. Her head was uncovered, and her coal-black hair, braided around her head in the manner of a medieval nun, glimmered in the mid-afternoon sun.

Despite her grace and beauty, she had lately seemed even more fragile than before, as if she were constantly at the point of exhaustion. She breathed with difficulty and spoke in a low, whispery voice. In the past, these symptoms would be apparent for a few days at a time and then fade, and she would seem to regain her strength and some of her health, and her dark eyes would brighten again, reflecting light from deep within, like obsidian in moonlight. But this most recent decline had lasted a month or more. So I was watching her with a mixture of rapt admiration and fearful concern, when I first heard and then saw, about fifty yards beyond her at the center of the flat, grassy plot halfway between the bee yard and the Live Oak Lake landing, the sudden arrival of a sink. The sound of the collapsing ground was very loud, all out of proportion to the visual effect, as a rough circle of loamy, grass-covered ground the size of a washtub sank six or eight inches below the rest and then opened at the center like the dark eye of an ox. Sadie, startled by the event, stopped walking for a few seconds, when, with apparent interest and curiosity, she began to move steadily toward the sink, as if to examine it up close.

I had never seen the actual emergence of a sinkhole before, only the later evidence of it, the aftermath. But many times, late at night lying in my bed in the dark, I had imagined their unseen cause and effect with a vividness that made me shudder and leave my bed and walk around the room, until the image dissipated and went away. So I understood immediately that the ceiling of a half-flooded, subterranean room beneath the flat, uncultivated meadow where Elder John and Brother Hiram had plans for an orchard of grapefruit trees was starting to collapse. I imagined large, porous chunks of limestone cracking and breaking off beneath the surface and tumbling into black space and water, pulling roots and loam and all the plants that bloomed on the surface down with it, loosening the pale sedimented rock and black soil, pulling it all down, as the ceiling of the dark room below rapidly crumbled and the collapse spread out from the fallen center.

At the first sound of the breaking ground, Brother Hiram had pressed his hands flat against his ears and was now staring up at the sky in stark terror, as if he thought we were being attacked by artillery fire. The roar of the underground collapse went on for many seconds. It sounded like the earth itself was in pain. Then it went silent for half as long, before erupting again, and I knew that more soil and limestone were falling invisibly into the black pit below. Silence again. And still Sadie kept walking toward the widening hole at the center.

I called to her, "Sadie, don't go near! Stay back! Stay back!" But she did not seem to hear me and kept approaching the small circular opening in the ground, as if it were an abandoned burrow and she only wished to know what sort of creature had made it.

I ran full-speed straight at her, shouting, "Get back, Sadie! Get back!" She had almost reached the washtub-sized hollow and the widening hole at its center when she finally seemed to hear my cries and turned to face me. She looked almost cross with me for shouting at her—she saw no danger before her, why was I so alarmed?—when suddenly the ground on which she stood broke and tipped, and the hole opened up like a giant mouth, and she lost her balance and fell down and clutched at the grass to keep from sliding into the sink's dark maw.

I heard screaming and yelling behind me—Elder John and some others, men and women roused from their work by my cries and now by the awful sight of Sadie being pulled toward the sink. The section of ground beneath her broke, one end tilted up and the rest dropped away, and she let go of the grass with one hand and reached out to me just as I arrived at the widening crack in the tilted wedge of topsoil. I grabbed her hand, but then the ground under me gave way, too, knocking me off my feet, and we both began to slide down into the cavern below.

Something strange happened then. As we fell, with no conscious thought of what I was doing, I wrapped my right arm around her back and the other beneath her legs in a single unbroken move and slung her up and across my right shoulder like a sack of grain, and at the same time kept my legs churning, as if I were at the end of a long, arduous climb up a steep mountain and were making the final mad scramble to the summit. There was nothing but the cloudless blue sky above to hold on to, and with my free hand I reached out and grabbed on to the sky, and using its leverage and my pounding legs, I brought Sadie and myself up out of the sink onto solid ground.

I carried her a safe distance away from the rapidly collapsing earth, and when I lowered her from my shoulder, I saw that she was unconscious. Slowly I walked with her draped across my arms up the long slope to meet Elder John and the others who were rushing toward us. There I laid her down on the grass and, suddenly exhausted, my head spinning, the sky above going black at the edges and receding in the distance, I lay down beside her and closed my eyes.

When I opened them again, Elder John was down on his knees holding Sadie in his arms, and she was coming out of her faint. Eldress Mary and several others rushed up to us and kneeled around me and Sadie and touched us gently on our shoulders and cheeks, as if to be sure we were still alive. Sadie and I looked into each other's eyes, and I felt at that instant an unbreakable bond forming between us. We were becoming one person, indivisible, our souls permanently mingled—or so I believed. We said nothing, just stared directly at one another and let the mingling get under way. We were surrounded by the brothers and sisters and they were all talking at once, but Sadie and I were alone together in a bowl of silence lit by a burnished late-afternoon sun.

After a few moments, the bowl of silence that surrounded me and Sadie broke, and the babble of voices slowly resumed, and the soft golden light cleared, as more of the brothers and sisters, including Mother and my brothers Raymond and Royal, joined the group, asking what happened, were we all right, was either of us hurt or injured, and so on. Until at last Elder John spoke.

He said, "Brethren, we must give our heartfelt thanks to the Lord above for saving our beloved Sister Sadie and Brother Harley. And we must give thanks to Brother Harley for his heroism." But they must not forget, he said, that I had clearly been inspired by the example of Jesus Christ and Mother Ann to love one another more than I loved myself. The Lord had protected me and Sadie, and Jesus and Mother Ann had put me forward as a model for all. The brethren in turn should be inspired by my example, Elder John declared. "I thank thee, Brother Harley," he said, "for thy example," and for the first time in a long while he gave me a warm, trusting smile and reached forward and clapped his heavy hand on my shoulder. "The quality of thy love for thy sister is pure and godly," he said.

He placed his other hand on Sadie's thin shoulder and said to her, "Thy love for Brother Harley hath likewise been purified by his heroism. Thou art equal to Brother Harley in the eyes of the Lord. By sending him to save thee and by protecting him in the commission of that heroic act, the Lord hath shown His favor equally on you both. We are grateful to have witnessed this," he said.

He released us then and stood, and Sadie and I also got to our feet, and I felt as if he had ministered over our marriage. I reached for Sadie's hand, and she reached for mine, and for a long moment we remained standing side by side like a bride and groom before Elder John and Eldress Mary and our Shaker brethren. And then the party slowly made its way back up the long, grassy slope to the house, where there would be food and drink prepared for everyone and a happy celebration of our marriage would follow.

Meanwhile behind us the collapse of the ground slowed, until eventually the rock beneath held, and the loosened soil began slowly to fill the void, and in the passing weeks grass and flowers grew upon it, until there was nothing there to remind us of the event except for a shallow depression in the land, around which the Shakers would plant their grove of grapefruit trees in a circular shape, which would be admired by visitors to New Bethany for many years to come.

There was no food and drink prepared, of course, and no happy celebration of our marriage. Our wedding had taken place only in my mind, and I hoped in Sadie's. In everyone else's mind, the Lord and Jesus Christ and Mother Ann Lee, by making it possible for me to rescue Sadie, had made us brother and sister, Shaker brethren, which was cause enough for celebration. And the story of our near-death experience, told repeatedly with small embellishments and deletions at evening services, all in the interests of ecclesiastical exegesis, was soon shaped into a religious parable linking Shaker daily life to the will of God and the desires of Jesus and Mother Ann. I started to feel that Sadie and I were becoming characters in a chapter of the Bible and the sinkhole in the grove had become the gateway to hell.

Not long after this event, Elder John came to me one afternoon and suggested that I accompany him to the agricultural exposition and fair held annually up at Tampa, which was about one hundred twenty-five miles northwest by rail from St. Cloud. He had been elected by the Osceola County Farmers Association as their chief representative and was particularly proud that year of our pineapple crop and had entered New Bethany into competition for the Pineapple gold medal, an award that would guarantee large sales to Northern wholesalers. In the past, pineapples from New Bethany had won second and third place in the competition for the gold medal, and though they had sold well in Cuba, because of our ability to produce the necessary volume and carry it south by train from St. Cloud to Fort Myers for transshipment by sea to Havana, New Bethany pineapples had not yet penetrated the market in the cities of the North. Elder John was determined to win the gold medal and advertise it everywhere, from the Northern newspapers to the crates of pineapples themselves. He said to me, "If we win at Tampa, Brother Harley, we can become the pineapple kings of America."

I liked his enthusiasm, it was almost endearing, but mistrusted it. Why would a small colony of Shakers in south Florida want to become the pineapple kings of America? He said that he would like me to come up to Tampa with him for the fair and manage the New Bethany stand and show off our product and offer samples to the attendees. He told me that I was well-spoken and young and attractive, and the many people of the World who held a prejudice against the Shakers as a religion would not so easily apply that prejudice to me. I would make them think more kindly toward the Shakers, he said. Also, I was mathematically competent and could keep good track of our sales at the exposition. He wanted to give away small, bite-sized samples and sell whole pineapples from this winter's harvest and take orders at a wholesale price for shipment and resale later. In previous years Brother Edwin had manned the stand, but he had given away whole pineapples, our entire crop, as samples that should have been paid for and had taken no orders at the wholesale price. "The cost of the exposition for us has up to now exceeded by far its return. The Society of Believers," Elder John declared, "is not a charitable organization."

Nor is it a profit-making organization, I thought. But I was happy to have regained Elder John's trust and for the chance to leave the confines of New Bethany for a brief sojourn in the World. What made me even happier was his revelation that Sister Sadie would accompany us to the fair. He explained that due to the persistence of her illness, her spirits of late were low. Unlike the rest of us, she did not have a line of work to occupy her days, so he had invited her to come along with us to Tampa, he told me, with the hope that it would stimulate her mind and body a little and lift her spirits in the ongoing battle against her disease. She could help us exhibit our excellent pineapples to the eyes and taste of the World, which would have the added benefit of enhancing her feeling of belongingness at New Bethany.

I wondered if in reality his invitation to bring Sadie to the fair with him had actually preceded his invitation to me. It occurred to me that I was being brought along for appearance's sake, as a kind of chaperone. But whose chaperone? Hers or his? It was widely known at New Bethany, especially after the episode of the sinkhole, that I was Sister Sadie's special friend. She and I being non-Shakers, she might be seen by all, therefore, as accompanying me, not Elder John, to Tampa for three days and nights. If he brought someone else instead of me, Brother Edwin, for instance, as he did last year, or one of the orchard keepers, she might be seen as accompanying Elder John. He probably did not want that.

I had begun to think that the man was far cleverer than he was generally thought to be. He was already regarded by all who knew him as the cleverest of the Shakers, much more so than Eldress Mary, who was a trained accountant and stern guardian of Shaker beliefs, values, and behavior and was viewed as intelligent and diligent, but not clever. Elder John, on the other hand, was our master builder and architect and the superintendent of the works, as well as our resident theologian and explicator of the sacred texts. These skills and responsibilities required a high degree of imagination. He was creative. And thus clever. Making him capable, I thought, of deceit and hypocrisy.

I remembered how he had purchased those plots in St. Cloud in his own name, using Shaker money for the down payment and signing a promissory note that obliged New Bethany to pay the balance due plus interest five years hence, and I thought that perhaps he was creating a potentially profitable situation for himself, if at some future date he abandoned New Bethany for the World and chose to put the lots up for sale. I saw that the articles he wrote and published in the *St. Cloud Tribune*, which he described as merely a means to promote the virtues of the Shaker life and improve the agricultural and environmental practices of our neighbors, might also function instead as covert advertisements for the superior quality of our produce, thus improving our position in the open marketplace. And I noted again his desire to make New Bethany the pineapple king of America. It was as if he were managing a plantation, not a religious commune.

The night before we left for Tampa, we loaded our old green John Deere wagon to the rails with crated pineapples, and before daylight the next morning we carried the crates in the wagon drawn by a pair of our draft horses to Narcoossee aboard the *Coquina* and from there by road to St. Cloud. Elder John sat up front on the narrow springboard seat and drove the horses, and Sadie sat close beside him. The John Deere had high sideboards and canvas-covered hoops like a Conestoga, and I was stashed in the back with the stacked crates of pineapples and our cooking implements and tarps and bedrolls for our housing at the fair. I watched carefully from the shade, on high alert for any attention Elder John paid to my Sadie, and conjured thoughts and plots for him like a novelist inventing the mind of a villain.

Every once in a while, he would turn to me and deliver a brief lecture on the ins and outs of the cultivation of excellent pineapples. He was preparing me, he said, for my interactions with buyers. With his lectures he may have been showing off a little for Sadie's benefit, but the truth is, up to that point I had worked only with the bees, except when called out in October and late spring to help with harvesting citrus or one of the other crops, and knew next to nothing about growing and selling high-grade pineapples. I had no particular desire to become a farmer or orchard keeper and was happy enough as an apiarist, but I thought it would do no harm to keep him talking to me instead of Sadie, so I feigned interest.

He said he wanted me to sound like an expert when dealing with customers, as he would often be away from our stand negotiating bulk purchases with the wholesalers and attending meetings with his fellow county representatives and delegates and swapping information and news with the other farmers. I asked him, "If I'm only running the sample stand and selling pineapples from the crates, why do I need to sound like an expert? Especially when I'm clearly not one?"

"When a man purchases something from someone who appears to possess precise knowledge of his product and how it's made, and the purchaser enjoys that product, he will return for more. It's the returning buyer we want," he drawled. "Not the one-shot." He had dropped his Shaker manner of speaking shortly after we landed at Narcoossee, reverting to his friendly Kentucky-farmer affect, which always made him seem warmer and less intimidating. "The man who thinks you're only a barker," he went on, "that man won't quite trust his satisfaction with the product. He'll question his pleasure. He won't return for more. I want you to come across, Brother Harley, as having had deep experience in the cultivation of pineapples. So you're not taken as some kind of fairway tout. You get me, son?"

"Yes, sir, I get you. You don't think it's deceitful of me, though? I mean, pretending to be an experienced grower of pineapples."

"Not if you learn what I'll be teaching you as we go along today. To sell someone a phonograph player a fellow don't need to know everything Mr. Edison knows about electricity. He don't need to know how to build a phonograph player himself," he said. His intention was to provide me while we traveled to Tampa with a basic user's manual for the proper cultivation of pineapples. "The fellow who knew all there is to know about apples, the daddy of the industry, was Mr. George L. Russell, who claimed there's thirty-seven varieties," he began. "And Mr. Russell, he believed that your Smooth Cayenne type is the finest all-around apple. Which is what ours is. That's what you call them, by the way, apples. Not pineapples. That'd give you away right off."

We were a few miles east of St. Cloud, crossing a vast, flat expanse of scattered slash pines and low greenery. The marl road cut a narrow, raised pale-gray stripe through the watery plain. Clusters of snowy-white egrets strolled on brittle black legs among pink and white fleabane and pickerelweed. Elder John pointed out that this type of land may look fruitful, but it would be no good for growing apples. Too much muck in the soil. Too wet. You need, at the very least, dry, sandy soil where longleaf pines grow, which will produce a good enough crop, yes, but only for three to five years. So what you really want is a high spruce pine hammock, like what you see at New Bethany, with a mix of muck and sand. You can grow excellent fruit indefinitely on that sort of land. However, the hammocks tend to be destitute of humus, he pointed out, so you have to add a little muck to the top or spread some cow manure. But not too much, he warned, or you'll injure the keeping quality of the apples, which is important when you're shipping them to distant locations.

Sadie laughed and said, "Elder John, you're going to confuse him. That's more information than poor Brother Harley can possibly hold on to."

"No, it's not," I said. "I have a steel-trap mind and an excellent memory. In fifty years I will still remember everything that he's telling me today."

She laughed again. "Oh, Brother Harley, you are such an audacious young man! Just take care that your audacity doesn't lead to impudence," she warned.

Her language, as always, charmed me—"audacious" and "audacity" and "impudence." Elder John chuckled and nodded in agreement, but continued talking as before, as if I were his student and were making written, not mental, notes while he lectured. He instructed me to be sure to say that at New Bethany we protect our apples from sunburn by covering our pinery sheds, not with thin cloth, like most growers, but with airy latticeworks made of wooden slats three inches wide aligned to the daylong passage of the sun. This allows for an even distribution of shade and sunlight from sunrise to sunset and lets the fruit mature before ripening and helps slow the evaporation of moisture. Apples grown out in the open, like the common Red Spanish variety, cannot compete in tenderness of fiber and delicacy of flavor with our wood-shedded Smooth Cayennes, and they are by comparison diminutive in size, he said.

At St. Cloud we transferred the load from the wagon to the waiting train and boarded the horses at the livery stable there. Many other local farmers and cattle ranchers were on the same train, hauling their produce and animals to the fair. Once we were settled in our seats, Elder John resumed his lecture. On and on he went, reciting all the best ways to prepare the soil and the proper quantities and proportions of blood, bone, and potash to use for fertilizer and when to apply it, how to propagate the plants with slips and suckers, the virtues of raised beds, the best seasons for planting, the need to weed the plants with a scuffle hoe so as to avoid going too deep and disturbing the roots—all that and more, which, indeed, as I bragged, I have not forgotten to this day. He said that the best apples, like ours, will weigh in at eight to twelve pounds. If packed in excelsior, a dozen apples to a crate, they will keep for two to four weeks for shipment to the North, and ought to sell this year for no less than six dollars per crate, he noted.

By mid-afternoon, we were nearing Tampa and could smell the salt air off the Gulf, and Elder John was lecturing me on the myriad medical uses of pineapple and its juice, claiming that the fruit will cure malaria and dyspepsia and has long been used as an antiseptic and in the treatment of diphtheria. To demonstrate its excellence as a digestive aid, he suggested that while at the fair I purchase a few small pieces of roasted pork or beef and every now and then place a morsel into a glass jar filled with pineapple juice and let folks watch it dissolve the fibers of the meat. "Speaking of which, Brother Harley, be sure you point out the strength of the fibers of the plant leaves," he said. "Tell them how it's superior to the best New Zealand and English flax, and that the leaves can be used in the manufacture of rope and even of cloth. Tell them that all one has to do is soak the fibers in cold water and dry them in the sun, and they'll turn white and soft and be ready for use."

He was formidable. Tireless and interested in everything that walked or grew upon the planet, and a deeply religious Shaker besides. And he was a tall, robust, physically gifted man. And hand-some, but in a rough-hewn way that made you think he couldn't possibly be vain. And yet he was vain. He liked his full beard and could occasionally be caught combing it smooth as if preparing to be photographed for a portrait. He dressed with Shaker simplicity and practicality in field clothes, but his overalls and work shirts and boots were always clean and tidy, no matter what kind of work he happened to be engaged in. The man next to him in a ditch might be spattered with mud, his boots slathered with manure, but Elder John would look like he had just come from his office.

The path that led to his position as coleader of New Bethany was circuitous, and for a Shaker of that era, unusual, inasmuch as he was from the South and had joined the Society of Believers up in Mount Lebanon when he was a very young man. Shakers avoid col-lecting personal histories and eschew gossip and rumor on principle, so what I knew of his past I had to glean from casual remarks and observations dropped by the side in conversation with him and with a few of the older brethren, like Brother Edwin, the head carpenter, and Sister Hazel, our schoolteacher.

No one seemed to know his whole story, however, only pieces of it, and many of those pieces didn't quite interlock with the oth-ers. For instance, he was born in Tennessee in 1870 to Quaker par-ents, poor farmers who, to avoid the growing violence of the Ku Klux Klan, migrated north as far as Kentucky when he was a boy. In 1887, Congressman William Culbertson, a Kentucky Republican, appointed him to West Point, which is highly unusual for a young Southerner with his background, especially back then. He must have been singled out early for his gifts, and to accept the appointment, he would have been obliged to abandon his parents' Quaker pacifism, if not quite their manner of speaking. But no further military service was ever mentioned by him or anyone else, which suggests that he was either expelled from West Point before being commissioned or discharged from the army later for some sort of offense.

One evening at New Bethany, hoping to find answers to some of these questions, I asked him directly how he became a Shaker. We were seated side by side in the meetinghouse, waiting for prayers to begin. He said it occurred when he was in his early twenties and was "spiritually adrift." He told me that he was employed for a few years as a prison guard at the Auburn Prison in upstate New York and was in despair over the inhuman, punitive nature of his job. He added that when he attended his first Shaker meeting at Mount Lebanon, he had recently assisted in the execution of a man at Auburn Prison. "I went to the Shaker meeting mainly in order to get the free dinner that went with it," he said, smiling. "But I was fed for a lifetime that night. I quit my job at the prison the next day and asked to be taken in by the Shakers, and I have never been hungry since, neither physically nor spiritually. And I've never had to assist in the killing of any man or woman since, either."

He deflected any further inquiry by describing in detail the execution at Auburn Prison of a man who had murdered his wife with an axe, the first execution in the world by electric chair. He said that he had earlier acquired some basic knowledge concerning electricity and had been asked by the warden to help design the chair, and he and two other guards were called on to help strap the murderer into the chair. The first charge was 700 volts applied for seventeen seconds, leaving the man unconscious with burnt clothing and flesh, but still alive. So they prepared a second charge of 1,030 volts and applied it for a full two minutes. "You could see smoke coming from his head." After a long pause, he said, "It would have been better done with an axe."

I remember wondering if, instead of having been employed as a prison guard, he might have been an inmate himself, one who happened to have some knowledge of electrical engineering, probably gained at West Point. He was too educated to have been employed as a guard, and he did seem to know an unusual amount about Thomas Edison. Possibly he had been imprisoned for committing a crime while a cadet at West Point or, if he was indeed commissioned in the army, soon after. Maybe, that fateful night when he showed up for supper and prayers at Mount Lebanon, he had just been released from Auburn Prison. In those days people often joined the Society of Believers in order to start their life over, just as Mother had. In some ways, it was not a difficult transition from prison life—or the military, or life at Rosewell Plantation—to Shakerism. They were all, in a sense, utopian societies, and many of the skills that made it possible merely to survive in prison or in the army or at Rosewell were the same skills that allowed one to thrive as a Shaker.

From others I learned that in 1892 Elder John—known back then as Brother John—had been instructed by the trustees at Mount Lebanon to travel alone to Narcoossee, Florida, to investigate the possibilities of founding a Shaker colony in the region. He would have been just twenty-two, young for taking on such a heavy responsibility, but as the sole Southerner in the community, a man with both a farming background and training as an engineer, he was probably the most qualified Shaker to evaluate the land and estimate the costs and time and number of settlers it would take to convert it into a thriving, self-supporting commune. Hundreds of thousands of acres in central and south Florida had been thrown open by the federal and state governments for purchase and settlement, making land cheaper there than anywhere else in the nation. After a month of reconnoitering the watery flats and hammocks surrounding St. Cloud, Kissimmee, and Narcoossee, he returned to New York and reported to the trustees at Mount Lebanon that there was unlimited excellent farmland available for three dollars an acre. Very little of it needed to be cleared, although he conceded that some of it was underwater and would have to be drained.

The Shakers were no longer growing in numbers like they had earlier in the century, when religious revivals had swept large numbers of converts to their doorstep, and the emergence of state-run orphanages and poorhouses were eliminating what for years had been a major source of new young recruits—orphans and abandoned women. In fact, their numbers were shrinking. They had no pressing need to launch new satellite communities like they did back in the 1840s and '50s when they expanded into Ohio and Kentucky and Illinois. And more and more of their members were elderly or would be soon, and the image of living out one's old age, then as now, in a semitropical clime must have looked attractive to them.

Whatever the reasons, the trustees at Mount Lebanon decided to dip into their collective savings and send Brother John back down south to arrange for the purchase of seven thousand acres of marshland and hammock and sawgrass plain and scrub forest. They agreed to subsidize the creation of a new colony just outside Narcoossee on Alligator and Live Oak Lakes. Eldress Mary went with him, along with six other Shakers, three men and three women, among them Sister Hazel and Brother Edwin. They were the founding mothers and fathers of the New Bethany family.

Now, just fifteen years later, with Sadie Pratt and me as his faithful squires, Elder John was entering the ring at the South Florida Fair in triumph as the elected representative of all Osceola County farmers. The community he led with Eldress Mary and the farm they comanaged were the most prosperous and admired community and farm in the entire region, famous for the quality of their crops and livestock and their farm buildings and habitations, their mills and canals and engineering marvels, their ingenious crafts and seeds and seedlings, and for their hospitality and the honesty of their dealings with their neighbors and near and far-flung customers alike.

In those days the South Florida Fair and Agricultural Exhibition was the peak economic and social event of the year. It took place over three days on a thirty-acre park adjacent to the Tampa Bay Hotel, the old campgrounds used by the United States Army during the Spanish War. The crammed main exhibition hall was the size of a modern airplane hangar, with a half dozen smaller halls scattered about the grounds. There were rides and games of chance and a racetrack and grandstand, an auditorium for public lectures and theatrical and musical performances, sideshows with P. T. Barnum–type freaks of nature and exotic animals for people to gape at, indoor restaurants and outdoor cafés, picnic tables and barbecue stands, and a tree-shaded camping area on the banks of the nearby Hillsborough River, where the exhibitors could set up their tents or park their wagons for sleeping. That is where Elder John and I lugged our four large duffels and claimed a pleasantly scenic spot on a grass-covered knoll overlooking the dark, slow-flowing river below. I was now as tall as Elder John, though not as broad, and strong for my age and enjoyed proving it, especially in front of Sadie.

While Elder John went off to the main exhibition hall to check on our pineapples and set up our stand, I pitched our tarpaulin with ropes and poles and unpacked our bedrolls and cots and cooking gear and set up the portable grill that Brother Wayne Tilley, the blacksmith, had manufactured for the occasion in the New Bethany foundry. We had brought a light folding canvas chair with us for Sadie, where she sat and watched me as I worked.

It was near dusk, and Sadie looked weak and tired from the long day's journey. I wondered if it may have been reckless of Elder John to have brought her along on this trip. I had noticed her several times on the train trying to disguise her need to cough and saw her struggle to catch her breath when we walked across the huge fairgrounds to our camping spot. But if he had not invited her, he would not have invited me—or so I then believed. He wouldn't have needed me to cover his true intention, which I was sure was solely for him to spend time away from New Bethany in the company of Sadie Pratt.

I was eager to wander back to the midway and immerse myself in the sights and sounds and smells there, but did not want to leave her alone at our camp. She must have sensed my conflict. Without my saying anything, she urged me to go now to the fair and see everything before it got dark. "This is your first chance to see the World in all its glory and all its folly in one place," she said. "I need to rest, Harley, and Elder John will return shortly, so I'll not want for company."

"I'm sure he'll be happy to keep you company," I said. "And happy for my absence," I added in a low voice.

Which she heard. "If I didn't know better, Harley, I'd think you were a little jealous of Elder John. But really, you needn't be. I love him, certainly. He's been steadfast and loyal and caring since the day I first visited New Bethany. And I love you, too, for many of the same reasons."

"Do you think his intentions are wholly honorable?"

"Of course! He's a Shaker, an elder!"

"He's also a man, a man with feelings and appetites," I said. "Like me," I added, venturing forth, entering a danger zone.

"Yes, I know. But he is a Shaker elder, and you are not." Then she laughed and said, "Now, go! Go on to the fair, Harley, and enjoy yourself. Get a taste of what life in the World is like. Then come back and tell me all about it. Because, like you, I'm not a Shaker yet. If I felt stronger, I'd go with you. It would be fun to venture into the World with you."

"Oh, my goodness, yes, it would!" I said. "Maybe you'll feel stronger tomorrow, and we can do that."

"I don't think Elder John would approve. Besides, he'll want you to tend to the pineapple exhibit and will likely expect me to help you and keep you company there. Now's your only chance, Harley. Go on," she said, and smiled prettily and waved me away with the back of her hand.

I took her extended hand in mine and kissed it and turned and danced off toward the fairgrounds and the midway. The World! In all its glory and folly, just as she promised. I felt like I'd been told by my Sadie to sally forth and risk my innocence for her and return to her afterwards carrying the gift of forbidden knowledge.

Of course, Sadie already knew quite a bit of the World from her childhood and youth in Rhode Island up to the onset of her illness and her withdrawal first to Sunshine Home and then to New Bethany. In fact, she knew even more of the ways of the World than I thought. But I, raised by Ruskinites in one utopian commune and then a second, and indentured afterwards at Rosewell Plantation, and for the last five years confined pretty much to New Bethany, I was altogether new to it. The midway at the South Florida Fair was my first exposure to the temptations and dangers and oddities of the World, to its beauty and chaos and sensuality, and to its startling, even shocking revelations as to my own desires and curiosity and fears. For the next few hours, as it slowly grew dark and all across the fairgrounds the lights came on, and in the midway the discordant noise of the spinning rides and calliopes rose and merged with the shouts and siren songs of the barkers and touts before their tents and exhibits and the roar from the grandstand as the thundering horses rounded the far turn and headed for the finish line, I was both in Heaven and in Hell and unable to distinguish between the two.

I had no money jingling in my pocket, no bills, not even a penny, so I had to stand numb-struck outside the tents that advertised with garish signs and paintings the presence inside of a two-headed calf and a lady with a long black beard and an ape-man from Borneo and Siamese twins and a woman with the face of a dog and a fire-breathing Komodo dragon, and was forced to imagine how they would look in the flesh, if I only had five cents, for these were things I had never seen illustrated before or even dreamed of. The smell of barbecue and roasted ears of corn and grilled sausages and peppers and onions filled my face and made me ache with hunger. I was jostled by White men in bowler hats swilling tankards of beer, shirtless Black workers with their ropes and sledgehammers stepping around me to set up more tents and more spinning rides, slender, mustachioed, brown-skinned men smoking cigars, wearing white guayabera shirts and loose trousers, and their pretty wives and children, all speaking rapid-fire Cuban Spanish, and gangs of young White toughs my own age with ropey muscles and jutting jaws punching on each other's shoulders and shoving one another good-naturedly as they pushed past, daring me with their glares to step in their way. I saw a huge black bear chained to a post looking more mournful than fierce. I saw an elephant wearing a turban. I saw a brightly painted wagon with a cage atop it and a tawny, mottled Florida panther locked inside, sullen and bored, ignoring the small boys who were trying to poke it through the bars with sticks.

I was called out by a pair of young women, or maybe they were teenaged girls dressed as women, with scarlet lipstick around their mouths and eyes blackened with kohl, wearing parti-colored blouses that exposed their bare shoulders and throats. "Hey, big fellow, you looking for company tonight?" the first one said, and I shook my head no. The other grabbed me by the arm and pulled me close, and I found myself thrilled by the mingled odor of her sweat and flowery perfume. While she held me enthralled, her friend, who was prettier and a few years older and whose makeup was not so garish, slid her hands in and out of all four of my trouser pockets in a flash like a professional finger smith. Finding nothing, not even an empty wallet, she backed away and shook her head.

The younger one said, "When you get your pay, honey, c'mon back. We'll try it again."

I said that I didn't work for pay.

She laughed and repeated to her friend what I had said, and she laughed, too, and the two of them walked quickly away from me, as if I had insulted them.

It was dark when, still bedazzled, I returned to our campsite. I might have stayed out there on the midway late into the night, had I not been hungry and had I not been so eager to bring my findings back to Sadie. In my absence, Elder John had returned from the exhibition hall and had a fine bed of red coals glowing beneath the grill. Sadie had moved her chair next to the fire pit and was tending to a bubbling pot of stew made with black beans brought from New Bethany and a ham bone that she said Elder John had purchased from a pig farmer's exhibit sales counter. I stood over the pot and closed my eyes and inhaled. She said she had flavored it with paprika and an onion and honey and cinnamon.

Elder John stood beneath a live oak tree a few feet away, sharing out a jug of apple ginger cider with a stranger, a short, nearly bald man in a white linen suit and starched white shirt and a Western-style black string tie. Elder John waved me over and introduced him as Dr. Cyrus Teed and said my name, "Brother Harley," and we shook hands. He was a pale, citified fellow of late middle age. His face and hands were soft and pudgy, his bright blue eyes cold and intense behind spectacles, and although I had remained silent, he stared at me with his mouth half open as if I had just said something astonishing.

Elder John flashed a slight, knowing smile and said, "Among his people Dr. Teed is known as Koresh. Which is ancient Persian for Cyrus, is it not, Dr. Teed?"

"It is indeed."

"And therefore his people are known as Koreshans," Elder John said. "They number in the hundreds—"

"Thousands!"

"*Thousands*. They have a thriving settlement down Fort Myers way, out there on the banks of the Estero River estuary. Very pretty spot," he added. "Three hundred and twenty acres, he was just telling me. They're not farmers or herdsmen like us, though. More like regular business people. Shopkeepers."

"Correct. We have a bakery, a general store, a concrete manufactory, a weekly newspaper, and several other businesses that serve the wider community. Even a college, with students coming from all over the world to study Koreshanity with me."

"Koreshanity," I said. Sadie watched and listened by the fire. It was she I wanted to be speaking with, not Elder John in one of his sly, self-amused moods and this pompous little man with his weird invented name. I knew a little of the Koreshans, who were generally regarded by the Shakers and the World alike as fools and dupes. Koresh himself, Dr. Cyrus Teed, was viewed as a heretical charlatan. He claimed to be immortal, believed in reincarnation, and argued that the universe was enclosed inside the earth rather than outside it, that the earth was hollow, the sun a gigantic battery at the center of the earth's interior and the stars and planets the reflected light of the sun. He called his theory "cellular cosmogony" and practiced alchemy, among other pseudo-sciences. But he also preached celibacy and communal living, like the Shakers, which made it difficult for the Believers to dismiss the Koreshans out of hand. Despite their religious and metaphysical differences, there was among all the utopian sects back then a fairly high degree of mutual respect, as long as they could find a few points of social agreement, like celibacy and communal living.

The truth is, at that time I myself shared almost none of the Shakers' beliefs, although I respected their essential goodness and devotion to one another and to work. Unlike Mother and my younger brothers, who had become true Believers by then, I still held on to the secular materialism of the Ruskinites that I had been taught as a child in Graylag and Waycross. Everything I had learned since then of human nature and the World only confirmed those early teachings. I was no mystic and did not wish to become one.

My twin, Pence, made a good external show of his commitment to Shakerism, but he had recently confessed to me that as soon as he turned eighteen he was gone from New Bethany. He planned go west, maybe to Texas or California, and become a cattleman, or else enlist in the army and become a cavalry man. He loved horses more than people, he said. He said outright that he did not believe in God or Jesus or the divinity of Mother Ann and did not intend to become a Shaker. I might have wanted to go west with Pence or even enlist in the army, had it not meant leaving Sadie Pratt. As long as she was at New Bethany, I would remain there, too. If she ever left New Bethany, I would follow her. I revealed none of this to Pence, however.

Elder John and Koresh resumed what sounded like a discussion concerning the ways the two communities might cooperate to influence the Florida state legislature and governor in matters of mutual interest, and I edged away from them and squatted down next to Sadie by the fire. Before I had a chance to tell her all that I had seen at the midway, Elder John invited Koresh to join us for supper, and he happily accepted. While the four of us sat together at a nearby picnic table and ate, Sadie and I mostly remained silent and the two leaders of their respective colonies continued negotiations for a joint lobbying effort at the state capital.

After we finished eating, Elder John and his new friend and colleague, Koresh, the reincarnated Babylonian king who in his previous existence had freed the Jews from captivity and returned them to Israel, decided that they, too, wished to visit the midway. Elder John asked Sadie if she would like to join them, but she declared that she had been weakened by the journey from New Bethany and was too tired to walk anywhere that distant. He said in that case I should stay at our camp and keep her company and watch over our belongings, and I happily agreed, and the two men of religion marched off into the carnival night.

When they were gone, she said to me, "I don't like that man, Harley. I don't trust his motives."

I assured her that I didn't like or trust him, either.

She said that she felt protective of Elder John, that he was too honest and openhearted a man to be dealing with someone like Koresh.

"I fear that Mr. Koresh has designs on New Bethany, somehow. I heard him say that he wants to come out and speak to the brethren about his visions and teachings, and Elder John in his kindly way agreed to that. Some of the brethren are weak-minded, you know, sweetly so, especially when it comes to religion. They could be influenced by a man like him to go over to Koreshanism, or whatever it's called."

"Koreshanity," I said, and gathered up our metal dishes and cups and prepared to carry them to the river to wash. "Actually, I think Elder John may have his own designs. I don't feel protective of him at all," I said. "He wouldn't mind having a commercial base for New Bethany's produce and livestock down near Fort Myers. He'd like to be able to combine Koresh's shops and shopkeepers and warehouses by the sea and rail lines with our inland farmers and herdsmen and shepherds and beekeepers. He could make good, prosperous use of easy access to the wider market of Fort Myers and the port for shipping our produce and cattle to Cuba and the cities of the North. No, I think Elder John has big ambitions for New Bethany," I told her. "And for himself."

This shocked Sadie. She accused me again of being jealous of Elder John because of his attentions to her. "You don't want me to love him at all," she said. "You think I love him more than you! And you think I love him in a romantic way, don't you?"

I didn't respond to her charge. Everything she said was painfully true. Silently, I carried our supper dishes down to the river and by a large, flat rock sat down, rolled up my sleeves, and began to rinse them clean. It was nearly dark there, lit only by the moon reflected off the water and by the night sky, paled by the lights of the midway and the racetrack beyond. Then suddenly she was kneeling beside me.

She placed a hand on my bare forearm and said, "I'm sorry, Harley. It was wrong of me, wrong to defend Elder John by impugning your motives. We are close, he and I, it's true. In some ways as close as you and I. But in other ways, not as much. You and I are nearer in age than he and I. He's more like a father to me, Harley, the father I never had, and I've revealed to him things that I would not have dared reveal to you. Things that happened to me in the past that I was ashamed of. And he comforted me and showed me that I needn't be ashamed."

"But Sadie, anything you could tell Elder John you could tell to me."

She kept her hand on my forearm and remained silent for a few moments. Finally, she said, "Yes, Harley, you're right. You're no longer a boy. I've treated you like a boy for too long." Then she told me that her doctor back in Rhode Island, who was married and a much-admired member of the Warwick community, had tried to seduce her. When she rebuffed him, he feared that she would tell her mother or some other confidant and it would get back to his wife. He was afraid to continue treating her as a patient, and she was reluctant to go on seeing him in any capacity, so when he offered to send her to Sunshine Home for treatment, she accepted his offer. He paid for her travel to Florida, and for the first year he covered the costs of her stay at the sanitarium. She was ashamed for letting him pay for her care and wanted no contact with him. After a year of not having heard from her, and believing that she would never return to Warwick and probably had died from her illness anyhow, he stopped paying Sunshine Home. That's when Eldress Mary allowed her to become a ward of the sanitarium, and then, when Sunshine Home closed, a ward of New Bethany. "Elder John knows all this," she said. "I confided in him. And now you. But no one else knows, not even Eldress Mary."

"Why did you tell Elder John?"

"Well, he is an elder. He's a good man. And he's used to hearing the confessions of the brethren."

"Yes, from the males. But not the women. Why didn't you go to Eldress Mary instead? She hears the women's confessions. You had nothing to confess anyhow. It's obvious that the doctor in Warwick was the sinner, not you."

"I didn't think I had done anything wrong, but still, I felt ashamed. I had taken money from him. Can you understand how that affects a woman? My thinking was confused, and as Elder John is a wise older man, I thought he could help clarify my thoughts. And he did, or I wouldn't have been able to tell all this to you now. He made this conversation possible. Besides, as you know, a woman who makes her confession of sins to the eldress is taking the first step to becoming a Shaker. I wasn't ready for that. I'm still not."

"Nor am I. But before long I'll be of an age where it'll be expected of me."

"What will you do?"

"It depends on what you do," I said. "As long as you are at New Bethany, Sadie, I will be at New Bethany. I'll do whatever makes that possible."

"Even lie? Even make a false confession to Elder John?"

"Yes, even lie."

"Before God?"

Her face was close to mine. She turned to me, and her eyes looked so deeply into my soul and saw me with such astounding clarity that it was as if I had never been seen before, as if all my life until this moment I had been invisible, even to myself. I said, "Yes. I am willing to lie before God. That's how much I love you, Sadie."

"And I will lie for you," she said. She leaned forward a sliver and tipped her head toward me, and I returned the gesture, and then we kissed. A long, hungry, devouring kiss, and I knew, as it was happening, that everything was different now, that there would always be this moment, and the rest of my life would be divided between *before* this moment and *after*.

REEL #9

Maybe it's luck, maybe it's only a meaningless coincidence, that I reached the end of that reel just as I was telling about the first time Sadie and I kissed and declared our love for each other. In any case, swapping out a filled reel of tape for a fresh blank one gave me a chance to get up from my chair and leave the porch and walk through the house and clear my mind of its turbulence, which I needed nearly as much when telling about that first kiss and declaration of love as I did when it actually happened, some sixty-four years ago.

I was a seventeen-year-old boy in love with a twenty-four-year-old woman who, while not yet a full member of a society sworn to celibacy, was a novitiate and a ward of that society. I was a resident novitiate in the same society myself, a secret nonbeliever, and was expected to ask for full membership as soon as I turned eighteen. For all I knew at the time, this woman, whom I loved above all others and whom I would continue to love for the rest of my life, was dying of tuberculosis. She might recover, of course. But when Sadie first came over from Sunshine Home to live at New Bethany, Eldress Mary had let it slip that the Sunshine Home doctor had given her barely six months at most. That was over a year ago, however, and she seemed now only a little worse than when she first arrived.

I didn't know what was true and what wasn't. Though she had not yet told me much about her past, especially regarding her romantic life, I knew that at least one man had attempted to seduce her. She had not lived in as cosseted and affluent and patrician a manner as I had imagined, and well into her adulthood she had been living unprotected in the World, so very likely there had been others who had tried to seduce her, for she was a young woman and beautiful and passionate. For all I knew, there may have been someone who had succeeded in seducing her. Possibly the doctor in Warwick, despite her claim to have rebuffed him. Or more than one. And what about Elder John? I could not count him out, regardless of her description of him as the father she never had. All these thoughts and fancies and fears went roaring through my head that night sixty-four years ago, as we embraced and kissed again and again on the rock down by the Hillsborough River, when Sadie abruptly pulled away from me and looked over my shoulder to the knoll above, and when I turned and followed her gaze, I saw the silhouette of Elder John, hands on hips, staring down at us.

He stood a hundred feet away and uphill and in semidarkness. I didn't know how long he had been watching us or what he had actually seen, but by the time we scrambled back up to the camp-site, he had settled at the foot of a live oak tree and was reading a newspaper and said nothing to us. As if in passing, Sadie casually mentioned that I had suffered a shoulder cramp, a muscle spasm, and she had been able to undo it. She had learned how to massage away shoulder and back cramps and muscle spasms while aiding the patients at Sunshine Home, she said. The patients often felt their muscles tighten and seize when they resumed physical activity after a lengthy period of inactivity, she went on.

I was impressed by her quick and easy and digressive explanation of our embraces. "Lugging those duffels from the train station must have done it," I lamely added. "After a long day's inactivity, no doubt."

"No doubt," Elder John said. And that seemed to be the end of it. Although for the remainder of our time at the fair, except when he himself was with us, he kept us apart. From early morning till evening, I manned our stand at the exhibition hall, giving out samples and selling pineapples and making the spiel he had taught me in our wagon coming up from New Bethany and on the train to Tampa. Meanwhile he tasked Sadie with small chores at the campsite or accompanied her on strolls through the midway or brought her along with him when he met with the wholesalers or when he displayed our pineapples to the judges. The rest of the time he urged her to take regular solitary rests in her folding chair by the river. "We don't want you to overexert yourself, or when we get home, Eldress Mary will surely give me what for," he said to Sadie. "She only allowed me to bring you along if I promised that I'd make you rest in a quiet place whenever possible."

Dr. Teed, or Koresh, passed by our stand at the hall several times, helping himself to handfuls of samples, and at one point he walked off with a whole pineapple without paying for it. When I called him on it, he claimed that Elder John had told him to take one for himself to show to his Koreshan brethren down at Estero, and I let him go.

Later, I asked Elder John if this was true. He laughed and said, "No, it's not, but it doesn't matter, as long as it opens the door for an order from the Koreshans' general store." But Elder John had a greater interest in the Koreshans than selling them pineapples. "He may be a fraud or just a little cracked, that Dr. Teed, but he's got a bunch of followers down there who could easily become ours, which would save their souls and contribute to our population of workers and in that way help advance the commercial interests of New Bethany. I do have to look after that," he said, as if reciting instructions from the trustees at Mount Lebanon. "Our commercial interests."

After three days, we broke camp and departed for home on the morning train, and at mid-afternoon we retrieved our wagon and horses from the livery stable in St. Cloud. New Bethany's pineapples had received the gold medal, which pleased Elder John immensely, for he had been immediately rewarded with more orders from Northern wholesalers than he could fill with this season's entire crop. From St. Cloud to Narcoossee, Elder John drove the horses, and the whole way he talked proudly of the gold medal and the Northern markets. Sadie sat beside him, as before, and I stretched out behind them in the wagon box, emptied now of all but our duffels and tarpaulin, and mostly listened.

"Just to keep up with demand we'll have to expand our pineapple cultivation to at least twice its present size," he told us. "We'll need more workers before spring. This is worrisome, though. Our market is growing, but our membership has not kept pace." He kept returning to what he saw as a serious labor shortage. Demand had exceeded supply, and he was clearly anxious about the imbalance and seemed to regard the conversion of the Koreshans as a possible solution.

I viewed it differently, and in front of Sadie, perhaps to impress her, I told him so. "Shouldn't the conversion of nonbelievers into believers be motivated, not by a wish to raise and sell more pineapples, but by Mother Ann's command to bring people from the World into the Shaker fold?" I asked him. "I mean, for example, shouldn't we be motivated more by a desire to save the poor, deluded Koreshans from the thrall of a fraud like Dr. Teed than to expand our pineapple acreage? I know that converting the Koreshans into Shakers may well help us grow and sell more of New Bethany's produce. But it should do so only as an unintended consequence," I asserted.

Elder John didn't have many weaknesses, but I thought I had ferreted one out and wanted to expose it to Sadie. He was a man easily tempted by the prospect of profit. Not that he was greedy or covetous, for he had no apparent desire for luxury or physical comfort or for the envy of his neighbors. He was like a compulsive gambler who is more interested in winning than in obtaining the winner's actual prize. For him, life was a contest in which his main goal was to best the other contestants. Making a profit was just one way to do that. People like Elder John make good capitalists, effective salesmen, and successful politicians, but poor religious leaders.

If one is interested in having one's life tuned to the needs of humanity and having one's soul join God's immortal chorus, if one wishes to put his "hands to work and hearts to God," then, quite simply, one must abandon competition, winning, and the need to show a profit. One must abandon the belief that life is a contest. "We Shakers have to forget the bottom line," I said to him. "We must not try to gather in the lost and afflicted men and women of the World merely in order to expand the work force of the community so as to sell more pineapples to the World than the fellow who farms the land down the road."

This bold peroration did not seem to have the desired effect, then or later. And what was the desired effect? Looking back now, although I did not know it then, I can see that I wanted both to challenge and to impress Elder John. And I wanted to impress Sadie with my intelligence and with my logical and moral consistency, in contrast to what I regarded as his inconsistency and hypocrisy. But my long-range intent was to alienate Sadie from Elder John without diluting his loyalty to her. I did not want him and Eldress Mary to question their commitment to letting her continue to reside at New Bethany. If he decided that there was no chance of his winning her favor, no chance to keep her at his side, he might call off the contest between him and me and send her back to Rhode Island or to a sanitarium far away from Florida. Or, if he thought he was in fact losing that contest, he might decide instead simply to evict me from the community, which as an elder he was empowered to do, and still keep her at his side, and win the contest that way.

As it turned out, he did neither. He didn't send Sadie on her way. In fact, shortly after our return from Tampa, her health worsened, and that winter he and Eldress Mary invited her to move from her tent to a guest bedroom on the third floor of the main house, above the schoolroom and the floor where they each kept their own bedrooms. Nor did he evict me from New Bethany, not even in March that year when my brother Pence and I turned eighteen and thus were old enough now to leave New Bethany for the World if we wished. I did not declare one way or the other. I simply watched our birthday come and go, and thanks, no doubt, to the New Bethany labor shortage, I was not asked to choose between leaving and becoming a Shaker. I could remain as a resident novitiate.

Then, at a Sabbath meeting in early April, Pence publicly announced to the entire community that he had decided to leave

New Bethany and live in the World. He said that he intended to ride the rails to Texas like a hobo and work as a cowhand on one of the many ranches there. Mother and Raymond and Royal and Rachel, along with the brethren and the elders, embraced him and wished him well and made him promise to write regularly to his New Bethany family and return often to visit. I, too, embraced him and wished him every success out there in the World. But I was oddly unmoved by his departure and was almost relieved to see him go, as if it signaled a sloughing-off of a part of myself that I did not wish to keep. As if I had committed a crime and he were a witness for the prosecution.

But twins are blessed, or cursed, with a profound interdependency, and it's hard to sever it, because they share nearly every experience, especially within the family, from infancy, childhood, and adolescence into adulthood. Pence and I had been deliberately separated early on and removed from our original family and placed into a much larger, more dispersed one, so that by the time we turned eighteen we barely felt like brothers, let alone twins. From infancy through childhood, until we came to New Bethany, we had mirrored each other, like the two hands of a single person, and as the dominant twin, I was the right hand, Pence the left. When we looked at each other we saw ourselves looking back, only reversed. Since entering adolescence, with Pence working days and often overnight among the cattle and other livestock on the open range and me attached to the apiary near the main house and teaching in the schoolroom, he and I had grown apart. In accord with Shaker policy regarding family members, we slept in separate bedrooms in the men's quarters and ate at different tables in the dining room. In barely noticeable increments and without our knowing how it had happened, in small ways and large, Pence and I, despite the force of our attachment, no longer felt or acted like twins.

The morning of his departure, on his way to meet the *Coquina* at the lake, he stopped off at the apiary. He carried all his belongings in a rucksack. When you depart from the Shaker community, you are allowed to take away only what you brought on your back and carried by hand on your arrival. We Manns arrived from Rosewell

Plantation owning nothing more than the tattered clothes we wore and a few cooking implements, so that is what Pence took with him in his rucksack, along with a chunk of dried beef and a large piece of cheddar cheese and a half dozen hard-boiled eggs, he told me when I asked him the contents of his pack. He said that he regretted that he was not allowed to take away his braided whip or his tanned boar-skin chaps, which he had hoped to bring with him to Texas. He said he was sad to leave his horse, Bosh. He did not say he was sad to leave me or Mother or our younger brothers and sister.

We stood side by side and looked across the meadow and the circular grapefruit orchard to the lakeside pier and the waiting barge below. We shared an awkward silence for a moment, until finally I turned and faced him and clapped him on both shoulders and in a hearty voice wished him well out there in the World. "Time for you to go," I told him.

He nodded sadly and then said, "Harley, what about Sadie?"

Suddenly we were twin brothers again. "What about her?"

"What are you going to do?"

"Do? Only God can save Sadie. I'm not God."

"No, not that. You're in love with her. It's why you're staying on, isn't it?"

I said nothing in response. I could not lie to him. He knew the truth as well as I.

"Nothing can ever come of it," he said.

"No! She loves me as much as I love her!"

"She doesn't love *you*, Harley. She loves your attention. Come away with me to Texas."

"I can't!"

"They need beekeepers in Texas, too," he said. "I can be a ranch hand and you can be a beekeeper. We'll find work, and we'll live together."

"You don't understand!" I said, almost in tears. "Sadie and I love each other! She may die soon, and I can't let her die without me. But if she recovers her health, which is still possible, we can leave New Bethany together. We can join you out in Texas."

"Harley, she doesn't love you. Whether she lives or dies, she loves no one. Or else she loves another."

"No, that's impossible! You don't understand," I said.

"She loves no one, or she loves another," he repeated. "And you know who he is. And so does most everyone else at New Bethany. It's the main reason I'm leaving. The hypocrisy. Especially Elder John's. It's why you should leave, too."

"No, no, no!" I cried. "You mustn't say that. She loves me, and I love her, and I will stay here at New Bethany until she is well. Or until she dies from her illness. That's all that needs to be said."

We were silent for several minutes, and I managed to calm down and was able to more or less restore myself to myself and my delusions. "Now go, brother. Go and prosper out there. Write me letters, and I will write you back," I said.

He didn't answer, just slowly, sadly shook his head. We embraced, and he walked down the slope to the lake. He was tall and slim and looked like a Western ranch hand already, a handsome young cowboy.

Oh, Pence, oh, my beloved lost brother! My twin, my other half. My conscience. I should have listened to him. I should have believed him. I should have followed him when he went west, first to Texas and then drifting on to California together, where my presence at his side would have protected him from his melancholy and the loneliness and isolation that prompted him to enlist in the army, where he became a cavalry officer in command of the 15th Cavalry Regiment and went to war in Europe and got shot off his horse on the Western Front by a German sniper and never returned, dead and buried in Flanders Fields. Oh, my poor brother!

Everything in both our lives would have been different if on the day Pence told me that Sadie Pratt loved no one or not me but another, I had simply believed him and had admitted to myself the absurdity of staying at New Bethany. I would have gone out west with him, and he would not have gone to war, he would have lived on, perhaps even to today, deep into old age, as I have lived on, and we would have ended up a pair of garrulous old men who never married, never had children, two old brothers sitting side by side on a front porch of a ranch house way out west in Altadena, California, reminiscing together about our strange childhood and youth among the Ruskinites and Rosewell Plantation and the Florida Shakers, instead of him dead in a grave in Europe marked only by a white cross and me sitting here alone in St. Cloud, at the end of a wasted, foolish, solitary life, talking into a recording machine about a young man's impossible love and suspicion and an awful, unforgivable betrayal.

I think about all this, and it's still mysterious to me, but somehow, as long as Pence was living and working at New Bethany, there was an equilibrium to my life and the life of the community. They were nicely balanced, singly and together, and though I was taking certain secret risks with both my life and that of the community, no one and nothing was the worse for it. As long as Pence was there, the Shaker colony throve, and the people were content with their work and crafts and filled to overflowing with love of one another and with love of God and the Shakers' twinned saviors, Jesus and Mother Ann. Pence was not the cause of this peaceful time, I know. His presence was only associated with it, coincident. But the truth is, when he was among us, all this transpired as if it were to be expected. As if it were meant to be. There was no disruption.

When Pence was one of us, the daily and weekly and seasonal spiritual exercises and ceremonies proceeded apace in the way they had been codified and laid down generations earlier by Mother Ann and the early Shaker elders and eldresses, our founding mothers and fathers, unhindered by excesses of emotion or the sour tinge of skepticism or temptations from the World, marking the start of every day and all the stops along the way to day's end, as if guided by a cosmic clock and calendar. When Pence was among us and the season called for planting, the fields were plowed and harrowed, and seeds went into the soil, and the shoots rose from the dark, fertile ground as expected, and the plants produced their leaves and grains and vegetables in a timely fashion, and the orchards and groves were weighed down with fruits and berries, and the bees gave up their honey, the sheep their wool, the cows their milk and cream, the hens produced their eggs, and the swine and cattle, when they had given birth to large numbers of healthy offspring, sacrificed their bodies for us, and the harvest was abundant twice a year, for when Pence lived with us there was no frost and no drought or flood, and the livestock and the cattle were healthy and sleek, and there were no hurricanes or blight or plagues of locusts or uncontrollable wildfires to disrupt the peaceful cycle of birth, life, and death in the community. And during this time, while Pence still resided at New Bethany, though I was secretly surrendering to my foolish, obsessive love of Sadie Pratt and letting it nourish my relentless competition with Elder John, no one suffered from it, no one, not Elder John, not Sadie, not anyone in our community, not even me. It was only when Pence left that everything fell into disarray and the suffering began.

The first sign of the darkness descending came within days of my brother's departure from New Bethany when, just as the bananas were about to be harvested, a sudden, unprecedented late-spring freeze blackened and destroyed the entire crop. A cold front from middle Canada had inexplicably slipped down through the prairie states, spreading as far south as Tennessee and the Carolinas, where it got overridden by a cyclonic irruption off the Gulf. The warm rains from the south fell through the cold Canadian air below and caused an unrelenting ice storm all across the Southeast, and when the front and its chilled rains finally moved east to the Atlantic, the skies cleared, but the trapped Canadian cold lingered, and for a day and a night the temperature in central and north Florida did not rise above twenty-five degrees.

There was nothing to do but cut off the banana stalks at the ground and bury the plants and the blackened fruit and start over—two hundred ten-foot-high stalks and leaves and a thousand pounds of bananas tossed like corpses into trenches. It would take nearly two years before new banana plants could produce fruit again. The strange, aberrant spring freeze also killed the blossoms of all our citrus trees, ending the season early for oranges and lemons and grapefruit and cutting in half our anticipated yearly revenue from citrus. Its effect on the apiary was equally calamitous. The bees were stunned into listlessness by the sudden cold, and when a day later they woke and began to search again for nectar for their honey, the blossoms they sought were lying dead on the ground in a bed of melting frost. Brother Hiram and I were obliged to clear and shut down nearly half our hives that spring, making the dear man so despondent and grief-stricken over his starved and dying creatures that he decided to go back to his unwelcoming family in Maryland, leaving me to tend the remaining bees alone.

At the same time, several other brethren, men and women who had no skills other than those of a laboring farmworker or orchard keeper, also decided to depart from us, for there was not enough work for them in the fields and groves of New Bethany to pay for their board and shelter, nor was there work at any of the farms and citrus plantations nearby, for the region's entire agricultural industry was all but destroyed by the freeze. Elder John urged the workers to stay and switch over to making turpentine from the pines off the hammock, a dirty, grinding kind of labor much despised. But the workers, all of whom were White—and not all of them Southerners, either—thought making turpentine was best done by Blacks, and they were reluctant for that reason alone to undertake it. They were unmarried, childless men, mostly novitiate residents, not true Believers, so it was easy for them to pack up and leave New Bethany and migrate further south to the farms and orchards outside Miami, which had gone untouched by the frost, or shift north to Georgia and the Carolinas, where they were harvesting crops of a hardier kind that could withstand an occasional freeze.

Suddenly the population of New Bethany had shrunk to nearly half its previous size, and the community was facing both a severe shortage of resident workers and much-diminished crops. Even those crops that survived the freeze, like potatoes and cabbages and onions, survived only in part, so that we who remained at New Bethany could barely feed ourselves with the products of our fields. We could not even adequately feed our livestock, many of which went barren that spring or miscarried or simply refused to breed.

With the dispersal of so many workers and our much-lowered population, we still had too many people living at New Bethany to feed and too few to produce the food. About a third of the remaining residents were not confessed-and-sworn members of the Society of Believers. In recent years, under the leadership of Elder John and Eldress Mary, there had been a natural, inevitable shrinkage of the percentage of residents who were actual Shakers, with many of the members, as they died or moved away, being replaced by people like me and Sadie, men and women who professed a love for Shakerism, but for one reason or another showed little interest in actually becoming Believers. And a few were mentally deficient individuals or had a criminal past or were too spiritually eccentric for normal civilian life or, through no fault of their own, had been cast out of worldly society. Others, like Sadie, had nowhere else to go. And some, like me, were too attached to another resident to leave.

This might well have been the case for the Shaker communities in New York and New England, too, or out in Kentucky and Ohio. We'd been told that those families, like ours, had undergone serious population loss, due to the aging of the longtime members and, of course, to our vow of celibacy, making it impossible for the Shakers to be fruitful and multiply on their own. Standards for recruitment fell precipitously, especially at New Bethany, where most of the newcomers in '06 and '07 and '08, the years leading up to the Great Freeze, were lost souls and castoffs. We were in Florida, not upstate New York or New England or the upper Midwest, and Florida from its beginnings has served as a catch basin for the world's detritus. It's where you go when your prospects elsewhere have ended, and you've not yet settled into despair, and you still think there's a slight chance you can start over, and no one will notice your previous failings or hold them against you while you gather your bearings and begin again.

I like to think that it all starts with the Seminoles, who once were Cherokees, driven out of the Carolinas and Georgia by the early Americans, a purge that went mostly unnoticed, and the African slaves and indentured Whites in flight from the Southern plantations, escapees and refugees who knew they'd not be pursued with much energy, and after the Civil War, the poor White sharecroppers who, looking for a piece of land of their own, claimed it wherever they saw it. For all of them, Florida was a place to heal their wounds in hiding and start their lives over.

Or go back further, to the Spanish and French privateers and pirates who, failing to get a decent landhold in the Caribbean, grabbed on to this vast, flat, semitropical wilderness that no one else wanted. And before them, the conquistadores who sailed east a generation too late to conquer anything worth conquering, Santo Domingo and Cuba and Mexico and Peru having already been taken, so they made Florida a part of Spain and then a part of France. Even the Indian bands who eons earlier migrated down from the highlands and prairies of the continent proper to this uninhabited marshland, where the land mass had only recently risen dripping from the mingled waters of the Atlantic and the Caribbean Sea and the Gulf of Mexico—even they were lost souls and castoffs. Even they were detritus.

Or come forward to our nineteenth and twentieth centuries, with the arrival of the land speculators, the Yankee fortune-seekers buying up thousand-acre tracts of mostly underwater land for pennies on the dollar from the federal and state governments and reselling it in five-acre plats to lesser speculators, everyone lending and borrowing other people's money to keep the transfers going, until the federal and state handout became a boom and the boom became a bust and the last person holding the debt went bankrupt.

And in my own lifetime, it's been the refugees from Europe's wars and pogroms and the survivors of the concentration camps who have migrated to Florida, and a few decades later, people in flight from Cuba and Haiti and Central America have splashed ashore, while all along retirees from the Northern states have come seeking a place in the sun to finish out their allotted fourscore-and-ten snoozing on a park bench or casting a lure from an aluminum Sears, Roebuck motorboat on the flats or hitting golf balls, while behind them their children and grandchildren and everyone else's children and grandchildren arrive in station wagons, drawn south as if by a state-sized sinkhole to the American dream world, the Magic Kingdom, Disney's playtime plantation. My world.

It has been this way here in Florida for millennia, and it probably always will be. It was the same back in '07 and '08 and '09 at New Bethany—first the boom, when the number of our residents and the acreage under cultivation expanded greatly and we won the gold medal at the South Florida Fair and the farm prospered beyond all expectations or need. And then, after Pence departed and the Great Freeze arrived, the bust, and the New Bethany colony shrank to fewer than a dozen men and women, one of the women my own mother, and six children, three of them my younger siblings.

The colony was now barely able to feed the colonists. And we were indeed a colony, but like seventeenth-century Jamestown without the help of the Powhatans or Plymouth without the Wampanoags. We had our Seminoles, but they weren't much interested in helping New Bethany. They had long ago slipped into hiding in the Everglades and had only recently emerged from the swamp to begin discussing with the governor and the state legislature the prospect of opening casinos on reservation lands. Boom and bust and boom again. For as long as Florida has existed, that's how it has gone here. And now New Bethany was trapped in the bust end of the cycle, waiting for the boom to return.

If it had just been the Great Freeze that afflicted us that year and the resulting drop-off in the number of our resident workers, the community, under the leadership of Elder John and Eldress Mary, most likely would have recovered and prospered as before, and in another year or even less would have attracted new and past colonists wanting a piece of that prosperity. Elder John's and Eldress Mary's tireless energy and force of personality and competence seemed only to increase under stress. The two moved and thought and talked faster than ever and were more meticulously organized and even more certain of their opinions and strategies than in the past, and they stayed calm throughout. We, the brethren and novitiates who remained, worked longer hours, regardless of the nature of our work, and voluntarily joined the field workers, when we normally would have taken a little leisure time for study or prayer or letter writing. But in midsummer, just when it appeared that the coming harvest from our gardens and fields was likely to be sufficient to meet all our standing orders and still leave enough to fill our own larders and bins and feed our residents and livestock until the following harvest, we realized that we had been without rain for an exceedingly long time.

By early August we knew that we were experiencing a drought, and at the nightly and Sabbath noontime services Elder John and Eldress Mary led us in prayers for rain. But the rain didn't come. The soil dried out and turned crumbly and then to dust, and the leaves of our plants shriveled and went from green to yellow to brown, and those fruits and vegetables that matured at all came in at half their usual size and weight. The sun beat down relentlessly. Day after day, week after week, we looked west in the evenings in vain for clouds to gather above the Gulf and at dawn looked east toward the Atlantic, but no clouds came. Despite the heat, thick and heavy with humidity, the usual sudden late-afternoon showers never fell to earth. We watched the rain evaporate in the sky before it reached the overheated ground.

We lugged buckets and hauled barrels of water in wagons from the canals and lakes and cisterns and watered the crops and animals as best we could, and Elder John had us, men and women alike, dig irrigation ditches in the fields close enough to connect to the steadily shrinking bodies of water and marshes before they turned to muck and mud. Our dug wells and water tanks were going dry, and the windmills, whenever an errant puff of air blew through, had begun to pump air. Brothers Amos and George abandoned their cattle to forage as best they could out on the arid range and came in to the farm and joined us in the attempt to save our crops. The elderly Shakers, like Sister Beth, who had recently retired from the print shop, and Brother Ezekiel, whose leather shop had effectively been taken over by my brother Raymond, joined the effort, and the children, including Rachel, who was then only seven years old, were told to shut down their schooling and join their teacher, Sister Hazel, in the bucket brigade. Even Sadie tried to help, but when carrying her water bucket filled from Live Oak Lake to the nearby pineapple yard for three days in a row, though she had complied with Elder John's instructions to walk slowly and rest often, she nearly collapsed of exhaustion and had to retire to her bed.

This greatly concerned and frightened me. After seeing her stumble and drop her bucket and nearly fall and with Eldress Mary's help go into the main house, I brought my concern directly to Elder John.

He and I were near enough to the house to have seen what happened. We had been at work in the cabbage field together digging a narrow channel for irrigation and were about to open the banked end of the ditch to an inlet we'd cut from the adjacent canal. Though he was the chief engineer and operations chief for the elaborate network of trenches and ditches and pipes that he'd designed and that we were constructing all across the farm, as well as manager of the day-and-night bucket brigade and wagon-borne barrels of water taken from the lakes, he also labored hard with pick and shovel in the fields under the relentless sun alongside the rest of us. Much as I wanted to fault him for something, for *anything*, I could not.

But I tried anyhow. "Sister Sadie should not have been told to join the bucket brigade," I said. "Especially in this heat."

"I agree, I agree," he said. "I told her to stay inside. But she insisted on joining us, brother. She said she was ashamed for not helping. You should go and speak to her. She trusts you and loves you and will more likely do as you say than what I say. Go," he told me. "I can finish the trench here myself."

And so I did. I wiped my face with my handkerchief and put down my spade and walked quickly away from the field of shriveled cabbages to the main house and went inside. I looked into the kitchen and the dining room and the main office and hallooed for Eldress Mary, but she didn't seem to be there. No one was in the house. They must all be working in the fields, I thought, so I took the liberty of going up the center stairs unannounced. The house had three floors, the first for general and collective use, the second given over to Eldress Mary's and Elder John's private quarters with a bedroom, dressing room, and small office workspace for each and the empty schoolroom separating the two suites. A narrow stairwell led from the schoolroom to the third floor, where I knew three bedrooms were kept for visitors to New Bethany and a fourth had been used for nearly a year now by Sadie Pratt. In my six years at New Bethany I had never ventured this far in the house, not even when I was spending most of my days as a student and teacher in the schoolroom below.

At the top of the stairs I came to a short central hallway. The space was attic-like, low-ceilinged and dimly lit. A pair of windows less than a foot off the floor at either end let in light. It was ventilated by the open windows and insulated with palmetto thatch and was surprisingly cool. The smell of the oiled cypress plank floors and roughly finished pine rafters and palmetto thatch filled the air. There were four doors off the hall, three of them open, one closed. I went to the door that was closed and softly knocked.

There was no response. "Sister Sadie, it's me, Brother Harley," I said. I assumed Eldress Mary was with her, so I added, "Elder John sent me to check on you."

Still no response. The door was unlatched, and when I touched the handle, it swung open unaided to a sizable corner room located on the shaded side of the house. The windows on two of the walls were open, and when I shut the door behind me, a light late-afternoon breeze passed between them. Sadie was alone, lying in her narrow bed. She had what looked like a damp cloth over her eyes and forehead. Her slender body was covered with a sheet. She appeared to be wearing the same pale-yellow cotton frock she had on earlier. A pitcher and a half-filled water glass and an unlit kerosene lantern were on the bedside table. The only other articles of furniture were a small chest of drawers and a narrow, head-high wardrobe and a low bookcase with a dozen or so books and a writing desk—old-style Shaker furniture crafted in local pine by Brother Edwin and the New Bethany brethren. It was a beautiful, calm room.

"Sadie, it's me," I said. "Are you all right?"

She removed the cloth from her face and tried a faint smile. She was very pale, and her dark eyes were hard and glowed like polished black stones. Speaking rapidly, she said, "Oh, Harley, I feel so ashamed of my weakness, I don't want to be up here like an invalid, I want to be out there helping the family, I want to carry water like the others or dig trenches like you." She spoke as if her thoughts and feelings were impossible to contain, and she didn't give me a chance to respond. We hadn't talked intimately for many weeks, partly because of the communal nature of life at New Bethany and partly out of a need for discretion, but also because we both knew we were being watched with mild wariness by the brethren, perhaps especially by Elder John and Eldress Mary. The Shakers were celibate and intent on keeping the sexes physically apart, yes, but they weren't naive. A young woman and a young man in their midst who had not yet confessed their sins and committed to Shakerism needed to be watched carefully. And I admit it, I was lustful, and I believed that Sadie, despite her illness and frailty, was filled with the female version of lust, although I had no clear idea of what that might be like. Also, I felt that our kisses and embraces months ago by the river at the fair had established a permanent bond between us, a secret trust that we shared with no one else, and I wanted to build upon it and believed that she did, too.

She moved aside a bit and while she talked she patted the edge of her bed, a silent command for me to sit, and I complied. She said that Eldress Mary had ordered her to stay in her bedroom and not come down for her meals, that someone would check on her periodically and bring food and drink to her along with anything else that she might need. Continuing to speak rapidly, her words tumbling over one another, she said that this kind of caring only caused her more pain and shame, and she would rather be expelled from New Bethany, cast out, like Eve out of Eden, to wander alone in the wilderness, than to be seen as useless and a burden of care, and she said that with everyone else in the New Bethany family making such an extreme sacrifice of their bodies and time and energy, their caring for her only exacerbated her illness, rather than diminished it. As if to prove her point, she began to cough and had to turn away from me, and when she did the top of her thin yellow frock, which was unbuttoned at the throat, slipped free of her shoulder, and I saw her beautiful long neck and the soft white curve of her shoulder and partially her breast.

I could not stop myself. I reached forward and touched the bare skin of her shoulder with my fingertips, as if needing to determine that she was real, as if to prove that I wasn't dreaming, for I had so often dreamed of seeing her lying like this in a disheveled state— her body partially naked and exposed to my sight, and in my dream

I reach forward and touch her. I was having trouble believing what I was seeing. Or doing. I did what I had done so many times in my dreams, some of them waking dreams. I had by then violated so many of the restrictions and prohibitions decreed by the faith of the people I lived with that it was a small step from our kisses and embraces and my dreams and fantasies to placing my hand on her naked shoulder and drawing her to me. Or did she come to me of her own volition? I could not tell the difference. We were both equally to blame for what happened then.

In the years that followed I have thought back to that dusky summer afternoon ten thousand times, to those few moments leading up to the moments that were outside of time, when Sadie and I first made love. I remember clearly in vivid detail all that preceded it—my walking from the cabbage field to the house, calling for Eldress Mary, going up the stairs to the second floor, then to the third, entering Sadie's room, sitting at the edge of her bed. I remember her words, her bare shoulder, I remember touching her cool skin. But then, though I know the facts of what happened next, I have no memory of it. It could have been hours or a day and a night or mere seconds, I could not say how long we lay together as consummating lovers, for I have no conscious memory of it, only the knowledge that it took place.

I can reason that it did not take long, for my memories resume with the sound of someone ascending the stairs from the schoolroom below and Sadie twisting away from me and pulling her clothing together, rebuttoning her dress as she left the bed and ran barefoot to the door. She stood by the door holding it shut and waited, until there was a quiet knock. We heard the easily recognizable voice of Sister Beth: "Sister Sadie, are you awake?"

Sadie looked at me in an oddly calm way and spoke toward me, away from the door, so as to be heard on the other side as if from a distance. "Yes, but I'm resting."

"Is there anything I can get for you, dear?"

"Not now, thank you, Sister Beth. Perhaps in an hour, some sassafras tea?"

"All right, dear. I'll come back in an hour."

We stood there, rearranging our clothing and listening to Sister Beth descend the stairs. Then we embraced and stared into each other's eyes and knew fully what we had done and that we would do it again as soon as we were able to be alone again. In silence, speaking only with our eyes, we began planning our next meeting.

REEL #10

I wasn't quite out of tape there. I had another five or six minutes left, but it seemed a useful place to stop and change reels. I needed to clear my whirling mind.

Some of the memories evoked in making this account have given me great pleasure, true. But some have brought pain and regret. And tears. My memory of that afternoon and making love to Sadie for the first time is as much one of pain and tearful regret as it is of love and ecstasy. Not because we were violating a cardinal rule upon which nearly every other Shaker rule was based, and not because it forced us into living with secrecy and lies, but because it initiated a sequence of events that in time would prove catastrophic for both of us and for many other people, men and women and even children, whom I loved and who were wholly innocent and undeserving of what our love affair eventually brought down on them.

Breaking the rule of celibacy was less of a sin than the secrecy and lies it required, for neither Sadie nor I was a Shaker as such. We had not confessed and taken the pledge. Had we been open about our love and the carnality of its nature and publicly confessed it, Elder John and Eldress Mary and the other Shakers, and even Mother, would not have been shocked, given our youth and the strength of our mutual attraction, nor would they have judged us for it. They simply would have asked us to end our love affair at once or leave New Bethany.

The Shakers were not deluded about human nature. They understood the temptations of the World and the difficulties of resisting them, perhaps especially for men and women who were young. Besides, during those years, late in the history of the Society of Believers, the monastic aspect of Shaker life was less a condition than an aspiration. Some of the early puritanism had been diluted. Joining with them, living among them as novitiates and working alongside them with common interests, sharing their commitment to communist and pacifist and feminist values and accepting their particular hierarchical distribution of authority among trustees and elders and eldresses and brethren and novitiates, sharply differentiated our life at New Bethany from life in the World. But in those latter days in the history of the Shakers it was not so immeasurable a difference as to force us to make a hard choice between them. And the Believers' somewhat eccentric version of the Christian faith? Their elevation of Mother Ann to the status of a deity on the level of Jesus Christ? For those who were not orthodox to begin with, those who were lukewarm Christians, that was easy enough to go along with. Even for people like me and Pence, who had been raised as spiritually inclined agnostics, and for Sadie, too, who had been raised, she told me, as a Roman Catholic and now considered herself lapsed. It was relatively easy for us to subscribe to "hands to work and hearts to God" and to accept "the gift to be simple."

It was about this time, the late summer of '08, when after nearly seven weeks without rain the drought had still not abated, Dr. Cyrus Teed, the man who called himself Koresh, showed up unannounced at New Bethany. Before the evening meal Elder John and Eldress Mary welcomed and introduced him to the assembled group and invited him to sit at the elders' table. Koresh, in his foppish white suit and professorial spectacles, bowed and thanked them for their hospitality and declared to the exhausted Shakers—the dozen men and women and six children who had spent every day and night for over a month fighting to save the farm and community from destruction and dissolution—that he would deliver his lecture to the brethren afterwards in the meetinghouse. He told us that the title of his lecture was "On the Spiritual and Metaphysical Implications and Advantages of Koreshanity and the Rebuttal and Dissolution of Universal Error."[*] He promised that his lecture would expand our minds and liberate us from our erroneous ways of perceiving reality.

I was seated at the adjacent table and tried to read Elder John's face, but it conveyed nothing more than polite interest in the topic. When Koresh sat and immediately began to eat, Elder John patted his forearm and made him stop. Then, as we had been taught was the custom, we all lowered our heads and silently, individually, expressed humble thanks to God for His abundance. After a moment, we raised our heads and opened our eyes, and as he often did, Elder John gave a brief peroration. He said that in bringing this fierce drought unto the land God was putting us through an ongoing test of our loving dedication to one another. He quoted a psalm: "God setteth the solitary in families. He bringeth out those which are bound with chains, but the rebellious dwell in a dry land." And as was his wont, another Bible verse, from his favorite disciple, John: "As Jesus said unto the woman of Samaria, 'Whosoever drinkest of this water shall thirst again, but whosoever drinketh of the water that I shall give him shall never thirst, but the water that I shall give him shall be in him a well of water springing up into everlasting life.'" He finished with "Amen, my beloved brethren."

We all repeated his "Amen" and began to eat. I glanced down the line of tables to where Sadie was seated with Sisters Beth, Hazel, and Rosalie, and caught her eye. Since the afternoon of our lovemaking the week before, she had confined herself to her room, as instructed by the elders, and tonight was the first time she had appeared again in the dining room with the others. She was pale, even paler than a week ago, and moved carefully, as if enduring slight, all-over pain. Leaning forward, she held her spoon above the soup bowl a few

---

[*] A lecture that is the basis for his book, *The Cellular Cosmogony; or, The Earth a Concave Sphere, Pt. I, The Universology of Koreshanity* (with Addendum: *"Astronomy's False Foundation"*). Estero, FL: Guiding Star Publishing House, 1905.

inches from her lips and pursed her lips and blew, and turned and smiled down the line of tables at me, for she knew my thoughts, just as I knew hers. We were both remembering our few moments of bliss and contemplating more.

I quickly looked away from her knowing smile, her beautiful lips, her frail white hand, or my response would have given me away to Elder John, who was seated nearby, listening to Koresh natter on, but all the while watching me, as if to keep from breaking into a broad smile himself, as if he too had secrets, in his case a non-Shaker loathing of the white-suited man opposite him and a plan somehow to use the man to the advantage of New Bethany, or to his own, whichever came first.

Just as Sadie and I could read each other's thoughts, so, too, in a parallel way Elder John and I knew what the other was thinking—perhaps because from early in our relations I had viewed him with a conflicted mixture of skepticism and admiration, and, despite the difference in our ages, he had viewed me similarly. We were both clever in many of the same ways. Perhaps he saw in me a younger version of himself, just as I saw in him an older version of myself. It was a troubling fix I was in, simultaneously reading my Sadie's romantic thoughts on one side and the skeptical, mocking thoughts of Elder John on the other, and having my matched thoughts read by both.

Later, after the meal and the tables were cleared and we had adjourned to the meetinghouse for Koresh's lecture on Koreshanity, it was the same. We three, Elder John, Sadie, and I, were triangulated in our silently amused, straight-faced response to Koresh's lecture, so that the opinions of one of us were the opinions of all three. The others, even Eldress Mary, seemed enthralled by his words and by the mostly incomprehensible diagrams he drew in chalk on the standing blackboard he'd had us bring over from the schoolroom. He spoke for an hour, though it seemed like ten hours, with great confidence and fluidity but not much lucidity. He said that his colony, Estero, was "the vitellus of the cosmogonic egg," and claimed that it was the New Jerusalem and within a decade would become the largest city in the world, "ten times the size of New York, its streets laid with gold and running like spokes in all directions like the streets of Washington, DC." He argued that the earth was hollow, and it contained within it the entire universe, and we humans and everything we think of as the world live not on the outer surface of the earth, but on the inner shell, looking down or up, depending on where we're located on the shell, onto all of God's creation, including the sun, moon, and stars. There was much else, but I remember that he based his theory on the biblical book of Isaiah: "Who hath measured the waters in the hollow of his hand, and meted out heaven with the span, and comprehended the dust of the earth in a measure, and weighed the mountains in scales, and the hills in a balance?"[*]

When everyone had left the meetinghouse, Elder John and I together carried the chalkboard back across the lawn toward the main house. Halfway there he stopped and asked to set the chalkboard down. "Stand, brother. Wait a moment," he said. "Do you smell smoke?"

"Yes, faintly."

"It's not good," he said.

I asked him where he thought the smoke was coming from, and he said, "Somewhere out in the Glades, probably. Miles to the south and west of Okeechobee, carried here on the evening breeze."

"That's too far to be a danger to us, right?"

"No. If the Glades south of Okeechobee are burning, it won't be long before the hammocks between us and the Glades catch fire and then the pine woods. The fires could grow strong enough to jump the canals and marshes. They might even jump the smaller lakes, they're so much shrunk by the drought. We may have to prepare to evacuate New Bethany. But don't say anything about it yet. We don't want the family to be frightened unnecessarily."

We picked up the chalkboard again and continued on in silence to the main house. Sadie was a short ways in front of us, headed for the schoolroom and to her bedroom on the floor above. I followed her with my eyes, as always. Elder John and I said good night to her and we both watched her go, all the while talking softly about the fires

* Isaiah 40:12

and the possibility of their overrunning New Bethany. He said, "If it comes to that, and we're forced to temporarily abandon our home, I'll need you to assume greater responsibility than has been asked of you up to now. You're the only young man among us who has good sense and understanding. If we abandon the farm, we'll have to take our livestock and as much of our poultry and our essential belongings with us as we can manage. We'll have to set loose the animals we can't take. Before we flee we will likely have to create a burned-over zone surrounding the farm in hopes it will preserve the buildings. We can't count on our neighbors for help. They'll be in the same fix as us. What we need is someplace safe to go to. I will want you to be my second in charge."

I assured him that I would take on any tasks he asked of me, and he smiled and said, "Thank you, brother."

Just then Koresh came up the wide stairs from the sitting room below, and we stopped talking. He walked past us and said good night in his cold, peremptory way.

Elder John said that he very much enjoyed tonight's lecture. "Tomorrow, before you depart for Estero," he said, "I would like to discuss a potential partnership between your Koreshans and us Shakers. Not a financial arrangement. More of a bartering," he added.

"Ah! Do you, now? Well, I have a plan of my own to offer," said Koresh with a smile. "I think you will find it very attractive and advantageous to us both. I'll reveal it on the morrow," he said. He turned abruptly away and crossed the schoolroom to the narrow stairs that led to Sadie's aerie and the guest rooms and mounted the stairs, leaving Elder John and me, amused by his remark and manner, to smile at one another knowingly and shrug our shoulders.

"The little fellow is not to be outdone," Elder John said.

"You mean, without having heard what you plan to offer, he's already opened negotiations?"

"Exactly, brother. Quick of you to notice. He's making a preemptive move. I have to admire him, though. The fellow may be a grandiose fool and a charlatan, but he's a born salesman. If he concentrated on selling Florida real estate, instead of trying to sell the world on his Koreshanity, he'd do extremely well."

"What sort of partnership can you imagine with such a man?" I asked him.

"Well, if the fires force us to leave, we'll need someplace to shelter. For providing it, he will want to be paid somehow. We have much to barter with."

I now thought I understood Elder John's intentions. His immediate intentions, that is. I saw that his plan to protect us from the fires by moving us to Estero was a tactical move, for which he might in exchange barter some of our crops and livestock, the fruits of our labor. But I reasoned from there, without evidence, that his overall, long-range strategy was to seize management of the Koreshans' colony from the hapless Koresh and thereby get easy access to the deep-water port and railheads. His ultimate goal, so I believed, was to make New Bethany into an economically thriving corporation of sorts, producing goods up here on our seven-thousand-acre plantation that could be warehoused, distributed, and sold at a profit down at Estero and shipped from there to the rest of the country and the Caribbean and possibly even Europe. He could produce and sell wholesale to the world everything we grew, from pineapples to citrus to cattle to cabbages and cotton, and everything we manufactured, from our seed packets and crafted furniture to baskets and brooms and dozens of other Shaker-made items. He could create and rule his own little Shaker kingdom.

This is what happens when a calculating, rational man gains control of an enterprise that was created for the purpose of elevating the spiritual life of its members, I thought. Elder John was more rational than Koresh, perhaps, but no less calculating. It helped that he was handsome and had plenty of personal charm. I saw myself as learning from a master.

"What will you offer to pay Koresh for sheltering us and our animals?" I asked him.

"Well, you go to war with the army you have, not the army you wish to have," he said with a smile.

"And we, the New Bethany brethren, are we your army?"

He laughed and said, "It's a small force and a weak one, but we're armed with our vast land holdings here and the wonderful bounty we produce. I learned in my discussions with Koresh at the South Florida Fair a while back that he covets our land. But he has neither the funds to purchase acreage on this scale himself nor the ability to make it arable."

"And you believe that letting him use our land will give us power over him?"

"Not power. Equivalence. Whoever controls the land controls whoever wants to make use of it," he said. "It's a simple equation. And Koresh wants to make use of it. He needs it to feed his people. As the fires approach and we grow increasingly endangered, he'll think I'm negotiating from weakness, when in fact, since we control what he needs, and he controls what we may need, there's nothing to negotiate. Which means I'll be negotiating from strength. I'll offer what we have in exchange for what he has, and both our needs will be met."

I listened respectfully to him and learned what I could. Since my arrival at New Bethany at the age of twelve, I had listened to him and, as much as I could, learned everything that he wished to teach me. He seemed to have selected me early on as his favorite student, the one whose mind and heart he most wanted to influence. He lent me books and gave me instructions on how to read them, and he did it in a wholly trusting manner and did not quiz or test me afterwards, did not ask me what I thought, and did not ask me to relate those great and profound books to the teachings of Mother Ann or Jesus or the Bible. It was as if he wanted to transfer the contents of his mind to mine. He merely passed me Montaigne's essays, the writings of Emerson and Thoreau, even ancient writers like Marcus Aurelius and Plutarch and Aristotle and Plato, books that often seemed impenetrable at first but that gradually opened and gave me entry, and he did not speak of them again, except with a casual, knowing reference to a specific notion or insight. We did not possess shared life experience, as our early lives had very little in common, but by lending me his favorite books, we might have shared knowledge.

Yet I remember thinking that evening, as we talked about Koresh and the approaching fires, that Elder John was possibly deceiving himself. The man called Koresh was obviously a charlatan, but he was nobody's fool.

But perhaps the one who was deceiving himself was me. I couldn't see it then, but I can now. Driven by an innate skepticism and my all-consuming, possessive love of Sadie and a filial competition with the man who had in significant ways replaced my father, I was attributing motives and schemes to Elder John that he did not necessarily possess.

I said to him, "You're very wise in these matters, Elder. But in a non-Shakerish way. Where did you learn all that you know about negotiating and controlling people? Surely not in your dealings with Shakers. Was it in your readings of the non-Shaker writers? Was it during your early years in the World?" I was aware that much of my own view of human nature had been shaped by my family's brief time at Rosewell Plantation, where I first learned of mankind's essential wickedness and depravity, so I asked Elder John directly, "Where was your view of human nature formed?"

This was not a frivolous or an idle inquiry. I really did want an answer to my question. I admit, I was finagling a little bit, for I also wanted to get him telling me about his personal past, about his life before he became a Shaker at Mount Lebanon and his early years there, before he came to Florida and participated in the founding of New Bethany. Elder John Bennett was an unusual man, especially for a Shaker. I wondered if when he was a young man, he was like me. That's really what lay behind my question. If when he was a young man, he was like me, then it would be easy to imagine him being in love with Sadie Pratt and she in love with him—as my brother Pence had warned the day he left New Bethany for the west. Easy to imagine him as calculating as the man called Koresh. Easy to imagine him as ambitious for New Bethany as a corporate chieftain. Easy, then, to imagine me someday taking his place. For I was all these things.

He said, "My view of human nature? You're right to wonder, brother. It didn't come from my dealings with the Shakers, who, to be sure, aren't like the rest of mankind. They are trusting and live mostly in the sweet hereafter. The rest of mankind, however, the people of the World, even the world of Koresh, are mistrustful and are therefore untrustworthy, and they live only for the moment and are acquisitive and materialistic and hungry for power and sensual gratification. I guess I first learned this as a boy, the child of poor Kentucky sharecroppers who were treated little better than slaves. Like you at Rosewell. And I had it confirmed in the military, where young men are taught how to kill with efficiency and skill. And I learned it again later at Auburn Prison, where I saw that the primary purpose of imprisonment was exploitation and total control, right up to and including execution, legalized, state-sanctified murder. So that by my mid-twenties, when I met up with the Society of Believers, I was ready to confess my sins and commit to communism and pacifism and love of one another in the spirit of Jesus and Mother Ann. But the truth, for better or worse, as your question suggests, is that I never forgot what I had learned earlier about human nature." He laughed and said, "Especially when it comes to dealing with men like Dr. Cyrus Teed, our Koresh, who is very much a man of the World."

"When you were at Auburn Prison, were you there as a prisoner or a guard?" I asked him.

The question did not seem to catch him by surprise. He had a ready answer. "Both. But it makes no difference, brother. In a prison, whether one is an inmate or a guard, both are controlled by the system. The same as in the military, where it makes no difference if you are a buck private or a general. Or in a business, whether you're a lowly worker or the presiding officer of the corporation. You either surrender your freedom to the system, or you walk away from it. There's no middle ground. I walked away from it. That's why and how I became a Shaker. That's all you need to know, my brother."

His answer dazzled me, both for its elusiveness and for its clarity. Elder John seemed to be saying that there was no essential difference between victim and victimizer, between the oppressed and the oppressor. That both were equally controlled by the system that created and maintained and enforced their relationship. The slaveholder and the slave, the prison guard and the inmate, the landlord and the renter, the lender and the borrower, the seller and the buyer, the rich and the poor—Elder John was saying that neither can exist without the other. The only moral position, therefore, is to refuse to be one or the other and reject the system that maintains the relations between the two. Simply walk away from it, as Elder John did when he became a Shaker. It's a paradox, yes, but he believed that in bowing to the Believers' yoke, he had acquired his freedom.

I was still young, and despite having been raised by utopians, this struck me at the time as not so much a wise as a strange way to think. Less so today, however, now edging past eighty years of age. And especially less so in the aftermath of having sold the old New Bethany landholdings that I'd purchased piecemeal over the years, all of it, every last carefully collected piece of the seven thousand acres. By making myself the seller, I was in league with the buyer, collaborating in my own deception. Just as, when I purchased the properties, I was in league with the sellers.

But that's another story, isn't it? Not the one I'm trying to tell here. And I don't want to talk about that, the story of my final, great, and terrible humiliating folly, even though when I went to Disney World for the grand opening, blunt recognition and unavoidable acceptance of it is what prompted me to begin speaking of the history of New Bethany and my role in causing its downfall. For I had seen with startling clarity that the two are connected, the fall of New Bethany and the rise of Disney's Magic Kingdom.

It's not yet clear to me exactly how they're connected. Except that in both cases I know that I, Harley Mann, am the material and formal and efficient and final cause of both the fall of one magic kingdom and the rise of another. Perhaps, as I continue telling the story about me and Sadie Pratt and Elder John Bennett and the brethren of New Bethany, I'll begin to understand how the two are connected.

Or perhaps not. What does it matter, anyhow, if my life remains a mystery to me? Who cares if Harley Mann dies without ever learning how or why his youthful delusions and follies are matched by those of his old age? Or why, in between, from youth to old age, he remained for all intents and purposes a Shaker without a Shaker family, adhering nonetheless to the Society of Believers' prohibitions and principles, a celibate, abjuring alcohol and tobacco and all other stimulants, a nonbelieving Believer, a Shaker pariah, a man in some perverse but fundamental way affirming the Shaker way of life by building his hut just beyond the closed and locked gate of New Bethany. Who cares, other than Harley Mann himself? Everyone who once might have cared is gone now, dead and buried or else beyond caring about these long-ago events and circumstances.

After Elder John left the schoolroom for his adjacent quarters, I stood alone at the top of the stairs for a few moments and pictured Sadie in her room overhead, undressing and readying herself for sleep. My thoughts kept switching back and forth between the words of Elder John and the imagined picture of my beloved in candlelight slipping between the bedcovers and silently saying her prayers and then, as I hoped, thinking of me. Elder John had given me much to ponder tonight, much to question—about myself, the World, the relations between the World and Shakerism, and how to live with both.

Elder John and Sadie were the two opposed poles of my life, and there were times, like tonight, when I felt drawn to them in equal measure. I could not imagine putting either of them out of my life, rejecting one for the other. And yet I could not see how I could continue to adhere to both. My desire for his approval and respect and the continuation of his mentorship lay in sharp conflict with my desire for her love and the continuation of our sensual expression of that love. These were more than mere desires; they were needs, life-saving needs. I believed that I could not survive without either, and yet I could not live with both. One or the other would have to be rejected, expelled, expunged. But I could not choose.

The next morning the wind had shifted and was out of the north now, and I could not smell any smoke. The threat of the distant fires seemed almost a fantasy. The sun still beat down from a cloudless sky. I watched from where I was clearing an irrigation ditch in the cabbage field as Elder John and Koresh walked side by side down from the main house to the pier. I heard the steam whistle shriek across the mangroves from the canal between Alligator Lake and Live Oak, signaling the approach of the *Coquina* from St. Cloud.

The two men were talking animatedly, or at least Koresh was. Elder John appeared to be mostly listening. The lake was surrounded by a wide aureole of mud between the water and the old pre-drought shoreline, and as the side-wheeler edged up to the pier, the flat hull of the barge scraped against the muck beneath. Koresh was lucky. This would likely be the last trip out from New Bethany until the rains refilled the lakes and canals. After the Great Freeze and now with the drought, we had no crops to ship downstream to St. Cloud anyhow and nothing to receive, and there were no arriving visitors. The white-suited, cane-wielding Koresh had the boat to himself. He stepped aboard, and the barge scraped its way back onto the lake and disappeared around the bend.

A few minutes later, Elder John joined me in the field and picked up a spade and began helping to clear the ditch. "How did your negotiation with Koresh go?" I asked.

"I learned from the captain of the *Coquina*, Shea, and his mate, Haversack, just now that the fires are burning their way north between three and four miles a day. So we have at most ten days. Unless it rains. Pray for rain, brother, whether you believe in the power of prayer or not."

"It didn't go well with him, then."

"He'll shelter us all right, if we have to flee the fires. But he wants title to half our land in exchange. I turned him down."

"You didn't make him a counteroffer? Isn't that what you do in a situation like this?"

"No. Remember what I told you last night. You either surrender to the system, or you walk away from it. There's no middle ground. Dr. Cyrus Teed is first and foremost a capitalist businessman. That's his system. He can't help himself. We mustn't let it become ours. I just told him that he misunderstood the nature of our request, that we wished only to exchange our kindness for his. But we're neither buyers nor sellers. So we'll just have to circle our buildings and livestock with a burn line and make our stand right here. Meanwhile, pray for rain, brother."

Soon, day and night we smelled smoke, regardless of the wind direction. We abandoned our fight against the drought, and under Elder John's direction we marked off with stakes the cultivated acreage surrounding the buildings and barns and corrals, including the apiary and orchards and vineyards and the fruit and berry patches. We made a circle of nearly ten acres and began to cut out the trees that till now had served as shade for the workers and animals and cleared the underbrush and raked away anything that could serve as flammable tinder. Equipped with shovels and brooms and pieces of carpet and carrying water-filled rubberized backpacks with hose attachments designed by Elder John and manufactured overnight in the woodworking shop, we divided our people into two work crews of five and six, one under Elder John's direction and one under mine, and began setting small fires along the perimeter of the zone that we hoped to save, simultaneously nurturing and extinguishing the fires, keeping the flames steady but low, laying down a wide, charred, circular track designed to hold our beloved New Bethany compound in its blackened hands.

It was hot, hard work, and we stayed out there from sunup until long after sunset, and when it became too dark to see our way from one marker to the next, we split our crews into shifts that alternated every four hours, keeping at it throughout the night. While one shift grabbed a bit of cold food and a few hours' sleep, the other continued to set fires and beat at the flames and keep them in line. Except for feeding the livestock and collecting eggs and milking the cows, all other tasks were suspended—no meals were prepared in the common kitchen, and for the first time in my memory there were no nightly religious services. The lathes and saws in Brother Edwin's woodworking shop went silent. My brother Raymond and Brother Ezekiel closed up their cobbler shop, and Royal and Sister Beth abandoned their printing press and sign shop. The herdsmen, Brothers Amos and George, drove most of the nearly feral cattle out onto the open range and brought in and corralled behind the barn the old seed bull and enough young heifers and calves to restart the herd if the fires caught up with their scattered mates.

We could have used my brave brother Pence, long gone to Texas, and Brother Hiram, my beekeeping mentor, who I hoped was safe and calm in his parents' Maryland home, and the ten or twelve other workers, most of them healthy male novitiates, opportunistic temporary Shakers who had joined the colony in the years when New Bethany was prospering, but who had abandoned us when our crops began to fail from the Great Freeze and then the drought. But those who had remained were faithful to our cause and uncomplaining and, despite the advanced age of a few, like Sisters Beth and Hazel, tireless.

More than at any other time in all my years at New Bethany, we were truly a united family of Believers. Even Sadie, who was too weak to shoulder one of Elder John's backpack water tanks, ignored his protestations and joined his crew and wielded a broom against the slow creep of the burn, steering the low flames back onto their proper path whenever they crept away from the markers or threatened to flash and flare into a wall of fire. With our faces and hair wrapped in wet kerchiefs and hats and our hands in gloves, we wore waxed raincoats and capes to protect us from the sparks and hot ash and cinders that flew from the burnt-over ground. We were almost unrecognizable, one from the other, male from female, young from old. Even White from Black, for I could not distinguish Sister Beth from the rest.

Yet throughout those long days and nights, whenever I paused and looked around me, I could immediately identify and separate Sadie's slim form from the others'. No matter how far from me and my crew she was working, and even in the dark of night, illuminated only by the long, flickering lines of orange-and-yellow flame eating the ground cover, turning its remains to ash and char, I could spot her frail frame flailing at the fire with a broom, stopping to wipe her fevered brow, taking a sip of water from a dipper and pail and resuming her labors. I saw Elder John several times an hour approach her and watched him put his arm around her thin shoulders and seem to comfort and query her before stepping away and going back to his own post nearby. He seemed to be always near her. Even when she left the field, no doubt at his insistence, to eat and to sleep for a few hours before returning to work, as long as she was visible to me, Elder John stayed near her. No matter that I had my own crew to manage and direct and was often many hundreds of feet away from Elder John's crew, I still saw all that.

The smoke grew heavier and was a nearly constant presence all through the day and night, stinging our eyes and clouding our vision and causing many of us, especially Sadie, to gasp and cough and steadily weep. Towards dusk late one afternoon, I saw that she had dropped her broom and was bent over by a relentless coughing spasm, and I went to her and placed my hand on her shoulder and said as calmly as I could, "Sadie, you must go inside, you must go to your room and close the windows and lie down. You must, Sadie. This smoke will kill you. Please go inside."

She shook her head no and continued to cough and gasp for air as if she were being drowned by it.

Then, suddenly, Elder John, who must have been watching my movements as closely as I had been watching his, was at my side, and he, too, placed a hand on poor Sadie's shuddering shoulder. "I will not allow thee to work out here any longer," he said in his deepest, darkest voice, a biblical patriarch's, a tone he rarely invoked. Stated in his most authoritative diction, it was a command, not a request. Not to comply would require open rebellion. He rarely made a disagreement or difference of opinion into an irreconcilable impasse or turned a request into an order. He preferred to govern with the consent of the governed.

And then Eldress Mary appeared beside us, and without a word, she took Sadie gently by the hands and led her like a child slowly away from us in the direction of the main house, across the blackened field and into the cloud of gray smoke.

Elder John shook his head mournfully. "I should not have allowed her to leave her bedroom in the first place," he said. "It was a mistake. But she insisted."

"If the exertion and the smoke kill her . . ." I began. I didn't know what I would say next.

He finished my sentence for me. "It will be my fault."

"Yes."

"And you will not be able to forgive me. Am I right, Brother Harley?"

"Yes."

He sighed and said, "I will not be able to forgive me, either. We both love her, brother. Differently, perhaps, but equally."

"I do not think so. Not equally. Or you wouldn't have allowed her to come out and work with us. If you loved her as I do, you would have forbidden it. You have the authority, Elder, but you refused to exercise it," I told him.

"Yes, you're right. It was a mistake," he said. "Worse than a mistake. I tried to treat her as if she were merely one of the brethren who wanted to get up from a sickbed and help us save New Bethany from the fires. As if it was her will and the Lord's will in tandem, and not mine. I was wrong. I acted as if I knew the Lord's will. That's not a mistake, that's a sin. I pray that I won't need your forgiveness, brother. Or my own. Or the Lord's."

"For Sadie's sake, I hope your prayers are answered," I said, and walked quickly back to my crew on the far side of the field.

It was dusk now, darkened more by layers of gray smoke than the plunge of the sun behind the western horizon. But the darkening sky was not the streaked vermilion-and-turquoise velvet curtain that we were used to seeing at this hour. It was a dull, peach-colored sheet, shading from pale yellow in the west to a burnished orange in the east, the glow cast against the smoky sky, not by the red, rapidly descending sun, but by the burning surface of the earth itself. All afternoon great flocks of birds that don't normally move in flocks—ibises and egrets and herons and anhingas—flew in broad waves from south to north. And birds that rarely leave the mangroves and swamps, roseate spoonbills and limpkins, crossed above our fields in pairs and small bands and passed over our shrunken lakes and kept going. Smaller birds, martins and jays and swallows, usually calling noisily to one another as they tumbled and twirled like circus performers through the branches of the shade trees and orchards, were nowhere to be seen.

The cattle in their pens and the oxen and horses in their stalls and our other livestock were unusually restless and seemed to be calling out to one another in confused alarm. The sheep and goats kicked and butted their enclosures, and the pigs clustered by the gate of their pen and peered out anxiously between the slats and grunted and snorted at us when we passed. The poultry, our hens and ducks and geese, stopped laying and went silent and huddled together inside their coop, and the rooster had not welcomed the dawn for several days now. Nor had we heard the mourning doves' chuckling coos at dawn, nor the squawking of the grackles at dusk.

It was all very strange, and then it got stranger. The belly-deep grumbles and growls of the alligators that lived along the shores of the lakes and canals shifted to a higher scale, rising almost to a nasal whine that made them sound distressed and anxious. We were used to the gators' primitive bellows and low, arrogant grunts, which we knew were their territorial claims and mating solicitations, but we'd never heard them make this thin, high-pitched, almost fearful sound. Because of the drought, the lake and canal levels were down, but they were not yet completely dry, and as long as the gators stayed in the depths of their deep water-filled holes, they were safe from the fires. But we wondered how the usually somnolent creatures knew that the fires were growing closer by the day. Who or what told them? The odor of the gray pelt of smoke that hovered above the water, perhaps? Or the recklessness of possums and raccoons and the small Everglades deer that had fled their sanctuaries in the wooded hammocks in search of safety, gathering beside these depleted bodies of water, leaving their tracks in the muck and mud in the mangroves surrounding the alligators' watery wallows, where previously they would not have dared venture, risking the nearby presence of their antediluvian adversary? Their instincts and habits and needs were not made for this altered world. A natural order was being upended, and even a creature as unevolved as the alligator could sense it. The world had a smell and a sound and a look that was new and that was therefore alarming to all the creatures of the swamp and the sawgrass plain and the hammocks.

The black bears, too, behaved strangely. Bears tend to be solitary and very skittish near humans, but I remember something I'd never seen before, a pair of bears, two young males, lumbering across the yellow pasture on the far side of our burn, traveling not away from us, but toward us, as if bringing news from the deepest recesses of the Glades. Then a day later we saw four more bears, adults and cubs. They emerged from the woods, came toward us and stopped a hundred yards or so away, keeping their distance, and watched us work, as if we were engaged in building a sanctuary as much for them as for ourselves. The next day we counted a dozen sightings of bears, singly and in pairs, stepping from the depths of the marshes and woods at different spots to stand and sit and lie in the shadows near the outer ring of our burn, patiently waiting for us to finish constructing our palisade of scorched, blackened earth.

Finally, after seven days we had succeeded in surrounding our compound with the firebreak. By then we could see and hear the approach of the flames from several sides at once. We saw yellow-and-orange flickers and flashes of fire on the far side of the mangroves along the canal linking Live Oak Lake to Alligator, and we saw, barely a half mile from us, flames leap from branch to branch along the line of live oak trees atop the hammock. The fire crackled like distant gunfire, and smoke billowed into the darkening sky. There were no more birds of any kind passing overhead, no more of the small creatures, possums and raccoons and rabbits and armadillos that for the last few days had scampered across our land fleeing the approaching inferno. We saw a family of wild hogs troop past, and a pack of coyotes and a bobcat slink through the yard and bypass the barn and move on. Even the water rats and otters had fled their wet homes for safer swamps and glades north of us. Every creature in the kingdom, except for the Shakers of New Bethany, was on the run before the onrushing fire.

On the seventh night Elder John called us together, and out there on the front porch of the main house he led us in prayer for the coming of a deluge of biblical proportions. He said that the deluge would come, not to wipe from God's creation the sinners and heretics and blasphemers, drowning the wickedness of man which had become great on the earth, but to save us from the hellish flames. In a brief homily he compared us to Noah and his family, and he compared our compound to the ark that God Himself had ordered up and that Noah and his sons had built, and he compared our livestock and poultry and sheep and goats and swine to "every living thing of all flesh," both fowl and cattle, and every living thing that creepeth upon the earth, which following God's command were saved two by two.

The following morning, pulled by the immense heat, the wind

shifted around and now blew back in the direction of the approaching wall of fire, as if being inhaled by the towering flames. Elder John gave the order to start the back-burn. We would fight fire with fire. We lit bamboo torches topped with oil-soaked rags and ignited the clumps and piles of brush and sawgrass that we had stacked at the outer ring of our charred break, and the wind-drawn flames of our smaller fire began to advance quickly upon the larger fire like an advance force of grenadiers. We stood away from the heat and watched our fiery troops with great anxiety, for if this tactic combined with the firebreak did not work as planned, we would be trapped inside a closing circle of flames and we and our animals would be incinerated.

I turned and looked around at the sweating, fearful, soot-covered faces of the Shakers, my brothers Raymond and Royal, my mother and my sister, Rachel, Elder John, Eldress Mary, all the loyal brothers and sisters of New Bethany, and saw in the distance beyond them my beloved Sadie standing on the porch, watching over us like an archangel. We held on to our torches and stared at her. She looked otherworldly. A woman from a world different than ours, sent here to protect us. Her head and shoulders were covered with a long crocheted shawl white as snow, and her face was a silvery-blue mask carved from a block of ice. She gripped the edges of the shawl tightly in her fists as if to keep it from being yanked away from her body and gazed without expression, as if in a trance, across the wide lawn to the meadow where we had gathered together to witness the final battle in the war between the fires—nature's fire, sent by God, and ours, deliberately set.

That's when I saw the panther. Out of the cloud of smoke and swirling ash and cinders billowing between the oncoming inferno and our back-burn, the beast emerged like a dark-hearted demon, Beelzebub or Astaroth, as if it had been created in that flaming crucible and had been long imprisoned there. First came its leonine, white-muzzled face and thickly muscled shoulders and then its long, smooth, wheat-colored body and black-tipped tail. It was a yellow-eyed male panther, over one hundred fifty pounds and nine or ten feet long from its nose to the end of its tail.

It was the first time I had seen a living uncaged panther. There was the sad, caged panther at the fair, and I had seen four of them one time in Narcoossee shot dead, the shooter and his local guide posing beside them for a photograph, the quartet of panthers' powerful, elegant bodies hung like slabs of meat from a rack, their beautiful heads slumped, their eyes closed like sleeping cats, the heads ready to be severed from the bodies and shipped back north and mounted on a clubroom wall. And out on the range I had from time to time come upon the half-eaten carcass of a cow or calf killed by a panther and dragged into the bush, hidden for a later meal. And I had heard admiring stories told by local hunters of the great cat's murderous temperament and its elusiveness and its ability to overwhelm and defeat the most powerful creatures of the Glades, even including the black bear and the alligator. But I had not imagined its furious grace and power, its unbridled rage, the twisting quickness of its long body as it swung its massive head from side to side and warned us off with sulfur-yellow eyes and black lips curled back from primeval fangs.

The fire-maddened beast leapt across the back-burn and came down in our midst. Not daring to turn our backs and run, caught between terror and fascination, we backed away, holding our torches high and giving the panther as much quarter as it wanted. In a miraculously calm voice, Elder John told us to make room for the animal to escape, don't close him in a circle, give him a way to put the fire behind him, and we complied by breaking into a ragged line, opening a space for the panther to flee both the fire and the torch-wielding human beings. He took a step and then another and made a long leap away from us, and with a loosely bounding stride, he crossed the wide yard in the direction of the main house.

I watched in horror, then, as Sadie stepped down from the porch and walked slowly toward the approaching panther, as if to greet him. Her arms were extended in front of her in greeting, and she had a peaceful smile on her pale face, like a sleepwalker soothed by her dream. Her dark, deep-set eyes were wide open—in surprise, it appeared, or delight, or curiosity, a mingling of emotions that made her expression unreadable. She opened her mouth slightly, as if to inhale or to speak softly.

The great cat seemed about to meet her head-on and crush her bones with his momentum and weight. But at the last second he ducked to the right and cut around her and loped on toward the house. Sadie dropped her hands and turned and watched him pass, almost as if disappointed that he had not leapt upon her and had not torn her frail body to pieces with his fangs and claws.

It was an incomprehensible desire, but I could not imagine that she wanted anything less than to be slain by the panther, or she would not have walked down from the house straight toward him. She would not have given herself up to the beast. She had conceived a terrible way to die, an unspeakably cruel way to commit suicide, cruel to herself, but also to all of us who would be forced to witness it, and cruelest perhaps especially to me, who loved her, who had held her in my arms and kissed her lips and made love to her and longed to go on making love to her for as long as both she and I lived.

With the pandemonium and roar of the fire towering behind me, and the panther, maddened by fear of the flames and the torch-bearing humans, crossing the yard toward the house, and with Sadie running after the panther as if hoping for him to turn back and attack her, I believed at that moment that she did indeed want to be killed. If not by the panther, then she would do it herself by turning back and throwing her body onto the fire like a Hindu widow committing suttee. I did not want her to die alone, then or ever, slain by the panther or by the fire. If she must die, even if of her own volition, then we should both die together.

And to make it happen, that we both should be killed at the same time and not she alone then and I alone years later, I put down my torch and broke away from my Shaker brethren and ran toward Sadie and the panther, not to save her, but to be with her at the end, to share it with her. The secret of our furtive love affair would never be known, that was my only comfort. I reached out to Sadie and took her hand in mine and together we ran toward the panther. At that instant, our suicide pact was sealed.

The panther had reached the porch steps, where he turned and faced us as if he had taken possession of the house and would slay us if we attempted to enter. He opened his great mouth and showed us his terrible fangs and warned us off. But hand in hand, Sadie and I kept coming, closer and closer, walking straight toward him, for we no longer needed to chase him down, we had the beast at bay. We had settled on what we wanted from him. Secrecy and death. That is what was left to us. We thought, we believed, we behaved as if this were our only path forward.

But wait, look at us. I was barely nineteen years old, naive, and wildly, obsessively in love, my mind saturated with romantic literature and philosophy and leavened with biblical tales and teachings of moral heroism and sacrifice and redemption. Sadie was only seven years older than I, but mortally ill for a decade, her mind disrupted and enflamed by her illness, her sense of her worthiness and value to me and to the Shakers who had cared for her and to the world at large diminished by her belief that she would soon die. And we were both torn between the longings of our heart and our devotion to the Shaker way of life and were rent by guilt for our secret sins, our lovemaking conducted in the dark shadows cast by the light of Shakerism. We were both torn between unbelief and belief. All this drove us toward the panther that day. Self-sacrifice seemed the only uncorrupted act available to us. It was as if God Himself had loosed the panther on us, like Darius, the king of the Persians, setting the lions on Daniel, who refused to worship the king and instead prayed to the one true God of the Israelites.* Sadie and I, unlike Daniel, had worshipped Darius, the king of the Persians. And God had sent the lion from out of the fiery furnace, not to punish, but to redeem us.

We were not to be redeemed. Our lion fled from us. When we were close enough to reach out and touch his face, he turned away, as if we were no longer worthy of his attention, and he walked regally down the length of the wide porch to the end and stepped to the ground there and disappeared around the corner of the building and was gone from our sight.

Elder John was the first of the Shakers to reach us, and the others all followed and gathered around, stunned and relieved, staring silently at me and Sadie as if we were ghosts or angels. Except for

* Daniel 6:1–28

Elder John, who merely stared at us, as if he had read our minds and knew what we had failed to accomplish and why. My mother and several others touched us on our cheeks and shoulders to be sure that we were real. But no one said anything, then or later.

After a few moments, everyone turned away from us and returned to the meadow and the firebreak and went back to the work of setting the back-burn against the approaching wall of flame. Elder John's tactics of combining the firebreak with the back-burn now seemed to be working. The greater fire, on reaching the blackened, burnt-over ground that encircled our compound, had retreated and turned and was now burning through the mangroves along the canals and lakesides, searching for an alternative route around our sanctuary.

By sunset, the great Glades fire of '09 had moved away from us altogether and was no longer a danger to New Bethany. Elder John and Eldress Mary told us to convene in the meetinghouse to offer up prayers of thanksgiving and asked us to enliven our prayers and re-establish our unity with joyful song and Shaker dance, which we gave ourselves over to for nearly two hours, even though we were physically and emotionally exhausted. And no one said a word about Sadie's and my encounter with the lion.

And neither Sadie nor I spoke of it to one another. The long-prayed-for deluge did indeed follow within days, and it ended the drought. Though the rains didn't last for forty days and nights, they extinguished all the remaining fires large and small across the Glades, and in a few short weeks the fields and forests and the swamps were greening again. Even my bees returned with their queen from wherever they had hidden during the conflagration and were thriving in their hives, and our fields were under fresh cultivation, and the orchards were putting out new blossoms.

REEL #11

That was a convenient place to stop. It was near the end of the reel, anyhow, and I happened to look out the window on one of my all-too-frequent trips to the bathroom and noticed that the sinkhole in my driveway has started to open up again. It isn't much of a sink, barely the size of a ten-gallon hat, but it needs to be broken open and refilled and paved over a second time. More gravel and sand, more asphalt, five or six workmen standing around leaning on their shovels, watching the dump trucks and the roller and charging me for their time.

I probably should wait until the sink finishes its underground dissolve and let it open up as far as it will and then fill in the crater and repave the entire driveway, instead of patching it. The truth is, I don't really need to get my car out of the garage. I have no plans to drive anywhere soon, no place to go, no one to visit. If I need groceries, I can walk over to the Piggly Wiggly or call and have them delivered.

To get on with the story of New Bethany, then. Before I run out of blank tapes. I guess I should go back to 1909, the year of the freeze and the drought and the fire. Elder John joked, when the fire was over, that all we needed to complete the list was a plague of locusts or a torrent of frogs, and the Egyptians would be forced to recognize God's authority and our status as His chosen people and let us go.

Elder John was an optimistic man of supreme self-confidence, and now that New Bethany had survived and was once again thriving, he could crack jokes about how we had suffered. Anyone else would have been too superstitious or too pious or too afraid of a literal plague of locusts or frogs to make light of it. Anyone else would not have been willing to take the measure of the freeze and the drought and the fire and then with good-humored optimism say, "Well, my brethren, we got that behind us, so let's joke about how it could have been worse and get back to work." Without Elder John to sum it up for us and oblige us to look at our *annus horribilis* squarely and show us that in fact it was an *annus mirabilis,* out of fear and discouragement we might well have closed down the settlement and sold off the land and buildings then and there and either gone back north to Mount Lebanon or else scattered individually across the country, abandoning Shakerism and joining the people who live in the World.

That's what I wanted to do. If after the freeze, the drought, and the fire New Bethany had collapsed, Sadie and I wouldn't have retreated north to the Shaker capital in upstate New York with the others. No, we would have left the Shakers altogether and gone to live in the World, probably someplace close by, like St. Cloud, where I would have dedicated myself to curing Sadie of her illness. I had plenty of commercially viable skills by then and could easily have found sufficient employment to support us both in a modest but adequate way. I told her this, presenting it as an actual plan.

She smiled as if complimented, but waved it away. "I could never ask that of you, Harley. Or of anyone else, either," she said. "I live with a death sentence. It's not so onerous for the brethren here to take care of me, when I can't take care of myself, or to pay for the cost of my room and board, since I have no financial resources of my own, because the burden and the costs are distributed among the entire community of Believers. But I couldn't give myself over to the care of one person alone. It would be too cruel to you, too selfish of me. You are young and healthy, Harley, and have a long life ahead of you."

"But what would you do if New Bethany was forced to shut down?" I asked.

We were meeting at the bee yard almost daily for half a day at a time then. She had asked Eldress Mary and Elder John for permission to learn beekeeping from me, and they had happily granted it. This was during one of her periods of slight recovery, several months after the fire, when she was capable of performing small tasks for brief interludes, but not able to work a full day or undertake anything that was physically demanding. It gave us time to be alone together and to speak intimately of our love for one another and other matters that we didn't want to share with the others. We did meet privately on rare occasions for lovemaking in her room and kept secret rendezvous elsewhere on the property, but weren't able to do it without elaborate planning and scheming, like a spy and counterspy arranging to pass secret documents to one another.

She said that if Elder John and Eldress Mary decided to close New Bethany and return north to Mount Lebanon with the remaining brothers and sisters, if they would still have her, she would go with them. She wanted to spend her dying days with the Shakers, whether here or up there. "As long as you are somewhere nearby," she said. "So you see, Harley, if you love me, you'll have to remain a Shaker a while longer, whether here or somewhere else. At least until I die." She smiled and cocked her head in her to-me-provocatively flirtatious way and turned to helping me switch out a set of combs from one of the old weather-beaten hives to a new one I had recently assembled.

Often, in response to a clever remark by Elder John, she cocked her head like that and raised an eyebrow and smiled slightly without showing her teeth, and it always angered me. She flirted with him the same way she flirted with me. When I brought it up to her, telling her that it upset me, she explained that it was to throw off any suspicion that there might be something more than mere friendship between her and me. It was strategic, she said. It kept people from thinking there was something exclusive and private about our relationship. She said, "If I give Elder John the same attention in front of the others that I give to you, no one will suspect that you and I are more than just friends."

I was besotted with love for Sadie, insane, the way only a very young man in love can be. During those autumn months, we were sneaking off to kiss and embrace and even to make furtive, hurried love once or twice a week, sometimes more, for she went through a period then of partially recovered health. Also, the flames of my ardor were fanned by the danger and the secrecy and the deception required by our love affair. It made my pulse constantly race. I was afraid of nothing except of being found out. I was not even afraid of catching her disease. Other people with tuberculosis might be contagious, but not my Sadie. I remember it now as madness, as a sustained hallucination, but at the time I believed it was an expression of my mental and moral clarity. My secret reality, as I saw and experienced it—reinforced by my belief that it was the same for her—was superior to all other realities. Superior, even, to Elder John's.

Yet he was my mentor, the man I had been emulating since I was twelve years old. For nearly a decade he had been teaching me how to think skeptically and rationally, like my long-gone father, while still adhering to the Shaker way of life. Elder John made Shakerism normal and even desirable, the way my father had made the Ruskinite communistic way of life normal and desirable. Elder John showed me by example and word the metaphorical nooks and crannies in Shaker theology and faith that allowed me to view the religion as a continuing lifelong quest instead of a fixed and permanent resting place. He was Jesuitical, and yet he eschewed dogma. He trusted my intelligence and intellectual honesty enough to place in my hands books and writings that other, more orthodox Shakers, like Eldress Mary and my mother, would have viewed as heretical, and he taught me how to bend those works and the thoughts they contained so that they melded with the teachings of Mother Ann and the Christian Bible, and he showed me how to interpret the fundamental Shaker principles so that they did not contradict the secularists. I knew that he was grooming me to be his successor, the son that he, as a Shaker, could never produce otherwise. And I wanted to be that person.

But I wonder now if I would have come to love Sadie so passionately if I had not feared that Elder John loved her passionately, too. In the early days, when I was still a boy and my attraction to her was little more than a boy's infatuation with a beautiful young woman, I was perhaps overly conscious of any attention paid to her by him, as if I were competing with her for his affectionate regard, the way I would have competed with my brother Pence if he, and not Sadie, had been the recipient of Elder John's kindliness and teaching. But that never happened. From the start I was the one singled out for his special care and confidence, I was his favorite, not Pence or any other male member of the community. So instead I competed with Sadie, as if we were siblings and Elder John were our father.

But as I grew older, my infatuation with Sadie turned to romantic love, and gradually I began to feel, not competitive with her for his fatherly attention, like a brother with a sister, but its opposite, competitive with him for hers, like rivals. And then I became a man, and romantic love got carnal and became obsessive love, sexual and possessive, and I grew overtly jealous of Elder John, suspicious of Sadie's descriptions of the innocent nature of their relationship, her rationales and excuses for the many hours a week they spent together in private in the main house while I labored in the apiary, the evening walks they took together following prayer services in the meetinghouse, the warmth of their sidelong glances during mealtime or while dancing and singing afterwards, their mutual solicitude and expressions of concern for each other's health and well-being, which each of them confided to me, as if I were the wise, knowing, and sympathetic confidant of both.

It occurred to me that if my Sadie was so skillful at conducting our love affair and concealing it from the others, including Elder John, with whom she spent so much of her time alone, then she was capable of conducting and concealing from everyone, including me, a love affair with Elder John. When one has taken up lying, as I had done, it's natural to assume that everyone else is lying, too. A person who has successfully created a false identity will be quickly led to question the authenticity of everyone else's identity. One cannot live a lie without believing that one is surrounded by liars and nothing is what it seems and no one is who he or she claims to be.

And so gradually I came to believe that both Sadie and Elder John were lying to me, that he and she were as much secret lovers as she and I. To this day, more than sixty years later, I still do not know if I was right or wrong in that belief. But maybe if I reveal everything that I do know, whoever someday listens to these tapes will be able to come to a conclusion one way or the other. It would not matter much, of course, a tawdry love affair between a very young man and a somewhat older woman living on a religious commune, a story of long ago, except for the scandalous consequences of the young man's jealousy and bitterness and anger. The fallout, as they say.

My attentions to Sadie intensified over the autumn and winter, and so did my jealousy and suspicions. Although I did not confront her directly, I did grow sulky and insecure and required frequent reassurances from her that she loved me above all others and that I was the only man allowed to kiss and fondle her and make love to her. At the same time she was growing weaker and her symptoms of consumption were becoming more dramatically evident. She was even thinner now than she had ever been. When I held her in my arms I felt obliged to embrace and handle her lightly, out of fear that I could easily break her fragile bones. Her dark eyes seemed to be lit from behind, as if her brain were on fire, and her chalk-white skin was dry and hot to the touch, as if she were feverish and the fever were trapped inside her body, burning from the inside out. Her cough had returned and was now so constant that she could not speak more than a few short sentences before needing to stop and cough and gasp for breath. And when she did speak, her words burst from her lips in beaded chains of plosives between sharp, shallow intakes of breath. She was in a state of constant high excitement, a kind of mania, but was unable to say clearly what had so excited her.

Before long, she came less frequently to the apiary and then ceased coming altogether and left the house only for an hour or so every three or four days to walk alone, or sometimes accompanied by Elder John or Eldress Mary or one of the sisters, for a short stroll to the flower beds and bird feeders and to wave feebly to me across the lawn and then return to the house. There seemed to be someone at her side at all times, usually one of the women, occasionally Elder John, escorting her to the dining room or to evening services or up the stairs to her bedroom, attending to her as if ready to catch her should she fall.

I did not dare any longer to steal away from the others and with a glance and a hidden gesture signal her to meet me outside alone or down by the canal in the boathouse, where we had conducted so many of our secret rendezvous, and in the predawn hours I no longer silently slipped up the stairs in the main house before the others had risen from their beds and on cat feet passed the closed doors to Elder John's and Eldress Mary's private quarters and on up the narrow stairs, to meet in Sadie's bedroom and lie in her bed with her for thirty or forty minutes, trembling with wild desire and the thrill of deception and the risk of discovery, while the rising sun spread lengthening panes of light across the polished floor and the morning breeze gently filled the muslin curtains like sails.

Then for nearly two weeks Sadie did not appear among us anywhere. Finally, in as casual a manner as I could muster, at breakfast one morning I asked Elder John a question I already knew the answer to. I asked him if Sadie had left us and returned to her home in Rhode Island.

He said, "No, no, not at all. Her health has been declining, however. I know you've missed her company," he said. "Why don't you go up to her room? Sister Hazel will give you her breakfast tray, and today you can be the one to deliver it. That will please Sister Sadie as much as I'm sure it pleases you, brother."

I thought I caught his tone—ironic, almost sarcastic. Triumphant.

"Perhaps it will please her," I said. "Perhaps not. But weren't you in the habit of checking on her yourself at the start of the day? Since she's been housebound, I mean, with her health declining and unable to join us down here."

"Yes. But let her see your much-loved face for a change, instead of mine. When she sees my face, she's usually in pain, and I'm only there to urge her to take her medicine. But that was an hour ago, so she'll be free of pain by now and will welcome you. She may be a little lethargic and sleepy, however. Morphine does that."

Pain. And morphine. I asked him if a doctor had come out to see her, Dr. Cardiff, who used to care for the patients at Sunshine Home.

"There is nothing Dr. Cardiff can do to help her now," he said. "He sent out a packet of morphine from St. Cloud with instructions on how to dilute it and told us to administer it ourselves, which is what we've been doing. And it seems to relieve her for several hours at a time, though it leaves her weaker afterwards. It's a hard choice." He paused a few seconds as if to gather his thoughts. "Pain versus increasing weakness. It's a downward spiral, I'm afraid, more than a simple circular spiral. The illness feeds the pain, but the medicine for the pain weakens her ability to fight the illness. Go up and see her, brother."

I left the table at once and went to the kitchen and fetched Sister Hazel's prepared breakfast tray of porridge and tea and quickly made my way up the two flights of stairs to Sadie's room. The door was closed. I knocked gently and said, "Sadie, it's Harley. I've brought your breakfast."

There was no answer. I waited a moment and announced myself a second time.

Still no answer. I opened the door and entered. The window was shut, the curtains drawn, and the room was dark and humid and warm. She was lying in her narrow bed facing the wall. I put the tray down on her desk and sat on the edge of the bed. Her long hair was loose and tousled and covered her face and neck like an ashen shawl. Her white cotton nightgown had fallen slightly off her shoulder, as pale as the fabric itself. I touched her lightly on her bare arm. Her skin was dry to the touch, like the chalky cloth of her nightgown.

A third time I announced myself: "Sadie, it's Harley. I've brought your breakfast."

She murmured an answer that I couldn't make out.

I asked her to say it again.

"Not hungry."

I begged her to drink some tea, as if for my sake, not hers, just a few sips. "And take some nourishment, please."

She said nothing, and then I broke and said, "Oh, Sadie! Please don't go. Don't leave me. I need you, Sadie."

She turned slightly and pushed her hair away from her face and looked at me through half-lidded eyes and said, "Harley, I'm going to die."

"No, you're not going to die. You'll get better soon, like you always have."

"It's right for me to die now."

"Don't say that."

"To punish me."

"Punish you? Why? For loving me? Then we both should die. For I'm as guilty as you."

"No, Harley, not that. I'm pregnant."

She turned away from me and faced the wall again. I was silent for a long time. I could hear her raspy breath and realized that I was not breathing, I was panting, like a dog in pain. I heard my blood thump past my ears. I stood up and walked to the window and opened it wide and let the morning breeze flow into the hot, stifling room. Everything in the room, even Sadie herself, appeared small to me and far away, as if I had suddenly been lifted to a great height and were looking down, like a bird from the topmost branch of a tree.

When finally I spoke, my throat was constricted and my voice was a croak. "How do you know . . . ?" The question trailed off and hung in the air for what seemed many minutes.

She answered by saying my name: "Harley."

It was enough. My question was ridiculous. I did not dare ask if she might be mistaken. I said, "What . . . what shall we do?"

"Nothing. I'm dying now. I'll be gone before it's known, anyhow. Except by you."

"No! You can't. You have to get well again, Sadie. You must get well, and then we can do whatever we must, to . . ." Again I trailed off.

"Until we . . . what? Nothing can be done."

"We can leave New Bethany. We can live in St. Cloud, and we can marry, and you can have our baby. Dr. Cardiff is there, and he and I together can bring you back to health again. I know we can. The pain will go away. You can have our baby."

She said my name again: "Harley." It was a gentle dismissal, a rebuke.

"This is not over," I said. "I won't let you die."

She was silent for a moment. "You won't let me die?" She uttered a short, acidic laugh. "What if you are not the father, Harley?"

Her words rolled over me like thunder. This was my worst fear compounded. If I am not the father of her unborn child, then who else could be? Without asking the question I knew the answer.

Everything was a lie, then. No one was who I thought. Nothing was as it seemed. Not Sadie, not Elder John, not even me. I was a fool, an easily deceived fool. The two people I loved most in the world had conspired to deceive me and had laughed at my love for them and had treated me for months, for years, like a lovesick boy. Which was only as I deserved, for that's what I really was, a naive, trusting, lovesick boy. I saw that fully now.

But if Sadie believed she was dying, why would she even tell me that she was pregnant? And possibly by someone other than me? I wondered if she had confessed the same thing to Elder John.

Of course! She must have. If she told me, then surely she told him, too.

And that was the reason he sent me up here this morning, I thought. So that I would be alone with her, and she would reveal to me that she was pregnant, and if not by me, then by him. So that, just as I believed he might be the father, he could believe the same of me. And then I could tell myself that the unborn child was his, and he could tell himself it was mine. And thus neither of us could say he was the father. We were both freed of responsibility.

That must be his plan, I decided.

But how unspeakably cruel of them! Of him, especially. Not Sadie. For she was mortally ill, her mind addled by morphine and terrible pain. And she was the one who was pregnant and was very likely on her deathbed. She had deceived and betrayed me, yes, but I almost deserved deception and betrayal and had practically invited it, for I was a fool, a childish fantasist, vain and reckless. I could not claim that she had been gratuitously, selfishly cruel to me. Not like him, Elder John, the hypocrite. He was my enemy, not Sadie.

I thought, yes, she betrayed me and lied to me and played me like a vain, worshipful boy. But maybe . . . maybe she loved me anyhow. Because of my innocence, not despite it. Especially at the beginning of our romance, when I was indeed still innocent. Maybe she loved me because twice I had shown myself willing to sacrifice myself in order to save her, first from the sinkhole and then from the panther. And maybe she loved me because, like her, I was not a bona fide Shaker. We could play at being skeptics together and ironists and agnostics, while still appreciating the Believers' way of life, warming our cold, proud, youthful intellects at the Shaker fire.

But meanwhile, all along she was being seduced by Elder John. He was older and wise-seeming and custodial, and he was handsome and learned. And he had authority at New Bethany, which allowed him to make sure, after the closing of Sunshine Home, that she was properly cared for throughout her illness, even if she remained a Shaker novitiate, like me, and not a proper Believer.

Because of her illness and poverty, she needed him more than she needed me. I had sensed that early on. It's probably why I was so jealous of him. To her, our romance was just that, a romance. Seductive, distracting, flattering. But her affair with Elder John was life-saving. His favor and protection provided her with a home and a coterie of devoted attendants. He gave her New Bethany. And along with New Bethany, he gave her me, a clever, amusing boy saturated with worshipful affection and admiration and, eventually, adolescent lust. How could she have turned her back on all that? No, I could not blame her. Not the way I blamed him.

In as level a voice as I could manage, I said to her, "There's nothing that says I'm not the father and much that says I am. But even if I am not the father, Sadie, I will behave as if I were." I sat on the edge of her bed again and touched her bare shoulder, which now felt feverishly warm and moist.

"I will be dead before anyone knows I'm pregnant," she murmured. She went silent for a moment, then breathed in and said, "I can't live any longer with this pain. My entire body is a wound, Harley. An open, festering wound."

"What about Elder John?"

"He refuses to help me die. Both he and Eldress Mary. They won't help me."

"I mean, he knows you're pregnant, doesn't he?"

"Of course not! No one knows . . . except you."

"But you said I might not be the father."

"No. I asked, would you want me to live if you thought . . . if you thought someone else was the father."

"And you have my answer. If I'm not the father, I will behave as if I were. And I do want you to live, Sadie. I want you to live without pain and illness. I want you to live because I love you. And because you might be pregnant with my child."

"That's not . . . possible now. This pain and illness, Harley, it will only end with my death. I need you to help me, Harley."

"I will help you. I will."

She spoke slowly and clearly, but with great effort, as if she were scratching the words onto a slate. "I wanted you to believe that I was pregnant . . . and that someone else might be responsible . . . so that you would help me die."

"What? No! I won't help you die."

"Elder John and Eldress Mary, they keep the morphine. They dilute it and use it . . . but only to soften the pain for a short while. Find it, and bring it and the syringe to me . . . and help me inject a dose large enough to end my life, Harley."

"No! I can't!"

"You must. It's time for me to go. I'm only a burden on New Bethany now. I can't work, I can't help anyone, everyone has to help me. I'm too weak to leave my bed. It's shameful. I'm ashamed. And the suffering, the pain . . . it only worsens by the hour. You must help me. If you love me. Please, Harley."

"No, I can't. Not this way."

"Then go to them, and plead with them to do it."

"If I did that, it would be cowardly. I'd sooner inject you with the morphine myself than ask them to do it. I won't, Sadie. I won't help you die."

"All right, then. Go away. Go. Leave me, Harley . . . leave me. Don't come back again."

I leaned down and kissed her lightly on the shoulder where I had been touching her with my hand. Her skin was hot against my lips. She recoiled and drew her nightgown back over her shoulder and curled further into herself.

I got up and walked to the door and opened it and stood there a few seconds and looked at her, so small and crumpled, so worn down by pain and suffering and fear. "Goodbye, Sadie. I love you. And I won't let this be the last time we are together. I won't obey you, Sadie. I will come back again," I said, and I stepped into the hallway and shut the door.

My head was literally spinning, and as I made my way back down to the dining room, I held on to the banister, afraid the dizziness would make me fall. I didn't know what to believe, what to think, what to feel. I didn't know what to *do*. My beliefs and thoughts and feelings were coming from all directions, colliding like small animals driven mad with fear of some huge unknown predator. What was that dark beast standing in the shadows, that omnivorous predator? It was some crystalline, irrefutable fact, some true thing that could neither be misinterpreted nor misunderstood, but which refused to make itself known to me. I knew it was there, just beyond my comprehension, and that it could explain everything and could show me what to believe and think, what to feel and, most importantly, what I should do. But I couldn't see its shape or outline, only its dark presence, and could not name or define it even by saying what it wasn't. It was like loneliness when you are not alone, sadness when you are filled with laughter, fear when you are being brave. It was grief before death. Disbelief lurking behind belief.

As I reached the bottom of the stairs, Sister Hazel and her three small charges passed me on their way up to the schoolroom. My real sister, Rachel, now eight years old, smiled up at me as she passed and brushed my wrist with her fingertips. Raymond and Royal were no longer students. Their hands were now dedicated wholly to work and their hearts to God. The other two schoolchildren, even younger than Rachel, were the son and daughter of a recently arrived Seminole, whom we called Sister Doreen, a woman in flight from a husband who had attacked her with a knife.

By the time I reached the dining room, the tables had been cleared, the dishes and tableware and pans washed and put away, and the brethren all gone off to perform their usual appointed tasks in the fields and shops and barns. I glimpsed Eldress Mary at her office desk, bent over her accounts receivable and expense ledgers. From the parlor window I saw Elder John and Brother Amos out by the barn hitching the oxen to the harrow. Mother and Sister Rosalie, on their way from the washhouse to the clotheslines behind the main house, lugged baskets of wet laundry past the two men. It was an ordinary spring day at New Bethany, nothing out of place, nothing unusual, nothing awry.

Except for the pregnant young woman dying in agony alone in the room two stories above.

But was she really pregnant, and if so, by whom? I couldn't wholly believe anything she had told me. But no matter how contradictory or conflicted it seemed, I couldn't deny any of it, either. If she had wanted to sow confusion in my mind as to the truth of her pregnancy—first telling me it was true, then suggesting that someone other than me was the father, then denying it all and claiming that she had made these false claims in order to manipulate me into helping her die—if she had wanted me weak and uncertain, then she had wholly succeeded.

Also, she had raised anew the old nagging question of Elder John's involvement with her, its true nature and consequences. For years, my natural inclination had been to suspect him of attempting to seduce Sadie, to make his relationship with her evolve in small, barely perceptible stages as he went from being her patriarchal protector and sponsor to becoming her secret lover. I had long been afraid that he wanted to take her away from me and replace me in her heart with himself, and now she had all but confirmed my fear.

And was she really dying in agony? She had been living with this disease for over seven years, enjoying long periods of apparent good health, alternating with relapses and declines, followed by a gradual return to health. Tuberculosis often struggled with its victims like that, especially when the victim, like Sadie, was young and otherwise healthy and living in a healthful climate and home.

And did she really want to die? Was the physical pain, combined with her shame for her pregnancy—if indeed she was pregnant—and for being a burden to the New Bethany family and, though she did not say it, her guilt for her secret love affair with me and probably an affair with Elder John, too, was that enough to drive her to suicide?

But Sadie feared and despised death. She loved every aspect of being alive and never tired of contemplating and attending to the world that surrounded her. Over the years that we were confidants and lovers she had shaken me out of my melancholy and pessimism again and again. She had passed her temperament into mine like an electric current and had enlivened my morbidity beyond anything I could have generated on my own. If there was anyone longing for death back then, it was not Sadie, it was me, a self-romanticizing adolescent boy struggling to resolve unresolvable conflicts between freedom and security, honesty and mendacity, belief and unbelief, trust and mistrust, love and hate. Had it not been for Sadie, it sometimes seemed to me that an early death was the only way I could untangle myself from the dialectical chains that bound me.

I lingered in the parlor a few moments longer, looking out the window at Elder John. He stood by the open barn door, giving instructions for the day's harrowing to Brother Amos, who sat up on the driver's seat of the spindly harrow with his long goad at the ready, while the yoked chocolate-brown oxen waited patiently at the front of the machine for direction. It was early April, time to chop the soil and set out the seed potatoes. Elder John carried in his head the planting, tending, and harvesting calendar for every crop on the farm. He was like a walking, talking Florida *Farmers' Almanac*. He freed the rest of us from having to track our own work cycles, liberating us to go out and, without having to think of it, complete our assigned tasks at the right time of day and place and season. None of the rest of the brethren at New Bethany worried himself or herself over the larger overall scheme of his or her work, not even Sister Rosalie over her poultry or old Brother Ezekiel, the cobbler, who, because of his arthritic hands, was about to retire and be replaced by my brother Raymond. Everyone's daily and seasonal schedule and assigned task came from Elder John. We were like the pair of docile oxen hitched to the harrow, and he was our drover as much as our herdsman.

Except for me and my bees. After the opening of the sinkhole drove poor Brother Hiram mad and he abandoned New Bethany for his parents' home in Maryland, Elder John came to me one afternoon at the apiary. Falling into the Quaker manner of speech that he reserved for making important announcements, he said, "Thou art the sole beekeeper now, Brother Harley. The science of beekeeping lies entirely in thy hands, no one else's. No one here but thee has the capacity to learn all there is to know about the care and feeding and breeding of the bees and the harvesting of their honey, and I have not the time to do it myself. Go and order and study the books and reports that thou will need to master the apiary science. I will trust thee to manage these tiny creatures and their valuable sweet crop entirely according to thy best understanding, without interference from me or anyone else. If it goes well, and I'm sure it will, then I will soon place thee in charge of the orchards and the flower gardens, too, where the bees love to feed."

That was over a year ago, before the freeze. It was the first overt sign that he was grooming me to eventually replace him, and with it an implicit promise that I could do so without needing to become a true Believer. Though I had never stated it in so many words to him, or to anyone other than Sadie and my brother Pence, Elder John knew that I was an unbeliever. He also knew that, if to go on living among the Shakers I was obliged to confess my sins and declare my belief in "the duality of the Deity, Father and Mother God, the mighty dual spirit as manifested in Jesus and Ann Lee, immortal life, progress of the soul, faithfulness, lawfulness, equality of the sexes, equality in labor, equality in property, temperance in all things, justice and kindness to all, and celibacy," I would do it. I subscribed to some of these Shaker beliefs, yes, but if I pledged myself to that entire packet, I would be lying. Which would make me a hypocrite.

Elder John knew that about me. Just as I knew about him that he was lying. And therefore, though he was the best of the Shakers, he was a hypocrite. I wished to emulate him in every way, even in that.

How did I know he was lying about his faith and belief, when he hid it so well? No one else seemed to suspect it. To an outside observer, he was the exemplary Shaker. He led our evening prayers, after all, and heard the confession of sins from every adult male who chose to become a committed member of the New Bethany family, and whenever there was a need to apply biblical exegesis to one of the brethren's real-life moral or ethical questions, it was Elder John, not Eldress Mary, who got consulted. Like the accountant she was, Eldress Mary taught by rote and rule, by the book, as they say, and had none of Elder John's poetic sensibility or his affection for nuance and ambiguity and allusion. She wasn't interested in complexity, whereas he seemed to seek it out, even in places where it didn't exist. He did not make a show, as she did, of his dedication to the seven primary principles that undergirded the Shakers' way of life, but nonetheless he could enumerate and explicate them like a medieval monk, and often did so, chanting them aloud, as if idly humming an old folk tune to himself.

But to a skeptical and admittedly competitive insider like me, there was the occasional fly in the ointment. As the Bible has it, "Dead flies cause the ointment of the apothecary to send forth a stinking savor: so doth a little folly by him that is in reputation for wisdom and honor."* Or as Thoreau said, "Some circumstantial evidence is very strong, as when you find a trout in the milk."†

The fly in the ointment and the trout in the milk: I would not have known and could not have cited the phrases if Elder John himself had not steered me to those very texts, the Old Testament book of Ecclesiastes and the journals of Thoreau, which had been published a few years earlier and which he gave me to read, all three volumes,

---

* Ecclesiastes 10:1

† *The Journal of Henry David Thoreau* (Boston: Houghton Mifflin, 1906)

saying, "Thoreau was a very wise man. You should drink from his cup, brother, if you wish to be wise and not merely smart."

As for Ecclesiastes, which he said was his favorite book of the Old Testament, Elder John had instructed me to study it, not just read it for the poetry and the clever parallelisms, and to think deeply about the many meanings of the word "vanity" and the causes of "a vexation of spirit" and the relationship between the two. Which I dutifully did—I think I was only about fourteen at the time, and the idea of vanity was to me little more than a superficial notion that I confused with conceitedness and self-centeredness, and I had not even begun at that age to examine the nature of my spirit. But I did recognize myself in those ancient Hebrew verses and quickly realized that Elder John was forewarning me.

A self-invented person like Elder John, the Kentucky sharecropper's lad, more so than one who has followed the path laid down for him at birth, tends to see embodied in his neighbors his own weaknesses, sins, and fears. As Montaigne wrote, "Confidence in the goodness of another is good proof of one's own goodness."* The opposite is just as true. It's telling that Elder John saw in me tendencies that he thought could be identified and corrected by the ancient Hebrew preacher who speaks the verses of Ecclesiastes. No one else who knew me, not even my own mother or my twin brother, fussed about or even noticed my vanity or the vexation of my spirit. Only Elder John, who therefore must himself have possessed the same tendencies, vanity and a vexatious spirit, or he would not have recognized them in me.

That he steered me to the writings of the modern New England transcendentalist Henry David Thoreau, calling him wise, even though Thoreau's religious leanings tipped away from Shaker beliefs by about one hundred eighty degrees. As if he sought to counter religious orthodoxy with wisdom and wished to create in me an ally who was a Shaker but not a true Believer. He succeeded, of course, but in so doing he exposed his own disbelief and his hypocrisy.

Then there was the matter of his purchase of four lots in St. Cloud

---

* Montaigne, *Essais*, book 1, ch. 14

in his own name with Shaker funds, brought to our attention by the delegation of trustees from Mount Lebanon and resulting in Elder John's temporary demotion and replacement with the lovable Elder Thomas Halsey. That it was pure financial speculation, which could ultimately benefit him, and involved usury, didn't—

[*Here Reel #11 runs out, apparently catching Harley Mann by surprise.*]

REEL #12

It's not dark yet, there's still a few hours of daylight left, so I'll talk a while longer and try to get to where I was going when the previous tape got filled. I can pick up the rest of the story tomorrow, for there is much more to reveal. Much more to confess. More to assess.

It was shortly after the midday meal, the same day as my early-morning visit to Sadie in her bedroom that had left me so shaken and confused. We had all returned to our labors, when Eldress Mary came out onto the porch of the main house and clanged the bronze bell that called the brethren back from the fields and barn and shops and brought me up from the bee yard. I had been planning another visit to Sadie's room as soon as I thought it would go unnoticed. I intended to test everything she had told me, but the call of the bell and the gathering of the brethren disrupted my plan.

Usually, when Elder John or Eldress Mary rang the bell in the middle of the workday, it signaled a need for all hands to join in a common task, like loading or unloading the barge from St. Cloud so it could quickly turn and return. I glanced down at the dock and along the shore, but there was no sign of the *Coquina*. This meant we'd likely be marched off together to somewhere out on the land and lined up like Pharaoh's slaves by Elder John to lift or move or carry some heavy thing, or many heavy things, for one of his building projects, a dam or a bridge or maybe even a pyramid. He was forever organizing us into impromptu work parties of ten or a dozen laborers, male and female, young and old, to complete some Herculean task. And we all willingly put down our tools and ceased whatever specialized work we were doing at the time and joined the party and put our collective shoulder to his big wheel. Hands to work and hearts to God. No one ever complained. Elder John's building projects were the glory of New Bethany and the envy of our neighbors far and wide, who had no such access to a large unpaid labor force. Not since the end of slavery, anyhow.

So we gathered around Eldress Mary at the porch, some of us on the lawn nearby, others coming out of the kitchen and the sewing room to stand around her, all of us waiting for our marching orders. I hung back a ways from the others, and I remember thinking, We're like schoolchildren. Or worse, like servants about to be told by the master of the house that an important visitor is coming and we must make the house ready.

Then Elder John, bareheaded and slump-shouldered, stepped from the parlor onto the porch and stood next to Eldress Mary. He did not resemble his usual self when about to take charge of his ragtag troop of Believers. His face was gray and slack, as if he'd suffered a grave disappointment. He was the furthest thing from a commanding presence, and I think everyone, including me, was surprised and a little frightened by his appearance. We all went suddenly silent and watched and waited for him to speak.

But it was Eldress Mary who spoke. In a calm, clear voice, she said, "Today our beloved Sister Sadie Pratt has passed. She is no longer suffering and has gone to sit at the side of Mother Ann and Jesus Christ in Heaven. Tonight, after the evening meal, we will hold a funeral service for her in the meetinghouse. Her earthly body will be laid out so that we can all say our goodbye to her and raise our voices in prayer and song to help hymn her soul to Heaven. We will bury her body tomorrow at noon in the Shaker cemetery. Brother Edwin will build her coffin this afternoon, and Brother Royal will make the marker for her grave," she declared. "You may all return to your work now," she added. She turned and walked back inside the house, and Elder John followed.

The brethren dispersed without much conversation or apparent concern, as if Eldress Mary had announced an unexpected change in our usual supper time. Alone and frozen to the spot, I stayed, however. There was for me at that moment only one fact in the entire universe—my Sadie was no more. She had been instantly transformed from a defining presence into a defining absence. Others had died, Elder Thomas Halsey, old Brother Theodore, and several other New Bethany brethren I was close to, and many had left the community, never to be seen or heard from again, like my brother Pence and Brother Hiram, but their deaths and disappearances had not altered the nature of reality. Not even when my father died in Waycross those many years ago had such a definitive absence occurred. There was always something left behind, not a ghost, but a persistent presence that only gradually faded away. After a rent in the fabric of my life, there were still the torn pieces of cloth, which could eventually be reattached and the world made whole again.

Time seemed to have stopped, but gradually I was able to move my body, and time resumed its flow. I took a few steps toward the porch, slowly at first, then running, and I rushed into the house and up the stairs. I burst through the schoolroom, startling Sister Hazel and the children, and dashed up the second flight of stairs and entered Sadie's bedroom. Eldress Mary stood by the bed, carefully arranging Sadie's nightgown and blankets around her, as if tucking her in for the night.

She stepped away and showed me Sadie's dead body. She did it dispassionately, with a small wave of the hand, as if the body were no more than the physical evidence that Sadie had died. Only her face and throat were visible. As if sculpted in clay, her skin was pale gray now, no longer white. Her eyes were closed, but not as if she were sleeping. She seemed to have winced and deliberately shut them herself in the seconds before she died.

I stood by the bed and silently wept. After a few moments, I found my voice and asked Eldress Mary, "Were you with her when she died?"

"Yes. She was at peace with God. And she was not in pain. Her suffering was over, just as she wished."

"Was Elder John with her, too?"

"Yes, he was here. We both prayed over her as she left us."

"Did you hear her confession of sins before she died?" I asked.

I suddenly wanted her to have died a Shaker, even though her confession would have indicted me as much as her. Somehow it mattered to me, though at that moment I could not have said why. I decided that if Sadie died a Shaker, I would live as one. I would follow her. I would make an honest confession of my sins to Elder John, and I would become a celibate for life, a true Believer. It would be a way of making Sadie my wife, making me her husband. My bride would be an absence, a lifelong nonexistence. And every time I thought of myself as a Shaker, every time I was addressed as Brother Harley, whenever I prayed to Mother Ann and Jesus Christ or sang the Shaker songs or joined the Shaker dances, she would be pulled back briefly into existence.

Eldress Mary hadn't answered my question, so I asked it again. "Did she make her confession before she died?"

"That lies between me and her and God," she said.

"I need to know! Did she die a Shaker?"

"It will say it on her grave marker. That's all you need to know, brother. Now go out and tend to your bees. I have to prepare poor Sister Sadie's body."

"Where is Elder John?" I asked. He would know whether Sadie had made her confession before she died, and I believed that he would tell me. Eldress Mary wouldn't have revealed any of its details to him, but if it had taken place, she was obliged to tell him so. Whether Sadie died as a Shaker could not remain solely between Eldress Mary and Sadie and God. Elder John had also to approve.

He would have no reason to withhold this information from me, and several for wanting to offer it up. He might think that it would prompt me to make my confession, too. He knew that once Pence left, it was only my love of Sadie that kept me here, and with Sadie gone, there was no reason for me to stay on and eventually replace him and turn into Elder Harley, his heir apparent. Unless I became a true Shaker. Indeed, I had decided that I would do it. If Sadie had confessed to Eldress Mary, I would confess to Elder John that Sadie and I were lovers and that she told me before she died that she was pregnant and that in my vanity of vanities and vexatious spirit I believed that he was as likely the father as I. I would confess that I had for years hidden my unbelief, that I was secretly agnostic and faithless, that I had been a lying hypocrite. Then he would know all my secrets and sins.

Eldress Mary said that Elder John was to be found in his rooms at prayer and I should not disturb him. "He is very much saddened by the death of Sister Sadie. He had grown exceedingly fond of her."

I said, "And so was I. Exceedingly fond of her."

She fixed me with a steady, unreadable gaze and said, "Yes. You were. Exceedingly."

She was giving me my answer. So Sadie did make her deathbed confession. She had died a Shaker. Eldress Mary now knew everything about Sadie's secret love affair with me and knew that she either was pregnant or had lied about it to me. She also knew the truth about Sadie's relations with Elder John, one way or the other, whether it had been an innocent flirtation or a sordid, carnal love affair. And if Eldress Mary knew all Sadie's sins, then she knew all mine, too, for they were inextricably linked. And if Elder John had sinned with Sadie, it was more than possible that Eldress Mary now knew his sins as well.

But why would she protect him, then? Why would she protect me? She could denounce both of us to the trustees, and was in fact obliged by Shaker canonical law to report our violation of the cardinal rule of celibacy, and we would be cast out of the Society of Believers. New Bethany's most trusted and honored elder and the novitiate widely known as his chosen successor sent off to wander in the wilderness among the people of the World, permanent strangers in a strange land, shunned by their brethren, their true spiritual family, and by Mother Ann and Jesus in Heaven and God above, derided and pitied, even by the people of the World, for their fallen state. A defrocked priest, among nonbelievers, is an object of pity and condescension, someone who has failed to live up to his own spiritual and moral ambitions, a man or woman who set his standards too high for normal human beings and has been brought low, sent back down to where the people of the World, whose spiritual and moral standards are more realistically set, live out their messy, compromised daily lives.

Eldress Mary had more than merely suggested that she had heard Sadie's deathbed confession of her and my and Elder John's sins: *Yes . . . you were . . . exceedingly fond of her.* But she had given no indication that she intended to denounce me and Elder John to the trustees in Mount Lebanon. There was time enough for that. In the meantime there was the funeral to attend to and the burial, and the report to the trustees had to be made in writing, the truth of which Elder John and I had to attest to and sign.

I went to the door of his quarters on the second floor and knocked lightly. Behind me in the schoolroom, the children, under Sister Hazel's direction, were learning to sing "Down Low in the Valley." It was a song much loved at New Bethany, mainly because it was "received," as the Shakers say, instead of "composed," by Sister Minerva Reynolds, who was one of the oldest Shakers to come down from Mount Lebanon back in the 1890s with Elder John to help found New Bethany. She died here that first summer and was buried where Sadie would soon lie. I listened to the words sung by the children in their high, sweet voices, and tried to apply them to this fraught moment, but could not.

> Down low in the valley, where angels meet,
> The voice of our Savior we hear saying,
> Come, O! my chosen, ye lambs of my fold,
> To the fountain in Zion draw near,
> While the waters are troubled let each one step in,
> For all may here wash and be clean.
> Through the gift of repentance a balm will be found,
> A balm to heal every wound.

There was no response to my light knock on Elder John's door, so I tried again and this time heard him say, "Yes, who is it?"

"It's Brother Harley. May I speak with you?"

He opened the door and stood before me as he had earlier on the porch, slump-shouldered and downcast. I apologized for interrupting him and said I'd return later if he preferred.

He said to come in. "I always welcome your company, brother. Perhaps especially at this moment of grief and reflection."

It was the first time I had entered Elder John's private chamber. The bare room was somewhat larger than Sadie's, but with no more furniture than hers and no decoration or display of personal items, no family photos or niceties, just a small desk and straight-backed chair, a bookcase, a narrow bed and armoire. A monk's room. The bookcase was three short shelves and appeared to carry books that he was presently reading, as several of them lay open and others had pages marked with little scraps of paper. The main New Bethany repository for books was off the parlor downstairs, a small room called the library with floor-to-ceiling shelves filled with books and journals, practical and agronomical and philosophical and religious texts, presumably selected and acquired over the years by Elder John and mostly read by him alone and, under his direction, by me. He waved me to the desk chair and sat himself on the edge of the bed and wrapped his knees with his large hands.

"So," he said, "our little Sister Sadie Pratt, she has left us. A mercy for her, but a terrible loss for us. All the brethren loved her. But I know you especially loved her. I think she kept you from being lonely here."

I agreed and said that she was as close a friend as I had at New Bethany.

"I worry about you. Your twin brother, Pence, has left us, and now Sadie."

"Eldress Mary told me that you and she were present when she died," I said.

"Yes, we were. We were with her at the end."

"Early this morning, I went to her room to visit her," I said. "And she was in great pain. She was in despair and very confused." I paused for a few seconds and then said, "She asked me to help her die."

"She did? Well, yes, she badly wanted an end to her suffering."

"She asked me to find the morphine in your quarters and bring it to her and help her inject a dose that would end her suffering, even though it would end her life."

"She asked that of you?"

"Yes. She wanted a dose large enough to kill her."

"What did you do?"

"I refused. I thought that she was more intent on dying than she was on ending her physical pain. The small doses that you and Eldress Mary had been administering were adequately treating her pain, weren't they?"

He was silent for a moment, as if absorbing the implications of my question. Finally, he said, "No, they were no longer adequately treating her pain. We were following Dr. Cardiff's instructions exactly, but the morphine was not easing her suffering anymore. Not even for a few hours at a time. Her disease had begun to destroy her internal organs, not just her lungs, Brother Harley."

"Do you think Sadie wanted to die?"

"Yes."

"Why?"

"To put an end to her suffering. The poor girl, it was horrifying to see her face all contorted, to hear her cry out in agony, when she knew that she would never recover, when she realized that she would never return to her life among her beloved companions, her New Bethany family. Yes, she wanted to die. She knew it was coming, and she wanted it to hurry. She begged for a lethal dose of that morphine. I'm not surprised that she wanted you to help provide it. I'm sorry that you had to hear that request from her. Of course, you had to deny it." He added that Sadie died believing in God and Heaven and the divinity of Jesus Christ and Mother Ann, and here he resumed speaking in his old-fashioned Quaker way, as if he had taken off one hat, the Kentucky farmer's straw, and put on another, the preacher's broad-brimmed black fedora. "She hath gone to live eternally now, to live in blessed peace and comfort, no longer in pain, no longer diseased and dying. Thou must not feel sorrow over her dying, Brother Harley. Thou canst rightly miss her presence in thy daily life, but thou must take comfort from knowing that she hath been released from her long-suffering, diseased earthly body."

"Please," I said. "Speak to me plainly." At one time, I had been puzzled and then mildly amused whenever he switched off his sharecropper manner of speaking and turned on the Quaker preacher's archaic voice and grammar. But over the years the practice had come to grate on me, and I began to wonder what his authentic voice and grammar were like. How we speak is who we are, after all. How I'm speaking here is, for better or worse, who I am. But it had begun to seem that Elder John was neither the Quaker sharecropper's son nor the Shaker preacher. He was someone else, a third person, one who never spoke, one who remained silent and invisible and unaccountable.

But then for the first time the real Elder John was speaking, and he became suddenly audible and visible and, at last, accountable. He spoke with the soft accent of a college-educated Southern man. He said, "I am sorry, Harley. You are right, you of all people deserve to know the truth of how Sadie died. No one else should ever know, however. Will you promise to keep what I am about to tell you wholly between us? You must never reveal it. For Sadie's sake, but also for mine and Eldress Mary's."

"Yes," I said. "Of course."

"And I don't want Eldress Mary to know that I have told you this, either. I'm breaking a vow of secrecy that I made to her. Do you agree to that, brother?"

"Yes."

"All right, then. This morning, not long after you left Sadie's room, Eldress Mary and I injected Sadie with the rest of the morphine left by Dr. Cardiff. We did it so that she could die, brother. She begged us to do it. And when we had done it, she thanked us. She closed her eyes and seemed to go to sleep. I held her hand and felt her pulse until it stopped. She did not suffer, Harley."

Nothing he said surprised me. Only that he said it.

I inhaled deeply and was silent for a moment. Then I said, "So you did what I refused to do."

"Yes. But you were right. To refuse to help her die."

"Why? If you and Eldress Mary were right not to refuse?"

"We were jointly responsible for her being at New Bethany and caring for her while she lived with us," he said.

"And you think helping her to die was caring for her?"

"Yes, I do. She was in terrible pain and in a matter of days she would die on her own."

"And you and Eldress Mary vowed not to reveal it to anyone, not even to me?"

"Yes. Although it appears that now I have broken that vow."

"Before she died, did Sadie make her confession to Eldress Mary and become a Believer?"

"They spoke privately out of my hearing. Which is how it's done, woman to woman. I assume that, yes, Sadie made her confession and statement of belief, and that she died a Shaker. Sister Sadie."

So now the three of us, Elder John and Eldress Mary and I, were linked by secrets revealed mingled with secrets kept, with broken vows of silence laid over broken vows of celibacy, with confessions protecting lies and lies protecting confessions. Everything known was nullified by everything unknown, and vice versa. This is how the truth gets appropriated and remade in one's self-interest. This is how the truth gets obliterated.

Which is what I did from then on, obliterated the truth and remade it in my self-interest. It's what I believed Elder John and Eldress Mary were also doing. We judge and refuse to judge others the same as we judge and refuse to judge ourselves. The liar thinks that everyone lies, and the truth teller believes that everyone is honest. For many years, since the day I first fell in love with Sadie, I had been a liar. I said only that I was her friend. And when I became her lover, I told no one, which was a type of lie. And for many years I lied by simple omission, by never correcting Elder John's and Eldress Mary's assumption that I was a faithful Shaker novitiate and that, after I came of age, I would declare myself a Believer and that I, as Brother Harley, would eventually become Elder Harley, replacing the man who now sat across from me on the edge of his bed, his hands wrapped around his knees, his large, bearded head bowed as if in reflection or prayer, a man who had suddenly unburdened himself and in the process had unexpectedly taken on a whole new and greater burden.

"Helping Sadie die," I said to him, "was a crime. Whether it was a sin is a wholly different question. But you murdered her, and murder is a crime."

"Euthanasia," he said. "We didn't murder her. It was euthanasia. We helped her die. I don't concern myself over its being a crime. I care only that it was not a sin. And it wasn't. It would have been sinful for us *not* to have helped her die. Sometimes, brother, we have to break the law in order to keep from committing a sin."

"So was it sinful for me to have refused to do it?"

"No. You were not responsible for her care. We were, Eldress Mary and I. And we were exercising that responsibility."

"Call it what you will, Elder, it's still a crime. Euthanasia is as illegal as murder. Which is the reason you and Eldress Mary vowed not to reveal the truth of how Sadie died, isn't it?"

"Yes."

"Although you have now broken that vow," I added.

"By telling you."

"Yes, by telling me."

"Perhaps I should regret that?"

"No, you needn't regret it. I'll keep your secret," I said. "If you will keep mine."

He looked up at me, and puzzlement crossed his face, which I took to be feigned. He said he had no knowledge of any secrets of mine. He said he knew nothing about me that I had not told him myself or showed him with my visible, known behavior, and though I had not yet made my confession to him, he anticipated that when I did, it would contain no surprises, no dark secrets, nothing worse than normal youthful exuberation and errors of judgment and minor deceptions.

I was quite sure that he was lying and that he was well aware of the nature of my relationship with Sadie. Either Sadie had told him or he was told by Eldress Mary, who would have learned of it from Sadie's confession.

Of course, it was entirely possible that when making her confession, Sadie had *not* told Eldress Mary about her love affair with me. And it was possible that when she claimed to be pregnant and said I might not be the father, Sadie was lying to me. But I could not believe that. I chose to ignore what she said at the end, before she told me to go away and not see her again. *"I wanted you to believe that I was pregnant . . . and that someone else might be responsible . . . so that you would help me die."* So, yes, while it was possible that her friendship with Elder John might well have been just that, filial friendship, none of those likelihoods and possibilities satisfied my beliefs and suppositions.

And now I possessed concrete, specific proof that Elder John had participated in her murder. Instead of me confessing to him, he had confessed to me. He and Eldress Mary had murdered my Sadie. They did it, not to end her pain and suffering with mercy and loving-kindness, but in order to hide the fact that she had been sexually involved with me and possibly with Elder John, and that one of us had made her pregnant. That was why they wanted to make the funeral and burial take place quickly and more or less privately here at New Bethany. And why he called it euthanasia, even though it was a crime, because if ever they were arrested and charged, it would be for euthanasia, which was less of a crime than first-degree murder and was not as scandalous as the truth.

And the truth? If Sadie had lived another month or two, the World and all Shakerdom would know that the beautiful, consumptive novitiate living with the Shakers at New Bethany had been impregnated by one of the supposedly celibate males. The scandal would destroy what remained of New Bethany as a viable community and farm and would cause irrevocable harm to the reputation of Shakerism as a whole. Elder John and Eldress Mary couldn't let her live that long. They had to make sure that she died of tuberculosis and a virgin.

The only remaining question circled around Elder John's confession to me. Was it to draw me into a conspiracy with him and Eldress Mary, so that I could not reveal what they had done without putting myself in jeopardy? They surely knew that I was the only person at New Bethany likely to suspect them of helping Sadie die. And they knew, because of my admitted love for Sadie, that I would likely initiate an investigation into the circumstances of her death. Better, perhaps, not to take a chance on that and instead try to capture my silence by making me a co-conspirator.

So this is where it now stood for me. Honor my promise to Elder John and tell no one, not even Eldress Mary, what he had confessed, which would make me as legally responsible for Sadie's death as they were, an accomplice in the murder of the woman I loved. Or go at once to St. Cloud to the office of Sheriff Thomas Prevett and tell him what I knew of the circumstances surrounding the death of Sadie Pratt. Not everything I knew. Only the part about their having killed her.

In old age, the actions we most regret are those made when we were young and not so much foolish as hurt and angry. Too blinded by pain and rage to see the formal cause of our action, we act only on its material cause. I was confused and deceived by the vanity and vexatious spirit that Elder John and the book of Ecclesiastes had warned me against. I believed that my pain was caused by the death of my beloved and that my rage was directed at those who were responsible for her death. I went no further back in my life and its circumstances than my just-concluded conversation with Elder John.

I walked from New Bethany over to Narcoossee on the canal tow-path and caught a ride to St. Cloud on the returning afternoon barge. Captain Shea recognized me as one of the New Bethany Shakers, his best customer for shipping goods to and from St. Cloud, and waved me aboard and gave me free passage, which was lucky, as I carried no money of my own. Shakers were supposed to have no need for money of their own.

Late that afternoon a lanky, freckle-faced deputy near my age walked me into Sheriff Prevett's dark office on the first floor of the St. Cloud City Hall. The sheriff was a large, pear-shaped, nearly bald man in his mid-forties, in comportment and appearance more of a small-town mayor than a police officer. He reminded me of pictures I had seen of ex-president Grover Cleveland. He looked up from his newspaper when I entered and pushed away a half-eaten plate of rice and beans and fried chicken.

"Late lunch," he said, and smiled apologetically. He wiped his mouth and handlebar mustache with a cloth napkin and asked what he could do for me. He wore a wrinkled white shirt with sweat circles under the arms and wide red suspenders. He had a molasses-thick Southern accent and a relaxed, helpful smile, and his smile didn't fade when I told him that I had come to report a crime.

He pointed me to a wicker chair by his desk, and I sat down. A large four-bladed Wheeler ceiling fan turned slowly overhead. I had never seen an electric-powered fan before. I had never been to town on my own before or spoken to the sheriff or any other official or merchant. I was always in the company and under the supervision of Elder John or Eldress Mary. I remember that it was a very hot, humid day, and I was thirsty, and when he offered me a glass of water, I eagerly accepted it and drank it down in one gulp.

He refilled my glass from the pitcher and said, "Now, young feller, I don't believe we've ever met, so tell me your name and where you live. And tell me the nature of this here crime you're reporting."

I said my name and that I lived at New Bethany out beyond Narcoossee on Live Oak Lake.

"With the Shakers."

"Yes, sir."

"Good people. Honest and friendly. And are you one of them, a Shaker?"

"Not exactly. My mother is, and we've been living there about eight years, my mother and my brothers and sister and I."

"I see. Now what's this crime you've come all the way to town to tell me about? Something happen out there at New Bethany?"

"Yes, sir. A young woman resident, Sadie Pratt, she died this morning. She died of an overdose of morphine that was administered by the elder and eldress, who are in charge of New Bethany—the managers, you could say." I had rehearsed my little speech on the *Coquina* so that my agony over Sadie's death would not cause me to choke or break down while making it.

"Really? That's a very serious charge, young man. Murder, wouldn't you say?"

"Euthanasia."

"All right, euthanay-sis. You're sure it wasn't no accident."

"Yes, sir. It was not an accident. Nor was it a natural death. One of them, Elder John Bennett, he confessed it to me today, this morning, only a few hours after it was done. He said they did it to end her suffering from tuberculosis, but until today they were treating her with small doses of morphine prescribed by Dr. Cardiff. They injected her deliberately with a very large quantity of morphine, which they knew would kill her."

"This is all very surprising to me," he said. "I know Elder John pretty well, and the other one, Eldress Mary. Good people, ideal citizens. Sober and honest. And of course I know Dr. Cardiff. In all the years you people've been settled there, we've never once had cause to go out and arrest anyone or even serve papers. And this young woman who died, was she a Shaker?"

I said, "Not exactly. Like me." I told him that she had been convalescing at the Sunshine Home sanitarium until it closed about three years ago, and at the invitation of Elder John and Eldress Mary, she had come to live at New Bethany.

"Can you tell me why Elder John confessed this to you, son?"

His question took me by surprise, and I didn't have a ready answer. "I don't know why. He knew that I . . . that I was very close to her. We were . . . best friends."

"'Best friends.' You and this young woman. Well, now, that's quite a loss."

"Yes. And I saw her earlier this morning, and she asked me to bring her the rest of the morphine and inject her with it, because she wanted to die. But I refused to do it. When I told this a little while later to Elder John, he said that he and Eldress Mary had not refused. He said they had injected her with the morphine, and she had died from it. They killed her."

"He told you that? He said that straight out?"

"Yes, sir, he did. And now they're planning a funeral service for tonight, and they will bury her tomorrow at New Bethany in the Shaker burial ground. Which seems awfully quick to me."

"Well, that's no doubt on account of the heat and humidity. But I see your point. I have to take your accusation seriously, son. Assuming everything you say is true, of course. I have no reason to worry it ain't all true, do I?"

"No, sir."

Sheriff Prevett said that in that case he would go out to New Bethany first thing and speak with the elder and eldress and anyone else who might know what happened. He would ask Dr. Cardiff to come along, since the state requires a proper death certificate before burial. "We'll go in the morning by one of the patrol boats," he said. "That one road beyond Narcoossee, it ain't really a road and gets too mudded out this time of year to take the automobile. It's a brand-spanking-new Ford Model T, and I'd be mighty displeased if I got it sunk in the swamp. If you don't have a place in town to stay overnight, you're welcome to bunk at our house and accompany me and the doc tomorrow in the boat," he said.

I said I wanted to be present for Sadie's funeral service tonight and asked him why couldn't we go out there in the boat right away. "Besides," I said, "wouldn't Dr. Cardiff need to examine Sadie's body before they prepared it for the funeral and burial?"

He said he'd have to check with Dr. Cardiff as to his availability. The doctor was, among other things, the county coroner, and his office was down the hall from the sheriff's. He hollered for his deputy, whose name was Rebus, in the outer office and told him to see if Doc Cardiff was available to go out to New Bethany and write up a death certificate on a woman who'd died out there. "What'd you say her name was, son?"

"Sadie Pratt. She was a patient of his for many years."

"Yes, tell him that, Rebus," he said to the deputy. "He won't want to go out this late in the day, but that might unstick his ass from his chair."

A few minutes later the deputy returned and said Dr. Cardiff had a patient with him, but he'll be able to go out to New Bethany. "He knows the girl and the folks taking care of her. He says he'll meet you at the city pier in a half hour."

Before long, Sheriff Prevett, Dr. Cardiff, Deputy Rebus, and I were making our way along the eastern shore of East Lake Tohopekaliga in the sheriff's bright-white flat-bottomed dory. The afternoon sun hung halfway down the western sky behind a pale veil of cloud cover, and the water was smooth as black glass. Dr. Cardiff was a small, slim man in his late fifties with a tippler's complexion and a white Vandyke beard and wire-rimmed spectacles. He wore a Panama hat and a loose-fitting three-piece linen suit and string necktie and kept his black leather medical satchel beside him. I sat in the stern beside the deputy, who operated the motor, and the sheriff and Dr. Cardiff sat in the shade under the canopy.

The boat, about twenty feet stem to stern with a six-foot beam, was the first gasoline-powered watercraft I had ever seen. It had waist-high gunwales and a canvas sunroof and had a two-chined hull, the deputy told me. Powered by one of the new two-cycle, air-cooled Waterman Portos, it could transport four or five people and a fair load of goods through the shallow waters of the region and deep into the Glades. The sheriff was proud of his boat and said it was named *Belinda Blue*, after his eldest daughter, Belinda. I pretended to be interested, but my mind was elsewhere.

As we neared the cut where the Narcoossee canal linked to the lake, I started to anticipate what would happen when I brought Sheriff Prevett and his deputy and Dr. Cardiff out to New Bethany to confront Elder John and Eldress Mary over the death of my Sadie. Their equanimity and moral easefulness and lack of remorse had angered me, and my anger had shielded me from my grief. Until now I had held one thought in mind—to make them accountable for her death. I hadn't imagined the moment when they would actually be forced to tell it to an officer of the law.

But now that I had reported their criminal act to the legal authorities and had found myself in the company of those authorities, one of their party in fact, as if I had been deputized like Rebus, riding with the Osceola County sheriff and county coroner across the wide, dark lake and up the narrow, mangrove-lined canals past Narcoossee and on toward New Bethany, my home since childhood, to help bring about the destruction of my family of Believers, my only community of like-minded men and women and children, the people who had trained and educated and sheltered and fed and clothed me from childhood to adulthood, I began for the first time to regret what I had done and was doing now and to fear what would come next. My anger at Elder John and Eldress Mary had softened and receded somewhat, and my grief over the death of Sadie, like a leviathan, began to rise from the dark depths of my feelings and seemed likely soon to surface and overwhelm me, and by the time we reached Live Oak Lake, I had ceased speaking and did not even answer questions put directly to me.

Though the sun was still a long ways from setting, it was early evening as the sheriff's patrol boat entered Live Oak Lake and tied up at the New Bethany pier next to the Shaker dories. Beams of golden sunlight fell through the trees onto the dark water and across the broad lawns surrounding the main house and outbuildings. We walked up the lane from the pier, past my bee yard and the orchards and flower gardens. The sheriff and Dr. Cardiff and Rebus walked three abreast a few steps ahead of me, speaking with admiration of the plantings and the foursquare, neatly maintained buildings and barns and fencing, praising the Shakers for their industry and their use of "scientific farming," the doctor called it. The sheriff pointed out the windmills and cisterns and wellhead and aqueducts to Deputy Rebus, who had never been to New Bethany, and praised Elder John's hydrologic engineering. "The man's a mechanical genius," he said. "Wouldn't you agree, Harley?"

I did agree, but said nothing in response. I knew he was trying to draw me out as to the nature of my relationship with Elder John, but I was afraid that if I spoke I would picture Elder John in my mind, and then Sadie's face would appear, and I would choke and gasp for air and begin to sob. So I remained silent.

There was no one anywhere in sight as we passed the meeting-house and approached the main house. I remembered that it was dinnertime, and everyone would be seated at table in the dining room. But then Eldress Mary, in bonnet and white shoulder coverlet and long black dress, came out onto the porch and stood at the women's door with her bell in hand. Elder John, also with bell in hand, wearing his black suit and open-collared white shirt and black broad-brimmed hat, stood at the men's door, and simultaneously the two began to ring their bells in slow four-four time. A moment later, here came the rest of the New Bethany Shakers, females in one line emerging from Eldress Mary's door, males coming out the other, all of them dressed in their Sabbath best, stepping in time in separate parallel lines to the slow clang of the bells, *one-two-three-four, one-two-three-four, one-two-three-four,* a small group of pilgrims totaling just over a dozen, but because of their symmetry and disciplined order and spacing and their uniform dress and slow, ritualized walk, there seemed to be many more.

Sheriff Prevett and Dr. Cardiff and Rebus stepped aside and followed the mourners across the lawn and down the crushed limestone path to the meetinghouse, and I came along a few steps behind. The two lines of Shakers parted at the front of the low building, and the males and females entered their designated doors, and the sheriff's party and I entered accordingly and sat on the benches at the back of the room behind the other males. The females were seated across from us. Sadie's unadorned pine coffin, bathed in light from the setting sun, had been placed in the middle of the room on sawhorses.

The top of the coffin had been removed, but I did not look at her. I could not. When everyone was seated and silent for several minutes, Elder John stood, and the funeral service began. I have only the vaguest memory of it, as my mind was in a frightening whirl. I remember that he praised Sadie, and there were several old Shaker hymns chosen and led by Eldress Mary and a prayer to God and Jesus and Mother Ann that was spoken by Elder John. And I remember that throughout the service everyone stared at the coffin and at Sadie, and no one looked at me or the members of the sheriff's party. It was as if we were invisible or simply not there.

The room spun, and the voices of the speakers and singers echoed off the walls and ceiling and seemed unnaturally loud. There was a final long peroration by Elder John delivered with everyone standing and clapping hands slowly in time to his cadences, not as applause, but as a drumbeat, so that his closing words seemed more a chant than a speech. He then directed Brother Edwin to shut the coffin, and the carpenter came forward and placed the wide top board onto the coffin and fastened it at the end and sides with a mallet and an even dozen wooden pegs, his mallet keeping time to the slow rhythmic handclapping of the mourners. By now even the sheriff and the doctor and the deputy were clapping. But I did not join in. I could not speak, I could not sing, I could not clap my hands. I could not meet the eyes of anyone present, not my mother's or my brothers' and sister's, not the eyes of my Shaker brothers and sisters, and emphatically not the eyes of Elder John and Eldress Mary. And I could not bear to look at Sadie's body in the coffin. I hung my head and looked at my feet, the picture of shame.

Yet for all the appearance of shame, it was something else I felt. Grief, loss of the person I had loved above all others, yes. And, strangely, relief. The kind of relief that Elder John had described when he said that Sadie's long suffering had ended. And a deeply selfish relief that at last the years of my secrecy and lying had come to an end. And fear. I was suddenly afraid of what was about to happen. My life, which since childhood had been defined by my sharply defined place in a familial community of like-minded Believers, even though I myself was not a Believer, was about to end. Grief and relief and fear, they mingled and combusted and incinerated all the forms and norms on which I had based my deepest sense of selfhood—my love of Sadie Pratt, the years of secrecy, that double life I'd led for so long, and my days and nights as a member of the New Bethany community of Shakers.

As the mourners departed from the meetinghouse and the sheriff and Dr. Cardiff and the deputy followed them out, I stood by Sadie's closed coffin for a few moments and saw for the first time what lay ahead: nothing other than the deliberate, self-imposed exile of a true isolato.

When I stepped outside the meetinghouse, the Shakers had dispersed, except for Elder John and Eldress Mary, who were standing nearby, talking with Sheriff Prevett and Dr. Cardiff. I started for the men's dormitory, and Rebus followed me. The sheriff had likely told him to keep track of me. I stopped at a slight distance and turned and watched the sheriff and the others, but could not hear their words. They were a somber group, mostly looking at the ground, as if struggling to find the answer to a riddle, while one or another of them spoke.

Rebus said to me, "We should watch, don't you think? This could get right interesting."

After a few moments, Elder John and Eldress Mary and the doctor broke away from the group and walked to the main house. Sheriff Prevett ambled over to me and Rebus. He said to me, "Well, son, you made the initial complaint, so I got to ask you to come back to St. Cloud in the morning. The state's attorney will want to take down your statement. That's Honorable John C. Jones, soon to be the Democrats' nominee for lieutenant governor. So we got to go by the book. Old John C., he's gonna love this one. High visibility." He said the doctor had gone up to the house to fill out the death certificate and get the elders' signatures as witnesses to Sadie's death and added that he'd be taking both elders in tonight for questioning with a stenographer present. There wouldn't be room for me in the boat, he said, or he'd bring me in with them and let me bunk at his house. "The elders will have to bunk in a jail cell, unfortunately."

Rebus asked him straight out if they admitted to killing the woman.

"Oh, yes. That's why I got to go ahead and arrest them. They didn't try to hide it none. Said it was the kindest thing to do. And to be honest, I have to agree with them. But now, thanks to young Mr. Harley Mann here, I got to charge them with intentional murder and bring in Attorney Jones to determine if it's second- or first-degree murder. He's got to decide whether to charge one of the elders or both of them and take it to a grand jury and county judge. By then we'll likely be dealing with newspaper reporters from all over the state. A real mess. Complicates things for Doc Cardiff, too."

"What'd he say was the cause of death?" Rebus asked. "Since he didn't examine the woman's body."

"You practicing to replace me, Rebus?" he said. "No, Doc Cardiff was plenty familiar with her condition. He agreed to certify that her death was caused by organ failure due to consumption. Which is certainly true. As far as it goes."

"And not mention the morphine?"

"We'll let Attorney Jones and the court decide on that, Rebus." Turning to me, the sheriff said, "Son, let me ask you something directly. Something you likely won't get asked tomorrow, when it'll be on the record, since the two elders admit they did exactly what you claim they did. But I'm curious. Why did you decide to turn them in? The young woman was close to death anyhow, and in great pain. Those elders are decent, honest, religious people. You and your family have been living out here with the Shakers for, what, eight or nine years. Knowing them all personally like you do, you could've easily let it go. Nobody'd be the wiser. Nobody would fault you. It's what I would've done in your place, to be honest. It's what Dr. Cardiff would've done. It's probably what Rebus here would've done. What made you decide to come all the way into St. Cloud and report it to me, instead of just letting the Shakers have their funeral and put the poor woman in the ground?"

We stood there for a long moment in the darkening lane between the main house and the men's dormitory, the sheriff, the deputy, and I, waiting for my answer, but at that moment—as at this moment now, all these many years later—I had no answer, and so I remained silent.

Finally, the doctor and Elder John and Eldress Mary emerged from the main house and walked across the dew-wet lawn toward us. The two elders each carried a small cloth bag, and the doctor carried his satchel. All three kept their gaze straight in front of them and did not turn to me as they passed. The sheriff said, "All right, let's get a move on. It's going to be a little tricky heading back to St. Cloud in the dark. Easy to make a wrong turn and end up in the Big O."

They left me standing there alone. I watched them walk down the lane to the lakeside pier. Elder John followed the deputy aboard and sat in the stern next to him, where I had sat coming out. Sheriff Prevett helped Eldress Mary onto the boat, and he took a position in the bow, presumably to navigate their way through the growing darkness, and Eldress Mary and Dr. Cardiff sat side by side in the middle. Rebus got the motor started with a single pull of the cord, and the sheriff untied the line to the pier.

In seconds, the boat had crossed the black waters of Live Oak Lake and entered the canal and disappeared behind the mangroves at the far shore, and soon the sound of the motor faded, and all was silent, except for the groans of the gators in the lakeside mudflats and the steady chirp of tree frogs among the mangroves. The brown, broad-winged evening bats were out, a colony of them fluttering down from the topmost rafters of the barn and flitting across the grounds, clearing the air of mosquitoes and moths. Their wings were twice the size of their bodies, and their open mouths were twice the size of their heads. I watched the ravening creatures swirl past for a while.

I was unsure at first of where to go, what to do, and then I walked to the meetinghouse and went inside. Four tall beeswax candles burned in wooden wall sconces, filling the room with soft, watery light. I sat on a bench near Sadie's coffin and stayed there until morning, and whenever one of the candles began to gutter and die, I got up and replaced it with a fresh candle from the box that someone had set on the floor at the foot of her coffin. Now and then I dozed off and each time was wakened by the start of a cacophonous dream. At dawn I let the candles burn all the way down and die. As the cool first light of day filtered through the tall windows, I left the meeting-house and began the long walk down the towpath through the rising mist to Narcoossee to meet up with Captain Shea and the morning barge to St. Cloud.

REEL #13

For a long time last night, I found myself standing over my eight-foot-by-eight-foot topographical plaster of paris map of New Bethany, and this morning, before returning to the tape recorder, I spent a few hours dusting it off and repairing the several broken bits of plaster and repainting where the colors have faded and flaked off. I've kept it near me—in my realty office and, after Mr. Disney's minions bought me out and I shut the business down, here at home in the center of what would otherwise serve as a dining room—for so long that I'd almost forgotten it existed. It's like a large, unwieldy piece of furniture, an old Shaker sideboard or cupboard that is never used and gets overlooked, forgotten, lost to one's awareness, until it unexpectedly emerges from the background shadows and is seen in the foreground as if for the first time, and it appears beautiful and profound.

I long ago forgot what drove me to make the thing in the first place and why I've kept it all these years. Possibly it was the same impulse that moves me now to tell and record this story in such detail and at such length. It took considerable time and effort to build, and when

I closed my office years ago, it would have been much easier to have broken it up and tossed it into the trash than to have lugged it home and set it up here. I must have wanted to make and keep nearby a facsimile of the truth of something crucially important to me and to many others that would otherwise be lost, something that was here long before it got replaced by Mr. Disney's Magic Kingdom.

It was the Shakers' magic kingdom, and mine. And Sadie Pratt's and Elder John Bennett's and Eldress Mary's, and my mother's and brothers' and sister's, and all the other Shakers', the people who in my youth I loved and lived with, hands to work and hearts to God. New Bethany.

Back then, the morning I made my solitary way to the St. Cloud City Hall to give my statement to State's Attorney Jones, as ordered by Sheriff Prevett, I could not have imagined what would become of those good people and that beloved place as a result of my action. Or I would not have done it. I would not have done any of it—I would not have refused to help Sadie die or broken my promise of silence to Elder John and made a criminal complaint to Sheriff Prevett or gone to St. Cloud the next day to be interviewed by State's Attorney Jones.

As I approached the City Hall, passing beneath gray swatches of Spanish moss dangling from the spreading branches of a row of live oak trees, I encountered Elder John and Eldress Mary again. They were descending the wide limestone steps of the brick build-ing, holding hands like a pair of devoted elderly siblings. They were still dressed in their funeral garments from the night before. We came to a stop and faced each other for a few seconds without saying anything. Their expressions were held halfway between anger and sorrow, and I did not know what to say. As a kind of courteous salute, I removed my palm-leaf hat. It was an awkward, inarticulate gesture of respect, but must have looked arrogant and immature to them.

"Judas," Elder John said. Nothing else. Then he and Eldress Mary, still holding hands, walked past me, and when they reached the street they turned in the direction of the city pier and were gone.

I entered the building and went to the sheriff's outer office, where Deputy Rebus sat at his desk, cleaning a long-barreled pistol. He looked up and smiled and said, "Pretty neat, eh? Colt .45 SAA. The ol' Peacemaker. Sheriff issued it to me this morning. I been wanting one of these little ladies a long time."

It was an attractive piece of machinery, the first handgun I had seen up close, though not the first firearm. Elder John kept a shotgun out at New Bethany and used it solely for killing a cow, pig, or sheep for slaughter and for putting injured or mortally ill animals out of their misery. It was a task he reserved strictly for himself, as if he did not trust anyone else to do the killing properly, and he was probably right. He had military training, but the rest of us were pacifists with little or no experience with guns. A few, like the herdsmen, Brothers Amos and George, had been deer hunters in their pre-Shaker pasts, but had not fired a gun in many years. I wondered if Elder John's readiness to put an injured or sick animal down or kill one for slaughter had made it easier for him to kill Sadie.

"You pass the elder and eldress on your way in?" the deputy asked.

I nodded that I had.

"Sheriff let 'em go. Didn't want to charge 'em till the state's attorney makes his determination. Figured it wouldn't do no good keeping 'em in jail, specially the woman, the eldress." He spoke as if he and the sheriff had made these decisions jointly, though when the sheriff came out of his inner office, Rebus went silently back to cleaning his Peacemaker.

The sheriff said, "Come with me, Harley," and escorted me back out to the main corridor, and we walked to the rear of the building and up the wide stairs. At the landing halfway up, he stopped and touched my sleeve and said in a low voice, "You can say you got confused, Harley. You can say you don't know what really happened when the woman died. If you sound wobbly, Jones likely won't go for an indictment, since there's no other witness to her death than the elders, and they can still change their plea and say it was a natural death. Attorney Jones likes his cases open-and-shut."

I nodded, as if I agreed, and we continued on to the state's attorney's outer office. It was spacious and more nicely appointed than the sheriff's. There were framed portraits of Governor Gilchrist and President Taft and walls lined with glass-fronted bookshelves, filled,

I assumed, with law books and bound statutes and depositions. A middle-aged woman with spectacles and graying hair in a bun sat behind a large, cluttered desk. The sheriff said, "Good morning, Heddie. This here's Harley Mann, the Shaker who come in yesterday with the euthanasia complaint out at New Bethany."

The woman named Heddie got up and walked to the frosted glass door behind her and gently knocked, opened the door, went in, and closed it again. After a few moments, she came back and took up a stenographer's notepad and pencil. "Thank you, Sheriff Prevett. Come with me, young man," she said, and led me into the state's attorney's office, closing the door on the sheriff.

I suddenly felt alone and abandoned and in a very dangerous place. In the far corner slumped the Florida state flag with its scarlet cross of St. John, there to remind us of Florida's ongoing loyalty to the Confederacy, and the American flag with its constellation of forty-six stars. Sadie's death was no longer the business of a good-natured small-town sheriff. It was now the concern of the state and the nation, stern, unforgiving entities overflowing with the power to capture, prosecute, imprison, and execute lawbreakers.

A pair of tall windows overlooked the leafy tops of the grove of live oak trees and the low rooftops of the town. Seated in a high-backed leather chair at his wide, uncluttered desk, sunlight streaming through the windows behind him, was the state's attorney, Honorable John C. Jones. He was a tall, angular, clean-shaven man in his middle fifties in a black suit and white dress shirt and gray necktie. His thinning, straight black hair looked dyed and was combed from one ear across to the other with pink stripes of his nearly bald scalp peeking through. He had an intelligent look, more crafty than reflective. His complexion was pocked and rough and pale. His eyes were bright blue and his eyebrows were gray and long and lupine. Not a handsome man, but impressive, weighty. The stenographer took a seat on the sofa to my right. Attorney Jones waved me to a straight-backed wooden chair beside his desk and swung around and gave me a long, hard look.

"This's a deposition we're taking," he announced. He spoke with a soft south Florida accent in a voice surprisingly high and thin. "Do you solemnly swear that you will tell the truth, the whole truth, and nothing but the truth, so help you God?"

I so swore, and he continued, while Heddie the stenographer scribbled on her pad. "You are Mr. Harley Mann, resident of the Shaker colony of New Bethany in Narcoossee in Osceola County, state of Florida." He asked me if that information was correct, and I said yes, and then he asked me to state the date and place of my birth.

"October 14, 1890. Indianapolis, Indiana. In a Ruskinite community near there," I offered.

"Ruskinite. Can you spell that?"

I did as he asked and added that they were sort of like Shakers, only not religious.

He wanted to know how long I had resided at New Bethany and what was my principal work there and if I was familiar with John Bennett and Mary Glynn. He called them "the defendants." When I had answered, he asked me if I personally knew "the alleged victim, Miss Sadie Pratt."

I said, "Yes, sir. We were close friends."

"'Close friends.' How close, would you say?"

"Best friends."

"*Best* friends. So you must have been very upset by the news of her death."

"Yes, sir, I was."

"Who brought you that news, and when?"

"It was Eldress Mary. She called us all together that morning, yesterday, and told us Sadie had died."

"Called 'us.' Who is 'us'?"

"The people of New Bethany."

"What did she say was the cause of death?"

"Well, she didn't say, exactly. We all just assumed it was the consumption. Sadie was sick a long time and lately had been noticeably weakening."

"When was the last time you saw Sadie Pratt alive?"

I realized where he was going with his questions, and I remembered Sheriff Prevett's advice to me on the stairway landing, that if I sounded wobbly, Attorney Jones wouldn't go for an indictment. I said, "I guess it must've been early yesterday morning, when I carried her breakfast to her room. Or was that the day before yesterday? No, early yesterday was the last time."

"You and she talked early yesterday morning, then. What did you talk about?"

"Not much. She was pretty sick and weak. And in a lot of pain. From the consumption."

"Was she taking anything for the pain, do you know? Any medication?"

"I think Dr. Cardiff had advised morphine. She said it made her sleepy."

"During this conversation, did it come about that Sadie Pratt told you she wanted to die?"

"No. Well, yes, she did, but maybe I thought it was just an expression, a way to tell me how much pain she was in. Like, 'I'd sooner die than go on like this.' The way people talk."

"I see. And when you spoke with her, did it come about that she asked you to help her die by injecting her with a large dose of the morphine?"

"Well, yes, but that, too, might have been just the way people talk, like she was telling me she was so weak she couldn't do it herself. That's what I thought, anyhow."

"I see. And then you left and didn't see her again?"

"Yes. That was the last time." I was remembering our final exchange, when I stood at her bedroom door and said to Sadie, "I won't help you die," and she said, "All right, then. Go away. Go. Leave me, Harley . . . leave me. Don't come back again." I said to the attorney, "Actually, that was the last time I saw her alive. It wasn't the last time I saw her. I went to her room later, after Eldress Mary told us that Sadie had passed, and I saw her then."

"Were you alone at that time?"

"No, Eldress Mary was there."

"And did Eldress Mary, the defendant Mary Glynn, did she say how Sadie Pratt died?"

"No, she didn't say anything about that. Only that she had died peacefully."

"And what about John Bennett, the other defendant? Did you and he speak about the death of Sadie Pratt that morning?"

"Yes, sir, we did, in his room."

"Was anyone else present at that time?"

"No, sir."

"Did it come about that John Bennett spoke to you about how Sadie Pratt died?"

"He said it was probably the morphine."

"Probably?"

"Yes, sir. It slows down your heart and other organs, and she was very near death then, as we all knew."

"Who did he say administered the morphine to Sadie Pratt?"

"He didn't say exactly. I assumed it was him, since he tends to take charge of things."

"So you don't know if John Bennett or Mary Glynn administered the final dose of morphine?"

"No, sir. I guess I don't."

He went silent for a long minute. Finally, he said, "Mr. Mann, yesterday afternoon you brought a complaint to Sheriff Prevett that the man and woman you call Elder John Bennett and Eldress Mary Glynn murdered Miss Sadie Pratt, did you not?"

"I think I said they *killed* her."

"With morphine?" he asked. Then he said, "Strike that, Heddie. It's conjecture." Turning back to me, he said, "Did it come about that when John Bennett told you how Sadie Pratt died, he also told you that he and Mary Glynn had deliberately injected Sadie Pratt with morphine in order to kill her?"

"I was pretty upset at the time. I thought that's what he meant, but I don't recall his words exactly. Maybe I only surmised it. It was more of a conjecture, you could say."

"You were upset, you said. Because of the death of your 'best friend.' Yet her death from consumption was expected, was imminent, was it not?"

"Yes, sir, it was."

"Tell me how close you and Sadie Pratt really were, Mr. Mann."

"Well, I'd known her since I was twelve years old, when my mother brought us down to New Bethany from Rosewell Plantation in Georgia. She helped me with my schoolwork and such, on account of her being so much older than me and better educated."

Again Attorney Jones was silent for a long minute. Trying a new tack, he said, "Mr. Mann, did you yourself have anything to do with the death of Sadie Pratt by morphine?"

"No, sir! I never even saw the morphine. I wouldn't know how to do an injection myself, anyhow. Besides, euthanasia is a crime in Florida."

"Yes, it is. A serious crime. Murder in the second degree. It can even be first-degree, if the perpetrator stands to profit from the death of the victim. So tell me about your relationship with the so-called elder and eldress, with Mr. Bennett and Miss Glynn. Were you close to them? Friendly, not so friendly, trusting, not so trusting? Did you all get along?"

"Oh, we got along real good," I said. "Elder John you could say was my mentor, and Eldress Mary, she was like my spiritual advisor. I've been getting ready to become a real Shaker, and they were herding me in that direction. Schooling me. With us Shakers, if you're a man, you confess your sins to the elder before you become a bona fide member of the Society of Believers, so I was getting set to make my confession to Elder John."

This seemed to frustrate him enough to get him out of his chair. He walked to a cabinet and drew a slim cigar from a humidor and lighted it and puffed on it in silence. Turning back to me, he said, "If he was your mentor and you were going to be confessing your sins to him like he was a Roman Catholic priest, and the other, Miss Glynn, was your spiritual guide, then why the hell did you turn them in to Sheriff Prevett?"

"Well, sir, we Shakers believe it's a sin to disobey the law. It's how we get our reputation for being so law-abiding. It would have been a sin if I did *not* report to the sheriff what I thought was a possible crime, even if it was Elder John and Eldress Mary who committed it. Especially since I would've had to confess that very sin later to Elder John. So in a sense I was only *not* doing what I believed he and she would *not* want me to do. I didn't concern myself over whether it was a crime. That's up to the sheriff and you, sir, and a judge and jury. I cared only that by not reporting it I would be committing a sin, and by reporting it I was not committing a sin."

"You put out more double negatives than a damned Tallahassee lawyer," he said, and laughed. "Heddie, strike my last remark. You can close your notebook. I believe we're done here."

With that, he told me I was free to leave. "Maybe if you hurry, you'll meet up with your Shaker friends on their way home," he said. "Sheriff Prevett let them go this morning without charging them. Be interesting to hear what they have to say to you."

I thanked him and left his office feeling like I was the one who'd been let out of jail. I quickly walked from the City Hall and headed for the pier, hoping to get there before the *Coquina* departed for Narcoossee. I did not especially want to accompany Elder John and Eldress Mary back to New Bethany, but the afternoon barge was my only way to get home. By having discouraged Attorney Jones with my wobbliness from seeking to indict Elder John and Eldress Mary, I now thought that I could make things right with them. I planned to attempt it tonight at the meetinghouse, when in front of everyone I would ask for their forgiveness. Surely, they would forgive me when they understood that my true intention, as I had explained to the state's attorney, was to avoid breaking the law and thereby to avoid committing a sin.

Sadly, I would soon learn how wrong I was. About the elders and the rest of the Shakers, but also about my true intentions.

As luck would have it, the *Coquina* was still tied up at the pier. The elders were already aboard, seated solemnly side by side on the main deck, out of the sun beneath the canvas canopy. I came aboard and, to avoid the elders, went up to the wheelhouse and joined Captain Shea and the pilot, Salty Haversack. I negotiated another free ride with Captain Shea, this time all the way over to New Bethany. He was taking the elders home, he told me, and they had paid full fare. But the next time I wanted a free ride, I'd have to work off the fare as a stevedore, he said.

I said, "I wouldn't mind working as a stevedore full-time, long's I could learn how to be a pilot while doing it." I asked Salty Haversack if he'd be willing to teach me.

Haversack said, "I ain't close to retiring. Why would I learn you how to replace me? You want to be a Glades pilot, young feller, you got to go somewhere a long ways off from here."

"You planning to quit the Shakers, then?" Captain Shea asked.

"I'm thinking on it."

"Wouldn't have anything to do with the passing of your friend Miss Pratt, would it? I heard Doc Cardiff say this morning that she died the other day."

"Too bad. She sure was a pretty one," Haversack said.

It had nothing to do with the passing of Sadie Pratt, I said. I explained that I was the age when I was required to decide whether I wanted to be a permanent, bona fide Shaker. I was just considering what kind of work I might do if I left New Bethany for the World. "I'm looking into my options," I said. "Before I make my decision."

The truth is, this was the first time I had seriously imagined leaving New Bethany without Sadie on my arm, the first time it was more than a romantic fantasy, and of course the captain was correct, it had everything to do with Sadie's death. She had left New Bethany, and now it was my turn.

Captain Shea said, "Salty's right, no need for another pilot out of St. Cloud. It takes most of a lifetime to know what you're doing, anyhow. Same with guiding hunters and fishermen from up north. If you want my opinion, a smart young fellow like you ought to get himself into real estate. It's the future here. You buy up acreage with government-guaranteed money that's borrowed from the bank, and you sell off the acreage in little pieces. There's people doing it all over here in Osceola County and on the Florida east coast, people who don't know wetlands from dry, swamp from hammock, and they're making money hand over fist on land that's mostly underwater. I hear they advertise in Northern newspapers, and people up there buy the lots sight unseen, ten dollars down and the rest borrowed from the seller. Most of them don't build anything on the plots and default on the loan, so you get to sell the land a second time. Easy as taking candy from a baby."

One of those babies, I remembered, had been Elder John, whose loan on the four lots he'd bought in the name of New Bethany was about to come due. But Captain Shea's words made a positive impression on me and advanced by several steps my desire to leave New Bethany.

It was a little strange, I suppose, for me and Elder John and Eldress Mary to be passengers together on the *Coquina* all the way back to New Bethany and not once acknowledge each other's presence, strange for them to sit half-hidden beneath the tarpaulin on the main deck below while I remained cooped up in the wheelhouse with Captain Shea and Salty Haversack. But in calling me Judas, Elder John had written me off and out of the biblical world he normally inhabited, and it would take some serious doing on my part to gain re-entry, a thing much better done in front of the entire New Bethany family of Shakers than I could manage on board Captain Shea's barge. Elder John was the one who needed convincing that, not unlike the original Judas, I may have done harm, but I had not done wrong. Eldress Mary was in a sense Elder John's enforcer, his Paul of Tarsus, and like the rest of the Shakers, she would follow his lead in deciding whether and when to let me back into the fold.

So when we docked at New Bethany, I stayed in the wheelhouse and did not come down and disembark until after the elders had gone ashore and disappeared into the main house. As I left the barge, Captain Shea said, "You and Elder John seem to be on the outs. You used to be his boy, like his right hand. I always figured he was grooming you to someday take over his job running New Bethany."

"Ask Sheriff Prevett, if you want to know why he's upset with me."

"Interesting. I'll do that, son. In the meantime, if you do quit the Shakers and want work as a stevedore, let me know, and I'll set you up with the harbormaster in St. Cloud."

I said I would and went on up to my room in the men's dormitory and tried to gather my scattered thoughts for tonight's public presentation. In a short while, the dinner bell rang, and I came down the narrow stairs and went to the dining room in the main house. I entered the room and approached my usual place at Elder John's table, and I saw that my chair was gone. Elder John and Brother Edwin, the head carpenter, and Brother Ezekiel, the cobbler, were in their usual seats, hands folded, ready for Elder John to say grace, but there were now only three place settings at the table, instead of four. No one had taken my place. The place itself had disappeared.

I came to a stop where my chair should have been, and Elder John got up, and without so much as a glance in my direction, he squared his shoulders and turned his back to me. Everyone else, even my mother and my brothers Royal and Raymond and my sister, Rachel, stood and turned their backs to me. For a few seconds I was confused, and then, as I looked across the room at my Shaker family of twelve, all of them standing with their backs to me, as if I were repulsive to look upon, I was frightened. In all my years at New Bethany, I had not seen anything like this. I was being turned out of the community, as if commanded by Paul of Tarsus in his letter to the Corinthians. "But now I have written unto you not to keep company, if any man that is called a brother be a fornicator, or covetous, or an idolater, or a railer, or a drunkard, or an extortioner, with such a one no, not to eat. . . . Therefore put away from among yourselves that wicked person."*

I was that wicked person. My people were not simply ignoring me or treating me as if I were not present or even as if I did not exist. They were actively denying my existence. Rejecting me. Expelling me from both the family of Shakers and my family of blood relatives. Being shunned like this is worse than being merely abandoned. It's a public shaming. It leaves the person isolated and cast out and utterly alone. And the more attached to the community one has been, the more painful the isolation and loneliness. It's a condition that is permanent and can't be argued against or haggled with. When you see that you have been cast out of your beloved community, you experience a profound and terrifying solitude. It's as if you woke one morning and found that during the night everyone on the planet had left for another planet, leaving you behind to forage on your own for the remainder of your days, a solitary, silenced scavenger among the plants and wild and feral animals that remain, and they are all fruitful and multiply, while you grow old in sterile solitude and wither and die unburied with no one to mourn for you.

* 1 Corinthians 5:11–13

There was nothing I could do or say, except turn and leave the room. By the time I got outside, tears had filled my eyes. I made my way to the fields of berries down near the canal and picked a few handfuls of raspberries and strawberries and ate them. It was my sole nourishment for the day. Wandering along the towpath where Sadie and I used to meet, I said to myself the little speech that I had planned to give tonight in the meetinghouse. It seemed weak now and self-serving. Pathetic and deluded. I could not imagine saying it. I was a man who since boyhood had been keeping secrets and telling lies, and as a result I had lost sight of the truth, and thus I could not say what was the truth, the whole truth, and nothing but the truth. And worse, if I gave my speech, I would be facing their backs, pleading in vain to those who have cast me out, begging for their understanding and forgiveness and trust, despite my inability to say the truth. Even if I could say it, they would not hear it, for their ears were as shut to me as their eyes.

That's when and why I wrote my letter to State's Attorney Jones. Isolated, cast out, hurt, and angry, and confused as to what was true and what was false, I went to my room and sat down at my small desk and with pencil and lined paper torn from my schoolboy copybook wrote only the second letter I had written in my lifetime. The first had been to my brother Pence shortly after he left New Bethany. I mailed it to him at General Delivery, Marfa, Texas, as he had instructed, but it had come back to me marked "Addressee Unknown." This letter, addressed to State's Attorney Hon. John C. Jones, Osceola County City Hall, St. Cloud, Florida, I intended to hand-deliver myself.

August 17, 1910
Dear Sir,

I wish to make several corrections and additions to the testimony I gave you yesterday. Elder John Bennett did indeed tell me that he and Eldress Mary Glynn administered the fatal dose of morphine to Sadie Pratt. He claimed that it was done at Sadie Pratt's request and made me promise not to reveal this to anyone. Also, earlier that day, when I visited Sadie alone in her room, she was able to speak coherently and seemed alert. Further and more importantly, she told me that she was pregnant, and implied that it was by Elder John.

I do not know if this was true, as she was sometimes inclined to exaggerate, and she was quite ill and was being treated with morphine. But if true, then Elder John Bennett could certainly be said to benefit from her death and thus would be guilty of murder in the first degree. Although the benefit to Eldress Mary Glynn is less clearcut than to Elder John, Sadie Pratt's death would also benefit the eldress, who, as a senior Shaker, would want to keep information like this from getting out.

If you decide to pursue the case, I am prepared to testify under oath to the above facts before a grand jury and in open court. If you wish to depose me a second time, I can be reached by mail or messenger, c/o Captain Bernard Shea, St. Cloud, Florida, for whom I expect to be employed soon as a stevedore.

Sincerely yours,
Harley Mann

As if a dam had burst, a tumult rapidly followed. None of us could swim against the coming rush of events. I barely slept that night, and the following morning I packed a gunnysack with my few personal possessions and left New Bethany without attempting to say goodbye to anyone and met up with Captain Shea in Narcoossee. In exchange for help off-loading the *Coquina,* he carried me to St. Cloud and introduced me to Captain Bigelow Bunting, the harbormaster, who approved my being hired as a stevedore, assigning me, as I hoped, to the *Coquina* crew. Captain Shea gave me permission to sleep aboard the barge until I received my pay and could afford to rent a proper room in town—it would be the first time in my life that I was to be paid for my labor. That same afternoon I took my letter, carefully folded and sealed with candle wax the night before, to the

City Hall and handed it to Attorney Jones's secretary and stenographer, Heddie. I had written on the outside of the letter: "To Honorable John C. Jones, State's Attorney. Confidential."

Early the next morning, as I helped load the *Conquina* with cases of tinned food for the shopkeepers at Narcoossee and a ton and a half of cut sugar cane to be ground and refined by the mill at New Bethany, I saw Sheriff Prevett and Deputy Rebus taking the patrol boat, the *Belinda Blue*, out onto the lake, headed northeast.

A few hours later, aboard the *Coquina* on the canal between St. Cloud and Narcoossee, we passed the *Belinda Blue* coming the other way with Elder John and Eldress Mary aboard. Captain Shea steered the *Coquina* tight to the mangroves to let the *Belinda Blue* pass by. The elders were not in handcuffs, but they were clearly under arrest and looked very downcast. The sheriff and his deputy also looked grim and did not raise their hands to wave to us. When Elder John and Eldress Mary saw me standing on the main cargo deck with the two other stevedores, they abruptly turned away.

We reached New Bethany before noon, and when I and the other stevedores started unloading the fifty bundles of sugar cane and stacking them on the Live Oak Lake pier, three Shakers, two of whom were my brothers Royal and Raymond, walked alongside the old John Deere horse-drawn wagon down the lane from the barn. They spotted me on the pier, and the three immediately pulled up, as if I were the carrier of a contagious disease, and retreated with their horse and wagon to the main barn and went inside.

When we had finished unloading the cane, Captain Shea took the bill of lading up to the house for a signature and came back shaking his head in what looked like mild dismay or simple confusion. He came aboard and went straight to the wheelhouse. As the barge pulled away from the pier and steamed slowly across the lake toward the canal, I stood in the stern and looked back at the only place I had ever thought of as my home. It was singularly beautiful. I loved the sight of the stoutly constructed pier and the three little fishing dories tied up there and the large white-cedar-plank warehouse with wagon-wide doors open at either end like a covered bridge and remembered that on the day we ended our long journey out of Rosewell Plantation it had been my first sight of New Bethany. I could see the crushed-limestone lane beyond that led in a long, rising curl past the grapefruit orchard and the apiary and flower gardens and the blossoming citrus groves on either side where I knew my bees were hard at work gathering pollen. At the crest on the right was the perfectly proportioned meetinghouse, its paired high windows and doors facing the lane, and beyond the meetinghouse the two men's dormitories and the matching pair of dormitories for females, and directly across from them the three-story main house with its wide front porch and matching entries, all the buildings classically symmetrical and foursquare and painted white, a perfect nineteenth-century New England village enclosing a village green, the whole of it set down on top of a vast swamp in Florida, defying geography and climate and reason. Beyond the village were the large barns, their cedar shake roofs barely visible from the barge, and behind the barns the livestock pens and the windmills slowly turning and the sugar and grinding mills. I pictured in my mind the hundreds of acres of hay meadows and gardens and corn and potato fields beyond and the lattices shielding the pineapples from the burning sun and the split-rail-fenced pastures where the cattle and oxen and horses grazed. I saw no one anywhere among the buildings and fields and cultivations, until, just as the *Coquina* reached the mangroves at the western edge of Live Oak Lake where the canal connects to Alligator Lake, my brothers Royal and Raymond and Brother Edwin emerged from the barn with the wagon and horse and started to make their way back down to the pier. I felt like a ghost departing unnoticed from his own funeral.

Later that day, when we got back to St. Cloud, I checked in with the harbormaster to get my work assignment for the afternoon trip. Though he was in fact little more than a clerk of the works, Captain Bunting had once been a lower-level US naval officer and now fancied himself as some sort of civilian-appointed admiral. A jowly, red-faced man with white chin whiskers, he wore a dark-blue suit jacket with fringed shoulder boards and a double row of gold buttons and a naval officer's white, high-crowned cap with gold braid across the brim. He gave me my afternoon orders, mostly moving stacks of milled boards from warehouse number 3 to the *Coquina*, then asked me if I knew or was kin to the two Shakers they brought in this morning from New Bethany.

I said I knew them, but was not kin to either.

"The deputy told me on the q.t. they're being held for murder, pending a coroner's inquest on the body of the victim," he said. "You aware of any murder taking place out there? I always thought the Shakers were a peaceable bunch overall. Pacifists, even."

"They are peaceable," I said, and asked him what a coroner's inquest was.

"Not sure. I think the county coroner, that's Dr. Cardiff, he goes over the body and determines the cause of death. The victim here was a young woman. Evidently she was done in by the two Shaker leaders, the deputy told me, to hide the fact that the woman had gotten pregnant by the male leader. That'll be one for the newspapers, eh? Is it true the Shakers are supposed to be celibate?"

"Yes."

"And they keep the males and females, adults and children alike, completely separate at all times, even at meals?"

"Yes."

"And they even keep male and female animals in separate pens?"

"Yes, except when they need to be bred."

"Okay, so that means the Shakers know about sex. They're not ignorant of it. They're just not supposed to practice it on themselves."

"Yes."

"Even between husbands and wives?"

"Yes."

"Well, unless they get busy converting folks into Shakers, they're going to run out of Shakers," he said, and laughed and went back to his inventory and shipping lists. As I left his office, he turned in his chair and said, "That young woman they supposedly murdered, did you know her when you was a Shaker?"

I did not want to be drawn any further into this conversation. "Yes, but not well. She wasn't a Shaker herself."

"I heard she was a real looker."

"So people say," I said, and went out.

I slept aboard the *Coquina* that week on a pile of straw and under a thin blanket that Captain Shea lent me and knew next to nothing about what was happening over at the courthouse and the county jail. Then one night Deputy Rebus dropped by the marina. He said he came down to make some minor repairs to the outboard motor on the patrol boat, something about cleaning the carburetor, which seemed dubious, because of the hour, close to nine p.m. I sat on the pier next to where the patrol boat was tied up and dangled my legs over the silken black water, while he removed the cover of the small two-cycle motor and in the fading evening light made a show of examining its parts.

He said he and the sheriff were going out to New Bethany tomorrow with Dr. Cardiff and Attorney Jones, and as we talked I came to believe that he had been sent down to the marina by the sheriff to forewarn me. To give me one last chance to recant. I knew the sheriff was smart, and he liked me and the elders and did not want this case to go to trial and see the elders sent to prison or worse for murder. I had started the process, and now only I could stop it.

I asked Rebus the purpose for tomorrow's visit to New Bethany, and he said it was to oversee the disinterment of Sadie Pratt. "Your Captain Shea, he'll have to bring the coffin back here on his barge so the doc can do the autopsy. Our boat's too small for all them people plus the coffin," he said. "A shame they got to dig her up. That was a right nice and tight coffin them Shakers built for her."

"Why would they need to do such a thing?"

"They got to determine if she really was pregnant, so's Attorney Jones can make his case to the grand jury. And I guess the doc can tell how much morphine she had in her, too. And if she really was at death's door from the consumption, like the elders said." He shot me a hard gaze, as if to be sure that I understood the implications of his words. "They got to be sure everything you said checks out."

I did understand. If I recanted now, before the disinterring, and said that my letter to the state's attorney was a lie, I could put a halt to everything. That's what he was telling me. Otherwise, they will dig up Sadie's beloved body, and Dr. Cardiff will dissect it on a table in his office as if it were the body of an animal. He will learn that she was indeed pregnant, and even if her diseased lungs are shown to have brought her to the point of death, her veins will still be flooded with morphine sufficient to kill her, and it will be assumed by everyone that the father of her unborn child was Elder John Bennett and his accomplice was Eldress Mary Glynn, and that Sadie Pratt was killed by them, not to give her a merciful death, but to cover up a secret sexual liaison between the beautiful young woman from Rhode Island and the esteemed, much-older leader of a famed religious group known for their claim to practice strict celibacy. Attorney Jones's prosecutorial task will have been made easy, and his political ambitions, bolstered by the statewide publicity the trial was certain to attract, would be greatly advanced, and after the fall election, John C. Jones will be the lieutenant governor of the state of Florida, and Elder John Bennett will be convicted for murder in the first degree, and his accomplice, Eldress Mary Glynn, will be convicted of murder in the second. Elder John will be sentenced to death, and Eldress Mary will be sentenced to twenty years in prison, where she will die of old age.

The deputy screwed the cover back onto the motor and climbed up onto the pier and stood over me for a moment. "So you're sticking to your story?" he said. "Sheriff Prevett can't tell you this himself, on account of it would be a conflict of interest, but he ain't personally happy with the way things are going. He didn't like having to charge them two, no matter what they actually done or didn't do. Judge Parker set bail at five hundred dollars, and with the Shakers being so well liked and all, the sheriff got some local folks to come up with the bail money, and the judge released them on their own recognizance."

"So they're back at New Bethany now?"

"I took them back out myself day before yesterday. You must've been laboring in one of the warehouses," he said, and smiled. "Or they might've wanted to have a word or two with you."

"No," I said. "They wouldn't."

He asked me again if I was sticking to my story.

"Since it's the truth," I said, "it's the only story there is."

He said okay, he'd report that to the sheriff, and went on his way.

I walked for hours aimlessly along the darkened streets of St. Cloud before returning to my straw nest aboard the barge, haunted and repelled by the ghastly image of Sadie's body being taken from the earth's warm embrace and laid out on a cold steel examining table to be probed by Dr. Cardiff's scalpel. I slept very little that night.

The following morning I was part of a four-man crew on the *Coquina,* when Captain Shea and Salty Haversack dropped off a load of milled boards in Narcoossee along with a pair of Northern deer hunters and their guide. From there we went on to Live Oak Lake, where we tied up at the New Bethany pier next to Sheriff Prevett's patrol boat, the *Belinda Blue.* Waiting for us were the doctor and the sheriff and his deputy and the state's attorney, and at their feet, Sadie's dirt-encrusted coffin. There were no Shakers in sight.

I and the other members of the crew, three sturdy young Black fellows from St. Cloud, were told by the sheriff to load the coffin. The other stevedores folded their muscular arms across their chests and shook their heads no. One of them, Neilly Fabben, who seemed to be their spokesman in their dealings with White people, turned and said to Captain Shea, "Begging your pardon, Cap'n, but we ain't carrying no dug-up dead folks." I remember Neilly's name because years later, after he became a surveyor, we worked together when I was buying up the Shaker landholdings.

"If they won't do it," I said, "neither will I."

Captain Shea said, "You boys don't get to decide what to carry or not to carry," and told us to get to work.

Neilly said, "If we gots to walk the towpath all the way back to St. Cloud, we ready, Cap'n, 'cause we ain't carrying no dug-up dead bodies."

"Then you'll all be out of a job when you get there. You, too, Harley. Plenty of strong young boys hanging around the harbor looking to work for fifty cents a day."

Neilly and I and the two other stevedores glanced at each other one to one and collectively shook our heads no, stubborn as mules, and refused to move. We would take our chances, but we weren't carrying no dug-up dead bodies, especially me, and especially not the body of my beloved Sadie.

Finally Sheriff Prevett stepped forward and said, "Never mind,

Shea, me and Rebus can do it. She don't weigh hardly nothing, any-how, and the box is light and tight as a tick. C'm'ere, Rebus, give a hand."

Rebus grabbed one end, and the sheriff got the other, and they lifted the coffin easily, almost as if it held Sadie's ghost, not her body, and carried it aboard the barge. They set it down on the deck at midship and returned to the pier. The sheriff said to Captain Shea, "See you back at the harbor in St. Cloud," and he and Deputy Rebus and Dr. Cardiff and State's Attorney Jones took their seats in the *Belinda Blue*. Rebus got the outboard motor started, and the patrol boat quickly crossed the lake and went beyond the mangroves and entered the canal and in seconds was gone from sight.

Captain Shea said to us, "I'll be reporting this insubordination to the harbormaster, boys. What he does with it is up to him. Up to me, I'd let all four of you go. Except for Mann, maybe. The dead girl in the coffin was his friend, so maybe he had reason not to want to handle it." He fired up the boiler, blew the steam whistle to signal the departure of the *Coquina*, and we slowly moved off from New Bethany, carrying our box of darkness. My fellow stevedores, for their reasons, stayed as far to the stern as possible, and I, for mine, stayed with them.

I see I've come almost to the end of another reel of tape. It's still early in the day, so I'll just take a minute and switch it out for a fresh one and then continue with my story.

REEL #14

That damned sinkhole out there in the driveway! It won't go away. No matter how many times I fill it in and pave it over, a few days later it comes back, as if there's an underground river dissolving the limestone subsoil, causing the surface soil and pavement on top to collapse and fall in.

If this ramshackle old shotgun house and all its contents and the garage and my Packard, which is everything I own in the above-ground world, got pulled into that dark underworld, I'd be upset, yes. But not very much. For me, personally, the greatest loss would be these tapes I'm making, the story I've been telling all these weeks. I'd hate to lose my plaster of paris model of New Bethany, but I don't really need it anymore. I used to spend hours a day and half the night looking at it, reflecting on it, remembering and reliving everything that happened there. But I notice that lately, when I pass from the kitchen out here to the porch, I barely give it a glance. My miniature New Bethany has gradually disappeared, as if it's being dissolved by my tape-recorded words.

The truth is, everything I own, except these tapes, is replaceable. I'm eighty-one years old, and at my age, very little, other than my knees, needs replacing. Soon all I'll want is a narrow bed and a chair and a hot plate. For my few remaining purposes, a single room with a bath and kitchenette in the decrepit, roach-infested St. Cloud Hotel downtown would be more than adequate.

I might prefer it. I'd be living again the same as I lived when over sixty years ago I collected my week's pay from the harbormaster, Captain Bigelow Bunting, the first pay for work I'd ever received, and spent a day's wages to rent a room by the week on the third floor of the rebuilt St. Cloud Hotel. The original St. Cloud, the only hotel in town then, had been constructed on New York Avenue a few short blocks from the lake out of boards and timbers salvaged from the abandoned Disston Sugar Company warehouses. When the hotel burned in '08, the structure collapsed onto the bodies of over thirty unidentified tenants, men, women, and children, burying them in hot ash and cinders. The bodies were never recovered and properly buried. After the new hotel was built on top of the ash heap, the ghosts of those lost souls were said to haunt the building, and few travelers or snowbirds were willing to stay there. Gradually it fell into disrepair, until the only tenants in later years have been drug dealers and prostitutes.

But back in the fall of 1910, right after it was rebuilt, with bricks this time, instead of wood, and eighteen-inch-thick walls, the St. Cloud Hotel was a grand place for a young man to have a room of his own. There wasn't any plumbing up there, just a wash basin and bedpan, and for the first few years no electricity above the ground floor. For a few pennies a day you could take your meals among the potted ferns in the large, high-ceilinged dining room and watch the visitors from the North shake off their icicles and thaw out their frozen bones and plan to purchase a piece of land here in paradise and build themselves a winter home. I used to sit alone at a small corner table in the hotel dining room, the Old South Room, it was called, for breakfast and supper and listen to those snowbirds and tourists talk. It's when I first began to see the wisdom of Captain Shea's advice to get involved in buying and selling real estate.

I myself never saw any of the well-attested ghosts while I lived there, other than the ghost of Sadie Pratt, who haunted me night and day, but especially at night, while I lay in my cot and obsessively returned to our lovemaking rendezvous at New Bethany down by the canal in the evenings and our quick, furtive encounters at dawn in her bedroom. When we lay back on the moss in our hidden grotto beside the towpath and listened to the frogs and nightbirds and the plash of fish and gators and other creatures of that watery world, I studied her lovely, pale, moonlit face, her coal-dark eyes looking deeply into mine, plumbing my thoughts and emotions as no one ever had before, making me feel real in an entirely new, electrically charged way. And in the silky-gray predawn light of her bedroom, I gazed lovestruck upon the gentle curve of her cheek and the slight lilt of her upper lip and the slope from her chin to her slender neck and bare shoulder, while she let me unbutton her blouse and touch her breast, first with my fingertips, then with my lips and tongue. She was my ghost, and I embraced her, and when she faded and was about to leave me, before I drifted off to sleep, I pleaded with her to return the following night, and she did return again and again, and she haunts me still.

During those first few days following the disinterment of Sadie's body, while her ghost was becoming my sole companion, rumors began to float through the town, even among the Black stevedores at the waterfront, that the young Shaker woman was pregnant when she died, and she did not die from the effects of tuberculosis, but at the hands of the two senior Shakers from New Bethany. The male elder was said to have impregnated her, with the eldress serving as his accomplice. When the harbormaster, Captain Bunting, asked me what I knew of the circumstances surrounding her death, I said that I had been told by the state's attorney not to discuss the matter. When Neilly Fabben, my fellow stevedore, asked me if the rumors were true, I said that the state's attorney had sworn me to secrecy, giving the impression, no doubt, that I was privy to information that corroborated the rumors. It went the same with Captain Shea and Salty Haversack and everyone else in town whom I encountered on a daily basis—the night manager of the St. Cloud Hotel and the staff of the Old South dining room, the various shopkeepers and ship- pers and boatmen and workers I had quickly become friendly with at the warehouses down along the piers, even the shopkeepers and farmers out in Narcoossee who came to the *Coquina* to receive their goods when we pulled in from St. Cloud. By refusing to respond to the rumors, I inadvertently confirmed them.

Then late one afternoon, I returned to the hotel from the dockyard and went to the front desk to get my key from the residents' box. A young man in wire-rimmed spectacles and straight blond hair parted sharply in the middle stood by the counter, evidently waiting for me. He identified himself as Patrick Keane, a reporter for the *St. Cloud Tribune,* the paper where Elder John had published his essays on Shaker agronomy and I published mine on beekeeping. Mr. Keane wore a rumpled, loose-fitting seersucker suit and dangled a cigarillo from the corner of his mouth, the picture of a small-town wise-guy journalist. He said he wanted to ask me a few questions about what he called "the Sadie Pratt case."

As I had grown accustomed to saying, I told him that I had been instructed by State's Attorney Jones not to discuss the matter. "He's waiting for the coroner's inquest to be completed before deciding on the charges. You should be interviewing him, not me," I said.

"Yeah, well, I just came from Jones's office. And I spoke earlier with Sheriff Prevett. Jones told me Dr. Cardiff's report was turned in yesterday, and Circuit Judge W. Standard Parker instructed Prevett to release the two Shakers from jail. I'm told that you were the one who first accused the Shakers of murdering Sadie Pratt, so I wondered what your thoughts on the matter were."

This news stunned me, and for a moment I was speechless. I reached over Keane's shoulder and took my room key from the box as if intending to leave the reporter's question unanswered. Instead I stumbled to a nearby sofa and sat down. "What . . . what was in Dr. Cardiff's report? The judge and the sheriff set them free? Why?"

"Yeah, they're free, all right. The woman anyhow. She made bail. The man, Bennett, he couldn't swing it, I guess. The deputy, whatsisname, Rufus or Rastus, he's taking the woman back to New Bethany tomorrow morning. I'll visit Bennett in his cell, if he'll talk to me, and I plan to go out to New Bethany and try talking to the woman later."

"It's Rebus," I said. "The deputy."

"Yeah, right, Rebus. Anyhow, Jones isn't very happy about it. He was probably hoping for an easy conviction, since he's running for lieutenant governor. He was thinking it'd be a sweet little high-profile murder case guaranteed to get a lot of statewide coverage. But it's looking a little tricky now."

"The coroner's inquest, Dr. Cardiff's report. What did it say?"

"Didn't read it myself. Jones said he couldn't release it to the public, due to privacy concerns. But Sheriff Prevett, he let it slip that the report proved the woman, Sadie Pratt, was definitely not pregnant. Also, her tuberculosis was so advanced that the disease is what killed her, not the morphine she was taking for pain. Case closed, right?"

"Yes. I suppose so."

"Unless you don't believe the doc's report. That's the only case the prosecutor can make. Assuming he goes ahead and tries to convince a grand jury to indict them." He paused for a few seconds. "You got any reason to question the good doctor's report, Mr. Mann?"

"Dr. Cardiff is a man of science," I said. "I'm not."

Keane said he might come back to me after he talked to the Shaker woman. We shook hands, and he clapped me on the shoulder, as if to bolster my spirits. "Cheer up, Mann. These people, the Shaker elders, they're your friends, right?"

"Yes, they're my friends. But if they did something wrong . . ."

". . . You wouldn't want them to get away with it, would you?"

"No, I wouldn't," I said and turned away, and with images of Dr. Cardiff performing his autopsy and the elders returning to the welcoming embrace of their Shaker family swirling through my mind, I slowly climbed the stairs to my room.

By the following morning the reporter, Patrick Keane, had spread his news across the entire region. The headline of the *St. Cloud Tribune* blared, "Shakers Exonerated by Coroner's Report!" The byline was Keane's, and his long front-page article detailed the history of the case. He wrote that an anonymous accusation of euthanasia filed with Sheriff Prevett on August 15 had "raised suspicions that the death of Miss Sadie Pratt, a twenty-seven-year-old native of Warwick, Rhode Island, and resident of the New Bethany community of

Shakers, was not attributable to natural causes." The article said that Elder John Bennett and Eldress Mary Glynn, "the respected leaders of the New Bethany Shakers," were arrested on August 16 and then released for lack of evidence. They were rearrested on August 18, however, when State's Attorney John C. Jones reportedly received additional evidence that a crime had been committed in the death of Miss Pratt. There were strong suspicions that the young woman had been made pregnant by Bennett and that her illness was not so advanced as to have caused her death. In an aside, Keane noted that "the Shakers are famous for practicing strict celibacy." On orders from Circuit Judge W. Standard Parker, he wrote, Miss Pratt's body was disinterred, and the Osceola County coroner, Dr. Timothy Cardiff, performed an autopsy, which determined that the woman "was not seen to be pregnant and had died of natural causes." The two Shaker leaders were refusing to speak to the press or to the general public about the case. State's Attorney Jones was said to be considering whether to seek an indictment from a grand jury, regardless of Judge Parker's and Sheriff Prevett's wish to drop all charges.

The *St. Cloud Tribune* for September 4, 1910, was widely read in Tallahassee, the state capital, where there was great interest in any news concerning State's Attorney John C. Jones, the Florida Democratic Party's nominee for lieutenant governor. Readers were also attracted by the suggestive mix of sex and religion. Northern Republican newspapers, like *The New York Times* and the *Chicago Tribune,* maintained offices and stringers in Tallahassee and other Southern state capitals to keep track of regional politics, and the case quickly came to the attention of the national press. It being Labor Day weekend, there wasn't much other news, so the various agencies and reporters based in Tallahassee copied and sent to their New York and Chicago editorial offices the slightly scandalous story about the death of a young woman in a Shaker colony in the Florida Everglades. By Tuesday, September 6th, all America knew the names of Elder John Bennett and his presumed paramour, Sadie Pratt, and his female accomplice, Eldress Mary Glynn, and the desire of the state's attorney, John C. Jones, to pursue charges of first- and second-degree murder against the two Shakers, despite the objections of the Osceola County sheriff and circuit judge, who were regarded locally as friends of the Shakers.

Thus there was great and growing interest in the story, and consequently, over the following few days, Attorney Jones was interviewed by the New York and Chicago journalists for follow-up stories and by reporters from newspapers in Jacksonville and Atlanta and Washington. Attorney Jones seemed to enjoy the publicity and with each new interview sounded increasingly likely to convene a grand jury for the sole purpose of indicting the two Shakers for murder. Democratic Party chieftains saw an opportunity to get their candidate portrayed statewide and even nationwide as a zealous champion of the law and an opponent of illicit sexual activity. Editorial pages far and wide called for a grand jury. In the end, Judge Parker and Sheriff Prevett realized they had no choice but to once again charge the two elders with murder and clap them back in jail in St. Cloud and let Attorney Jones convene his grand jury and seek an indictment and proceed to what was expected to be an exciting, closely watched trial.

While all this was happening, I kept my head low and went to work every day and otherwise holed up in my room on the third floor of the St. Cloud Hotel, as if the unfolding drama had nothing to do with me. And for a spell I did believe it had nothing to do with me. Until the evening I was startled by a knock on my door, and when I opened it, there stood Eldress Mary.

She wore her usual Shaker bonnet and white lace shoulder covering and long black dress. Her round, sun-burnished face had faded to a pale gray from being locked in a jail cell, and she seemed uncharacteristically fatigued and frail and vulnerable. She said, "I would like to speak with you for a few moments."

I bade her come in, and she entered the room and shut the door behind her. I sat on the bed, and she sat down on the straight-backed chair next to it and began to speak in a tentative manner that was unusual for her, always so certain. She said that Sheriff Prevett, having raised her bail bond a second time from a committee of local citizens, had again released her from jail. Unfortunately, due to the negative publicity and gossip regarding Elder John's presumed role in the case, the sheriff had been unable this second time to raise bail money for him, so Elder John still languished in his cell.

She said that before returning to New Bethany tomorrow to await the convening of the grand jury, she had taken a room at the hotel and had learned from the night manager that there was another Shaker living in the building. "I asked the name, and the other Shaker turned out to be you," she said. "At first, I wanted only to avoid seeing you, Brother Harley, for you have been cast out of the family. But then I thought, since the Lord has placed us so near to one another, it might be of use to Elder John and myself and to you, if this one time I did not shun you, and we exchanged truths."

"I'm not sure I even know what's true anymore," I said.

"I meant, to exchange your truth and my truth, thine for mine, one for the other."

To contend with the pain of having been expelled by both my Shaker family and my blood family, I had built a hard shell around me, a carapace of not caring. Eldress Mary's willingness to suspend the shunning, even if only for this one meeting, cracked open that shell, and I found myself suddenly shuddering with gratitude and fighting back tears. "I'm not sure . . ." I said. "I don't know where to start."

She said, "Then I'll start with my truth. Yes, Elder John and I did inject Sister Sadie with the morphine that caused her death. She begged us to do it, and we did it. We did it in order to end her terrible suffering. We knew it was illegal, but we have never denied having done it, for we believed that it was the right thing to do."

I said, "That's the same information I brought to the sheriff. Even though I swore to Elder John that I would tell no one. I broke my promise to him and told myself that I made the accusation in order to avoid committing the sin of lying. But that's not my whole truth. I did it also because of jealousy and anger. Jealousy of Elder John's close relationship with Sadie, and anger at you and him for helping her die."

She said, "I told you that Sister Sadie died a Believer. Elder John reported to me that you took it to mean that I had heard her confession of sins, as is normally done when one becomes a Shaker. If so, then I misled you, Brother Harley. My truth is that I did not hear Sister Sadie's confession of sins. When Elder John injected her with the morphine, she said she wanted to die a Shaker, but the morphine acted very quickly on her, and she passed without speaking again. As her final request was to die a Shaker, I felt I had to grant it, even without hearing her confession of sins."

I wrung my hands, and I said, "When the sheriff released you and Elder John the first time and I was expelled from the New Bethany family, my grief and anger were doubled, and I suddenly felt all alone in the world. Early on the morning she died, in a moment of despair and desperation and in great pain, Sadie had told me that she was pregnant. Hoping to convince me to inject her with a fatal dose of morphine, she also said that Elder John might be the father. At the time, I suspected it was a lie, designed to make me jealous enough to help her die. But after I was deposed by Attorney Jones, and Sheriff Prevett released you and Elder John the first time, I wrote a letter to Attorney Jones, repeating Sadie's lie as if it were the truth. It's what prompted him to have Sheriff Prevett rearrest you and Elder John."

Eldress Mary said, "For several years I've thought that you and Sister Sadie had grown too close. Dangerously close. And yet, when I should have intervened, I did nothing about it. I couldn't have foreseen all this, but I knew that it would come to no good, and you would fall in love, and one or both of you would have to leave New Bethany. I brought my concerns to Elder John, and it turned out that he had the same concerns. But I wanted her to stay, for she had become like a daughter to me. And Elder John wanted you to stay, for you had become like a son to him. As you well know, we Shakers can have no children, Brother Harley, except those we adopt, and when we love them too much, we lose sight of what is best for them." She reached forward and took my hands in hers. Her hands were an old lady's hands, wrinkled and spotted, small and soft. My hands, held by hers, felt large and leathery. She said, "Instead of intervening and keeping you and Sister Sadie separated, we allowed you to grow too close. Much too close."

I said, "The morning Sadie died, when she first told me that she was pregnant, I did not suspect her of lying. I assumed at once that I was the father of her unborn child. Who else could it be? Even when she claimed later that Elder John might have been responsible, I still believed that I was the father of her unborn child. My truth is that I refused to help her die that morning, because I wanted her to live and bear our child," I said, and I lowered my head and began to sob.

She said, "Dr. Cardiff's coroner's report claims that Sister Sadie died of natural causes. That is, she died from the effects of tuberculosis. Elder John and I know that cannot be true. She died as a result of our having injected her with one hundred milligrams of morphine, instead of the forty-five milligrams prescribed by Dr. Cardiff. His report also claims that she was not pregnant. You and I cannot believe that he has told the truth there, either, can we? Dr. Cardiff is a kind man, and he is trying to help me and Elder John, but it's with at least one lie, probably two. Elder John and I cannot decide whether to accept his help." She paused for a few seconds, then she said, "What would you have us do, Brother Harley?"

It was not a test. I believed that Eldress Mary sincerely wanted my advice and counsel, and by asking my opinion on a moral question of this magnitude, she was giving me a chance for redemption. I said, "If your truth is that you and Elder John injected Sadie with an overdose of morphine solely as an act of love and mercy, with knowledge that it was a crime, then you should reject Dr. Cardiff's false conclusions publicly and accept whatever punishment the law requires for euthanizing a person. If my truth is that Sadie and I were unmarried lovers, then I should say it in public and accept the shaming and isolation that is my just punishment. I should also say publicly that when I learned how Sadie had died, I believed she was pregnant by me, because she told me so. I should testify that I was jealous of her relationship with Elder John and angry at him and you, which is why, in my letter to Attorney Jones, in violation of the law and of the Lord's ninth commandment, I bore false witness against you and Elder John. I should pray for forgiveness from the Lord and from you and Elder John and my New Bethany family, and I should accept the law's punishment for perjury. If we three are convicted and sent to prison for our crimes, you and Elder John for euthanasia and me for perjury, it will not be because we have lied. It will be because we have told the truth. Your truth and Elder John's and mine."

She nodded in agreement, and we both sat in silence. Finally, she said, "I can't remove the order to expel you, Brother Harley, without Elder John's permission. You must go to him in his cell and say to him that you and I have exchanged our truths. He will know what that means. You must offer to exchange your truth for his, just as you and I have done. He may or may not agree. But if he does agree, and is satisfied with what you offer up, then he and I and the rest of the brethren will discuss and pray over whether to revoke the decision to expel you and allow you to return to New Bethany as a novitiate. We will then pray over whether to invite you to make a full confession of your sins and become a member of the Society of Believers."

"But what if I don't wish to become a member of the Society of Believers?" I said. "What if I don't believe? What if the only reason I stayed on at New Bethany after my brother Pence left was in order to be close to Sadie?"

She remained silent for a moment. She released my hands and stood up. "Well, then there's no reason for you to go to Elder John's cell and ask to exchange truths," she said. "And considering what you have revealed to me concerning your secret relations with Sister Sadie Pratt, there's no reason for us to remove the order to turn away from you." She pointedly turned her back. Saying nothing further, she walked to the door and was gone, and I was once again, as I am today these many years later, unforgiven, cast out, shunned, a man with no family or tribe. I was an isolato lost among the people of the World.

[*A five-minute, thirty-seven-second silence occurs. Then Harley Mann resumes speaking.*]

A few moments ago, just as I finished describing my exchange with Eldress Mary and was at the point where she had renewed the Shakers' decision to cast me away, the house trembled and shook, and I heard glasses and dishes falling from the cabinets in the kitchen and books tumbling from the living-room bookcases. It felt like an earthquake and lasted no longer than thirty seconds. I rushed from the porch back inside the house and saw no further damage, except for several long cracks across my plaster of paris topographical map of New Bethany. I feared the sinkhole in my driveway might have suddenly expanded, but from the kitchen window it seemed the same size as it did yesterday and the day before.

I'm embarrassed to confess that for a moment, lost as I was in the telling of my story, my first thought was that Eldress Mary had invoked the wrath of God, a God I do not believe exists, but the strength of her belief was so great, she seemed to have the ability to bring Him into existence and loose upon me His punishing power.

For most religious people, like the Shakers and the Koreshans and Evangelical Christians and Muslims, the supernatural world easily displaces the natural. They'd rather believe in magic than nature, in the invisible world than the visible. But for me, ever since I was a boy living with my family among the Ruskinites, it has largely been the opposite. To honor those early formative years and my long-gone father's strongly held principles, over and against what has seemed to me little more than superstition and spiritualism and belief in invisible beings and worlds, all of which are aspects of Shaker belief, I have assiduously clung to scientific rationalism. Much as I tried, I could not avoid love, however.

But today, for the moment, anyhow, sanity has quickly returned, and I have decided that it must indeed have been a small earthquake that shook my house, not Eldress Mary's vengeful God. Earthquakes are rare in Florida, but not completely unknown. Though there are no fault lines or shifting tectonic plates in the Sunshine State, I have read that deep below the Gulf of Mexico there is a subduction zone, where the Caribbean Plate grinds against the North American shelf, conjuring volcanoes in the Antilles and earthquakes sometimes felt as far north as Kentucky and Georgia and even down here in south-central Florida.

Fortified by scientific rationalism, then, I continue with my story. I have come nearly to the end of it. After Eldress Mary left my room that night at the St. Cloud Hotel, a few uneventful days passed, until, on my usual early-morning arrival at the office of the harbormaster, I was met by Sheriff Prevett. He was not warm or particularly friendly.

He handed me a sealed envelope and quickly departed. Opening the envelope, I saw that it was an official court document that began with the Latin words *Subpoena ad testificandum,* summoning me to appear at ten a.m. on Wednesday, September 21, 1910, five days hence, to give oral testimony to the grand jury in the case of *Florida v. John Bennett and Mary Glynn.* It was not an arrest warrant, but it felt like one.

As directed, on the morning of Wednesday the twenty-first I walked to the St. Cloud City Hall passing a phalanx of reporters gathered outside, among whom I recognized Mr. Patrick Keane of the *St. Cloud Tribune*, and was directed to the room where the grand jury had been convened.

Despite the absence of observers, the chamber seemed crowded. Present were Sheriff Prevett and State's Attorney Jones and the stenographer, Heddie, and the defendants, Elder John and Eldress Mary. Deputy Rebus with his shiny new Peacemaker holstered at his waist stood guard by the door, and an aged clerk of the court leaned familiarly against the judge's bench. The entire gathering was presided over by Circuit Judge W. Standard Parker, a tall, solemn, clean-shaven man in his fifties with a luxurious mane of white hair, as handsome and self-admiring as an aging marquee star of stage and screen. Attorney Jones waved me to a chair beside his at a table below the judge's bench.

Across from us and to the right of the judge's bench was the jury box with the jurors seated in three rows. There were fifteen of them, local citizens chosen by lottery, shopkeepers and merchants and clerks of various ages dressed for the occasion in suits and neckties as if for church, with a few who appeared to be farmers in clean coveralls and work shirts. All the jurors were White, all were male. They looked weary and uncomfortably warm and seemed irritated, sour-faced, probably not pleased to have been called away from their jobs and fields merely to decide whether a capital case should be tried. An actual murder trial would have been different, more exciting. A jury might get to find the defendants guilty and hear the judge issue a death sentence.

The stenographer sat at a tiny desk on the left. At a second table

Sheriff Prevett sat between Elder John and Eldress Mary. I glanced in their direction, and the two Shaker elders turned in their seats and looked at the wall. There did not appear to be an attorney present to defend them, which at first surprised me, but I remembered that they had no intention of denying their culpability in hastening Sadie's death. Maybe they had already testified to that effect. I wondered if Dr. Cardiff had testified yet and if his coroner's report had been submitted and admitted without challenge as Exhibit A. I wondered if Attorney Jones had questioned Sheriff Prevett, and I worried about what Attorney Jones would be asking me, because I didn't know any of the testimony that had preceded mine. But I was prepared this time to tell the truth, the whole truth, so it didn't matter what he asked me or what the others had already testified to.

I was summoned to the empty chair beside the judge's bench, and with my hand on the Bible, was quickly sworn in by the clerk of the court. Attorney Jones, wiping his forehead with a handkerchief, ambled up to me and asked me to state my name and age and current place of residence. It was a soft opening that hardened as he went along. He wanted to know how long I had known the defendants, how long had I lived at New Bethany, and what was my line of work there.

"I was the beekeeper," I said.

He seemed to find that interesting and asked me a few questions about bees, which I was glad to answer in detail, until Judge Parker questioned the relevance of the line of questioning.

"I'm merely trying to establish the witness's intelligence and clarity of mind," Jones said, and the judge nodded permission to continue.

Then Attorney Jones turned to my relationship with the defendants, whom he referred to as "the Shaker elders, Mr. Bennett and Miss Glynn."

I said that I had known them since I was twelve years old, and Elder John had been my mentor and in many ways my model, since my real father had died when I was a boy. I described Eldress Mary as my spiritual and ethical guide, a role she played for many of the Shakers at New Bethany. I said that I greatly admired both of them and had a strong personal affection for them, especially for Elder John, who over the years had done a great deal to cultivate my mind by providing me with books I would otherwise never have read and by discussing the content of those books with me as if I were his intellectual equal. I knew I was volunteering more information than his questions aimed at, but I was not afraid of harming myself or Elder John and Eldress Mary, because everything I said was true.

He said it was odd that I should speak of Elder John and Eldress Mary in terms of such fondness and respect, when they appeared not to welcome my presence here this morning. Could that be attributed to the fact that I was the person who had first brought their self-admitted crime of euthanasia to the attention of Sheriff Prevett? Could it also be because of my letter to the office of the state's attorney, which implied that their crime was not simply the so-called mercy killing of a terminally ill person, as they claimed, but a cold, calculated, premeditated crime of first-degree murder?

"Very likely attributable to both my having told about Sadie's death to the sheriff and the letter I wrote to you shortly after," I said. "And I'd like to speak further about that letter, sir. But to fully answer your question, there are other reasons for the elders' visible antipathy toward me."

"Such as?"

"The nature of my relationship with Sadie Pratt."

"Well, why not begin there?" He then asked me to describe the nature of my relationship with "the deceased person, the young and beautiful Miss Sadie Pratt."

I wasn't sure where to begin, because I wasn't sure who I was speaking to. Was it Elder John, who no doubt had already been told by Eldress Mary that Sadie and I had been lovers and that Sadie had claimed on the morning she died that she was pregnant? Was it Sheriff Prevett, who wondered why I'd made the accusation against the elders in the first place? It never made sense to him. Was it Attorney Jones himself, who needed affirmation that my initial accusation and my letter to him were motivated by my close friendship with Sadie and a belief in truth, justice, and the law? Or was I speaking to the fifteen jurors seated across from me, the strangers who were trying to balance my letter to Attorney Jones—that she was pregnant by Elder John and was not dying of tuberculosis—against the findings in Dr. Cardiff's coroner's inquest—no pregnancy, and she was indeed terminally ill—over and against Elder John's and Eldress Mary's open confession to having committed the crime of euthanasia in order to ease the suffering of a woman about to die of tuberculosis?

It's no different now, sixty-some years later. Because I don't know who I'm telling this story to, I'm unsure of what to say and what to leave out, what to describe and what to pass over, how much background to provide and how much to forgo. To end my quandary and answer the state's attorney's question, I decided, then as now, that I was speaking to a listening angel of the Lord, though I don't believe in angels or, for that matter, the Lord. But it's a useful conceit. Thus I was speaking to everyone in the courtroom and to no one. Just as right now I'm speaking to anyone who listens to these reels of tape or reads a transcript of them, and I'm speaking to no one, for my words will likely never be heard or read anyhow. Then as now, it's as if my words were directed exclusively to a listening angel of the Lord and were merely being overheard, rather than heard, by whoever happened to be in the room.

I commenced by saying that my relationship with Sadie Pratt was one of passionate, obsessive love that began when we first met, when I was a twelve-year-old boy and she a nineteen-year-old woman. "For many years I thought she was my special best friend and confidante," I began. "And she claimed that I was the same for her, her special best friend and confidant. When she was a patient at the Sunshine Home sanitarium," I continued, "she was a frequent long-term visitor at New Bethany, but we did not have many opportunities to be together without someone else present. Then, starting three years ago, when she came to live full-time at New Bethany, we saw each other daily, and we became lovers, lovers in all but the very act of love. And then, less than a year ago, starting at the Florida State Fair in Tampa, we began arranging to be together secretly in order to commit the act of love. We lay together as often as we could do it in secret. Because of our obsessive love for each other, we lied, violating the Shaker insistence on truth telling, and we constantly broke the Shaker rule to maintain strict celibacy between men and women. We lied and broke rules in many other ways, too, especially me, primarily by pretending to be a Believer in the Lord and the divinity of Mother Ann and Jesus Christ and Heaven and a host of other beliefs close to every Shaker's heart. We were hypocrites. We did this so that we could stay together at New Bethany and continue being lovers. That was the true nature of my relationship with Sadie Pratt," I said, and added, "We did many bad things, we committed many sins, and we did it all for love."

Attorney Jones stared at me, his thick black eyebrows raised in surprise, his mouth half open, as if he were ready to speak, but was unable to remember what he had intended to say. He picked up and shuffled a few loose sheets of paper that had lain on the table and placed them back on the table again. Leaning forward, he appeared to carefully read the top sheet.

Finally, he said, "Let's address the letter dated August 17, 1910, that you wrote to me and delivered to my secretary the following day. In that letter you stated, and I quote, 'Elder John Bennett did indeed tell me that he and Eldress Mary Glynn administered the fatal dose of morphine to Sadie Pratt. He claimed that it was done at Sadie Pratt's request and made me promise not to reveal this to anyone. Also, earlier that day, when I visited Sadie alone in her room, she was able to speak coherently and seemed alert. Further and more importantly, she told me that she was pregnant, and it was by Elder John.' Is that correct, Mr. Mann?"

"Yes, I wrote that."

"And did you also write these words? Here again I quote. 'I do not know if this was true, as she was sometimes inclined to exaggerate, and she was quite ill. . . . But if true, then Elder John Bennett could certainly be said to benefit from her death and thus would be guilty of murder in the first degree. Although the benefit to Eldress Mary Glynn is less clear-cut than to Elder John, Sadie Pratt's death would also benefit the eldress, who, as a senior Shaker, would want to keep information like this from getting out.'"

"Yes, I also wrote that."

"Mr. Mann, were you telling the truth with this letter?"

"That's what I wanted to discuss with you, sir. I did tell the truth in that letter, but not the whole truth and nothing but the truth."

He gave a thin smile—more a grimace than a smile, actually. "You're still very clever with these double negatives, Mr. Mann," he said. "Tell us the whole truth and nothing but the truth, if you please."

"You mean, tell you what I left out of my account of Sadie's and my conversation the day she died and my meeting later with Elder John? Other than what I have just told you about the nature of my relationship with Sadie?"

"Yes. Tell us what you left out," he said, and sighed, for he doubtless knew what was coming and what it would do to his charge of murder in the first degree.

And so I proceeded to describe in detail my final meeting with Sadie. How she revealed that she was pregnant by me and asked me to help her die. How I refused, because I wanted her to have my child. How Sadie, hoping jealousy would make me willing to help her die, said that Elder John, not I, might be the father, but I did not believe her charge against Elder John and still refused to help her die, so she sent me away. I told him everything.

"So you don't believe that Elder John might be the father of Sadie Pratt's unborn child?"

"No."

"But you do believe that Sadie Pratt was pregnant when she died."

"Yes."

"So you don't accept the findings of the coroner's inquest that was conducted by Dr. Cardiff."

"Only one-third of his findings. I know that she was indeed terminally ill with tuberculosis. The second third, that she was not pregnant? No, I do not accept it. Nor do I accept his finding that she did not die from a fatal dose of morphine. I believe that Dr. Cardiff is trying to protect Elder John and Eldress Mary, who are his friends. Which is understandable, for they are only guilty of what they have confessed to, easing a woman who was suffering incurable, unbearable pain into her imminent death. Theirs was solely an act of mercy."

Attorney Jones said, "We'll let the grand jury make that determination, Mr. Mann. Thank you, that will be all."

Judge Parker loudly cleared his throat to gain our attention. "Before we dismiss him, would the defendants like to question the witness?"

Elder John leaned across Sheriff Prevett and whispered to Eldress Mary, who shook her head no. "We have no questions for the witness, Your Honor," Elder John said.

Judge Parker said, "What about you, Sheriff Prevett? Do you have any questions for the witness?"

Frowning and looking troubled, the sheriff slowly stood and faced me. "Mr. Mann, nobody in this room was closer to the young lady who died and the two defendants said to be responsible for her death than you. You knew these three people intimately, one might say. So tell us, son, how you think the grand jury should vote on Attorney Jones's charge of murder?"

"Point of order, Your Honor," the state's attorney said. "Mr. Mann's opinion has no relevance to the case."

"Overruled. Sheriff Prevett is right," the judge said. "The young fellow has lived in close proximity with the defendants for many years and thus has deep knowledge of their character. And he has admitted to a lengthy, let us say intimate, relationship with the deceased. Go ahead, Mr. Mann, tell us how you think the members of the jury should vote on the charge of murder."

I said, "I think justice will be best served if they dismiss the charge."

The judge said, "And the charge of euthanasia, how do you think they should find on that?"

Again, Attorney Jones tried to intervene and called for a point of order, adding that I was not a lawyer and could not speak to questions of criminal law.

With a theatrically raised flat of the hand, the judge silently shut him down. "Overruled. Go ahead, young man," he said to me. "On the charge of euthanasia, which, as you may know, is a serious crime in this state, a crime comparable to second-degree murder and punishable with a lengthy prison sentence, tell us how you think the jury should find."

I said, "Your Honor, I know it's a crime, but the state's attorney has a weak case that, if it goes to trial, will only get weaker. At trial, the defendants will be represented by a first-rate lawyer, for they have many friends who will be honored to pay for their defense. Their lawyer will go to the numerous complications and contradictions between my testimony and Dr. Cardiff's report and the defendants' confession, and he will point to the amount of hearsay and rumor and widespread newspaper coverage of the case, and he will note the possibility of prejudice against the defendants because of their religious and social beliefs and practices. Your Honor, I think justice will best be served by a grand jury decision to dismiss all criminal charges against the defendants."

The judge nodded as if he agreed. He said, "If you came here with the hope of defending your fellow Shakers, Mr. Mann, you have done well. You have paid the price of revealing your sordid personal life to us. In the process you have impugned the character of a young woman who is unable to defend her honor, which is unfortunate, perhaps unforgivable. But luckily, grand juries are forbidden to reveal what they have heard. Your testimony will remain permanently sealed. You are dismissed, sir."

REEL #15

And here is where the end begins. Here also, therefore, is where the beginning ends. It's the end of the story that shaped the rest of what has turned out to have been my long, solitary life. Most long lives like mine seem to be made of fits and starts, refits and restarts, rapid runs from one post to another, from optimism to disillusionment to optimism and back again, from dawn to dusk to darkest night to dawn again. It's the American way, I guess—a lifetime of starting over.

Not my way, however. My life, at least the last sixty-one years of it, has been the slow unspooling of a coil loosened that September morning in 1910 in the St. Cloud courthouse, when my testimony convinced the grand jury to vote in favor of dropping all charges against the Shaker elders.

I was in the crowd waiting outside in the shade of the live oak trees, where the Spanish moss floated in the light breeze like curtains of gray gauze, when State's Attorney Jones came out onto the columned portico to speak to the journalists. He had removed his jacket and necktie and had rolled his shirtsleeves to his elbows, as if about to deliver a stem-winding political campaign speech, and indeed, after mentioning almost in passing that the grand jury had declined to indict the two Shakers and he was therefore dropping all charges, he quickly swerved into a catalog of the changes he would bring to governance in the state of Florida, once he was elected lieutenant governor.

The tribe of reporters tried shouting questions about the Shakers' alleged crime of murder and the rumors concerning sexual relations between the male Shaker and the deceased young woman, but Attorney Jones ignored them and continued on with his speech, until the interest of the reporters and most of the crowd faded, and they drifted away to write their articles, and the crowd dissipated, leaving only me and Patrick Keane of the *St. Cloud Tribune* and a handful of local unemployed hangers-on for an audience, at which point Attorney Jones urged us to vote for him in November and turned and entered the building.

Patrick Keane noticed me standing nearby, and when I walked quickly away, he caught up to me at the corner of New York Avenue and tugged my sleeve. I stopped, and he asked if I had testified to the grand jury.

I acknowledged that I had made a brief appearance, but offered nothing more.

"Can you tell me why the state's attorney dropped the charges? Since the Shakers already confessed to bringing about the girl's death," he added, still holding on to my sleeve. "Did they retract their confession?"

I said, "The judge instructed us not to discuss what was said in the courtroom."

"He did, did he?" He gave a sly smile and a wink and said, "Well, I have a pretty good idea of what was said in the courtroom, friend."

I pushed his hand away and walked toward the St. Cloud Hotel, leaving him standing on the corner, scribbling into his notebook. I spent that night sleepless, communing with the ghost of my Sadie, importuning her to forgive me for having revealed our secret love to the elders and to the court and to the fifteen men of the grand jury and the sheriff and his deputy—as if they were everyone in the World. And then, when morning came and I descended the stairs to the hotel dining room, it turned out that I had indeed revealed our secret love to the world.

A copy of the morning edition of the *St. Cloud Tribune* had been placed on my usual corner table, either by the manager or at his direction by one of the Black waiters. The headline trumpeted, "Shaker Couple Cleared of All Charges!" The article, written by Patrick Keane, was illustrated with three portraits drawn by an artist purported to have been present in the courtroom, in which one could easily recognize Elder John and Eldress Mary seated at an imagined defendants' table. The third portrait was of an unnamed young man who closely resembled me with his right hand raised to be sworn in.

The restaurant was not crowded, a half dozen early-morning local diners, regulars whom I knew slightly, and several of the journalists from yesterday and a few travelers from the North, but I felt that everyone was watching me, waiting for my reaction to the *Tribune*'s front page. I read Keane's article quickly and felt the blood rush to my ears and face.

He summarized in the first paragraph Attorney Jones's passing remarks made outside the City Hall, but then went on to say that there was still much about the death of Sadie Pratt that remained a mystery. The main question, he wrote, concerned the grand jury's refusal to indict the two Shaker elders for murder, neither first-degree nor second-, when they had already confessed to the crime of euthanasia, a second-degree-murder offense. Despite their confession, the coroner's inquest claimed that the young woman's death was caused, not by an overdose of morphine, but by her long battle with tuberculosis. Then why, Keane asked, did the state's attorney ask the grand jury to indict the Shakers in the first place?

It was initially thought that Attorney Jones did so because he had evidence confirming the rumor that the young woman was pregnant as a result of a love affair with the male Shaker, John Bennett. Presumably, Bennett and the female Shaker, Mary Glynn, wanted to hide that fact. Yet we note that the coroner's inquest further claimed that the young woman was not pregnant. The Shakers' confession and the coroner's inquest cancel each other out.

Therefore, we cannot help but assume, Keane wrote, that testimony from an unnamed third party must have contradicted both the confession by the Shaker elders and the results of the coroner's inquest, thereby adding to the mix a plausible third narrative. Sealed by order of Judge W. Standard Parker, that unnamed person's testimony must have convincingly argued that someone other than John Bennett, a different male Shaker, perhaps, had been involved in a sexual relationship with the young woman. It would have to be a person who would have much to lose if the affair ever became known. That unnamed person might even have implicated himself in bringing about her death. This would render moot the Shaker elders' confession, which, in all fairness, they may have made by mistake. They had been providing Miss Pratt with small doses of morphine, as prescribed by Dr. Cardiff of St. Cloud, and in their honest naiveté may have believed that their care had been the cause of her death. The coroner's inquest would therefore have to be rejected as inaccurate, which is not uncommon, especially when a body has been disinterred, as was Miss Pratt's, and autopsied long after the time of death.

The mystery, then, is who is that unnamed third party? Name him, Keane wrote, and all the questions raised above will have been answered. Name him, and you may well have named the man who murdered Sadie Pratt, either to ease her pain and suffering, or else to hide the fact that, though they were members of the sexually celibate Shaker community, he and she were engaged in an illicit love affair, and she had become pregnant by him.

Thus the front page of the *St. Cloud Tribune* had all but named me, Harley Mann, as Sadie's secret lover, the father of her unborn child, and her murderer. Naturally, Patrick Keane's speculative, artfully lascivious story and the accompanying portraits got picked up and reprinted by newspapers all across the state and region and, a day or two later, by *The New York Times* and the *Chicago Tribune*, along with papers in Washington, Atlanta, and other Southern cities. Such is the power of the media that within forty-eight hours I was being accused and judged not only by the Shakers of New Bethany, but by the entire population of the United States.

No one in St. Cloud wanted to be seen associating with me.

Whether named or unnamed, I was marked as a national villain. On the local level, Captain Bunting, the harbormaster, told me that his wife had been outraged by my continued employment there. She had insisted that he not have a murderer and scandalous philanderer and religious hypocrite working for him, so I would have to find employment elsewhere. When I went to see Captain Shea, hoping to join the crew of the *Coquina* as a deckhand, Salty Haversack, the pilot, pointedly did not return my greeting and gazed out at the lake waters as if checking for rain, and Captain Shea refused to let me come on board. He said, "If I'd known what you was up to back then, Mann, I'd never have recommended you to work at the harbor. And I wouldn't have let you ride for free back and forth between St. Cloud and New Bethany like I did."

At the St. Cloud Hotel, when I returned from the harbor and asked for my room key at the front desk, the manager came out of his office cubicle in back and told me that I'd have to move out of my room by the end of the week. "Nothing personal," he said. "But too many of our residents and customers have been complaining about you living and dining here." Even my fellow stevedores, the three young Black men led by Neilly Fabben, were careful not to be seen in my company. Early the evening of the day that I was given notice by the St. Cloud Hotel, they saw me walking toward them along the wooden sidewalk on Pennsylvania Avenue and stepped down onto the street and slogged through the mud to the other side. It would be many years and a different era before Neilly and I could work comfortably together, me as a realtor, him as a surveyor, although even then, whenever the subject of our shared time working for the old harbormaster, Captain Bunting, came up in conversation, he steered us away from the subject, as if we had never been stevedores together when we were young men, side by side loading and unloading barges and boats on East Lake Tohopekaliga.

Oddly, the only person in St. Cloud willing to speak civilly to me and treat me kindly was the deputy sheriff, Rebus, who turned out to be a true Samaritan. He never admitted it, and I never asked him to, but it occurred to me that he was likely the person who had let the content of my testimony slip to Patrick Keane, and now he regretted having done it and was trying in some small way to make up for it. He was an honest man, but none too bright, and was too proud of his access to inside information, and the journalist, Patrick Keane, was a sly fox who could easily have induced the deputy to reveal what he'd overheard in the courtroom.

At the end of the week, with only a few dollars left from my final week's pay in my pocket and no idea of where to go next, I packed all my worldly possessions into a gunnysack and moved out of the St. Cloud Hotel, and the deputy and I literally bumped into each other on the hotel porch. He came up the steps as I descended them, unable to decide whether to turn right or left when I reached the plank sidewalk.

He said howdy and shook my hand and said he'd heard I'd lost my job and was being kicked out of the hotel. He asked me where I was planning to live and if I'd found any work in town to pay for it.

I told him that I was homeless and jobless.

He suddenly brightened and reached into his pocket and pulled out a folded envelope. "Sheriff asked me to bring you this letter that come for you. It was sent in care of the City Hall. Guess whoever wrote it knew you wasn't at New Bethany no more."

There it was, after nearly two years of silence, a letter from Pence, with a return address in Hawthorne, California. He must have somehow learned of my plight and was writing to help and advise me and wrap me in brotherly love in this moment of my greatest need. I opened the envelope and sat down on the porch steps to read it. Rebus squatted next to me and looked over my shoulder and tried to read it, too.

It was very short, written in pencil on lined paper, a single paragraph of three sentences: "From the newspapers it seems like you have lost your mind. I guess you betrayed everyone, especially Mother, and have turned out to be a murderer too. I can no longer think of you as my brother, so do not write back." It was signed simply "Pence Mann."

"Who wrote that?" Rebus asked.

"My brother."

Rebus patted my shoulder and said, "That ain't exactly brotherly, if you want my opinion."

I tried to explain that given the nature of my family and its bed-rock belief in principles before all else, even before love—a predilection inherited from our father, enforced by our early Ruskinite communist years, and then reinforced by the Shakers' devotion to hands to work and hearts to God—Pence's letter made perfect sense. But the deputy—a good, sentimental Christian, I was learning—didn't get it. It's difficult to explain the power of dogma to someone who is temperamentally so undogmatic that he doesn't fear dogma. He barely knows what it is.

"My pastor told me to do unto others as you would want them to do unto you," Rebus said. "He called it the Golden Rule. So I figure, if I got fired by the sheriff and my daddy kicked me out of the house, I'd be just like you. I'd want someone to come around and do unto me. I can help you out for a spell, at least," he said. Years ago, he and his father had built a hunting camp out beyond Narcoossee on a small piece of dry land his father owned. It was located on a low hammock not far from Sunshine Home, the old tuberculosis sanitarium. "It ain't much, but it'll keep the rain off of you, and there's a tin stove and a privy." He offered to take me out as far as Narcoossee in the sheriff's patrol boat when he got off work, and I could walk the rest of the way. He said I could camp there as long as I needed. They no longer used the shack, as the dove and duck and deer population out there had been overhunted in recent years. "Get yourself some cans of beans and coffee and dried beef and a bag of rice, and I'll meet you down at the pier at half past five," he said.

That is how I came to live for the next few years like a twentieth-century Robinson Crusoe, a castaway on a wooded islet in the middle of a vast swamp, but within sight of the larger island nearby, where my Sadie had first tried and then failed to recover from her illness and my love for her had blossomed and bloomed and filled my heart and mind with its intoxicating perfume. Now it was the first thing I saw when I woke and looked out the single small window of the cabin and the last thing at night when I stood outside and studied the stars and listened to the hoot of the owls and the splash and guttural moan of the gators.

The larger, neighboring island rose from the waters in the distance as if in a dream of a fairy-tale princess's palace, and to myself I called it Sister Sadie. The smaller, the islet where I slept and cooked my meals and gathered firewood and sewed and patched my few articles of clothing and from whose shore I fished in the swamp for supper after my store-bought food ran out, where I harvested figs from the strangler fig tree and sea grapes and persimmons and sprouts off the cabbage palms and made coffee from chicory roots and stole eggs from the nests of moorhens and grebes—that island I named Brother Harley. This way Sadie and I were together again, resurrected, me from a kind of death in life, and she, a gleaming presence rarely out of my sight, free at last from illness and pain, resurrected from mere memory, which is a kind of life in death—both of us, our love no longer tainted by gossip and rumor and scandal and the judgment of strangers, no longer burdened with secrecy, face-to-face again and linked like two islands in an archipelago bridged beneath the watery surround.

Though I was living off the land for most of my food, from time to time I managed to earn a few dollars cutting cane in the fall and chopping the burned-over soil in spring for the new cane crop on one of the small plantations outside Narcoossee, where no one knew me. It was a three-mile hike down the crushed-coral lane, and at the end of each day when I returned to my islet I was greeted by the sight of Sister Sadie's bright-green palace rising from the watery plain that surrounded us. And when I woke and looked out, she was still there to welcome and smile upon me.

One afternoon, when departing from the sugar plantation for home, I took a shortcut behind a wagon barn and discovered a small, run-down, abandoned apiary that I hadn't noticed before. It was overgrown with weeds and brush, and in exchange for half the harvest, I volunteered to clear and restore it. In a few months I was gathering enough honey to sweeten my meals, and I made beeswax candles, so that after dark I had light to read from the books I was borrowing from the little one-room Narcoossee library. Soon I was able to set up a stand in town and sell off the excess honey to local house-wives and cooks, so I quit cutting cane, which I hated anyhow, and turned to selling honey and beeswax candles instead.

Before long, with little need to make cash purchases in Narcoos-see, since most of my provisions were provided by the plant, animal, and aquatic life found around my island home and the swamp, I had stashed considerably more cash money in a Maxwell House Coffee can than was required for my personal upkeep. Raised in utopian communes by communists, both secular and religious, I had never learned what to do with capital. I was more a simpleminded stranger to money than its antagonist. Now, suddenly, with a wad of bills and a pile of coins, I was a relatively wealthy young man—relative to my previous condition and to anyone I had ever lived with or known well enough to ask what one did with capital. That's when I remem-bered Elder John's long-ago purchase in his name of four lots in St. Cloud. He'd done it with money borrowed against future earnings from the sale of crops and products manufactured by the Shakers of New Bethany. I wondered what Elder John would advise me to do with my newly accumulated capital and wished that I could ask him.

Rebus, my only friend, had been coming out to my island once every month or so, whenever he had business in Narcoossee for the sheriff or to help his father establish a real-estate office there, and he had kept me loosely aware of events occurring at New Bethany. Ever eager for news of my immediate family and the larger Shaker fam-ily, I asked after Mother, especially, and my brothers Raymond and Royal and my sister, Rachel, but also Elder John and Eldress Mary and all the brethren. I still felt strangely and strongly attached to New Bethany, almost as if I were away only temporarily on Shaker business and would soon return to their warm, familial embrace.

Rebus brought little news of my immediate family, except that they remained in residence out there. But he had much to say about Elder John. He'd heard that within weeks of being released from jail, Elder John had gone off to visit the Koreshan community down near Fort Myers and hadn't returned. Their leader, Cyrus Teed, or Koresh, had recently died, and after a few months his followers had given up waiting for his promised resurrection and had finally removed his poorly embalmed, decomposing body from its open bier and sealed it in a marble mausoleum. They were still a prosperous group with a profitable, subscription-supported newspaper, *The Flaming Sword*, and owned many shops and warehouses for storing and shipping their crops north and had even incorporated the commune as the city of Estero and lately had formed a political party to put forward candidates for county offices and the Florida state legislature. "From what my daddy tells me," Rebus said, "your old boss's been made their chairman or president or whatever they call their leader now. He's taken over from the dead fellow, the one named Koresh, and he's been whipping them Koreshans into shape. Daddy thinks highly of Mr. Bennett," Rebus said. "He says, now that Bennett's running Estero, he ain't likely coming back to New Bethany. He says he'll prob'ly end up governor of Florida." Which was not far off. Elder John, now known as Reverend John Bennett, built a successful agricultural import-export business in Fort Myers, was admitted to the bar in 1917, and commenced practicing law in Fort Myers. He later entered politics by means of an appointment to the Florida State Senate as secretary from 1918 to 1921. Subsequent state positions were as general counsel of the Florida Real Estate Commission, 1921–1925, and member of the Florida House of Representatives in 1926. On November 3, 1928, voters elected him, by then known to the press as the Quaker Cracker, as a Democrat to the United States Senate to fill the vacancy caused by the death of Senator Park Trammell. He was re-elected in 1934 and 1940 and served until his death in Washington, D.C., on September 18, 1946. During his time in the United States Senate he was chairman of the Committee on Enrolled Bills while serving with the Committee on Public Buildings and Grounds and on the Special Committee on Reconstruction of the Senate Roof and Skylights. He never married and left no survivors. At the time of his death his net worth was said to be over $700 million, which he left to Florida Southern College in Lakeland, Florida, to endow professorships and scholarships for the study of American utopianism. Two buildings designed by Frank Lloyd Wright and a campus pathway between the Usonian Visitors' Center and the Esplanade have been named for him.

Rebus also told me that Eldress Mary had taken a fall. "She busted her hip or something, and she's failing, and several of the old crew of Shakers run off somewheres, and the two young herdsmen, they're long gone, and the cattle have run wild, and now the Shakers don't have enough hands to bring in the crops and hay and are starting to sell off their livestock and poultry, because they ain't able to feed them."

I worried about my mother and siblings, naturally, and urged Rebus to ask Mother next time he was out there if there was anything I could do to help them. That would be a good way for me to use up my capital, I thought. "Ask her when no one else is around," I said. "Tell her I'll send money or buy food or supplies in Narcoossee and ship it over to New Bethany for them."

Ten days later he appeared again at the cabin and reported that he heard from Dr. Cardiff that Eldress Mary had died of a stroke, and the remaining Shakers were planning to depart from New Bethany for their headquarters someplace in upstate New York. Rebus figured that would include Mother and my brothers and sister, but he wasn't sure, as he hadn't had any occasion to go out there himself. This was in early January, the winter of 1911–12, a bad time to move north. But according to the doctor, Rebus said, the remaining New Bethany Shakers seemed determined to go anyway. Dr. Cardiff, who had been close to Eldress Mary, had been asked to purchase eight one-way train tickets to Albany, New York, leaving St. Cloud the morning of January 15th. "I think the doc paid for their tickets out of his own pocket," he said.

I decided to be in St. Cloud on the fifteenth and see for myself if Mother and my siblings were among the eight Shakers leaving for Mount Lebanon, New York, and if they were, I'd try to say goodbye to them in person, and I would tell them that I was remorseful over what I did to New Bethany, and I would ask for their forgiveness.

Captain Shea wasn't likely to let me ride the *Coquina* from Narcoossee, so I resolved to get to St. Cloud on foot, a daylong walk. I packed a day's food into an old rusting tin ammunition box left in the cabin years ago by Rebus or his daddy and added my Maxwell House can of saved-up capital and set off on the morning of the fourteenth, keeping to the towpaths along the meandering skein of canals linking the lakes and following the Seminole trails around the lakes, until I got to the old St. Cloud–Tampa Turnpike, and arrived in St. Cloud before dark.

I spent the night sleeping fitfully on a bench outside the train depot. Luckily, no one rousted me, and it did not rain, and when I woke, sunlight was spreading across the glittering waters of East Lake Tohopekaliga, and the cloudless sky was a newborn pinkish shade of blue. Cormorants off the marshes and seagulls off the Gulf wheeled and looped over the lake and rose and merged and floated upward on the morning offshore breeze and broke from their flocks and dove and skimmed separately over the low waves.

I sat on my bench and watched the birds and waited, feeling profoundly alone in the world, a twenty-one-year-old man just arrived from nowhere and going nowhere soon, with no one waiting here to greet him and no one coming here for him to greet. Except for an early-arriving Black baggage handler, I was by myself on the depot platform. After a while, an elderly White clerk arrived and opened the ticket office. Neither man took notice of me. It was the dwindled, solitary end of almost everything in life that I had known and loved. At the same time it seemed somehow like a new beginning, one of those rare moments when the past is rapidly receding into faded, fragmented memory and the future has not yet arrived.

As I sat there, I remembered other static, first-light, early-morning moments like this, going back as far as Waycross, when Father died, and I would wake before the others in our shedlike hovel at the edge of the Okefenokee Swamp and stare out the window at the neighboring shanties of our fellow Ruskinite communards and not know how I had got there or where I would go from there. I was a boy, but a lost boy. And later, when we were debt slaves at Rosewell Plantation, I would leave our tent before sunrise, with Mother and my brothers and baby sister still sleeping, and walk to the privy, and shivering from the cold, I would stand at the edge of the foul-smelling ditch with my skinny legs spread to pee and stare up at the pinking sky and watch the stars get snuffed out one by one by the coming light. At those times I felt different and distinct from everyone I knew and loved and from all the strangers in the world, for I was the child whose father's dying words had made him the man of the house, separating him from the others, even from his mother, differentiating him from the others, and charging him with a task he could never fulfill. Then I remembered how, after we were rescued from Rosewell Plantation by Elder John and were brought to New Bethany, everything changed, everything except the feeling of separateness and difference that came over me whenever the others were praying and singing the Shaker songs and uniting in the dances and marches in the meetinghouse or when Sister Hazel in the schoolroom taught us the Shaker beliefs, and I saw how that old familiar feeling had made me into a secretive hypocrite, for I could not let go of it. Separateness and difference—I had come to embrace the feeling and had begun to think of it as my essential nature, my true self. It fit and suited me perfectly. Despite its discomfort, I have tried since then to preserve it at all costs. Separateness and difference. It's what generated my obsessive love for Sadie and freed me to pursue her. It's what has sustained that love throughout all the years since her death.

It was close to mid-morning when I first saw them. They were walking along Pennsylvania Avenue on the narrow wooden sidewalk, headed toward the depot. At the front was Dr. Cardiff, and clustered tightly together behind him, the New Bethany Shakers in their dark Shaker garb, the females wearing white bonnets and the males in wide-brim palm-straw hats, and each lugging a large satchel or an overstuffed gunnysack, even little Rachel, the sole small child in the group. Citizens of St. Cloud and tourists and visitors from the North stared and stepped out of the Shakers' path to let them through and stared again when they had passed. There was Sister Hazel, my old schoolteacher, walking with a cane, and stout Sister Rosalie, who for twenty-five years had managed the poultry side of the farm, and Brother Theodore, who must have been nearly one hundred years old, hobbling along with his back hunched and legs bowed by crippling arthritis, and Brother Ezekiel, the bald, white-bearded cobbler, almost as old now as Brother Theodore, and there were my nearly grown brothers, Raymond and Royal, suntanned, tall, slim farm boys peering excitedly around at the stores and shops and offices and the cars and trucks, seeing for the first time what passes for civilization out here in the World, and my sister, Rachel, clutching her sack of belongings with one hand and Mother's hand with the other, and there was Mother herself, looking fearfully around at what had so excited her twin boys—the World, the World and all its temptations, which they must now pass through unscathed, uncorrupted, unmarked, in order to reach the sublime protection of their Shaker sanctuary in the distant North and from there at the appointed time ascend to Heaven to join the chorus of angels and sit at the feet of Jesus and Mother Ann. These were the last of the New Bethany Believers, the remnant of a remnant, pilgrims like the first Shakers, driven out of England one hundred thirty-eight years earlier, who, led by the living Mother Ann, purchased a wooded, rock-strewn plain between the Mohawk and Hudson Rivers and began to clear the land and build their magic kingdom. This branch of the kingdom, New Bethany, was done now. Finished. And it was I who had destroyed it.

I stood and walked to the edge of the platform and watched them approach the depot. The doctor was the first to notice me standing there. He acknowledged my presence with a nod and continued on and climbed the half dozen steps to the platform and went to the opposite end, as far from me as he could manage. The others, all eight, caught on to my presence with a collective split-second glance and did not look at me directly or signal in any way that they had seen me. As if following an invisible leader's silent command, they stared straight ahead and followed one another up the steps, with my brothers stooping to assist old Brother Theodore and Sister Hazel, who appeared to be lame. Once on the platform, they all turned their backs to me, except for Rachel, who peeked over her shoulder and gave me a shy half-smile. Mother pulled on her hand, turning her, and they all walked to the far end, where Dr. Cardiff, pocket watch in hand, peered down the track.

I did not know how to approach them, or even if I should, so I waited and watched them as if we were strangers waiting for the same train to arrive. Then, after a while, I heard in the distance the three short alto chimes of the steam whistle signaling the approach of the South Florida passenger train running north to Tampa and beyond. Quickly, I moved toward my New Bethany family, my people, the only people I have ever truly known and loved, and I called out to them, "Mother! Brothers and sisters! Please, listen to me a moment before you leave!"

They kept their backs to me. The locomotive was now in sight a thousand yards down the track. I could hear the huge pounding pistons and the grind of the six steel drive wheels against the track and the slowly rising scrape of the brakes as the train began to slow for the stop at St. Cloud. I shouted above the noise, "Brethren, brethren, please forgive me! I wronged you! I confess it, brethren, I wronged all of you, every one! Forgive me, please."

The train pulled into the station and came to a hissing stop, and the Shakers all turned, and for the first time since the shunning began, we stood face-to-face. "I can save New Bethany," I said to them, more calmly now. "If you stay and allow me to become one of the family again, I can bring New Bethany back to life. I know everything that Elder John knew about managing the farm. He taught me all he knew. If you forgive me for my sins and transgressions and stay here, if you don't leave New Bethany, I promise to build it back to what it once was, and we can all live there together again in love and harmony with hands to work and hearts to God."

I opened the tin ammunition box I'd brought from my island and took out the Maxwell House Coffee can and held it out to them. "I've got money that I saved up, cash capital, and I'll give it over to New Bethany, all of it. Capital! We can buy new seed and livestock with it and seedlings for the citrus groves, everything we'll need to restore New Bethany to its old ascendency."

They stared at me, even little Rachel and Dr. Cardiff, as if I were a mad stranger, pitiable and slightly threatening. Behind me, the conductor called, "All aboard!" and the brethren formed a line and passed by me in silence, single-file, eyes straight ahead, and entered the train. Dr. Cardiff came and stood next to me, and through the windows of the car he and I watched the Shakers find their seats one by one. And then the conductor pulled up the steel steps and shut the doors, and with a blast of steam the great pistons began to churn again, the drive wheels to turn again, and the train slowly left the station and disappeared around the bend at the north end of town, and except for the chatter of the lakeside palms in the offshore breeze and the mocking cries of the errant seagulls off the distant Gulf, all was quiet again.

The doctor waited beside me a moment longer, then moved across the platform and stepped down to the street. Turning to me, he said, "Them being gone, it makes you the last of the Florida Shakers, eh, Mr. Mann?"

"It does."

"How does that make you feel?"

"Forlorn," I said. "Abandoned and forlorn."

He laughed lightly. "I think that's what they had in mind for you, Mr. Mann." He gave me a dismissive wave, as if I deserved my fate, and walked up Pennsylvania Avenue the way he had come. And then I was alone again. The last of the Florida Shakers—when I had never been a Shaker in the first place.

What I did next surprised even me. The day before, when I left my Narcoossee sanctuary for town, I had not thought of doing it. I had in mind quite a different use for my accumulated capital. Later, when I was actually doing it, I was barely aware of having made the decision to purchase Elder John's four plots of land in St. Cloud. Yet there I was, standing at the counter of the Seminole Land & Investment Company office on New York Avenue with my emptied coffee can in front of me, counting out the bills and coins and nudging them with a knuckle over to the spectacled, bald clerk to pay off the balance due plus accumulated interest on New Bethany's debt to the Seminole Land & Investment Company, less the down payment Elder John had pilfered from New Bethany funds, taking full legal possession of four vacant five-acre lots in the town of St. Cloud. A lawyer might have successfully challenged the legality of the transfer, but, pleased as they were to get back their full investment plus interest, no one from Seminole Land & Investment cared to contest it.

I returned to my islet cabin outside Narcoossee by way of the old Seminole trails and the canal towpaths, arriving home in the dark, carrying in the tin ammunition box the deeds to the lots, and I told

Sadie's ghost what I had done and asked her to bless my enterprise. The following day I began my career as a buyer and seller of south Florida real estate by selling three of the four lots to Rebus's father, whose name was Morton Horton. He had recently opened a satellite real-estate office in the village of Narcoossee and was willing to purchase my St. Cloud properties for twice what they had cost me. The fourth lot I held on to, and that was where a year later I built this little shotgun house that has sheltered me for fifty-seven years. Mr. Horton quickly sold the other three lots, sight unseen, to buyers in Pennsylvania and New Jersey for twice what he had paid me for them.

So it went. The Florida land boom was under way, the supply of buyers was endless and self-replenishing, and I now had sufficient capital to purchase still more real estate and quickly resell it, often for cash, more often by loaning the purchase price to the buyer and later, when the loan was not paid back, repossessing the property and promptly reselling it at a still higher price. I plunged in, and was immediately successful, if success is measured in profit from speculating in real estate and moneylending, which in Florida in those days was like gambling in a casino where you also happened to own the casino. Once in a while, you'd lose, as I and Mr. Horton lost in the early Depression years, when we ran low on buyers and borrowers. But if you are the house, if you are the person dealing the cards and loaning money to keep the players in the game, in the long run you'll beat both the sellers and the buyers, no matter the size of the pot.

I incorporated myself as Shaker Real Estate & Investment Company and had business cards printed and asked Mr. Horton to rent me a desk in his Narcoossee office where I could conduct my business. From my years at New Bethany I was intimately familiar with all the land holdings thereabouts, from St. Cloud to Kissimmee to Narcoossee and beyond, and as Elder John's right-hand man, I had gotten to know personally many of the farmers and cattlemen who owned the land and was able to convince them that large chunks of their property, some of it seasonally underwater, were too wet for planting or grazing cattle and could be sold off in small pieces at a profit. Most of them knew little or nothing of the scandal that had tainted me in St. Cloud and were glad to do business with me. I advertised Shaker Real Estate & Investment Company in Northern newspapers, where the word "Shaker" implied honesty and diligence. I had the phrase "Hands to work and hearts to God" printed on my stationery and business cards, and soon I had more eager inquiries coming in than I could answer.

Mr. Morton noted my skill in matching local sellers with distant buyers and maximizing the difference between selling price and purchase price, and six months after I moved into his office, he invited me, in exchange for a small percentage of my profits, to manage his Narcoossee branch under the name of Shaker Real Estate & Investment Company, while he ran the main office in St. Cloud, effectively making us partners. In time he would sell me half the company, and when he retired in 1941, I bought the other half, by which time Shaker Real Estate & Investment had eclipsed Seminole Land & Investment as the largest real-estate buyer and seller in the region, and though, out of habit more than principle, I lived simply, I was a rich man, a man who had come to own personally all seven thousand acres of the original New Bethany property.

It happened gradually. For many years, starting in 1913, after I abandoned my cabin on the little islet I called Brother Harley, the hammock that rose from the swamp across from the wooded island that I called Sister Sadie, and moved into the house I had built for myself in St. Cloud, I purchased piecemeal the portions of New Bethany that the New York–based Shakers put on the market through Mr. Horton's company. They sold off the land sporadically in five-hundred- and thousand-acre pieces, no doubt in response to their declining population and income and the demise and closing of their various colonies in other states. Eventually, I owned all of New Bethany.

I made the purchases under my corporate name, rather than my own, and did not resell any of them. Instead, I let the marshes and the swamp and the mangroves and sawgrass plains and palmetto thatches take back the fields, meadows, and orchards, and I let the canals and irrigation ditches fill with silt and runoff soil from our old plowed, fertilized, and harrowed planting grounds. I let the hurricanes and spring rains and drought and wildfire reshape the lakes and smaller waterways, and I let the elements burn and blow through, rain down upon and level and then reseed and level again the tree-topped hammocks and pine woods. I let my beehives collapse. I let all the buildings, the main house and the meetinghouse and the men's and women's dormitories and the barns and pens and shops and mills, suffer the burning sun and the pounding rains and lightning strikes and the raging winds of the hurricanes year after year, until clapboards and shingles began to loosen and fall away and chimney bricks to crackle and collapse and windows to shatter, and let raccoons and snakes and swamp rats and possums and feral cats and homeless drifters and the occasional convict on the run from a road gang take up temporary residence in the desolated, abandoned structures, and black mold began to creep up the walls and rain to blow through the upper stories and rot the floorboards, the water working its way down to the sills and foundation stones, dissolving the limey mortar and turning the timbers to doughy rot, and one by one the structures tilted and fell to the ground or were blown down or were strangled and crushed by the vines, until there remained nothing out there of our once-glorious plantation but scattered heaps of weed-and-kudzu-covered wreckage sinking into the muck and the returning waters of the no-longer-ditched-and-drained swamp.

When I moved out of my cabin and islet outside Narcoossee and took up permanent residence here in St. Cloud, Sadie's ghost did not follow me. The town was expanding and filling fast with strangers from the North, snowbirds and retirees and tourists, who knew nothing of Sadie's and my love affair or the old Shaker colony out on Live Oak Lake or the mysterious circumstances surrounding Sadie's death. The newly paved streets were crowded with automobiles and trucks and buses, and hotels and motels and small amusement parks and miniature golf courses were opening fast, and out at the edges of the city, where the streets became four-lane roads and turnpikes, trailer parks and car and boat dealerships with flapping, neon-colored flags and banners had started to appear like mushrooms after a rain. The city, like most of the state of Florida, was antithetical to the presence of a ghost.

And there was no evidence of Sadie in my new house, either. I owned not a single photograph or painting of her. I possessed no keepsake, not even a piece of her jewelry, a comb, a handkerchief. There was no evidence of her presence here, no memorial or shrine or image proving that she had ever lived and had been loved by me or by anyone else. She had migrated instead from her palace on the bright-green island once called Sunshine Home back over to New Bethany, and when I began to buy up the Shaker acreage, that is where I went to commune with her. I went out often and alone, first on foot and sometimes by rowboat, and in later years, after I cut a rough track through the palmettos and along the overgrown towpaths of the old Disston and New Bethany canals, I drove out almost daily in a company-owned jeep. I was like an archaeologist hacking my way through the jungle to the vine-covered ruins of an ancient kingdom's abandoned temple center, where the spirit of the kingdom's reigning goddess still presided.

I managed to locate our meeting spot in the boathouse down by the old canal towpath and cleared it with a machete so that I could sit and relive the moonlit hours we spent there locked in passionate embrace. I found the remnants of my apiary buried beneath a thick green quilt of kudzu and stood nearby in the weeds recalling our whispered conversations and confidences, bringing back to life the way Sadie and I had reinforced and strengthened our shared unbelief in the midst of a beloved community of Believers. I stood on the crumbled foundation of the main house looking at the piles of fallen ceilings and walls and smashed window frames and imagined that I could identify the narrow staircase that led me to Sadie's third-floor bedroom and the window we used to gaze from as the sun rose over the distant trees and fields and dissolved the morning mists. Near the fallen staircase, I found the rotting remains of the library, of which several hundred sodden volumes were salvageable. These I brought back to my house and dried in the sunlight and have kept close at hand, though I do not read them. They are talismans, not texts. And I found the wreckage of the meetinghouse, where I last saw Sadie's body laid out in a pine casket with candles burning around it, while I sat beside her through the night trying to pray her back to life and failed, because of my unbelief, and in my grief and rage began then to tear apart the close-woven fabric of love and trust that had kept New Bethany together.

It was a hopeless venture. Though I held the deed to the ruins of the kingdom and the land for miles around, alone I could not excavate the temple or the surrounding structures in order to properly honor and worship the woman who had reigned over me there. At last I saw the utter vanity of my project and the febrile nature of my need.

That was when I began to turn away from the ruins of the old kingdom and construct the plaster of paris model of my remembered New Bethany instead. I no longer went out there on foot, by boat, or in my jeep. I no longer believed in ghosts. Or, more accurately, in the ghost of Sadie Pratt, which had been more of a fantasy than a belief anyway, a self-indulgent fancy, like the naming of her island and my islet after the two of us.

To nourish and enliven my memories, I set that eight-foot-square model of New Bethany in the center of my office in Narcoossee, an oddity that struck the eye of everyone who entered, causing the visitor to inquire as to its meaning and origin, leading me to tell the story of the New Bethany Shakers, which explained the name of my company and little else, for, unlike this tape-recorded version of the story, it was a carefully edited version. One might call it a censored version, since it left out any mention of my having lived there myself and my love of Sadie Pratt and the unforeseen and tragic consequences of that love in the lives of my family and my Shaker brethren and Elder John and Eldress Mary, when one of my final interlocutors asked specifically, "So how come the Shakers abandoned the place?"

"As they aged, they began to die off, and because they were celibate, they could not replace themselves," I said. "They no longer had enough members to work the land or tend the livestock and could not feed themselves."

"Christ. And the place looked like this? Like the model you got set up here?"

"Yes."

"Jeez, it's beautiful. It's like a goddamn plantation. Right here in the middle of fucking south Florida."

"Yes."

"And you own title to all seven thousand acres of their land?"

"I do."

"These buildings and canals and orchards here in your model, are they still there?"

"No. Everything's gone now. Except the land and the lakes."

"We'd like to take a look at that land and those lakes."

"That property's not for sale."

"C'mon, Mr. Mann. For the right price, everything's for sale. This is America, for chrissakes. We flew up from Miami, we've got access to a private plane. If it looks from the air like it'll suit our purposes, we'll arrange a survey and make you a fair offer for the whole package. Sound good?"

"You say that your intentions are to use the land solely for grazing cattle?"

"Yes."

"How do I know you won't cut it into little squares and build subdivisions and trailer parks?"

"We'll put a clause in the contract that forbids us to subdivide. In perpetuity."

"In perpetuity?"

"Sure. In perpetuity."

AFTERWORD

It appears that Harley Mann chose to end his narrative there, at the end of the fifteenth reel. No additional tapes have been discovered either by myself or by my research assistant, the young woman who was the part-time librarian at the St. Cloud Veterans Memorial Library, where I rescued the tapes from the cartons of waterlogged books and periodicals about to be hauled off to the transfer station. She is no longer employed at the library and has left her home and family in St. Cloud and now resides elsewhere. I would like to thank her publicly here, but, as I said in my opening note, she prefers to remain unnamed in this account. Understandably, since it was she who facilitated my acquisition of the tapes in the first place and did not report me to the head librarian when I returned to St. Cloud for further research into the life and times of Harley Mann and New Bethany and Sadie Pratt, Elder John Bennett, Eldress Mary Glynn, and the others.

Beyond that, she made available to me the library's historical materials and early-twentieth-century newspaper and periodical archives, and she personally scoured the records kept by the St. Cloud Heritage Museum and Historical Society for materials related to New Bethany and the people who lived there. It was she who located Harley Mann's and Sadie Pratt's grave markers in the old, untended, all-but-forgotten Shaker cemetery at Disney World between the Rainforest Cafe and the Animal Kingdom. She showed me the nearby grave marked "Mary Glynn, 1839–1911, Shaker." It is not illegal to view these plaques, as long as one purchases a ticket to the Magic Kingdom, but since one has to depart from the designated walkways to get there, it is discouraged by Disney security guards.

I should also note that it was she, my research assistant, who provided me with the *St. Cloud Tribune* account of the untimely death of Harley Mann in January 1972. Untimely, for despite his advanced age he was neither ill nor infirm. His death was sudden and dramatic, however. Had he been more cautious, he might have lived another decade or even longer.

The manner and date of his death raise the question of who surreptitiously installed his and Sadie Pratt's and Eldress Mary's plaques at Disney World, and when. Shaker graves are typically unmarked and undated, nameless, except for the single word "Shaker," to signify the final absorption of the earthbound individual by the everlasting, universal light of Shakerdom.

According to the article in the *St. Cloud Tribune*, Harley Mann was killed in his sleep on the night of January 14, 1972, when a large sinkhole, the "sink" he mentions several times in his taped account, opened beneath his house. Apparently, it happened so quickly that he could not escape from the house in time to keep from being pulled underground with the structure. His body was never recovered, although, in the search for his body, parts of the house and some of the furnishings and other personal property were found and brought back to the surface. I assume that the fifteen reels of tape, carefully wrapped in plastic and tied with string, were among these salvaged items, along with many early-twentieth-century editions of scientific, religious, and philosophical books, all of which were donated to the Veterans Memorial Library by the rescue squad. Evidently, Mann's plaster of paris model of New Bethany was not recovered, which is unfortunate, as it would have provided us with a three-dimensional portrait of the Shaker colony in its prime and might have proved useful in publicizing this book.

The article in the *St. Cloud Tribune* mentions that Harley Mann, "a respected and successful realtor and longtime resident of St. Cloud," was unmarried and had no known surviving family members. However, my assistant, having typed the transcription of the tapes, tracked down a ninety-eight-year-old woman named Rachel Mann, living in a retirement home in Saratoga Springs, New York. Ms. Mann and I spoke on the telephone. She was alert and intelligent and responded openly to my inquiry, informing me that the late Harley Mann was indeed her older brother. She told me that she and Mann's two younger brothers, Royal and Raymond, both deceased, had been contacted in late 1973 by a probate attorney in St. Cloud, Florida, informing them of their older brother's death a year earlier. He read them the terms of Mann's last will and testament, in which he gave his entire estate over to the Shaker Museum at Old Chatham, New York. Mann had named his sister, Rachel Mann, as executor of his estate, which she said was "surpassingly large," although she would not say how large. She also refused to say if she was the person who, surreptitiously and no doubt illegally, installed her brother's and Sadie Pratt's and Eldress Mary Glynn's plaques at Disney World, but my assistant and I assumed that she either did it herself or hired someone in St. Cloud to do it for her. She did admit that she had been contacted around the same time by the retired Osceola County sheriff, Rebus Morton, who claimed to have been one of her brother's only known friends.

"My brother Harley was a very lonely man," she said. "But he made his loneliness tolerable by converting it to solitude. They are not the same, you know." Her manner of speaking was strikingly similar to her brother's.

"He seemed to have found love with Sadie Pratt," I said.

"I can't speak for her, whether she loved him or not. But no, he didn't love her. It was an obsession," she said. "Not love. Love and obsession, like loneliness and solitude, they're different states of mind. He was lonely for so long as a boy and young man that he became susceptible to obsession. But I was a child then and know only what was told to me by the others. I am glad, however, that if Harley could not find love, in the end he at least found solitude. Solitude is instructive," she said. "And a balm."

She said that she had remained a Shaker all her life, like her mother and her late brothers Royal and Raymond, until she was the last living Shaker at Mount Lebanon, where she, too, found solitude. "But unlike poor Harley, I have known love all my life. True love, the love of a Believer. And therefore I have never been lonely," she said. "Even now, with everyone gone." She thanked me for my interest in her brother's life and the history of New Bethany and expressed hope that my book would not damage the reputation of either.

A year later, in order to send her a copy of the edited transcript of Harley Mann's tapes, I tried contacting her, but the woman who answered the telephone at the retirement home said that Rachel Mann, the much-loved Shaker lady, had died the previous spring at the age of ninety-nine.

It took me another nineteen years to find an editor and publishing company willing to publish my book, possibly because of fear of the Disney Company's well-known litigiousness. I'm especially grateful, therefore, to the Knopf Doubleday Publishing Group, a division of Penguin Random House, for its willingness to bring to the public Harley Mann's melancholy account of his life and times.

ACKNOWLEDGMENTS

The Magic Kingdom is a novel, a work of the imagination loosely based on actual events. The real Russell Banks wishes to thank the following individuals for their help with research: his longtime assistant, Nancy Wilson, who searched the Internet and a thousand books and articles for details of Shaker life; Professor Daniel Patterson, who introduced him to the Shakers in his American literature classes at the University of North Carolina at Chapel Hill in 1964–67 and patiently read an early draft of this novel; and Christian Goodwillie, who gave him unfettered access to the extensive collection of Shaker materials held at the Hamilton College Library in Clinton, New York. Any factual errors concerning the Shakers are to be blamed on the real Russell Banks.

He also wishes to thank Ellen Levine of Trident Media Group, who has been his agent and friend for over fifty years, and Dan Halpern, who has been his publisher and friend for almost as long. Without their loyalty and support, this book would not exist.

A NOTE ON THE TYPE

This book was set in Celeste, a typeface created in 1994 by the designer Chris Burke (b. 1967). He describes it as a modern, humanistic face having less contrast between thick and thin strokes than other modern types such as Bodoni, Didot, and Walbaum. Celeste is highly readable and especially adapted for current digital printing processes which render an increasingly exacting letterform.

Typeset by Scribe, Philadelphia, Pennsylvania
Printed and bound by Berryville Graphics, Berryville, Virginia
Designed by Maggie Hinders

11-22

cu